DEEP
POCKETS

Linda Barnes

DEEP
POCKETS

St. Martin's Minotaur ▨ New York ≈

ISBN 0-312-28271-0

For my brother, Steve

Acknowledgments

A belated thank you to Nancy Hawthorne for her help on *The Big Dig*. My deep appreciation to Richard Barnes, Donald Davidoff, Hallie Ephron, Kate Flora, and Sarah Smith for their thoughtful reading of the manuscript in its early stages. Thanks again to my agent, Gina Maccoby, my editor, Kelley Ragland, and always, to Sam.

DEEP
POCKETS

CHAPTER 1

I hate running errands. I put them off and put them off, and then one morning the cat's got no food, there are zero stamps on the roll, and I realize I own no underwear minus holes. I understand some people like to shop for clothes, do it for pure pleasure and entertainment, but I count it as one more damned errand. When the tasks mount up and I can't put it off any longer, I make a list and set forth to Harvard Square. There are less pricey areas, granted, but the Square has its own post office and lies within spitting distance of my house.

I waited in line at the post office till my feet felt like they'd grow roots. I bought panties on sale at the Gap, mourned the passing of Sage's, where they'd always carried tons of my cat's favorite Fancy Feast, bought a few cans of an off-price substitute at the CVS instead. The wind tangled my hair, which helped me recall a shampoo shortage and led to cart-filling thoughts of toothpaste, soap, and lip balm.

I first noticed him as I was waiting, along with thirty-five other assorted students, panhandlers, and shoppers, for the scramble light at the intersection of Brattle and Mass Ave. His gaze lingered a moment too long and I wondered briefly whether I'd met him at a party or exchanged small talk with the man at a bar. He wasn't especially noticeable, a middle-aged light-skinned black man in a well-cut tweed jacket and charcoal slacks. Didn't hold a candle fashionwise to the young guy on his left wearing buckskin fringe. Still, I had the feeling I'd seen him before, and I thought it might have been behind me in line at the post office, or across the room at one of the writing tables, scribbling on the back of an envelope. When the traffic light changed, the herd charged across the street and dispersed, some heading for the subway, some the shops, some disappearing through the gates to Harvard Yard. I stopped at the Out of Town News Stand and gazed at the covers of foreign magazines. So did the black man.

The next time I saw him, he was standing outside the Cambridge Savings Bank while I was considering a bite to eat at Finagle a Bagel. He'd added a tan raincoat and a battered hat to his attire, and if I had to describe what he was doing, I'd have to say he was doing zip, simply loitering, which made him stand out from the crush of hurrying pedestrians. When I edged past, he fell into step thirty paces behind me.

Now, Cambridge is a crowded city, and Harvard Square is its hub. Teenagers cruise the streets, parading their finery, hoping someone will admire their most recent tattoo or pierced body part, but this guy hadn't been a teen in twenty years easy. I crossed Mass Ave again, turned right, then left on Church Street. I hurried past the movie theater and the Globe Corner Bookstore, hung a quick left on Palmer, a glorified alley, slowed down, and kept watch in the plate-glass windows of the Coop, purveyor of all things Harvard. Sure enough, he came hurtling around the corner, hurrying to catch up. I tried to get a better glimpse of his face, but it was obscured under the brim of the hat. I feigned interest in the fine-art posters displayed in the front window, then sauntered on.

I'd just finished working a case in which I'd managed to frustrate a bunch of survivalists-cum-terrorists. The Feebies, no less, had warned me to be on the lookout for revenge-crazed Looney Tunes. But the group allegedly out for my blood was the sort that wouldn't associate with black people, much less admit them as prized members and give them the choice assignment of taking out the half-Jewish bitch who'd foiled their finest scheme.

I used to be a cop, across the river in Boston. I worked Major Crimes and I worked Homicide, and there are no doubt former and future felons who hold a grudge. But I was pretty sure most of them would do a better job of shadowing. Truly, this guy was not good at his work. If he was an accomplished felon, I was queen of the junior prom.

He stayed too close, and then he stayed too far. He didn't know the basics, like walking on the opposite side of the street. He didn't use a shiner, a small mirror, so when he wanted to check where I was, he had to turn, risk a full stare, and look straight at me. He was strictly an amateur, but he was bird-dog stubborn and extremely patient while I visited Tower Records and sorted through stacks of bargain CDs.

The gent also looked prosperous. If I'd sent him away and he'd come out of jail dressing the way he did, he owed me thanks. My grandmother, my mother's mother, would have cautioned me to quit judging by appearances. *"Fun oybn puts, fun unten shmuts,"* she'd have warned in Yiddish. "Finery on top, filth underneath," meaning the guy could be some kind of stylish hitman, unswayed by the Hollywood idea of what a modern hood ought to wear. I considered strolling over to a beat cop, informing him that the elegant black man was tailing me, but I knew too many Cambridge cops to relish the horselaugh that would follow. Plus, I take pride in handling my own problems. My shadow didn't seem like much of a threat so far, but I wasn't about to lead him home or walk solo down some dark alley where he'd feel free to pull a gun if such were his intent. I could have lost him easily, could have hailed a cab or jumped a bus. Instead, I marched him around the Square while considering my options, then entered the Coop at the Mass Ave door, quickly stepped to the right into an open elevator car, and pressed the button for the third floor.

As the doors narrowed, I saw my man rush inside and take note of the departing elevator. I figured he'd wait for the next trip, and wait a while, too, since there was only the single car. I had plenty of time to turn left twice and secrete myself in an alcove, surrounded by books on medicine and near a handy fire extinguisher. Hidden from view, I stuffed my parcels into my backpack, turned my reversible jacket inside out, blue to gray, and yanked a knitted cap over my red hair. It took him four minutes to elbow his way off the elevator and start tracking me down.

I stayed behind him, veering from extreme left to far right, shielded by high bookcases, feeling like a crafty fox who'd turned the table on the hounds. The guy was tenacious, I'll give him that. He didn't approach the information desk or ask any Coop shoppers if they'd seen me. Instead, he walked briskly to the back of the store, glanced down the curving staircase, decided I hadn't taken it, and charged across the third-floor pedestrian bridge, passing the rest rooms and the phones and rushing into the connected Palmer Street Coop. There, he checked out the aisles of the textbook department, then worked his way down the floors of the Palmer Street building, ignoring dorm funishings, greeting cards, Harvard insignia bears and chairs, sweatshirts and baby booties.

He took the seven steps down into the Brattle Street building, exited, and did a brief survey of pedestrian traffic before stopping to consult a Rastafarian street musician who commanded a view of the door. I observed the interaction from behind a circular rack of crimson insignia bathrobes. The guitar player shook his head slowly, dreadlocks wriggling like snakes, and accepted a cash donation. The black man re-entered the Coop, passing within ten feet of my hiding place.

Tall, slim, maybe 180 pounds, regular features. He still wore the hat, so I couldn't check his hairline. Late thirties, early forties, a worried frown on a clean-shaven face. I still thought I might have seen him before today's post-office encounter, but I didn't know where, couldn't tag a name to the face or fathom a reason behind his dogged pursuit.

I followed him back up the stairs, across Palmer Street, and into the Mass Ave building again, where he took the elevator to the third floor and started working his way down through the huge bookstore, philosophy to periodicals to fiction.

He'd reached nonfiction before I grew impatient and approached.

When he saw me, a look of relief washed over his face, crinkling the corners of his dark eyes. When he realized I was heading straight toward him, the relief was replaced by panic. He grabbed a book off a pile and buried his nose in it. He was holding *The New Joy of Sex* upside down.

Maybe if he'd picked another book, or if a crease of anxiety hadn't furrowed his brow, or if he hadn't been quite so good-looking, I'd have shoved him against a wall, demanded ID, and threatened him with the cops. As it was, I made do with a firm hand on his arm.

"Store Security," I said. "Come along—"

"*You are not.*" His low voice was indignant.

"*Gotcha.* How do you know?"

He pursed his lips and thought about fleeing. He was my height, maybe an inch shorter. Six feet, narrow frame. With the shoes he had on, I didn't think he could outrun me. I watched his eyes as he considered his options. He closed them briefly, reopened them, and then pressed his lips together until they almost disappeared. His shoulders slumped, but he didn't appear defeated. The expression that crossed his face seemed more like resolve than despair.

"Miss Carlyle," he said. "May I buy you a drink?"

CHAPTER 2

I didn't return his smile. He knew my name and I didn't know his, which upset my sense of balance.

"Isn't it a little early?" I said.

"Coffee? Tea?"

"If following women around is your idea of a nifty pickup ploy—"

"This is, um, a professional matter." His fingers discovered he was still clasping the book, and he replaced it automatically on the table.

"I have an office for that, a phone number, too."

"I know. It's just that I hadn't— I didn't wish to— I hadn't quite decided—" His resolve seemed to be leaking away by the second.

A professional matter. I couldn't help wondering what sort of professional matter would compel the man to follow me through the Square.

"I could drink a cup of coffee, I suppose," I said.

"Yes, but I'd rather no one— I'd rather not be seen at the places I usually—places where I'm known—"

The Square is always crowded, the tables in the cafés jammed too close for private conversation. I considered and rejected several convenient spots. My home doubles as my office, but, like I said before, I wasn't about to guide a stalker, even an amateur, to my front door. It was chilly for mid-May, the hard winter refusing to release its grip, but warm enough to camp on a park bench or stroll by the river. I discarded both venues. If the man didn't want to risk being seen with me, neither fit the bill. I considered simply walking away, but curiosity won out.

"Come with me," I said.

Passim is a music club on Palmer Street, the alleylike stretch between Church and Brattle. It's famous as the reincarnation of the old Club 47, where Dylan and Baez used to play, even though the actual club was a storefront on Mount Auburn. Open for lunch, it's secluded and sparsely populated in the afternoon, the small stage and tightly packed basement tables approached by an outside staircase. The staff knows me because I'm a semiregular. I can leave the folky stuff alone, but if somebody's playing the blues, especially the old Delta blues, I'm in the audience. They don't sell alcohol or let you smoke, but where else can you hear the Nields one night, Paul Rishell and Annie Raines the next?

Skinny Sharon, on the desk, gave me a nod. I huddled with her briefly, and then my pursuer and I zigzagged past the kitchen, down the narrow hall near the bathrooms, and turned right into the back room, where the talent hangs between sets. I've used it before; it's nothing much—a couch, a couple of chairs, yellowed posters on the walls. Two hard-shell guitar cases were propped haphazardly against the sofa, and the place smelled of cigarettes and stale beer, indicating that the talent indulged in vices forbidden the audience.

I flipped on the overhead light and blinked in the harsh glare. "You want coffee?"

He gave his surroundings a careful once-over. "Actually, no. You?"

"I don't know your name."

He gazed around the small room as if searching for a hidden video cam. "Can we leave it like that for a while?"

"A short while."

I lowered myself into a folding chair and he did the same, both of us avoiding the enforced intimacy of the sprung sofa. The room was so tiny that our knees almost touched. His face was narrow, his forehead high, his nose broad. He had angular cheekbones and a strong chin. If you could wipe some of the worry off his face, he'd be better than good-looking, I thought. He smelled of spicy aftershave, and his tailor hadn't allowed room for a shoulder holster. I'd deliberately brushed against him in the narrow hallway to ensure that he wasn't carrying in a clip at his waist.

"Something I can do for you?" I asked.

He took a deep breath, the kind a man might take before plunging over a cliff into an icy lake. "Before I say anything, please tell me about your ties to Harvard."

My eyebrows rose. "You've been tailing the wrong person."

"Seriously, you don't have *any*?"

More than one local newspaper columnist has snidely referred to Harvard as "WGU," the "world's greatest university." Some tourists seem to think Harvard and Cambridge are interchangeable, one and the same, with MIT tossed in as a bonus. The students certainly think they own the place, and the Harvard Corporation actually does own a considerable chunk of the city to which I pay property taxes. Redbrick buildings and ivy-covered walls line both narrow streets and major thoroughfares. A constant influx of students keeps stores humming, rents astronomical, and foreign-language bookstores in business.

"I walk on their sidewalks. I cross the quadrangle, so I guess I walk on their grass, too. I've used a book or two from Widener, but I swear I returned them."

"You didn't go there?"

I'd worked nights as a cabbie to afford downscale UMass Boston. "Nope."

"What about your house? Harvard owns property all over that area."

Bastard knew where I lived. He must have picked me up there this morning. I didn't like that. I'd seen him for the first time at the post office.

"Not *my* property," I said.

"Ever do any work for them? Ever take a class there?"

I run a one-person private-eye outfit, and I doubt Harvard has taken notice, even though I'm perched in their backyard. I don't have a sign on my front door. The neighbors would never approve of such a thing, some of them having graduated from the hallowed halls of the WGU.

The extent of my Harvard connection: I used to park illegally behind the ed school before they put in the raised-arm sentry system. I figured he didn't need to know that, so I simply shook my head.

"Good. Excellent. Next, I need to know about confidentiality. I've never consulted a private investigator before, and I need to know to what degree I can be frank about my requirements."

"I'm a private citizen, not an officer of the court. If I'm working for an attorney, then his privileges can extend to cover me, as well."

I wasn't sure what this guy did for a living, but whatever it was, it paid. His understated clothes were expensive, his hands well kept, the fingernails manicured. His hands were ringless and very pale, the palms paler than my own. I've been going out with an African-American, an FBI agent temporarily on assignment in Boston, and the paleness of Leon's palms was nowhere near as pronounced.

My stalker bit his lip. "Therefore you could be compelled to testify in a court of law."

"Yes."

"Damn." He worried his lips some more and seemed at a loss as to how to continue. He had faint lines at the corners of his drooping eyes. I upped my age estimate, placing him at forty to forty-five.

"Are you ready to tell me your name?" I asked.

"Not yet."

A clatter of dishes and silverware penetrated the soundproofing, reminding me that people were finishing up lunch not fifteen feet away.

I said, "Prospective clients often consult me about hypothetical matters. Or they might talk about something that's happened to a friend."

"I have a friend," he said, seizing on the pretext and leaning forward eagerly, "who is being blackmailed. He is— He doesn't know what to do."

"Maybe your 'friend' should have made an appointment to see me."

He bit his lip. "I was— I should have— I didn't mean to alarm you."

"You didn't. About the blackmail, I hate to say it, but sometimes the easiest option is the expensive one. Pay up."

"You don't understand. My friend *has* paid. He thought it was over, but . . . it's more than that. . . . It's the threat. I find— My friend finds he can no longer live with the constant threat of exposure."

I don't know what I'd expected—police harrassment, a missing friend, an unfaithful wife—but blackmail took me by surprise. It's an unusual complaint these days. Blackmail isn't what it used to be because secrets aren't what they used to be. What with confessional TV, and talk-radio jocks hosting gay cross-dressers and their second wives, and Internet chat rooms devoted to perversion, it takes a certain type of deed to provoke blackmail, and, more importantly, a certain type of person to attract it.

"Tell me more about your friend," I said.

"He is in a position of trust."

"Working with money?"

"Working with young people."

"Very young people, or people the age you might encounter at Harvard?"

The mention of Harvard was enough to make his hands clench. "Do you know how few tenured faculty positions exist? Tenured positions at fine universities?"

"I can see where your friend might wish to keep his job."

"He does, believe me. He does."

The man probably looked familiar because I'd seen him in Harvard Yard, hurrying from class to the Faculty Club. A Harvard professor. Not one of the famous ones, not a local celebrity like Skip Gates. Still, the quality of my propective clientele was on the rise.

"Was your friend's action illegal?" I asked.

"What action?"

"I assume your friend is being blackmailed for a reason."

A fine sheen of sweat was visible on the man's forehead, and I wondered if he was going to balk at detailing his imaginary friend's offense.

"No, not illegal. I— My friend, upon consideration, would call it immoral, although considerations of morality—I don't know. Times changed, didn't they? The rules changed, somewhere along the line. Sex was—is—always about power, but we . . . we deluded ourselves, told ourselves how irresistible we were, told ourselves the same old bullshit stories. I deluded myself. I thought of myself as a man, not some powerful godlike professor."

I didn't interrupt, but I didn't like the way the conversation was going.

"She was of age, and, in fact, she initiated the, er, contact." He looked me directly in the eye. "I should say the affair, the relationship. What the hell do you call it without sounding like a fool or a cad? Understand that my friend is not proud of his behavior."

"I don't understand," I said. "Your friend, is he the master of house?"

"No."

"Is he some whoop-de-do professor of ethics?"

"No."

"What I hear, his behavior is absolutely normal, par for the course, unexceptional." I was understating the case; from what I'd heard, Harvard profs could sleep with assorted students of both sexes, not to mention barnyard animals, pay for prostitutes, call it research, and get away with a polite slap on the wrist if caught with their pants around their ankles.

"Times have changed," he said. "And my own particular circumstances make me vulnerable."

"Tell me about them. Beginning with your name."

"Please try to understand. I find myself unable to concentrate, unable to contemplate the future. I had everything, but I didn't know I had it, and now that I could lose it, I find myself behaving irrationally."

Irrational was right. A Harvard professor chasing an ex-cop through the Square.

"I find myself making foolish promises, going to church more often than I have since I was a child, begging forgiveness of some supreme being I'm not even certain I believe in. I feel out of control, in a way I can only compare to a mental illness. Excuse me. This is beside the point."

"The point being . . ."

"Leonard Wells mentioned you."

Aha. Leonard Wells is the FBI agent I'm dating. When I met him, he was calling himself Lee and I was pretending to be Carla, both of us working undercover on the Dig. "You asked Leon for help?"

"No, but he mentioned a connection to an investigator, and I thought of it as a possibility, a place to begin. I was taken aback when—"

"What?"

"I assumed you would be a black woman. When I followed you, I . . . I suppose I was trying to decide whether it made a difference."

"Does it?"

"Doesn't it always?"

His tone held me. It wasn't bitter, more flat and certain. Matter-of-fact. I let his words fade. It didn't seem there was anything I could say in response.

"Leon trusts you," he said. "Could you find out who this blackmailer is? I need to find out who's doing this to . . . to my friend."

"Then what? You planning to go to the police and have your blackmailer arrested?"

"Of course not. I'll talk to him, to her. I'll explain myself. Surely there must be some way I can stop this person from ruining my life."

"As a rule, blackmailers aren't big on chitchat."

"I'm an academic, a talker by profession. I'm a very persuasive man. Don't you think so?"

I almost smiled. I found his earnestness and naïveté touching, and I wondered how he'd come to know Leon. "You're telling me you have no idea who the blackmailer is?"

"I don't. I— My friend was discretion itself. He told no one; he never met the woman on campus."

" 'Told,' 'met.' Is there a reason you're speaking in the past tense?"

"The affair is over."

"Because of the blackmail."

"It ended before the blackmail began."

"If your friend was discretion itself, we have to assume that the woman—his student?"

"His student. Yes, but she seemed so much older, so mature for her years, so intriguing. I can't explain or excuse—" He studied his hands and adjusted his posture in the rickety chair. "My friend could never explain his infatuation satisfactorily to me."

"If I took on the investigation, I'd start with the woman. Would she be doing this, as a kind of revenge? Was it a bad breakup?"

He raised a hand to his mouth, rubbed his lips. For a moment, I thought he might refuse to answer, change the subject.

"The woman in question is dead," he said carefully.

"Dead," I repeated.

"Yes."

"How?"

He moistened his lips with his tongue and swallowed. "A fire. She was killed in a fire."

"An accident? What kind of fire? What happened?"

"I was out of town, at a conference. I don't really— I have tried to avoid the details of the disaster." He closed his eyes, his face a mask.

"Understand that my friend had ended the affair with Den—with the woman over a month before her death."

He waited for me to say something. I waited for him. It's a trick I learned when I was a cop: Don't be eager to fill the silence. You learn more by listening than by talking.

Inside the room, the stillness was absolute. Outside, the clatter of dishes was interrupted by the hum of the espresso machine.

"Perhaps you would not be interested in representing my friend after all," he said.

"Look, if the girl is dead, all you have to do is deny the story. Unless there are photographs."

"There are no photos. I was careful about—"

"Then why did you pay?"

"There are—were—letters. Tell me, are you interested in the case? If you don't agree to— I feel I've left my friend open to a new situation, a new peril. . . ."

"I'm not a blackmailer."

"I'm sorry. I didn't mean to imply that. Trusting people is not easy for me, and trusting a white person with this . . . It makes me uneasy to the depths of my soul. I'm not some showcase professor. I don't have a named chair or a university designation, not yet anyway, but I am a Harvard professor, and if this gets out, my whole life, my career, everything I've worked for is held by a perilous thread. God, I wish he could have held off, that this complication could have held off for another six months, another year—"

"The blackmailer's been in touch again."

"How did you know?"

"You wouldn't be talking to me if he hadn't been."

He nodded and stared into his lap. "I thought it was a one-shot deal, that it would be over."

"What does he want this time?"

"He's offering to sell me another letter."

"How many did you write?"

"I don't— No more than ten."

"E-mails or actual letters?"

"Letters. Handwritten. I know, it seems old-fashioned, stupid somehow. I never— I believed she had destroyed them."

"Does he want the same amount?"

"More. Five times what he asked before."

The blackmailer is a quick learner, I thought. And a greedy son of a bitch. A phone rang in the hallway, three times, five times, six.

I said, "You—your friend has a couple of options."

"What are they?"

"I already mentioned one: paying up. If you do, you're in it for the long haul. Don't kid yourself that it's one more time and you're out of the woods."

"There must be something I—he can do."

"I would suggest your pal tell all to his department chair and anyone else at the university with power over him, his wife, as well, if he has one."

"His wife would not be understanding."

"Limit it to people at the university, then. Tell them that he has a regrettable incident in his past that he would like to confess, in the hope that it will inspire members of the faculty to err in other ways and not his own."

"Hah," he said. "Understand that this was an undergraduate with whom my friend had an affair, and a white girl at that. My department chair would have my friend's head on a plate."

"No love lost."

"None."

"Could he be the blackmailer?"

"Frankly, I can't imagine it."

"Well, then, you could hire me to retrieve your indiscreet letters. Technically, it wouldn't be stealing. Letters belong to the recipient. In the event of the recipient's death, the sender has as strong a claim as anyone. I might be able to bargain with the blackmailer, convince him he ought to take what he's gotten so far and leave well enough alone."

"You said you thought a blackmailer wouldn't listen to reason."

"Put it like this: Everyone has something to lose. You could hire me to find out how to blackmail your blackmailer."

A slow-spreading smile widened his mouth and brightened his eyes. It wiped the creases off his forehead and took years off his age. "I like that. My friend would— I like the idea of that, the symmetry. You would find something in his life to hold over his head."

"I charge by the hour, plus expenses. I usually get a retainer and you'd need to sign a contract."

"But—"

"It wouldn't have to specify details, but I'd need to know your name."

He opened his mouth and sucked in a shallow breath. His hands were clenched so hard, his knuckles stood out like shards of white bone. "I think I—I need to think it over."

I got to my feet. "You're not ready." My action moved him off the dime.

"I am ready. Damn it, the situation is intolerable." He stood, too, and stared into my eyes like he was memorizing their color and shape, trying to see behind them into my mind.

After five seconds that felt like five minutes, he extended his right hand. "My name is Wilson Chaney, Professor Wilson Chaney."

Considering what I knew about him, I could have discovered his name in no time, but I didn't tell him that. I accepted his declaration as a leap of faith and shook his hand.

Don't get me wrong: Profs who boff students are not perched at the top of my favorites list. But I doubted this guy's livelihood was imperiled due to an amorous misstep. My demon curiosity had been aroused, rather than allayed, by his tale.

CHAPTER 3

I dumped parcels from my backpack, piling them on the dining room
table with a sigh of satisfaction. It wasn't often I returned from a
shopping trip with substantially more cash than the amount with
which I'd set forth. I liked the feeling.

"Anybody home?"

The house was cool and quiet, an oasis of dark wood and drawn
shades. I went into the kitchen, opened the fridge, and yanked the pop
top on a Pepsi. Dishes were stacked in the sink, no one had recycled
the bulging bags of soda cans on the countertop in recent history, and
the table was crusted with muck, but I wasn't about to let it spoil the
day. I had a new case. The prospect of interesting, lucrative work gave
the grimy kitchen a haze of cleanliness. I wouldn't even try to roust
Roz, the third-floor tenant, who's supposed to do the majority of scut
work in exchange for reduced rent; I wouldn't so much as tack a
scathing note to the bulletin board on the refrigerator door. She'd get
around to the kitchen when she felt like it, and that was good enough
for me.

I toted the Pepsi into the living room, which doubles as my office.
If I ran Chaney's blackmailer to ground in record time and earned

bonus, I'd make it a point to replace my old rolltop desk, the one destroyed in the fire, and finally bid farewell to the door and filing cabinet setup, which was too utilitarian for even my Spartan taste.

A red light flashed on the message machine. I pressed the button and Leonard Wells's voice rumbled like distant thunder.

"Hey, babe, finishing up on something and should be out of here by five, if you can believe it. I'll drop by and we can go for dinner, catch a flick, or maybe something else. See ya."

My pleasure in his deep voice diminished as I listened. I hadn't been going out with Leon for much more than a month, but I'd known him long enough to realize that he wouldn't call back to confirm. He'd show up on my doorstep, ready to go. His assumption that I'd drop everything whenever he got time to play was starting to unsettle me. Sam had never assumed I'd tailor my hours to his.

I sank into my chair and cursed. I'd made it through most of a week without thinking about Sam Gianelli, but there he was again, my off-again, on-again lover. We'd been a sporadic couple for more years than I could reasonably justify. We'd split for good just as Leon came on the scene.

I'd met Sam when I was nineteen and foolish. I'd thought he'd wait for me, but he'd married someone else, and then I did, too. Neither marriage lasted, and I guess I'd always assumed that Sam and I would eventually wind up together.

Now I considered the possibility that Sam's lack of availability had been its own reward. Maybe I'd turned him into some kind of dream lover, the unattainable male. Maybe one of his attractions had been that he rarely encroached on my space. Maybe the fact that he was unavailable had become the ultimate attraction. Maybe I'd gotten stuck in a goddamn solitary rut, content to work twenty-four/seven when I had a case, drive a cab or play guitar when I didn't. The only social engagement I currently tried to keep was my three-day-a-week volleyball commitment, and that was with women.

I consider myself way too young to rule men out of my life. I hope always consider myself too young. But Leon needed to inquire rather than assume. He was no dream lover, no one I couldn't have. He'd made it obvious: He was interested. When he had free time, he wanted to spend it with me.

So what the hell was I so busy for—what had I planned to do tonight that would interfere with dinner or a movie or the sexual tangle that Leon meant when he said "or maybe something else" with that furry rumble in his throat? Well, I'd planned to get a head start on the Chaney case, do the initial paperwork, some preliminary research, start asking questions. Maybe I should call Leon back and ask if we could just screw instead, take less time, and let me get my work done.

I swallowed and wondered why I resented the time and effort it took to start a new relationship. Was it because I wasn't finished with the old one yet? I wasn't sure how to keep Gianelli out of my thoughts, even when I was with Leon.

Work.

I'd taken notes on a spiral pad, like the incident-report log I'd gotten used to carrying as a cop. I slapped it down on my desk. Then I removed the blackmail note, enclosed in a plastic evidence Baggie, from the fold of my wallet. Chaney hadn't treated it carefully, but it might be worth trying for prints. First, I'd need to take Chaney's in order to eliminate them, and I wondered how he'd react to the request. Most black men I know have a gut distrust of cops and police techniques, but the black men I know don't teach at Harvard.

"Can't keep your dick in your pants, can't keep your bucks in the bank." According to Chaney, both demands began with the same crude sentence. He'd burned the first note, found the second shoved under his office door Monday morning, yesterday. It was written on cheap white paper, the kind that you buy in a tablet at the drugstore, and tucked into a sealed envelope.

"Can't keep your dick in your pants, can't keep your money in the bank. To bye back yr letter, 10/26, 'I love how you touch me,' ekcet, get 5 grand reddy by Friday. Hundreds, no sequence serial no.s."

My client thought the erratic spelling significant; I thought it was most likely a put-on. The message was printed in awkward block capitals that tilted slightly to the right, as though it had been written by a right-handed person using his or her left hand. The first message had come three weeks ago, a demand for a thousand dollars. The blackmailer had upped the ante quickly. Probably the first attempt had been a feeler. I wondered what would have transpired if the victim hadn't paid up so obediently.

I'd told Chaney I had no intention of intervening with or preventing Friday's payoff. I told him to get the money ready, to consider the five thousand dollars history. It was Tuesday; I don't guarantee three-day results.

At my request, Chaney had provided personal identification, including a photo ID and his Harvard faculty card. His check, drawn on a local bank, would have been good enough for me, but he didn't want any record of the transaction. I'd walked with him to the local Fleet branch, stood behind him in line as he cashed a check, listened to the teller greet him by name. He was who he said he was.

His retainer would make a pleasant bump in my bank balance. Retrieving, repossessing, even stealing his letters back would be tricky, although not impossible. Convincing the blackmailer that he'd been to the well just the right number of times might be trickier. Once I knew who the blackmailer was.

In exchange for the retainer, I'd given Chaney a receipt, my home phone number, my cell number, and Leon Wells's numbers, too, just in case, stressing that I needed to hear the minute the blackmailer made contact. If the blackmailer wanted to meet immediately, Chaney had orders to stall. I would need time.

Tuesday to Friday. I punched up my computer and did what Roz, she of the lackluster cleaning skills, refers to as "Googling the client." She says it dismissively, because a Google search doesn't reveal any of the deeper secrets she's able to squeeze out of the Web routinely, one of the reasons I discount her shortcomings as a housekeeper. She is a Web-cracker extraordinaire, and if she stopped cleaning entirely, which she may very well already have done, I'd still keep her around for her computer expertise.

I entered my client's name and was rewarded with a considerable number of hits. I wasn't sure how many a Harvard prof ought to rack up, so I typed in Alan Dershowitz's name (25,500), then Dr. Jerome Groopman's (2,850). Both men were pretty famous, but Wilson Chaney wasn't far behind with 2,267. The first hit was the Harvard Medical School directory, where he was listed as a professor, not with a named professorship like Groopman's or Dershowitz's, but not an adjunct professor or an instructor or a mere lecturer, either. He was cross-referenced to the ed school, which bore out his assertion that he held a joint appointment.

He was Dr. Chaney twice over, with a Ph.D. from the University of Chicago and an M.D. from Rutgers. He'd written articles that appeared in major medical journals, both *JAMA*, the *Journal of the American Medical Association*, and *NEJM*, the *New England Journal of Medicine*. I glanced at titles, punched up abstracts. The Web, as usual, gave more information than you could possibly absorb in a single sitting. I'd have Roz sort through the listings.

He'd written articles on the treatment of attention deficit hyperactivity disorder. They caught my eye, because here in the People's Republic of Cambridge, ADHD isn't simply a medical diagnosis; it's a divisive political argument. More kids in Massachusetts are diagnosed with the ailment than anywhere else in the nation, and some maintain it's a fashionable way of moving disruptive kids out of the public schools or medicating them into submission. My adopted sister, Paolina, had been ruled at risk for ADHD in the fifth grade. Turned out to be a false diagnosis.

Maybe not, I thought, glancing at the first paragraph of one of Chaney's pieces. The diagnosis had crumbled when challenged by a Spanish-speaking community activist who was supposed to be Paolina's advocate. Paolina had friends on Ritalin who were doing well, kids who were succeeding despite the fact that teachers had been ready to give up on them when they were unmedicated. And I wasn't sure Paolina's mother had done the right thing in harnessing her community to fight the diagnosis. Maybe Paolina would be in less academic trouble if Marta hadn't interfered.

It would be interesting to learn which side of the argument Wilson Chaney came down on. Or, more likely, to learn that, as with most arguments, there were way more than two sides. What counted now was that my client was who he said he was, a published and respected professor. He was also an absolute dead end when it came to suggesting identities for the suspected blackmailer.

I glanced at the clock, amazed at the amount of time that had passed, uncomfortably aware of how quickly it was racing toward five o'clock and Leon's arrival. I wasn't moving quickly enough. I hadn't done any research on the woman Chaney'd slept with. I considered calling Leon and canceling.

Give it a chance, Carlyle, I told myself. What the hell's wrong with you? The man is a prince. He's tall and dark; his voice is great. He's one of the good guys.

I have a friend, a true friend, never a lover, Mooney, who insists that the only guys I fall for are crooks and confidence tricksters, outlaws every one. I vowed to hang on to Leon long enough to make Moon eat his words.

I opened my notebook and concentrated on my chicken-scratch shorthand. Chaney's lover, Chaney's student, Denali Brinkman, was the blackmail trigger and the obvious place to start. At first, my client, an affronted gentleman had been reluctant to speak about her, certain she would never have betrayed the secret of their affair. A curiously naïve man, my client. When I pointed out that it was a simple matter of whether he'd talked or she'd talked, he'd admitted the truth of my deduction. Then once he started talking about Denali, he'd had a hard time stopping. The details poured out while I tried to pry facts out of his rose-tinted reminiscences.

She had been a freshman in his Introductory Educational Psychology class. It was surprising that he'd gotten to know her at all,

24

because he paid little attention to the freshman classes, the huge beginning-level crushes taught, as a rule, by graduate assistants. But he tried to give some attention to the entry-level classes.

I didn't like her being a freshman. Her age bothered me, made me wonder where I'd draw the line. If Chaney had been a teacher at the local high school where my little sister attends classes, would I have agreed to work for him? Kids who still live with their parents—is that the line? When does innocence end and experience raise its head?

In his version, the nineteen-year-old had come on to him. But did it matter? I reminded myself that it was his version. The woman in question wasn't around to tell her side of the tale, and few are the Harvard profs dumb enough to claim they made a play for a student.

She had been intrigued by one of his lectures and asked if she could set up an appointment to discuss it. Maybe if she'd been less attractive, he might have told her to submit her comments and questions in writing.

He hadn't wanted to come up with a physical description, and he maintained that he had no photos of the young woman. When pressed, he said she was blond, average height, average weight. Maybe a little on the thin side, but he admitted her figure was good. He sounded uncomfortable, regretful, and sad.

She was unusual, he insisted, gifted. Unusually bright, unusually warm, extremely outgoing with him, but terribly reserved in class. She wasn't like any other student or any other woman he'd ever known. She was a secret delight, and their relationship had grown intimate more quickly than he'd dared imagine possible. He resented my questions, and kept talking to avoid them. He *wanted* to talk about her; he just didn't want to answer my intrusive and awkward questions—like whether she was a virgin (no), or if he had ever altered any of her class grades (certainly not—what did I think he was?), or exactly how she had died (he knew no details, didn't want to know any). She rarely spoke about herself, but he'd gotten the impression of an unconventional upbringing, possibly from the flower-child quality of her first name. He didn't think she'd been born in Alaska, home of Mount

25

Denali, but knew she'd traveled a lot as a child—Europe, South America, and Asia. She was brilliant and an orphan and part American Indian, though she didn't look it.

Girl sounded like some fairy-tale princess to me. Too good to be true. Typical Harvard material, no doubt.

"Tell me about her friends," I'd said.

As far as he was concerned, she'd had no contact with anyone but him. She barely spoke to other students in class. She arrived and departed alone. They had never gone to a party, never socialized with another couple.

"She held herself aloof?"

"You make her sound snotty. She wasn't like that. She was *different*. She was most comfortable on the river."

"The river?"

"She was a rower. I didn't know the river at all. She showed me things about the river I would never have seen without her."

"It's not exactly private, the river." His admission of Charles River field trips seemed to nullify his protestations of discretion.

"Not the river here. I mean, she took me rowing nearby, as far as the Watertown dam, but that's as far upstream as you can go in a racing scull. She was a kayaker, too, and she took me where the Charles is—well, I never knew, but it's winding and it changes. Up in Waltham, in Newton—it was like we were a million miles from the Northeast, in a different country."

"Where did you have sex? Did you take her to your house?"

"Never."

"Your office?"

They had done it in his office and in a locked classroom, as well as in a Somerville motor court and a small Cambridge inn. She was a goddess, all the good things that had ever happened, and I was wickedly undermining her goodness with suggestions that she'd spilled the beans about her married lover.

I blew out a breath and considered his impassioned defense of Denali Brinkman, his refusal to discuss her demise. She was dead, elevated to the dream-lover status Sam Gianelli had achieved while still alive. She was flawless, rowing tirelessly on the river at twilight, bathed in a Technicolor glow, forever young.

I snapped my notebook shut. I had a place to start. Harvard freshmen live on campus, and one of the few facts that Chaney had retained was the name of the dormitory in which Denali had lived. Phillips House was within easy walking distance.

The doorbell rang, and damned if my wristwatch didn't agree with the wall clock: 5:35. Leon. I'd been so deeply into the memory of Chaney's words and actions that I'd forgotten, and what would a professor with a background in psychology say about that?

I put my eye to the peephole, a habit of mine. Leon Wells rocked on the stoop, moving almost imperceptibly on the balls of his feet in a way that would have identified him as a cop even if I didn't know he'd been one before his ascent, or descent, to the FBI. Leon is six two, handsome, the color of mahogany. His head is shaved and oiled, and his smile reveals even white teeth. He's part American Indian, like Chaney's girlfriend, but he shows it, with a hawklike nose and jutting cheekbones. He waited with an air of alert stillness, as though he'd be ready for anything that popped out from behind my door.

I wanted to ask about his friendship with Wilson Chaney, but I couldn't. I unlocked the door, which takes awhile. Two good standard locks, plus the dead bolt. Neighborhood's popular with thieves as well as Harvard grads.

"You ready?" he asked.

"Come in, get yourself a drink. I have to change."

"You look fine."

"It'll only take a minute."

I helped him locate a Rolling Rock, grabbed a package off the dining room table, and scooted upstairs. I'd bought black bikini underwear at the Gap. Why bother getting new stuff if you're not going to wear it?

CHAPTER 4

Leon left the house just before 6:30 A.M. I didn't give him the early-morning boot because of concern about gossipy neighbors. If I'd been concerned about the neighbors, I'd have made him sneak out while it was pitch-dark, 6:30 being way too late to escape the righteous bunch of early-morning joggers who live nearby. Leon left early because sometimes my little sister drops by before school starts to have a cup of coffee, pick up a change of clothes, or grab a textbook. She doesn't live with me full-time, but she sleeps here two nights a week when her mom works late. On those two nights, I never entertain gentlemen callers, and she never finds a man here in the morning. You might think my behavior hypocritical, and that's the point; she would think it vastly hypocritical that I, an unmarried woman, sleep with my boyfriend and yet strongly discourage her from sleeping with hers. She wouldn't see the difference, but I do. I'm over thirty and she's under sixteen, and that's the biggest difference in the world.

So I rushed Leon out the door, and of course she didn't show. I thought about going back to bed but then got up and went to play volleyball instead.

Three mornings, a week you'll find me on the court at the Cambridge Y, spiking the ball for the Lady Y-Birds, an assortment of academics, cops, firefighters, and one mild-mannered accountant. Wednesday morning, we started slow and droopy, found our rhythm a game and a half into the match, and whipped the Waltham Y team in a close third game. I've been getting back into volleyball slowly after taking time off to recuperate from a bullet wound in my left thigh. I'm still wary of diving for the ball the way I used to, but for a while, with the score stuck at 12-12 in the final game, I forgot about pain and played tough.

I celebrated the victory with a cold shower in a grim gray-curtained cubicle. The Y is not to be mistaken for some fancy health-club spa.

Chaney would call as soon as the blackmailer got in touch. I could have waited until then, but waiting has never been my strong suit, and identifying the perp didn't have to wait till money changed hands. I decided against my usual stop at the Central Square Dunkin' Donuts and turned toward Harvard Square instead, moving into a crush of pedestrian traffic that flowed far more smoothly than its automotive equivalent. Small shops line both sides of the street as far as Putnam Circle, where the stores on the right give way to red Harvard brick. I took a gentle left onto Mount Auburn, another left at Plympton, passing ethnic restaurants, stores with hand-carved furniture, used shops selling secondhand books, and cafés, taking pleasure in the old houses, the one-of-a-kind shops, the absence of Taco Bells.

Phillips is one of the so-called River Houses, although you can't actually see the Charles because other Harvard houses, notably Lowell and Winthrop, block the view. One of the smaller houses, Phillips isn't one of the original seven built when the house system began, but it was constructed to imitate the originals in style, with a hidden open court, carved pediments, and elaborate entry arches, designed to look like buildings at Cambridge and Oxford.

I tried side entries just for the hell of it but found them locked. I already knew the main entrance would be locked. All the Harvard Houses used to stay open during the day, but the tourists would come and use the bathrooms, since Harvard Square has almost no public toilets. When dormitory theft went up, the doors got locked, and the tourists went without. Occasionally, especially when I'm driving a cab late at night, I'll lurk in the vicinity and wait for some careless undergrad to charge in the door. I say hello and exchange small talk, cruise past the guard as though I were the entering student's buddy, get to use a decent bathroom. The guards in the front lobbies are supposed to make you sign in, but really they're more like concierges, giving directions, offering advice. I always get in.

Knowing the vulnerability of house security, I didn't ring the bell and ask to speak to the master or the senior tutor. I simply waited for a student to fling the door wide, then entered on her coattails, taking advantage of the fact that I don't look like a mass murderer. Part of me felt like scolding the cheerful student, a slim blond sprite, one of the golden children who invade the Square each year for the sole purpose of making the rest of the population feel old and jaded.

A tasteful printed directory listed both a female and male master, with suite numbers for each. The senior tutor was female, ditto the resident adviser. I tucked names and numbers away in my memory and started exploring corridors, entering the sorts of rooms where tea gets poured from silver pots and overstuffed furniture is tastefully arrayed on worn Oriental rugs. The scent of lemony wood polish blended with the smell of potpourri. The interior spoke of solemn tradition, a certain level of comfort, the expectation of continued success.

It sure didn't smell like the Police Academy. Didn't have the aroma of my alma mater, either. UMass Boston has its campus on Boston Harbor, and the redbrick and concrete-block buildings are cheap and earnest, like the daughters and sons of the working-class immigrants who make up the population.

By following an indistinct murmur, I located a cluster of students sitting in a room, watching daytime TV, some rerun of the latest reality show. I apologized for interrupting and mentioned that I was looking for a friend of Denali. I didn't mention Denali's last name. I mean, how many Denalis could there be?

My question brought silence, then a giggle as one of the kids, who hadn't tuned out of the show, reacted to a limp TV gag. There were four of them, two and two. A dark-haired girl stretched her long legs across a deep red velvet sofa. A stringy boy sat on the floor near her bare feet. Another girl was prone on the rug, knees elevated, a pillow under her head, a notebook resting on her flat belly. The boy in the armchair looked older, but mainly because he was trying to, cultivating a goatee and wearing gold round-rimmed glasses. His sweater had baggy elbows. He was the first to speak.

"You mean the dead girl?"

"Yeah, I'm looking for her roommate. She told me, but I can't remember the name. Karen, or something like that, maybe." I was making it up as I went along. According to Chaney, Denali had rarely talked about herself and had never mentioned the existence of a roommate.

"There's nobody named Karen here," the prone girl on the rug said, and an off note in her carefully controlled voice told me she might know the roommate's real name.

"Well, Denali was, like, never here, either," chimed the couch girl. "I didn't even know she lived in Phillips till—"

The boy in the armchair broke in. "Who wants to know?"

"Just me."

"You a reporter? You want our reaction to 'Grisly Death in the Ivy League'?" He used his fingers to float quotation marks in the air, his voice to punch up the capital letters.

"No."

He yanked a tiny cell phone from his pocket, hit buttons. I wasn't sure how many buttons he'd need to summon the Harvard cops.

"Miranda, this is Gregor in the Coolidge Room. A woman's here, asking about Denali. . . . No, I don't know how she got in."

Miranda Gironde was the name of the resident adviser. I'd wanted to meet her later, if not sooner.

"Gregor," I said, "you got it wrong. I'm asking about Denali's roommate. And I'm not a reporter."

"You're interrupting our show."

I wanted to smack his self-satisfied face. *Our show,* like they put it on the tube just for them. They were all studiously ignoring me, except for the girl on the floor, who stared with veiled interest. Again, I wondered whether she might have something to say. I shot her a questioning glance and she quickly looked down, affirming the hunch.

"Jeannie, let's meet tomorrow at eleven and go over the notes," Gregor said, noting the interaction.

"Can't. I've got an eleven o'clock at McKay," said the girl on the floor.

"Always supposing you're taking the damn notes." Gregor caught my eye. "You are interrupting an important group project. Close the door on your way out."

I left it deliberately ajar, which was childish, then paced the hall, hunting for other kids to interrogate. No one was in a small sitting room, or in a bigger room with a massive desk, a chandelier, and heavy drapes. I was back in the hallway again when I heard a door slam and light, quick tread on the stairs. Miranda—I assumed it was the resident adviser—was hurrying, a towel wrapped around just-shampooed hair. She leaned over the railing, quickly identified me as the outsider, and made her approach. She was flushed, maybe thirty pounds overweight, with a round face, tan skin, dark eyes, and dimples.

"I'm sorry," she said, "but all questions about Miss Brinkman are to be addressed to the dean."

Her severity, I thought, was forced. The lines in her face seemed naturally cheerful; a dimple threatened to display itself on her left cheek.

"Gregor misunderstood. It's not Miss Brinkman I'm interested in at all; I'm interested in finding her roommate."

"And why would you want to do that?" The rhythm of her speech was faintly Jamaican.

"To recover my property. Denali was storing a few things for me while I was out of town."

Her frown evaporated. "Oh, you know—knew Denali."

"I don't know why they thought I was a reporter. Have reporters been bothering you?"

"You wouldn't believe. It's been— You didn't come to the funeral."

"I was out of the country, actually. I only found out a couple of days ago—that she'd died." I let my voice tremble just a bit, like I was trying to bear up under the terrible news.

"Oh, there now. I'm sorry." The woman seemed programmed to believe what people told her, a serious flaw in a resident adviser. "Here, sit down." She led me into the larger, more formal room and asked whether I'd like some tea.

"Thank you." I'm not a tea drinker, but I figured she wouldn't toss me out with a china cup in my hands. She busied herself with silver and teaspoons and sugar in a small alcove while I wondered which dead white male had been honored by having his name given to this room. The old coot whose portrait dominated the space over the mantel had eyes like black ice.

"You look tired," I said sympathetically as she handed me a delicate cup and saucer.

She smiled and a dimple crinkled. "I'm not used to dealing with freshmen. Usually they're kept in the Yard Houses but this year, what with construction and remodeling, Entry B is practically all freshmen."

"Like Denali."

"Yes. Are you a rower, too?

I nodded, seizing gratefully on the offered identity. I liked Miranda. I bet she fed the kids excuses when they missed curfew. Except they probably didn't have any damn curfew here.

"I thought so, big girl like you."

"Denali's roommate might be able to help me find my things."

She sat across from me in an overstuffed chair. "I wish I could help. It might be they're gone—you know, in the fire."

The tea was sugary and strong. I sipped and set the saucer on the oval coffee table. I should have researched the fire and the girl before coming here; Leon's visit had interrupted the process. I'd walked around Phillips House in my search for open doors. I hadn't seen any evidence of a recent fire, but Harvard had the clout to have such things fixed overnight.

I said, "She told me she'd keep them in her room. That's why I thought her roommate—"

"Well, I shouldn't tell you this, but—"

I lowered my gaze and tried to look harmless. It always surprises me when it works; I never consider myself harmless.

"I wish I had known," she went on in a low voice. "It's not that Denali's roommate was unpleasant or anything like that. It wasn't that at all; it was how different things must have been for her, as used as she was to quiet and to open spaces. We have so few students with her background. I guess the chatter, the noise, got too much for her. We didn't realize—*I* didn't realize—that she'd moved into the boathouse to be alone. Believe me, no one had any idea she was camping there, until the fire, that is."

"The boathouse on Memorial Drive?"

"Yes. The Weld."

"She lived there? She had a key?"

"No, no. It's— They're remodeling, too. You can see—you could see—there was a temporary wooden thing. They're enlarging the boat-storage area. That's where she— I don't know how long she'd been living there, but she'd moved her things out of the suite. Not that she had much, poor dear. I wish her roommate had mentioned it to me, but you know, they hate to tell on anyone, and when someone doesn't come in, they make assumptions."

Shacking up with some man, that's what they'd think.

"Possibly Denali mentioned me to her roommate, told her where she'd put my—"

"I'm sorry," Miranda said firmly. "I've spoken to the girl and I'm sure she knows nothing about Denali's possessions. She feels terrible about this, and I don't want her upset all over again."

I wondered whether I could trick the RA into divulging the roommate's name. I didn't think she'd give it if I asked directly; I'd only raise suspicion. The tea felt astringent on my tongue, making me thirstier than before. No, I decided. I wouldn't ask. I'd try my luck down at the boathouse. Better than getting the party line from the dean.

I drained the cup and thanked Miranda for her help. She ushered me to the door and made sure the lock clicked shut behind me.

35

CHAPTER 5

A fatal fire at the Weld with a Harvard girl the victim. The story should have topped every newscast in town. I yanked my spiral notebook out of my backpack and thumbed through the pages I'd scrawled in Passim's back room. The second blackmail message had arrived two days ago, on May 15. The first had arrived three weeks ago, April 24. Denali had died the first week in April. I'd spent the third and fourth of that month in Philly, working on a case; I must have missed the initial coverage. And then I'd gotten caught up in the Dig business. I wondered if the WGU had stomped on the story. Harvard holds so many strings in its hands, it operates like a giant puppeteer orchestrating multiple marionettes. I made a note to check the *Globe* and *Herald* archives. I wondered if there were legal implications, a freshman not tucked up safely in her dorm. Maybe that was why Miranda had orders to funnel inquisitors straight to the dean.

Miranda had mistaken me for a rower, and the deception seemed feasible, short-term. I know the jargon, courtesy of Sam Gianelli, who took to rowing with the passion of a man whose mob-connected father loved only powerboats. *Single scull* and *weigh 'nuff* were terms I could toss off with authority. I'm still a regular head-of-the-Charles regatta viewer. I used to row from the BU Bridge to the Harvard Bridge and back again with Sam, going full speed on summer mornings. I shook the man out of my thoughts but kept the idea that I might learn more as a rower than as a private eye.

The day was bright and the wind stiff, the Weld Boathouse practically across the street. The lower Charles is edged with boathouses and yacht clubs. Boston University's is the newest, an Arts and Crafts cream-colored structure with vivid red doors, an aqua roof, and arched windows, but the Weld retains the title of most picturesque. From the Boston side of the river, it looks like an elegant Tudor mansion, set so close to the water that someone had the idea of installing ramps.

I admired the panorama, students lying on the grassy riverbank, reading and sunning, dogs romping through the grass. The Weeks Bridge, in the background, made me smile. It's a narrow pedestrian structure that connects the B school on the Brighton side of the river with the rest of the colleges in Cambridge. On summer weekends, the bridge is illuminated, and the Boston Tango Society holds dance classes there. My little sister always calls it "the Midnight Tango Bridge."

If somebody'd substituted a flock of white sheep for the flock of white geese near the Weeks Bridge and the students had been playing recorders instead of poker, the scene might have passed for pastoral. I couldn't see signs of a recent fire. I crossed the street at the light, backtracked, and started a clockwise circuit of the boathouse.

The eastern side of the building was blocked from Memorial Drive traffic by tall elms and overgrown rhododendrons. I could make out the remains of a structure behind the yellow tape, a few charred boards, a burned outline in the grass. The configuration of the structure was impossible to ascertain. The smell lingered. My house caught fire once, and sometimes I still wake in the night and think I catch the scent of burning wood. It wakes me fast, stone-cold alert, dread beating in my veins.

"Hey, miss, you okay?"

He was young enough to be a student, shaggy, with an untrimmed beard and long hair curling down his neck. He wore raggedy cutoffs and his shoulders were broad. No shirt. I hadn't heard him approach, partly because I was caught in my fire memory and partly because he was barefoot.

"I, uh, heard there was a fire at the boathouse," I said.

"You sure you're okay?"

He'd misinterpreted my reaction to the fire site, so I went with it. "No, um, I'm sorry. See, I knew her. The girl who—"

"You knew Denali? You on Harvard crew?"

"No."

"You knew her from before? Like from Idaho. Wow."

I hadn't heard about Idaho. Chaney'd just said she'd traveled. The shaggy-haired guy was waiting for me to say something. "I guess you knew her, too," I said.

"Yeah, like not well, but— Wow, like if the crew knew you were here, we could play Forty Questions. Like twice twenty, you know?"

"You rowed with her?"

"I'm Jaycee, on heavy fours over at Newell. I help out around here, too."

I nodded. The Newell Boathouse was Harvard's, as well. The men rowed out of Newell, the women from Weld.

"She was a single-sculler," he said. "Hell of a rower. Impressive. Damn shame she got injured. And then . . . well, the whole business was a crying shame. Thing was, we didn't know a lot about her. I mean, growing up on a reservation, and then all alone, rowing so she could travel." There was admiration in his voice.

I was starting to wish I'd met the dead girl; she didn't sound like one of the snots I'd run into at Phillips House. I wondered if they had driven her away, despite Miranda's claim to the contrary. I'd read about college hazing rites, about the cruelty of the group toward the outcast. I'd lived them as a cop.

"Did you know she was living here?"

"Hell no. Nobody was supposed to be living in there. Who'd even think somebody would? I mean, she was in a dorm, right? And this place was just a shell. No insulation, no nothing. They hadn't even joined it up with the rest of the building, so it must have been colder than hell, you know?'

I said, "She was storing a few things of mine. I don't suppose—"

"Well, you can see for yourself. If she kept 'em in there—"

"Maybe she had a locker in the main building or something."

"No way. That's one of the reasons the girls are waiting for the expansion. Can't store anything in the big house. Man, they catch you keeping shit in there, they throw it out."

"How did the fire start?" I was trying to see it in my mind, how a fire on a main road, easily accessible to fire department vehicles, could have turned fatal. I kept recalling the fire at my house, the billowing smoke, the acrid stink. I knew too well how easy it could be to take a wrong turn, make a fatal blunder. Maybe the building materials had been toxic. She might have been trapped under a falling beam, caught in some kind of explosion. Flammable stuff, paint and paint thinner, could have been stored in the shed. I hadn't asked Chaney if his lover had been a smoker.

Jaycee gave me a veiled look. "You don't know?"

"I just heard. I was out of town and—"

"Shit. I'm not sure I wanna be the one to tell you."

"Look, I know she died in the fire. What could be worse than that?" I remembered the heat searing into my lungs, the rising panic.

"Look, you wanna sit down?"

There was no place to sit except on the grass. "Just tell me. I can handle it."

He gave me a long look, decided I was okay. "Denali—she set it herself."

I'd been expecting some horrible image, a girl running from the building, aflame like a human torch. "What are you saying? She was an arsonist? She was trying to burn the boathouse down, and something went wrong?"

"No, that's not what I'm telling you. I know it's hard to believe, but she did it on purpose, left a note, the whole thing."

"You mean she killed herself?" Historical footage of Vietnam protests played through my mind like grainy newsreel, monks setting themselves ablaze. I looked at the charred planks and saw a funeral pyre. "Did anybody see? Was she alone? How did they—"

"I'm sorry I had to be the one to tell you," Jaycee said. "Really, from what I knew, she was a nice girl. You never expect anything like that. I mean, you read all the shit in the papers, but look at this place, look at the sunlight and the dogs. Why's anybody gonna do a thing like that here, right?"

He seemed honestly pained, more upset by the retelling than he'd expected to be.

"Jaycee, can I speak to you a minute?" The woman who came around the back of the boathouse was wearing a crew top and rowing shorts, and she was moving fast. She was almost as tall as I am; her shoulders were broader. She motioned the shaggy youth over, kept a suspicious eye on me while she spoke to him. I could see his back and just the top of her head. Jaycee spent the time nodding and bobbing his head. Then he went into the boathouse without a glance in my direction and the woman approached. She had authority in her eyes and some age on her. Late thirties, ocean blue eyes in a nest of premature wrinkles.

"Who are you?" she demanded.

"I'm trying to locate some things Denali was keeping for me. Nothing massive. Some CDs, a few books. I thought maybe she stored some stuff in the boathouse."

"I haven't seen you before."

"I haven't seen you before, either."

We locked eyes for a minute, and then she said, "Any questions about Miss Brinkman should be addressed to the dean." She had it down pat.

"Thanks." I smiled like I hadn't heard that one before, then turned to go.

"If you knew her, I'm sorry. She was a damn good rower." The woman nodded curtly and bounded up the steps to the boathouse. I waited until she was out of sight before hauling out my cell phone. Chaney answered after three rings.

I identified myself. "We need to meet."

"Listen, he hasn't called yet, and I don't want us to be—"

"If you want me to keep working for you, you'll meet me. *Now.*"

"I can't get away now. I've got— Okay, six-fifteen is absolutely the first time I can make it. How's that?" He kept his voice low, an irritated whisper.

I agreed to the time and punched the off button on my cell, thinking that if people would just level with me from the get-go, my job would be much simpler. Damn, if people would level with each other, they wouldn't need my services. But who's honest anymore? What does it mean, *honest*? Hadn't I just posed as the pal of a recent suicide, done too much bullshitting to judge?

CHAPTER 6

JFK Memorial Park is a manicured swath of green behind the school of government, studded with stately oaks and elms and separated from the riverbank by Memorial Drive. I sat on a bench and waited for Chaney in the deepening twilight.

When I suggested we meet near the scene of the fatal fire, he hadn't reacted one way or another, simply mentioned the bench at the northwest edge of the park, far from streetlamps. I wondered if he'd met Denali here, near Phillips House, near the boathouse where she'd studied and rowed and died.

Suicide. No wonder I'd been twice referred to the dean.

Earlier generations may have achieved identical suicide rates at prestigious colleges, but times were different then. Shamed families drew the drapes to shut out the sunlight and wondered how they'd failed, while friends and neighbors met silence with silence. Parents never dreamed of accusing universities of negligence, never hired attorneys. I'd spent my waiting-for-Chaney time at Widener Library, doing some research: Six students had killed themselves over the past ten years at MIT. I hadn't found a number for Harvard, but I was aware of two current lawsuits, one at MIT, one at Princeton. The MIT lawsuit concerned a girl who'd set herself ablaze in her dorm room. Denali would have read about her death in the papers, seen the gruesome TV coverage.

I hadn't seen Denali's death on TV. I'd been away. I'd found the relevant articles in the on-line archives. The *Herald* got the scoop; its initial piece gave credit to both a staffer and a correspondent. "Fatal Fire in Boathouse" was brief, a narrow column, a single paragraph. The timing must have been tight, deadline looming.

> Cambridge: A fatal fire engulfed an addition to the Weld Boathouse in an early-morning blaze. The wooden structure was totally involved when firefighters from Ladder Company 7 responded. The unfinished structure was presumed empty, but after the blaze was extinguished, firefighters searching the premises discovered a body. The victim has not yet been identified.

The next day's *Herald* article was front-page stuff, titled "Student's Body in Boathouse." The same two reporters shared credit for the longer piece. At first believed to be that of a transient, the badly burned body removed from yesterday's boathouse blaze is now thought to be that of a Harvard student rower. The name of the victim is being withheld pending confirmation of identity and notification of next of kin.

This article also said that the boathouse had been donated to Harvard by the George Walker Weld family in 1906. It gave the name of the construction company responsible for renovating and expanding the boathouse, and included a defensive quote from an electrical contractor. Another quoted source was Capt. Ed Flowers. I knew the name; he was the Cambridge fire marshal and the chief arson investigator. He said the nature of the blaze made it suspect.

Suspect meant multiple points of origin, use of an accelerant. Captain Flowers was the same man who'd investigated the blaze at my house. He was thorough and honest. Also nasty and suspicious. He'd assumed I'd set my blaze to collect insurance.

I thumbed through my spiral notebook. According to my client, Denali was an orphan and had no close relatives. I wondered how long it had taken the police to locate the next of kin. There was nothing in the next day's *Herald*. The *Globe* offered nothing new. Then, another single paragraph in both papers: The word *suicide* was modified by the adjective *suspected*. Denali Brinkman's name was given, along with a badly focused photograph of a racing shell. The woman rower, caught midstroke, was identified as the "college suicide." Her blond hair caught the breeze. Her face was a pale blur.

There was no follow-up in either paper, and I assumed the heavy hand of Harvard. How many names on how many mastheads owed allegiance to their alma mater? How many others hoped their children would one day be granted admission?

Suicides sometimes occur in waves, in epidemics of terminal despair. In South Boston one summer, young men hung themselves, jumped from high places, swam so far out into the bleak ocean that swimming back was not an option.

I waited eight minutes before Chaney approached from the opposite end of the park, passing behind the fountain, his dark sunglasses catching the last glare of the setting sun. I realized I was thinking of him by his last name, no longer giving him his honorific title. He wore his raincoat and a shapeless hat with the brim tugged low. If I'd been a cop, I'd have rousted him on suspicion.

He sat on the same bench, but at the other end, as though he didn't know me. "This is extremely inconvenient. Have you found him already?" He spoke while staring straight ahead, a man who'd seen too many spy movies.

I slid over on the bench, refusing the gambit. "You didn't mention that your girlfriend killed herself. Did you think I wouldn't find out?"

"I don't see how it's relevant." His face gave nothing away. Maybe he'd worn sunglasses so I couldn't read his eyes.

"You tell me the facts. I decide if they're relevant."

"The only thing that's relevant is the blackmail."

"What about the blackmailer's motivation? Would you call that relevant?"

"No one could hold me responsible for Denali's death."

"The thought never crossed your mind?"

He swallowed. "I don't have to defend myself to you."

I nodded. He didn't have to defend himself to me and I didn't have to work for him. Money had gone into my checking account, but it wasn't a one-way street.

He crossed his legs and arms defensively and stared off at a distant group of soccer players, kicking a ball near a KEEP OFF THE GRASS sign. The JFK fountain is a granite square. The water flows constantly, an endless sheet of glass, running over carved excerpts from the assassinated president's speeches.

Many wealthy conservative donors wanted Harvard to have nothing to do with memorializing the dead president. They refused the honor of having the Kennedy Library sited at Harvard. When there was talk of refusing to name the government school in his honor, the liberal city of Cambridge took action, changing the name of the street on which the school was located to John F. Kennedy Way, so that it would be associated with his name whether or not Harvard sought the distinction.

"I was stunned when I heard," Chaney murmured. "Stunned."

An elderly man walked a yellow Labrador down the curved path. Chaney waited until he was out of earshot.

"Listen to me. What we had was not the stuff of drama. What we had was a . . . a sexual thing."

"You know what she said and what she did, but not what she felt or what she thought."

"Her heart was not engaged. She broke it off with me."

"You said—"

"That was vanity."

"It was a lie."

He was silent for a while, but I didn't prompt him. I studied the granite memorial fountain and waited. It didn't look anything like a wishing well, too square and modern, but I caught the glint of pennies at the bottom. Tourists toss them instinctively; a fountain means pennies, wishes, keeping the kids quiet a moment longer.

"I never felt like I knew her," Chaney said. "It was one of the things that fascinated me. Basically, people are easy to read. Kids are; students are. There isn't as much infinite variety as you think when you're young, or maybe this place attracts certain types. I've seen so much ambition, so much ego, so much self-regard. Denali was interested in me, and not many of them are. I found it flattering. I don't kid myself; I'm no Einstein. I'm already old-fashioned. Most of the stuff I believe in, the kids deride. They don't want to know about educational theory; they want to know about drugs, quick fixes."

He was trying to figure out why she'd dropped him, not why she'd killed herself. I waited, hoping he'd speculate about that.

"She said once that early death ran in her family. That was the only time I remember her using the word *death*. I never imagined she was considered ending her own life."

"What do you mean, 'early death ran in her family'?"

"She— I don't see how this is—"

"Let me decide what's relevant."

"Her mother died when she was a child. Leukemia, I think, a sudden, virulent death. Her father died before she was born. She had no family, and the tribe was reluctant to raise her."

"The tribe?"

"Her mother was an American Indian, from one of those small Northwest tribes. Her father was Swiss, but she didn't learn that until much later. She had no brothers or sisters. She never went hungry, but there wasn't much kindness in her life. She didn't even know her father's name."

"It's not Brinkman?"

"His first name. The tribe never spoke it. He must have done something, displeased someone. She'd never even seen a photograph of him. She never talked much about her life, but every once in awhile— She was well traveled."

"How did a poor kid from an Indian tribe get to be so well traveled?"

"The woman who raised her made a lot of money from gambling casinos. They traveled together at first. There was a falling-out, but by then Denali rowed, and her rowing took her places. She'd done things you never hear about in Cambridge. She'd lived in the desert and worked on a ranch. In Switzerland, she met her great-uncle on her father's side, an old man, and he told her her father's name."

I wondered whether the great-uncle was the elusive next of kin.

"Harvard must have been quite a jump."

"She did well in my class."

"Did you know she didn't get along with her roommate?"

"No."

"Did you know she was living in a half-built addition by the side of the boathouse? With no heat?"

He swallowed. "I didn't know. It's not like I picked her up at her front door."

"Why did she break it off?"

"What does that have to do with anything?"

"Did she find someone else?"

"No!"

"How do you know?"

"I don't know. I—"

"Was she pregnant?"

"What?"

"Could she have been pregnant?"

He took off his sunglasses, and his eyes were fierce. "You're saying you think she killed herself rather than bear a black man's child? Is that what you're saying?"

"I'm saying she might have thought she had no way out."

"This is Cambridge, Massachusetts. This is the fucking twenty-first century. You're telling me she wouldn't have had an abortion."

"Some women won't. If she had religious—"

"If she had religious scruples, she probably wouldn't have killed herself. What you said bordered on racist, that she'd rather die than—"

"Don't put that on me. I might as well call you a sexist pig for not understanding that for some women, ending a pregnancy is not just a medical prodecure, but I'm not going to take that way out."

"You want a way out?"

"I want it clear: I wasn't hired to investigate a suicide."

"I don't want you to. I want you to handle the blackmailer. Will you do that? Look, I made a mistake. I slept with a student. If I were white or she were black, I might be able to weather the storm, but I can't, not with my department head against me."

I didn't say anything. The light was going out of the sky.

"Don't people deserve second chances?" he asked.

A good question, I thought. But irrelevant. Who the hell gets what they deserve?

"Call me as soon as the blackmailer makes contact."

I left him sitting on the bench.

CHAPTER 7

Paolina spent the night, so no Leon, not that I could have questioned him about his buddy, the professor. This whole business of her spending the night started as a cover story when Paolina's family moved out of the Cambridge projects. They wanted to stay in the city, but the areas that used to be cheap turned gentrified and high-priced, so they wound up in a tiny house in Watertown. Paolina used my address to continue at the local high school. She started sleeping over occasionally, when band practice ran late, or if she pulled a detention.

Then Marta found a part-time job as a bar hostess, and one of her friends agreed to stay with Paolina's younger brothers two nights a week. We institutionalized Paolina's occasional nights over. So far so good; Paolina seems to get along better with her mother the less she sees her.

She'd never had her own room before. I'm no great shakes at decorating, but I can paint. She'd wanted pink, but I'd balked at the girlieness of it all, and we'd settled on a deep rose. I was taken back by her choice of decor. Her walls are plastered with the usual magazine pics of rock stars, but the main focus is a huge poster of Medellín, Colombia, stuff of her heritage and her fantasies. Her drug lord

Colombian father may or may not still live in Medellín. I doubt it. The government's been trying to capture him so long, he's probably left the country. The poster echoes the warmth of the walls, with spectacular blue skies, fields of lush flowers, green cordilleros.

She never makes her bed. Not being a big bed-maker myself, I don't care.

The next morning, I got up early and made breakfast for my sister, even though it isn't part of our deal. My fault; our "deal" was made in ignorance. I didn't appreciate the dating complications. I didn't suspect the nutritional complexities. When she assured me she'd handle her own meals, I didn't understand that meant skipping breakfast, skipping lunch, eating take-out pizza for dinner when and if she and her pals could scrounge up the bucks. I'm not a nutrition nut; far from it. I eat junk food, love it, in fact, but breakfast is a time when your mother, or a reasonable substitute, puts food on the table.

Hey, how could I be so rebellious if I weren't a traditionalist at heart?

Orange juice, toast, scrambled eggs. I tried to give her a glass of milk, but she glared till I made coffee. She pours so much milk in it, it's practically healthy anyway.

It's been an uphill battle since we met, when Paolina was seven and I was still a cop. I miss the scrawny seven-year-old, the feisty ten-year-old, but I doubt I'll miss the fifteen-year-old with the pout and the overlipsticked mouth, the one who assures me that all the kids talk like that and who wants to know the fuck's my problem. This morning, she ate in a blur, left her dishes in the sink, and was gone before I could object to her tank top. Why her mother lets her buy clothes like that, I don't know.

Well, yes, I guess I do. Her mother dresses the same way. Marta, married twice, abandoned twice, four kids, no skills, considers the landing of a male meal ticket the be-all and end-all of life. Probably coaches Paolina in the proper tightness of clothes. And glories in Paolina's body, seeing her daughter's curves as golden lures.

I drank my coffee slowly. I hadn't gotten a hint as to where Denali

Brinkman might have stashed her love letters. I hadn't learned her roommate's name, but I'd taken the precaution of writing down every name that appeared on a Phillips House mailbox. The girl, Jeannie, if she lived there and wasn't just visiting to watch TV, was probably J. P. St. Cyr.

I needed to find out who was using the letters to blackmail my client, but my mind kept veering back to the fire. In the light of a new day, I found myself curious about exactly what had happened at the boathouse shed the night Denali Brinkman died.

The private-eye business is all about trading favors. It's about who you know and what they know—and what you can offer in return. I know Cambridge cops; more particularly, I know a sergeant who'd know what I wanted to know—namely, who'd responded to the fire at the boathouse—and I was in a position, due to a favor from a previous encounter, to ask. Kevin Shea gave me a song and dance, flirted lamely, and stalled around, but we both knew he'd kick up the name in the end, and he did.

I got dressed in a hurry, briefly debated between the T and the car, decided on the car. The risk was parking tickets, the benefit freedom, and I wasn't sure where I'd be headed after the cop house.

Central Square's station house is surrounded by funky ethnic restaurants and slightly seedy stores. The neighborhood gets better; the neighborhood gets worse. Right now, it's on an upswing. You can pay four grand a month for a three-bedroom apartment on Inman Street, and dine in splendor at Centro, an upscale Italian eatery entered through a dive called the Good Life.

Central Square is my stomping ground. I play volleyball at the Y, hang at the Plough and the Stars, eat at the Green Street Grill. I was never a Cambridge cop—Boston all the way—which means that fewer people hate me at the Cambridge cop house. They know me mainly as a PI, and most don't want to get too close, due to the natural antipathy between those who like to keep secrets and those who want to know the details.

I stopped by Dunkin' Donuts and got a dozen to go, half glazed, half chocolate. I'd just eaten a healthy breakfast, sure, but I'd only eat the doughnuts if Officer Danny Burkett wasn't interested, and the number of cops uninterested in doughnuts is minimal.

I held the fragrant white box against my right hip and paced the corner of River and Green, across the street from the main entrance, waiting for Burkett to make an appearance. I sniffed the breeze and caught spices from the Indian place down the block. Kevin had described Burkett as a rookie and a hotshot, and I could see that from the way he walked, the bold stride, the purposeful gait. He was close to six feet, fresh-faced and eager. He wouldn't want to damage his rep being seen with a private eye. On the other hand, Kevin outranked him, and he'd want to do his sergeant a favor. So he was in a bind. I watched him as he glanced around. Probably Kev had said tall redhead and left it at that.

"Officer Burkett?"

He made the connection and a faint blush tinted his cheeks.

"Shea didn't mention I was a woman?"

"Just said private heat. Carlyle?"

"Carlotta. Doughnut?"

He glanced at me with speculative eyes. Sometimes I tend to read too much into expressions, but I thought he was probably wondering whether I was sleeping with Kevin Shea. Mostly, it's just how cops think. I repeated the doughnut offer.

"I dunno. I eat that, I'll have to spend an extra hour at the gym."

"We'll walk while we eat. One cancels the other."

He nodded. "What you got?"

He took glazed and so did I, just to keep him company. It's not like a doughnut's a bribe; it's more of a relaxer. It helps to eat while you talk, loosens up the speaker.

We walked half a block, each getting used to the other's pace. He was shorter than I was, but he kept up. His boots were polished, his uniform starched and pressed. A man with long dreadlocks gave us a wide berth, and I remembered how it was when you walked around in uniform.

54

"That guy looks like a fucking drug bust on the hoof," the rookie offered.

"Yeah. Works the high school."

"Yeah?"

"My sister's at Rindge."

"Kids won't fucking tell you the time of day."

Rookies have to hold their own, and one way they do it is with their mouths. *Fucking this, fucking that. I'm a tough guy and don't you forget it.* I remembered the drill. Hell, I used to talk the talk.

I said, "Kevin tell you what I'm interested in?"

"Kevin never asked me to cooperate with private heat before. You special or something?"

"Bet your ass I am. April third, you caught a fire."

"That boathouse shit." He chewed his doughnut and admired his reflection in the CVS window.

"You remember the call?"

"Thing is, why should I tell you about it?"

"Kevin Shea's a good guy to work for, you think?"

We walked for a while. I didn't want to interrupt his internal debate. It wasn't an easy call. Sure, Shea may have told him to cooperate, but did he mean it? Was it some kind of test? Would the whole business come back and bite the rookie in the ass?

"You like working private?" he asked.

"Sure. Best part's the pension," I said with a straight face. "You gonna tell me about it, or am I wasting my time?"

"It's old," he said.

"Yeah."

"You work for fucking Harvard?"

"No."

"Nobody's saying anything's fucking wrong with how the department handled it, right?"

"Right."

He stared at me, like he was trying to decide how big a lie I was attempting to put over on him. "I brought my incident book."

"We can get to that later if you need to check details, but I'd rather just hear what you saw, what you did. I don't expect total recall." I put a faint challenge into my voice.

"Don't underestimate me. I'm fucking good." He broke into a sudden grin.

"You from around here?"

"East Cambridge, born and bred."

So we talked "Who do you know?" shit for a while. Since I grew up in Detroit, my local repertoire's limited, but I've picked up a lot of Cambridge lore from living here, talking to cops and firefighters. He accepted another doughnut, which I took as a good sign.

He remembered the fire.

"Hell, wish I didn't fucking remember," he said. "Freezing to death, like these bums do in winter, that's not so bad. You go to sleep, like, you don't feel the pain. But burns, shit. I burned my hand once, bad, when I was a kid. Christ, I'd been an animal, I'd have chewed the fucker off. You'd think a kid going to fucking Harvard—I mean, how can you be so goddamn unhappy, you're smart enough to get into fucking Harvard in the first place?"

I could have told him smart didn't mean happy, but I didn't want to stop the flow. We'd walked as far as the Main Street cutoff by the firehouse. We sat on a bench and I offered him the doughnut box again. This time, he took chocolate. He was going to have to spend a whole day at the gym to atone.

"You want specifics?"

"Whatever you got," I said.

"Okay. It's April third. I pulled graveyard eleven/seven, and the beef comes in early morning—I can get the exact time—after a god-damn boring shift. I'm in a car with Eddie Daley. You know Daley?"

"No."

"It gets back I said he's an old fat fart, I'll know it came from you."

"It won't come back."

"Well, it was up to him, we'd a missed the call. Came in as a fire, so we're backup; the fire guys are on it. It's dark, confusing, but things are okay. We block the street 'cause they gotta run the hose off a hydrant the other side of Mem Drive. The Harvard cops are all over it, and you know what they're like, former fucking Green Berets, think we're nothing but fucking trash."

"Uncooperative."

"Trained to keep that dirty laundry off the line. We go to a disturbance call at Harvard, the U cops get there first, they're flushing dope down the johns."

"They get in your way?"

"Nah. The place is just makeshift, made of wood. I remember thinking maybe bums got in, you know, find a fucking place to sleep. Light a candle, things go up. Like that warehouse fire in Worcester killed all those firefighters."

"You figure somebody's inside?"

"Nope. But the fire boys decide they better go in, case a bum got in, and by then the place is really burning and they can't get in, except for one team, and they think somebody's in there, but the captain calls them out 'cause the roof's going. Turns out she made a regular— whatchacallit—funeral pyre in there, accelerants and shit."

"But how did you make it as a suicde?"

"Didn't then. Treated it as a fucking supicious death. By the fucking book."

"Somebody could have set the fire."

"You think we're too fucking dumb to figure that? We talked to people, talked to her boyfriend. The guy's trying to be stand-up, but he's crying like a baby."

Her boyfriend. My client told me he was out of town. "Who?" I said. "Name?"

"Benjy? Yeah, Benjy somebody."

"You can look it up later." He was giving me good stuff, slipping into present tense, reliving it instead of just reporting it. I didn't want him to stop.

"Somerville boy—those Harvard babes can't stay away from the locals, ya know? Yeah, well, he fucking knew she was feeling down. She tried to break it off with him, told him she didn't want to fucking see him anymore. We traced her final evening. Had good luck with that. She goes to the gas station on Mount Auburn, the one at Aberdeen, gives 'em a story about running out of gas, buys a couple gallons. We got a good ID. Man, she didn't even have a car. Plus, she left a note. They usually do."

"How do you leave a note in a burning building?" Maybe that's what was bothering me.

"Left it at her dorm. Shoved it under this woman's door. Miranda somebody. Starts with a *G*."

Miranda Gironde, the resident adviser.

"So you treated it like a homicide?"

"Right up till the pieces started falling into place, saying she did herself. You know, maybe if we didn't find a note. Maybe if we didn't find out about how she bought the gas. I mean, the way it played, she douses herself with gasoline and lays down naked on this thing— whachacallit, the kids have 'em—a fucking futon. Lights a match. Fuck, you think nothing bothers you after awhile, drunks beating kids, puking in the backseat, but this one bothered me."

I wondered how long before he wouldn't feel anything at all.

"Smelled like roast pig," he said. "Didn't want to eat anything grilled for a while. The smoke just bit at the back of your throat. I thought maybe I'd be a fireman once, but man, I don't know how they fucking do it. That's not how I want to end up. You get shot, hey, you get shot; they can still fix you up for a nice funeral. You're not a crispy critter."

He was already getting the humor right.

"I need the name of the boyfriend, the next of kin, the people you interviewed."

I could see that he wanted to deny me the information. Then I could see him think about Shea, about having Shea owe him one.

Benjy Dowling was the boyfriend. Not a student, Somerville address. I'd already spoken to Miranda Gironde at Phillips House. A

Jean St. Cyr was in the mix, and sure enough, she was the roommate. The next of kin was Albert Farrell Brinkman, a Swiss businessman. They'd spoken to him by phone; he was elderly and unable to travel.

I said, "Who made the ID? The boyfriend?"

"Wasn't much to ID. One of those where the morgue asks if you'll please send a photo. Two choices: dental records, DNA. Took awhile, with the goddam reporters all screaming for the ID. Hell, we had to find the kid's great-uncle in fucking Switzerland."

"Next of kin send the dental records?"

"ME would know. I don't have it. Christ, those Harvard stiffs are lucky she didn't do it in the dorm," Burkett said. "Man, you send your kid to Harvard, you think she's gonna be with high-class kids. Imagine, sending your kid to Harvard, she rooms with somebody burns down the whole goddamn dorm?" He had a ring on his finger. Married. Maybe with a kid, a little girl he had dreams for.

"Other than the boyfriend, who was upset by the news?"

"Woman at the dorm, one found the note, she took it hard, but she coulda been scared for her job. She was shocked, you could tell, but not as shocked as she might have been. Shit, I don't know. Everybody deals with their shit differently, you know what I mean?"

I knew what he meant.

"Anything feel—I don't know—off about it?"

"Other than a kid killing herself for no reason, you mean?"

"Note say anything about being pregnant?"

"Nope."

"Remember it?"

"Don't have to. I wrote it down." He thumbed through a well-worn spiral pad. "It said she was unworthy, something about being unworthy to be there. Here it is. Three fucking sentences and out: 'Unworthy as I am, I apologize to those who tried to help me. Time to delve for deeper shades of meaning, ladies and gentlemen. Sorry, but I simply can't go on.'"

Delve for deeper shades of meaning? What the hell was that about?

This was her life, not some freshman class in literary criticism. *Ladies and gentlemen.* A litle sarcasm there? An acknowledgment of class differences?

I said, "So, you're okay with it being suicide?"

"Hey, not just me, Carlyle. I didn't make the fucking call. The ME, the arson guys, we all did our job with this one."

"Hey, I'm not saying you didn't."

"Finished?"

"What I mean is, are you satisfied with it being called a suicide?"

"Satisfied? What the hell's that mean, lady? A kid's dead, I'm not fucking satisfied. Look, I gotta go. My partner's gonna think I dumped him."

I gave him the rest of the doughnuts to give to his partner as a peace offering. Then I studied the names I'd scrawled in my notebook. Benjy Dowling, shaken-up boyfriend. Jeannie St. Cyr, former roommate.

Who did you trust with your love letters, Denali?

I flipped a mental coin.

CHAPTER 8

I wiped glazed-doughnut sugar off my fingers and glanced at my watch. Leaving my car in the lot behind Pearl Art, I walked up Mass Ave, skirting the Yard, passing the Fogg Museum and slipping between the ziggurat-topped Graduate School of Design and magnificent Memorial Hall. I might have found a parking space closer to McKay Hall, behind the Science Center, but it was doubtful at best, and I enjoyed the walk. One thing about a university town, people walk. Some folks in Cambridge and Boston consider cars an abomination; they don't even know how to drive.

The ones who do drive, most of them don't have a clue, either.

I found a convenient tree to lean against and waited for Jean St. Cyr, Jeannie, the roommate, the dark girl with the notebook on her belly and the questions in her eyes, who'd told nasty Gregor she couldn't meet him at eleven because she had a class at McKay. Across Oxford Street, a scrawny student tried to launch a kite despite an almost-total lack of breeze and an abundance of trees and telephone wires. I watched him fail over and over, wondered if it was a class experiment in futility.

I was starting to think I'd missed her, when I caught a glimpse of a girl speeding across the grass, her backpack flung across one shoulder, wearing a raggedy tight red T and bleached jeans. She saw me at the same time and stopped in her tracks, glancing quickly from side to side like a cornered animal.

I moved, and she ran like a deer.

She darted around the Science Center and made for the Yard. She was fast and agile, but hampered by the crowd near the gate. I was gaining, shoving kids out of the way, pushing past a clot of robed priests. She raced through the gate, sprinted to the right, away from the crowd, toward Memorial Church and Robinson. She was weighed down by her backpack, hampered by short legs and clunky shoes. She tripped and almost went down, regained her footing, and charged ahead.

I was on her heels, close enough to hear her pant. I didn't waste breath ordering her to stop. What the hell was I gonna do if she didn't, shoot her? I put my head down and ran hard, ran till I could grab her shoulder.

At my touch, she sank to the ground, like a stone plunging to the bottom of a pond. She was gasping for breath and crying. In a minute, I'd have a full-blown incident on my hands: *Hey, lady, what the hell you trying to do to that girl?*

"It's okay," I assured the closest hoverers. "My friend's okay. Just give her some space." There were murmurs of concern, but no one intervened; I don't look like a bruiser. I knelt beside her, inhaling the scent of fresh-mown grass, and put what must have looked like a comforting hand on her shoulder.

She wasn't going anywhere, and I wanted her to know it. Running makes a suspect look guilty as hell. Maybe I'd guessed right on whom to question first, the boyfriend or the roommate.

"Oh God," she said. "Oh God." Defenseless, out of breath, out of guts, tears rolled down her cheeks. My sympathetic side felt like patting her on the back. I kept it in check and waited till the crowd dispersed. Then I grabbed her chin and tilted her face so I could see into her dark eyes.

"You needed the money? Is that why?"

"What are you talking about?"

"Or did you want to teach the bastard a lesson?"

"What the—"

"You've got Denali's letters, don't you?"

"I don't have any of your stuff, honest!" She started wailing again, and a new audience began to gather, eager for a show. I helped her to her feet, careful never to release my grip. Her eyes were wide and staring; I wondered if she was taking some kind of dope.

"Come on, Jeannie," I said gently. "Let's take a walk."

Speak gently, it disarms folks. Call somebody by their name, people assume you know them. *No, Doris, don't butt in. It's not like it's some stranger trying to abduct a kid.* Abductors know it; they always use a name.

"I don't want to talk to you." She was too breathless from running to summon any volume. "I can't talk to you. I can't. Oh God." If I hadn't been holding her, she'd have fallen to her knees again. "It's all my fault. Everything's my fault."

If she collapsed, the guy in the rimless glasses was definitely going to come over and make a stink. She seemed so painfully young, so pathetically scared, I could hardly buy her as a blackmailer.

"Have you eaten today?" I asked.

She shook her head no. See, there it is; I'd tell Paolina.

I half persuaded, half dragged her to Mr. Bartley's Burger Cottage, a Harvard Square institution where the waitresses have seen everything, breakups and hysterics, drug ODs and marriage proposals, would-be grooms dropping to their knees on the saggy linoleum. After manhandling her into a booth near the rest room, I ordered a Pepsi for me and a breakfast burger for her, a glass of milk, as well.

By God, I'd make somebody drink milk.

"I'm missing class. It's, like, finals review."

I'd blocked her exit, sitting next to instead of across from her. To escape, she'd have to crawl under the table.

"I'm Carlotta," I said, "by the way."

She ducked her head like a turtle retreating back into its shell. "Jeannie."

"So how'd you get to be Denali's roommate, Jeannie? Luck of the draw?"

Nothing in these easy questions to cause another outbreak of hysterics. Her eyes slid sideways as she considered her plight. I had custody of her backpack. I had her socked into the booth. I was bigger than she was and I could run faster. She stared at me as if I were the matron of some terrifying prison camp.

"I guess they figured we'd have something in common. Like we were both freshmen, both hoping to be psych majors, interested in education." Her voice was small and hiccupy.

"Both in Professor Chaney's class?"

She responded almost eagerly, anything to shift the topic away from Denali. "Isn't he, like, wonderful? Like most of the lectures, with his TA, it's like she drones and we take notes, but when he comes in, everybody wakes up. It's like this big challenge, like he wants to hear what we think."

The waitress plunked dishes on the table; I was happy to let Jeannie prattle on about Chaney.

"Like this one class was about like who should get medicated? Like if we medicate students who are behavioral problems, instead of finding other ways to cope, what are we saying? I mean, I totally believe in all that chemistry shit. My mom, she's like depressed for no reason, and I figure if they could just like give her a blood test and readjust her serotonin, she'd be way happier. But Chaney wanted us to think about who we'd do that for, and why we'd do it, and whether we'd do it if the kid wanted it, or if the parent wanted it, or if the school wanted it. Like it might not be such a great thing after all."

Right, I thought. Start by filing the rough edges, pretty soon you're working with a cookie cutter instead of a file. Jeannie picked at her food, breaking the bun to pieces with nervous fingers.

I said, "What about Denali—did she like Chaney, too?"

Jeannie's eyes narrowed. "Everybody wants to know about Denali, and then when I don't answer, they think I'm hiding something. I don't know if she liked Chaney or hated his guts. I don't know where your stuff is! And I didn't make her move out. I liked her. I mean, like, I never had a roommate before. I don't have any sisters or brothers. She was pretty and smart, you know, blond and all, but really strong." Abruptly, she was crying again. The brunette waitress gave me the eye from behind the counter, checking to make sure I wasn't slapping the kid around. "Like, all the other girls, they got along fine with their roommates. They were like sisters."

I nodded encouragingly at the waitress, patted Jeannie on the shoulder. "But not you and Denali?"

"Like, I tried; I had a lot of friends in high school. Everybody told me my roommate would be like my best friend, but Denali didn't want to spend time with me or talk to me or anything. I mean, like the only time she ever started a conversation was when she had a toothache and wanted to know did I know a good dentist. Honest to God. And my mom's college roommate, she was, like, maid of honor at her wedding, and she's still her best friend. But that's in Illinois. You know, this place is so weird." She lowered her voice to a throaty whisper. "They tell you its not like cliquey here, not like high school, but everybody sorts themselves out: future presidents, business leaders, lawyers, and shit." She tried to force a smile, but it only made her look more miserable. "Then there're the also-rans." She didn't add "like me," but she might as well have.

"And Denali?"

"Oh, she was no also-ran. I mean, she was an athlete and everything, a rower. Maybe that's another reason they paired us. I'm, like, *interested* in rowing, but she was here on a rowing *scholarship*. She was world-class. She had, like, boxes of trophies. What, am I gonna talk to her about, like, the time I came in first at camp?"

She was thin and small, with a plain, earnest face and close-cropped dark hair. Her T-shirt was frayed, but it fit like a glove. It might have cost her twelve bucks at a discount store, but I thought it had probably run a hundred at a boutique on Newbury. She had rings on her fingers that weren't dime-store merchandise and small diamond studs in her ears. Her sandals tied at her ankles and her toenails were painted pearly orange.

Food was steadily disappearing off her plate; she seemed to be regaining some color. "I mean, how am I supposed to concentrate? This is, like, almost finals week, and here I am, talking about my ex-roommate instead of going to class. How can I study or anything when there's, like, this stupid lawsuit looming over everything?"

I'd been about to order another Pepsi, more milk. Instead, I froze and waited for her to continue. When she didn't, I repeated that single word *lawsuit*, raising my pitch to make it a question.

She moistened her finger and stabbed at some wayward crumbs. "Well, Denali's family—it's, like, a wrongful-death suit. Like she shoulda been in the dorm, and they're gonna make me testify, and then they'll blame it all on me, on how I was such a shitty roommate."

"Jeannie, look at me. Nobody kills herself because her roommate tries to be friendly."

"Worst of all, I didn't tell anybody when she left. I mean, I was, like, so embarrassed. What was I supposed to say? Excuse me, but my roommate moved out 'cause she can't stand me? I mean, I didn't know what to say."

"She didn't leave a note or say good-bye?"

"You knew her, right?"

"A long time ago," I said, lying.

"Well, believe me, she didn't do a whole lot of explaining. Like when she first moved in, she had almost no clothes, you know, and sometimes she'd borrow my stuff, but she'd never ask. It's not like I minded or anything. I didn't complain when she kept her kayak in the middle of the floor or her trophies under the bed. And when I said maybe we should buy curtains and bedspreads and stuff, she said no, the room was fine the way it was, just bare. I mean, she didn't even sleep on the bed, just rolled her blanket out on the floor."

Guilt poured off the kid in waves.

"I got mad at her because of the stinking kayak. I mean, why couldn't she leave it in the boathouse? Did she think somebody would, like, steal it?"

I shrugged, but I don't think she noticed.

"It was like the only thing she had. I mean, she hardly had anything, like she coulda put all her stuff in a cardboard box, another box for the trophies. I felt sorry for her. I didn't mind when she borrowed my clothes. I even tried to give her my sleeping bag."

"Jeannie, did she have a place where she kept special things? A place for jewelry or old photographs?"

"Like where she maybe kept your stuff?" She placed her tongue between her teeth and frowned in concentration. "Well, she had this old candy box, not even like Godiva, some drugstore thing. An old Whitman's Sampler box. Yeah."

"Did she leave anything behind, a slip of paper, something you might not have thought was important?"

She avoided my eyes, staring down at the table. "I found one of her trophies, a small one, under the bed. I was going to give it back to her sometime. I didn't throw it away. Do you want it?"

"If you don't mind."

"I *want* you to have it. I mean, you were her friend."

"Why didn't you tell me yesterday? Why did you run away?"

"They told me not to talk about her. They told me not to talk to anybody. Grayson and Miranda and this guy they sent over from Legal Services."

Grayson was one of the housemasters.

"You won't tell anybody I said anything? Like you're not gonna testify I said I didn't like her, are you? I didn't really mean it. She didn't like me, so I was glad when she left. And now she's dead and I just fucking missed my science class and I'm going to flunk out before they kick me out, and my parents will be so upset." She shoved her plate away and her head sank until her cheek met the tabletop.

When I was twenty-one, a close friend killed himself. Last person in the world to do it, I thought, so I didn't accept it as suicide. I saw it as another kind of murder, and I wanted to find the culprit. I blamed his parents, blamed his friends, blamed myself. Why the hell hadn't I been sharp enough, smart enough, to see it coming, head it off?

"Come on." I urged her out of the booth, plunked money on the counter, and raised my eyebrows at the inquisitive waitress.

Chaney seemed to have put his feelings for Denali Brinkman in a box, locked it, and buried it six feet under. Chaney might not blame himself for Denali's suicide, but this girl did. I grabbed her hand and explained where we were headed. For a moment, I thought she'd run again, but then I caught a glimmer of relief in her eyes.

Harvard Health Services is four floors up, in Holyoke Center. The waiting room was far from crowded, and after twenty minutes of "fill in the forms" inaction, I made myself unpleasant. The reception gorgon was brittle and defensive. Her nameplate said Jo, and she wanted me to know she was overworked.

"Her roommate committed suicide," I said.

"We follow protocols here. Policies. Who are you?"

"Somebody who knows what a protocol is, thanks. You want to wait till you've got another suicide on your hands, fine with me. I'm sure Legal Services will be enchanted."

Jo's foot started tapping as soon as I mentioned Legal Services. I wondered what a shrink would make of that. I also wondered if Denali Brinkman had a fat file in one of the color-coded rows that lined the wall behind the gorgon's counter.

When I finally got Jeannie into a chair in a psychologist's office, things improved. Dr. Rona Kupfer was a total contrast to the waiting-room witch, a motherly forty-five with a comforting smile and seen-it-all eyes. She wore a floral shawl to cut the chill from the air conditioning. Jeannie took one look at her and started to sob.

I wondered how I could find out whether Denali had made use of Harvard's psychiatric services. Then I wondered what the hell it had to do with blackmail. I pondered the fact that Denali Brinkman's family was considering bringing a lawsuit against Harvard. If the family— and who exactly was the family?—knew that a professor had been having an affair with their darling, that would be one more nail in Harvard's coffin.

Would Harvard protect Chaney? Or toss him to the wolves?

I gave Jeannie my card, not the one that says "Private Investigations," but the one that gives name, address, and phone number. She promised she'd call and tell me when I could come get Denali's trophy. I left her in Dr. Kupfer's gentle care and kicked my way through the dusty plaza in front of Holyoke Center. A flock of pigeons circled, landed, and started hunting for crumbs in the dirt. I wished them luck.

CHAPTER 9

If Jeannie St. Cyr had Denali's candy box, she was wasting her time as
a prospective psych major. She ought to be onstage at the Loeb Drama
Center, a full-fledged member of the American Rep acting company.

I wished I could raise two fingers to my mouth, whistle, and get
my car to speed over from Central Square like some Western hero's
stallion in a late-night TV rerun. The car was in one direction; my
house, my computer, and Dowling's Somerville address in the other.
Dead center between the two was Thompson Hall. And both blackmail notes had been shoved under the door of Chaney's Thompson
Hall office.

Why push notes under an office door when the U.S. mail provides
a beautifully anonymous delivery method? Nobody's gonna catch you
lurking by one of those million or so blue postboxes. There's certainly
a greater chance someone will notice you bending and placing a note
beneath a door.

Logically, the blackmailer should be someone who would, in the
ordinary course of events, be found in the school of education, a
native who could credibly say, if caught stashing the note, "Look what

I found!" That's why I'd gone for Jeannie St. Cyr, registered student, over a boyfriend with no Harvard connection.

Chaney had a larger office across the river at a Harvard-affiliated research site and a cubby at the Med School. He owned a house off Brattle Street. Why not deliver the note to the Med School, the research site, the house? Did Mrs. Chaney open her husband's mail? Do wives blackmail husbands? I smiled at the thought, rephrased it. Do they blackmail their spouses in such a literal way?

As I hurried up Mass Ave, I checked my cell, making sure the battery was charged. I knew Chaney should have the money by now, and I wanted to make sure he could reach me at any time. He was convinced the money drop would be the same as the first time, the faculty lot behind Thompson. I was pretty sure it would be different. The more times you go to the well, the more you expect the well to be guarded.

Hell, if I were the blackmailer, I'd choose a different well altogether. I walked faster, sneakers pounding the brick sidewalk. Late-afternoon sunlight slanted through the elms. Maybe my blackmailer was a creature of habit. Just because the scene of the crime was Harvard didn't mean he was bright.

Harvard's ed school looks a bit like a stepchild. Radcliffe Yard is nowhere near as grand as its big brother; even the grass is less well kept. The buildings don't share the redbrick Oxbridge look of the Harvard Yard structures. Some seem more like weathered clapboard houses than halls of learning. The small crushed-stone parking lot to the rear of Thompson Hall had places for ten cars max.

Not such a bad place for a money drop after all—sheltered from the street by a tall yew hedge, from neighboring buildings by high brick walls. I took note of entrances and exits, auto and pedestrian, decided where I'd position myself when and if the drop went down here.

Thompson Hall is an undistinguished modern cement and glass rectangle. Query: How difficult would it be for an outsider to shove a note under Chaney's office door? Building access should be easy enough; the ed school wasn't some nuclear launch site under Cheyenne Mountain. There was an obvious main door, double-wide, up three shallow granite steps. I used a less notable side door, then gravitated to the main foyer, where a chart conveniently gave the location of Dr. Chaney's second-floor office.

I passed unchallenged up the stairs. The building smelled musty, like old library books. Sunlight filtered through dusty casement windows on the staircase landing. The banisters were carved dark wood; the steps covered with institutional rubber tread. There was no visible security, just the sublime assumption that the people in the building were people who belonged. Everywhere I looked, heads were bent over tasks. No security guards, and what was there to secure? Desks and chairs? Educational philosophies?

At the door of suite 205, I hesitated. The numerals had been printed beside Chaney's name on the chart, but the word *suite* hadn't accompanied them. The door to suite 205 had a pebbled-glass half window, the look of a door that led into an outer office. I turned the knob.

"May I help you?"

She had fifties-style bouffant hair, sprayed to within an inch of its life. A pink sweater set stretched across her broad bosom, and, yes, her spectacles dangled from a chain. A veritable dragon lady.

"I'm looking for Professor Taubman's office?" His was the next floor up.

"He has no office hours today. May I please see your ID?"

"You mean today's Thursday? Shit. Excuse me. God, I thought it was Friday. Oh shit." I held up my wrist and stared at my watch. "I'm late at the Faculty Club."

I turned and moved, not so quickly that she'd think I was fleeing, which I was, but briskly enough that not one in thirty security-conscious secretaries would have pursued me.

So much for infiltrating Chaney's office. I wondered when the dragon lady went home at night, how a Somerville townie could rely on easy access. Might he have an accomplice among Chaney's teaching assistants, secretaries, colleagues, students?

I scribbled names and numbers while I walked back toward the car. The dragon lady's nameplate identified her as Esther Cummings. The department chair, George Fording, had digs on the third floor. The window on the driver's side of my Toyota was plastered with a city of Cambridge Day-Glo orange parking ticket. Exceeding the time on the meter. Damn.

At home, the dishes were still in the sink. No evidence that Roz was there, not that I planned to climb to her third-floor aerie to check. I yelled upstairs instead; I hate to go up there, because her artwork is scary. She does postpunk weird stuff and considers the third floor her canvas. The note I'd left for her on the fridge, asking her to sort through the Chaney Web references, appeared untouched.

I got a Pepsi to sustain me and sat down to play the keyboard, regretting the fact that I never took typing in high school because I wasn't gonna be anybody's coffee-fetching secretary. Made three errors entering Benjamin MacKenzie Dowling's name alone. I typed in his Claremont Street address. With his name and address, courtesy of Officer Burkett's incident book, I trolled for his birth date and Social Security number. Give me a name, address, DOB, and SSN, and I can find the rest.

Once I knew the golden four, I visited the Massachusetts Registry of Motor Vehicles site and discovered that Dowling drove a black '99 TransAm. I got the plate number. I debated phoning my friend Gloria and asking her to summon up Dowling's credit history. She owns the local cab company for which I sometimes drive, and she joined CBI, one of the largest credit-rating bureaus, at my urging.

The three major credit bureaus, CBI (aka Equifax,) TRW, and Trans Union are essentially off-limits to civilians. It's illegal to nab credit status, but the FTC, no less, says it's okay to access what's known as "header information." I decided to call up the header stuff on my own. Gloria likes to talk, and I wanted background on Dowling fast.

I punched keys. CBI was my first try, because they're the largest and handle most of the East Coast. I went on to TRW, then Trans Union, a sinking feeling in my gut. No credit record whatsoever.

Maybe if I hadn't suspected him of blackmail, I'd have shrugged it off, simply figured, Well, maybe Dowling hasn't had much luck, hasn't established himself financially. But the man drove an okay car. Who buys a car for cash on the barrelhead? I tried a dot-gov listing to see if Dowling had outstanding college loans. Nope. The lack of a credit history, any credit history, didn't sit right. Who has no debt? Rich folks who pay cash. Crooks.

Call it a hunch, but it's based on some of the oldest saws in the book. Criminals tend to start young; criminals are not that bright. They tend to get caught; they tend to repeat their bad behavior.

I dialed Gloria, but instead of asking her to run credit on Benjamin, I asked her to run a CORI, a criminal offenders record check. The Commonwealth of Massachusetts currently allows business owners to check the past criminal misdeeds of prospective employees. They finally got the message that cab companies don't want to hire habitual DUI offenders, that schools don't really want a rapist on the payroll.

As fast as I don't type, that's how fast Gloria does. Not that she'd devote her full attention to my request. I imagined her in her office, her wheelchair occupying its niche behind the phone console. Gloria's skin is so dark, it glistens. From the waist up, she's a whirlwind of activity, what with dispatching cabs, listening to the police scanner, eating junk food. I pressed the phone to my ear; sounded like she was munching Doritos.

My rookie pal, Burkett, hadn't mentioned the fact that Benjy Dowling had a record, but cops tend to give what they want to give. I wouldn't put it past even a rook to withhold information.

"Give me the DOB." Gloria's weight hovers at 325 pounds.

"Eleven/twenty-one/sixty-nine." The man was over thirty. Chaney was over forty. The girl had had a thing for older men.

"Bingo."

"What for?" Damn it, if Burkett had told me, I'd have homed in on Dowling like a hawk on a wounded chicken. Of course, I wouldn't have found out about the impending lawsuit, wouldn't have steered Jeannie toward needed help.

"A deuce for armed robbery. Concord sentence. Parole."

That surprised me. They've cut back funding for the parole office so much, most cons serve their full term. "Give the name of the PO?"

"Garnowski, J." She spelled it.

"Thanks a bunch, Gloria. I owe you."

"You got that right, babe. When you gonna pull a shift for me?"

"I'm working a case."

"Sam asked how you were."

I don't know how, but Gloria managed to load those five words with about a hundred shaded questions. *What's going on with you and Sam? Did you dump him? Did he dump you? When are you going to get back together, and why did you split this time?*

"Thanks." I pretended I hadn't heard, then hung up. Gloria adores Sam; she's his partner in the cab company, one of his few legal business ventures. I've never been sure how much she knows or wants to know about his mob involvement. Paolina adores Sam, too; she treasures the dream that Sam and I will marry someday, used to imagine herself trotting down the aisle in a pink dress, a flower girl tossing rose petals.

I seem to be the only one bothered by the fact that he recently caved in to his mob-boss father and agreed to take his place in the Gianelli hierarchy. Why can't I accept the party line, that he's not one of the goombahs, that he's simply trying to move the mob's money into legitimate enterprises? My hand was still grasping the phone, squeezing so hard, I was surprised the receiver didn't snap in two. I breathed in and out, let my muscles relax, and brought myself back to Chaney's problem.

Benjy Dowling was a con. Two years for armed robbery was real. It wasn't like kiting checks or possession of marijuana. I marveled at Denali Brinkman's luck. Against all odds, an orphan off an Indian rez gets into an Ivy League university. She sleeps with a prof and hooks up with an ex-con, behavior not recommended during freshman orientation. Made me wonder what lurked behind the blurred features in the grainy news photo. Some people attract disaster, thrive on a constant diet of argumentative scenes and lurid distractions. I wondered whether Denali was like that, a drama queen, or if things simply happened to her, if she was the calm center that summoned the storm.

CHAPTER 10

The flame was from a candle, a small votive illuminating my hands and the hands of the man sharing my table. Leon's hands, or Sam's hands? And maybe the flame wasn't from a candle, but the glowing tip of a cigarette. The tiny circle of flame grew and sparked, catching the whiteness of the tablecloth. The cloth flapped like a sheet as flame seared and devoured it, orange and blue, writhing and shuddering. Flames shot up like a geyser, catching the heavy curtains in the foyer, the old velvet drapes I'd tried to yank down to stop the flames, but there was no stopping them now. And then the flame changed and surged, and I knew the boats were burning, long, slender racing shells with their oars akimbo. The woman's face was out of focus, but I thought it might be Jeannie's, then my own, then the one in the photograph of Denali Brinkman. She was burning, too, and when I yelled for her to jump in the water, she nodded with that secretive smile still on her face, but she stayed in the boat, burning while I screamed that the cooling water was right beneath her, close at hand, so close.

I sat up, clutching the blankets, wondering whether I'd woken Paolina with my screams, but I knew Paolina hadn't spent the night. Neither had Leon, and the screaming came from the telephone. I readjusted to the reality of my own dark room, bedding flung helter-skelter, the ringing telephone. I don't keep the phone on the bedside table; too easy to reach out, pick up, hang up. I forced myself to place bare feet on cold wooden boards. The chill woke me and I moved quickly to intercept the shrieking phone. My client's urgent whisper got me dressed and out of the house in less than fifteen minutes.

Damn. Damn. Damn. Chaney was supposed to stall. The black-mailer's call wasn't supposed to come so soon. Yes, after midnight qualified as Friday, but the blackmailer was rushing the drop, and while I managed to reach Roz, who was sleeping at her boyfriend Lemon's dojo, who knew if she'd get into position in time? Who knew if I would?

The blackmailer must have picked the time because of the weather. I pulled my hood over my head, tucking wisps of soaked hair inside, and imagined him praying for just such a night. May, ha; more like November, chilly, with a nasty northeast wind that drove the rain into my face. My sneakers sank into the muddy grass near the edge of the river, and I regretted my choice of footwear. Rubber boots, heavy waders, would have been the thing.

Money drops in books and films take place at midnight. Midnight would have been a good time, trains still running, people on the streets. If it had been midnight, I could have anticipated a trip to China-town for a steaming bowl of hot-and-sour soup. No such luck. It was 3:37, the drop was set for 4:05, and anybody on the streets was head-ing to an early shift at a hospital or looking for someone to mug.

I hugged my shoulders, shivered, and told myself the empty streets were a good thing. Easy to follow the guy with so few people on the street. Easier for him to spot me, my subconscious snapped back. Or Roz. I told my subconscious to shut up. I knew we might not be able to follow him, or her. The key was identity—getting a photo, matching it to a suspect.

Lemon's dark paneled van would be parked on the bridge or cir-cling the rotary. I raised my head, but I could barely see with the damn rain sheeting down. Shielding my eyes with my hand, I let them roam the landscape, checking for new or different shadows.

The payoff spot wasn't the small lot behind Thompson Hall. The scene had shifted to the old stone bathhouse at Magazine Beach. For years, I'd thought Cambridge's Magazine Beach and Magazine Street were named for some sprightly Colonial digest that had built its offices in the area. Not so. Magazine Beach is the site of a military powder magazine built on what used to be an island in the Charles River. Captain's Island, it was called, and its isolated nature and defensible hill recommended it for the storage of highly flammable gunpowder. In 1899, the stones of the defunct powder magazine were reused to build a bathhouse for the new beach down by the filled marshes. When the beach closed in the fifties, the bathhouse was shut down.

These days, it's waiting for renovation; meanwhile, it's used to store equipment for the muddy playing fields nearby. Less than half a mile from the BU Bridge, it's isolated, ill-lit, and eerily deserted. The main path sends people forty feet up the riverbank, along Memorial Drive. The rusty pedestrian bridge at Magazine Street further discourages traffic. Night like this, even teens searching for a lover's lane would stay away.

My beeper was set to silent pulse. Roz, from her perch on or near the bridge, equipped with a night-vision scope, was supposed to signal any approaching pedestrian, any car that slowed and parked. Three times, Cambridge cops had sped by with cherry lights flashing. The same man had passed twice on Rollerblades. I rocked slowly on the balls of my feet, as though I were standing a beat. Rain dripped down my neck in spite of the hood, and I wondered if I had a hole in my jacket.

I poked my nose a few inches from my watch to check the time. My client was due in fifteen minutes. He had his orders. Park in the elementary school lot across the street, walk over the pedestrian bridge, cut through the baseball field, drop a backpack filled with cash over the stone wall behind the bathhouse. Get lost.

I'd parked in the turnoff near the MDC pool, built to make up for the polluted beach. The turnoff was posted NO VEHICLE ENTRY, and I was hoping my car wouldn't get towed or, more likely, stolen. I'd removed my bicycle from the trunk, stashed it behind a shrub. I was currently lurking behind the pool, doing an imitation of a bag lady. I thought it most likely the guy would have a car parked nearby, but who knew? Cambridge, you can't count on a car. He might be a runner, a biker, a blader. Any of those activities would camouflage him once he reached the path. Cops wouldn't stop a citizen exercising along the Charles. Even in the predawn hours. Even in a rainstorm.

I checked my watch again; it hadn't moved. Things weren't exactly going according to plan. My idea was that the guy would be in position long before my client showed with the money. What kind of urban blackmailer trusts to the fact that no street person is going to show in between drop time and whenever he finds it convenient to claim the cash? Cash isn't like a check payable only to you. Money is money, finders keepers.

My pocket jiggled. I saw a shadow cross the bridge and I tensed, ready to move. If it was my client, he was right on time, but as far as I could tell, there was no one in the vicinity to receive the package. Maybe Chaney had gotten the information wrong, the night wrong. Maybe this was a dry run, to see how well he obeyed orders.

It was Chaney, on foot. He did his stuff with dispatch, moving briskly. I'd warned him not to wait around, not to look for me or for the blackmailer. "Play it by the book and leave," I'd told him. He followed orders.

I focused on the backpack through the camera lens, barely distinguishing its rectangular bulk from the shadows and the bushes. I kept the camera to my eye and scanned the horizon. I waited for the beeper to shake and I listened. The occasional car thundered hollowly across the raised bridge over the rotary. I thought I heard a car pull into the turning where I'd parked. A stray dog snuffled at my bicycle. I shifted my feet, shooed him off, and took a quick hit from the flask in my pocket. I'd been strictly rationing the brandy because I didn't want to have to find a place to pee.

Rain poured down. The Charles is broad and placid at Magazine Beach. The sound of the river hadn't played a role in the night symphony, and it took me a while to classify the new noise, the soft rhythmic splashing, barely noticeable at first, then louder. Deliberate. It hit me suddenly that I hadn't taken the river into account. Denali Brinkman had been a rower; she'd have had friends who were rowers. I hadn't considered the river for what it was, a roadway. Damn. How could I follow if the blackmailer traveled on the river?

I ordered myself to relax. The important thing was identification. I trained my camera lens on the water, trying to get a fix on the rhythmic splashes. It was difficult to pinpoint the origin of the sound. Upstream toward Harvard and the Weld Boathouse? Downstream toward the lower Charles, the river basin?

The small boat came into focus, a kayak like the one Denali's roommate had described. Maybe Denali hadn't stored all her possessions in the boathouse. Maybe the kayak, like the blackmail letters, hadn't burned. I held my breath and pressed the shutter. I didn't need a flash. I had a fancy night-shot rig Roz had borrowed from Lemon.

I stayed in the shadows while the kayaker tied his craft off on a small tree and clambered up the bank, his feet making squelching noises in the mud. He used a small pencil flash to locate the backpack, then grabbed it. I focused on the money, took three more shots. The shutter click sounded as loud as one of the old cannons I imagined defending the site of the powder magazine in the old days, but the blackmailer didn't seem to hear. He wore a hood drawn up over his head, but I thought I caught the pale oval of a face. Good. If he'd had the presence of mind to wear a face mask, I'd have been out of luck.

I made a mental note of the black pants, the black hooded parka. Medium height, medium build. Rower's shoulders. My gut said the boyfriend, the ex-con.

I waited in the shadows till he pushed off. I could have followed him upriver or down, but if he crossed the water, made for the Boston side, I'd be stuck. I grabbed my bike and carried it to the car, dialing my cell phone as I moved.

"Roz, get up on the bridge. Heading toward the center of the Charles from Magazine Beach in a kayak."

"A kayak? Like a fucking Eskimo?"

"Find it, Roz."

"Can't see it." She sounded annoyed. "You didn't tell me to watch for boats."

"I know."

"Aren't boats supposed to have lights?"

"Yeah. I guess he forgot his."

"Dumb remark, huh?"

"See him?"

There are rules on the river, rules that govern which way you can launch from which boathouse, and under which arches of which bridge you can pass in which direction. The bow light should be red and green, red for port, green for starboard; the stern light should be white. But those rules were for racing shells and coaching launches, and I didn't think they held for blackmailers rowing kayaks in the middle of stormy nights.

"I think I see something down there," Roz muttered.

"Upstream or downstream?"

"Heading toward downtown, keeping midstream."

That would be the clever course, downstream to travel more quickly, keeping to the middle of the river till he could decide whether anyone was in pursuit. But where would he come ashore?

I started the car's engine. The heater felt glorious.

"Do you want us to follow him?"

"Us" meant Roz and Lemon. She's never learned to drive. I've been after her, have even volunteered as her instructor, but since Lemon jumps to chauffeur her around, she sees no reason to expand her skills.

"Follow a fucking boat?"

That was Lemon, in the background. He sounded sleepy and crabby, and knowing Lemon, he was probably high on whatever was stashed in the glove compartment. The chances of my Toyota or Lemon's van drawing a cop seemed higher than the chances of either of us getting a better photo op.

"Forget it," I said. "Go home."

I warmed my hands on the heater vents and thought about how neatly the blackmailer had handled the pickup. Then I drove to 157 Claremont Street, a triple-decker on a narrow street near the Somerville line. The parking was tight. I didn't want to stick the car in front of a driveway or a fire hydrant, didn't want anything to look odd or out of place. I had to circle the block three times before a man in green scrubs hurried out of an apartment across the street from my target and moved his well-placed Volvo.

Then I waited. I have a love-hate relationship with surveillance. It's filled with potential. Anything can happen at any time. You soak up the atmosphere of an area of the city you might not have appreciated before. After awhile, it gets goddamned boring. And then you have to pee.

At least it was dry inside the car. I took off my jacket and inspected it. Hole right in the damned collar.

Two hours and thirteen minutes later, a black TransAm with a kayak strapped to the roof turned into the narrow driveway next to 157. The garage door didn't operate from an automatic opener, so the figure in black had to get out and expose himself to the elements.

Bingo. The Claremont Street address was Benjy Dowling's. I didn't even need to snap another photo, but I did.

CHAPTER 11

I couldn't have been asleep more than twenty minutes when the phone rang. I rolled over and stared at it in dismay, hoping my glance would fry it, but I never considered letting the machine pick up. Ex-cops are tough; we answer the phone.

"Did he come? Did you follow him?"

Light streamed through the flimsy curtains and tried to blind me. I blinked. It felt like someone had removed my right eyeball, rolled it in sand, and reinserted it. "Professor Chaney?"

"Were you asleep? I'm sorry. I wouldn't have called so early, but I won't be reachable later today. I'll be at the lab, a conference with investors, not the sort of thing I can interrupt. So I just—I felt I needed to know."

"I got him," I said.

"Got who?"

"Not the sort of person you'll be able to convince with words."

"Is it someone I work with? Someone I know?"

"Look, go to your meeting and try to relax. There's a good chance this will all work out, and soon."

"You really think so?"

"Yes. Good night."

I hung up. It wasn't night, of course, but my body was confused. I tried to get back to sleep, but it wasn't any good. I'd sleepily reassured my anxious client that everything would work out even though I had no reason to suspect it would, and I couldn't rest with that on my plate. I wasn't making any progress on the case lying in bed.

I got up and hit the shower. Sometimes a long shower—hot water, hair scrub, cold-water finish—is almost as good as a night's sleep. I wrapped my dripping hair in a towel, my body in a red chenille robe, and went down to the kitchen to make coffee.

When I started at the Academy, I thought cops had it in for ex-offenders. The whole cop attitude, I thought, reeked of that final scene in the old film *Casablanca*, the one where the French cop says, "Round up the usual suspects." The French cop knows who did it, knows who killed the nasty Nazi major, but the usual guys are gonna get rousted, and probably one of them will wind up doing the time.

That's how I used to feel. Then I worked the city, and damn if the same guys didn't keep pulling the same shit over and over again. It pissed me off, the way they refused to learn from their mistakes.

What I'd learned on the streets told me Chaney hadn't a prayer of convincing Dowling that he hadn't struck gold with those love letters. If little Jeannie or one of her university pals had shown last night, the story might have been different. But Dowling was it, and I didn't see him as an easy nut to crack.

If Chaney couldn't reason with him, could I scare him? Did Dowling's landlord know he was renting to an ex-con? If not, I could threaten to tell the landlord, dangle it over Dowling's head. Then he, in turn, could threaten to reveal Chaney's secret. Standoff.

I fingered the pages of my case notebook. J. Garnowski, parole officer, was probably Jake Garnowski, former Boston cop. I could phone him and find out whether Dowling was still on the hook. If Dowling were still on parole, I could threaten to get him sent back to the slammer. And then Dowling could tell me to fuck off or he'd spill Chaney's story. Standoff again.

Ditto with his employer, his girl, his parents. I kept playing with it, retooling the scenario, hitting the same damn wall. Chaney had appreciated the symmetry of blackmailing the blackmailer, but the plan had one serious drawback: It would work only if the blackmailer were a citizen, not a con.

I contemplated plan B: retrieving Chaney's love letters.

CHAPTER 12

Daylight did nothing to improve the Claremont Street triple-decker I'd watched Dowling enter in the early hours of the morning. The gray clapboard siding and weathered white shutters needed paint. The parched scrap of lawn cried out for water, and gray dirt bloomed in the flower beds. The houses on either side had the same faded paint job, the same semiabandoned air, which made sense, since all three buildings were owned by Jimmy Flaherty, a small-time Somerville property owner with a bad rep for not maintaining his overpriced units.

I knew Flaherty owned the place, because I'd made a brief but necessary stop at my friend Gloria's cab company. It used to be called Green and White. Now it's Marvin's Magnificent Cabs, but all the drivers call it Black and Blue, because of the unfortunate color of the cars, and as a tribute to Gloria's deceased brother, Marvin, who was quite a bruiser. Gloria, dispatcher, owner, and queen, lives behind the garage in a specially adapted apartment. She is at Black and Blue the way prisoners are in their cells. I hadn't had to call ahead to know she'd be available.

It had taken her about three seconds to make 157 Claremont as a

Flaherty property. Then she'd really gone to work. I knew the name of each tenant in the three buildings. I knew that Mr. and Mrs. Jacob Hooper on the ground floor of 157 served as building managers for the complex. Dowling rented the top floor flat.

I wanted Chaney's letters, and given Dowling's record, I didn't think he'd return them even if I said "Pretty please." So I'd decided not to ask. If the man had lived in some isolated suburban house, I'd have handled the break-in solo. A triple-decker in a crowded neighborhood required a different strategy, something devious, like Gloria's youngest brother, Leroy.

Leroy used to be all sorts of things. He used to be in the NFL, till he bit somebody's ear off. He used to be a bar bouncer, till the bar's clientele started going elsewhere. Now he's Black and Blue's garage guy, the one who keeps the old Fords tuned and shepherds them through the Hackney Carriage Bureau inspections.

Leroy owns a truck. At various times, it's been known to say Highlights Interior Decoration, O'Casey Plumbing, and Vanderbilt Electrical. He keeps a set of ready-to-paint interchangeable panels behind a wall in the garage. Leroy and I had debated the proper wording while Gloria made her helpful phone calls. First, we thought we'd use Exterminator, but then we went to Pest Control. We finally settled on Hamlin Chemical because nobody wants the neighbors to know that their place is infested with bugs.

Leroy had parked the truck legally, a minor miracle in itself. The sign on the side looked great. We'd debated getting Roz to come over and do a logo, maybe a little Pied Piper figure, but Gloria had nixed the idea. The lettering was simple and dignified. The paint was dry.

Leroy and I wore coveralls. His said BRUCE above the left chest pocket. Mine said AL. I don't look much like an Al. If questioned, I'd be Alison, but I figured the subject wouldn't come up, since most people don't want to get up close and personal with bug-spray dispensers. I grabbed a heavy silver canister. Leroy helped me strap it into the harness on my back and then I did the same for him.

We stopped at the ground-floor digs of the Hoopers and showed some official-looking paper to a woman with smudged cheeks and a vague manner. She was a bit ruffled that Flaherty hadn't warned her about the spraying. Not that it wasn't long overdue, mind. But she was cooking, her husband wasn't home, and she didn't want any chemical residue in her barley soup.

She didn't question the paper. It looked good. We'd pulled Flaherty Realty's letterhead off his Web site.

Leroy and I argued with each other a bit and allowed that we could come by to do her flat another day. Or we could give the entire place a miss. No, no, now that we'd finally made an appearance, we should definitely do the second and third floors at least. That nasty Maguire woman on two complained all the time about bugs. Then Mrs. Hooper got worried that if we sprayed the other flats, all the cockroaches would rush into hers like an invading army. I told her that the stuff we used stopped the little critters in their tracks, and, bless her heart, she believed me.

When she opened the door to Dowling's apartment, Leroy and I lifted our face masks into position. Mrs. Hooper, right on cue, asked whether the chemicals we used were dangerous. We assured her that they were perfectly safe, but just to be sure, no one should enter the sprayed flats for two to three hours. That was why we sprayed when most people were off at work.

I was hoping she'd discuss Dowling's schedule. All we knew, courtesy of Gloria, was that he'd picked up his phone at 9:05. The answering machine had taken over at 9:50, but what did that mean? He could be asleep in his bedroom, with the covers over his ears. The landlady hadn't even bothered to knock.

Mrs. Hooper—she was Geraldine by then, and smiling cheerfully—assured us that neither of the tenants in 157 would be in till five o'clock. She worried that they should have been warned about the intrusion. Once again, we offered to leave. Leroy allowed that it was possible we'd be able to swing by again within the month. Geraldine dithered a bit, remembered her simmering soup, and left us to our work. Leroy and I exchanged grins; we're a convincing team. People tend to trust me on sight; Leroy looks scary enough that you don't want to ask him a lot of questions.

Both of us pulled on latex gloves.

I said, "Sing out if you find a Whitman's Sampler box. And keep it neat. The guy shouldn't know we've been here."

Not only were we searching for Chaney's letters, I wanted a reason to put Dowling back in the can. Leroy has an eye for a hot item. If twenty thirty-six-inch Sony TVs fall off a truck, he usually hears about it. I reminded him to keep an eye out for stolen merchandise as well, and had him start with the living room. I started with the bedroom because that's where most people store the items they hope to keep private.

Dark clothes were heaped in one corner, the T-shirt still damp. Any possible doubts about Dowling as the blackmailer vanished when I found Chaney's backpack underneath the pile. It was empty, and I wondered what the man had done with the cash. Most people don't walk into a bank with five grand in small bills, even though it's legal to do so. No clerk will even fill out a government form if you deposit less than ten grand.

Maybe he was out buying a used car. There are a couple dealers in Saugus who'll take cash, sell you a car for a day, then give you a check when you return it. The check's for a couple hundred less than you paid for the car that morning, but worth it for a quick laundering service.

The cash wasn't under the mattress.

A man who dumps wet clothes in the corner doesn't make his bed. Doesn't change his sheets too often, either. The place smelled of body odor and old cooking smells. I opened the bedside table's drawer. Most people keep their valuables, jewelry, watches, eyeglasses, close to the bed so they can grab them fast in case of fire. Silver's usually in the dining room, but this place didn't run to a dining room.

The bed was a saggy single, with a striped spread and mismatched sheets. Posters displayed members of the WWF in full battle array, including two curvy, muscled women who might, on second gaze, have been guys in drag. The posters had been pushpinned into the plaster walls; one hung crooked and loose.

I found myself wondering about Denali Brinkman again. Had Dowling invited the Harvard girl to share his unkempt bed under the World Wrestling Federation posters? Like her, I'd have preferred sleeping in the unfinished addition to the boathouse.

I had a bad feeling about the decor. I'd have been happier with a whole lot of creature comforts, sharp stereo equipment, wall-to-wall CD cases. This wasn't the room of a man who had a lot to lose. The bedside table was filled with different varieties of condoms. The closet ran to soiled jeans and cargo pants with holes in the knees. Two pairs of khaki coveralls, not unlike the ones Leroy and I wore, hung on a hook behind the closet door. I checked for name patches but didn't find any.

In the living room, Leroy was watching music videos with the sound turned off, which made the gyrations even more obscene.

"Hot?" This was more like it. Dowling had a massive TV. I've been to movie theaters with smaller screens.

"Huh?"

"The TV, Leroy, is it stolen?"

"Probably. I wouldn't mind lifting it. Cost money, that thing did."

"Take a picture of it, get the numbers off the back, and keep going."

"Dude's got Xbox and PlayStation, plenty of titles, most of 'em rentals. Probably boosted 'em."

Stealing videos from the local rental store wouldn't keep Dowling in the can long. Yeah, he had a record, but Massachusetts is not a "three strikes and you're out" state.

I moved into the kitchen. I once found a .38 in a freezer, scaring the hell out of a carton of mint-chip ice cream, so I always give kitchen appliances a careful once-over. Chaney's money wasn't in the fridge, imitating lettuce. I poked through the garbage bag under the kitchen sink. Looked like the staple of Dowling's diet was peanut butter and jelly on sliced white bread. I could threaten to turn him in to the local food co-op. On the Cambridge-Somerville line, pb&j on Wonder bread is actionable.

"Carlotta!"

Leroy, still in the living room, was beaming. He hadn't turned off the dancing girls and boys on the TV, but he'd glanced as far as a small desk in an alcove. Smack in the middle of the blotter: one Whitman's Sampler box.

"Leroy, check the john, okay? There should be cash somewhere."

"Gun in the toilet tank?"

"Whatever."

I lifted the lid on the Sampler. Seven letters, in envelopes addressed to Denali Brinkman at Phillips House, handwritten. Either they'd arrived before she'd moved out or she'd made regular stops at her dorm to pick up her mail. I left the box where it was but stuffed the letters in the generous pockets of my coveralls.

Mission almost accomplished.

A scraggly plant sat on the windowsill behind the desk. A nearby mug read IMPRO. It looked like he used the mug as a watering can. The left-hand desk drawer gave me a line on Dowling's everyday life. Rent checks, a couple of old phone bills. He had a cell phone, and that costs. He had a mother in a small Ohio town; she wrote him earnest letters twice a month. He hadn't destroyed them, so maybe he cared about keeping Mom's good opinion. Maybe Mom knew her son was an ex-con, maybe not.

There was a filing system of sorts, but only a few labeled folders. Others, unlabelled, looked used, but they proved to be empty. I couldn't find any bank statements. No checkbook. I glanced at the Whitman's box, set out like a gift on the desktop, and wondered why it wasn't hidden away like the cash.

There wasn't much in the way of paper. I lifted all the file folders out of the drawer. Where were the pay stubs? If the building manager was sure he wouldn't be back till after 5:00 P.M., didn't the man work? If he lived on his blackmail earnings, where were the other letters, the incriminating stuff he used to open other victims' wallets? There were two crumpled sheets of paper in the back corner of the drawer. I smoothed them on the blotter. Both were from Graylie Janitorial Services, one a receipt for $287, the other for $83. I stuck the pricier one in my pocket. There was no computer, no sign of peripherals for a laptop hookup. No printer, no scanner. No photos on display. I'd been hoping for a framed shot of Denali Brinkman, something more revealing than the rowing shot the papers had printed. He didn't even have a photo of his mom.

I found a plastic Baggie stuffed with marijuana under the cushion of one of two droopy armchairs facing the big-screen TV. I took its photo in situ, then raised my voice.

"Leroy?"

"Nothing in the john."

"Come in here, please." I held the Baggie up for his inspection. "You plant this?"

He gave me wide eyes. "Look at that shit; it's all stems and seeds. That's good shit; I'd smoke that shit myself."

"Does that mean you didn't plant it?"

"If I was gonna do a plant, don't you think I'd put enough shit in the bag so he'd go down for dealing, not just taking a toke? Gimme credit."

I could see his point. I nodded.

"So, can I take it?"

"Nope," I said.

If all else failed, I could pretend to be Mrs. Hooper and drop a dime on my dope-smoking tenant. Maybe, with his record, he'd draw more than a smack on the wrist.

"We done here?"

I walked through the whole place slowly: kitchen, bath, bedroom, living room. That was it. I felt unsatisfied and puzzled, uneasy. The apartment was unremarkable and unrevealing. There was no trace of Chaney's money. The Whitman's Sampler box filled with his letters had been left in plain sight. Empty file folders. No address book, no

Rolodex. Maybe Dowling kept a lot of his personal stuff in his car. Maybe he carried a Palm Pilot.

We gave the room a few hits from a can of commercial bug spray before we left, so it would smell right. Then Leroy asked Mrs. Hooper to let us into the second-floor flat. We played a few games of rummy and sprayed there, too. That place had some serious roaches in the kitchen, practically lapped up the Raid and begged for more. We sprayed a little in the hallway.

"Verisimilitude is all," Leroy said.

His vocabulary is outstanding.

I knocked on Mrs. Hooper's door and told her we thought there might be a major roach infestation in the garage. She looked nonplussed. She couldn't give us the garage key because she didn't have it. One of her tenants rented the garage and he had the keys.

Didn't she keep a spare set? I asked. Well, yes, she usually did, but they'd gone missing.

Dowling, I thought, probably stole them. He kept stuff in the garage that he didn't want other people to see. I was sorry I'd formally requested entry. I could have picked the lock or Leroy could have forced it. In the second-floor hallway, we debated our next move. The garage door was in plain view of the window over Mrs. Hooper's kitchen stove. The barley soup seemed to require frequent stirring. There was no way she wouldn't notice any hanky-panky with the garage door.

We carried our canisters back to the van, like it was time to refill, maybe time for a break. Mrs. Hooper's probably still expecting us to come back and do the other two buildings.

Leroy negotiated the narrow one-way streets, stopping at all the stop signs, keeping to the fifteen-mile-an-hour speed limit. I should have been pleased; I had the blackmail letters in my pocket. Dowling smoked dope, maybe had a hot TV. We turned at the KFC franchise and started heading back toward the river. I wasn't pleased. I'd wanted hard evidence of criminal activity that had nothing to do with my client.

"How the hell do you make somebody stop doing something illegal?" I was musing aloud, talking more to myself than to Leroy.

"This a bad dude, guy on the top floor?" The question surprised me. Usually, Leroy doesn't ask. It's immaterial to him.

I nodded, then realized he couldn't see me with his gaze directed straight ahead. "Bad," I agreed.

"But you don't want to take it to the cops?"

"No."

"Dude bothering you?"

"Not personally."

"That's good. 'Cause if he was—"

"I know. Thanks for the offer, Leroy."

"Lemme make you another one. How you stop somebody doing what's illegal? What you do is, you hire me to mess with him. I'll break his fucking leg. That'll stop him from doing what he's doing, least for a while."

Back at my place, after sliding Chaney's letters into a heavy mailing envelope and updating my expenses on the case, I found myself replaying Leroy's offer in my head, giving it serious consideration. I'm not saying the idea didn't bother me. I was concerned that I couldn't seem to find a better solution to Chaney's dilemma than grievous bodily harm. It made me feel like some kind of vigilante, some kind of gangster, on the opposite side of the law from the one where I consider I belong. But in a curious way, Leroy's words comforted me. When I discussed the next step with my client, at least I'd have more than one option.

CHAPTER 13

Chaney was right: That day, he was unreachable. I left message after message on his cell phone, which was all I could do, since he didn't want anyone to know he had business that involved a private investigator. He didn't want me leaving word with his dragon lady secretary, and I was specifically forbidden to communicate via his home phone, as his wife wouldn't take kindly to calls from females asking to speak to her husband.

When Leon phoned, I warned him I might have to cut the evening short, but I agreed to meet him for dinner. I took my cell along. Chaney would be able to reach me. It didn't feel like a dereliction of duty.

We ate bowls of hot-and-sour wontons and plates of spicy green beans and dun dun noodles at Mary Chung's in Central Square. Over dinner, we talked music and movies and he told me about his first wife, Sally, who'd hated his cop job from day one. I told him about my ex-husband, Cal, a Cajun bass player who'd turned into a coke addict and run off with a blues singer. The Szechuan spices were hotter than Leon expected, but he seemed to relish the flavor, downing glasses of Chinese beer to soothe his tongue. Sam Gianelli's name didn't come up. I assumed Leon knew we'd been involved; he's in law enforcement, where the gossip mill churns. Sam's name never surfaced, but there were moments when I almost felt his presence, as though he were a third at the small table.

I met Sam even before I met Cal, and I married Cal when I was a green nineteen. Sam knows me. I don't need to tell him stories about my younger days. He knows them. I am who I am with Sam; no temptation to reinvent myself by leaving out the ugly parts, retelling the tale. It's easy to misrepresent yourself with someone new. It's not even lying. You simply don't mention this error or that lapse. And it's not really lying, because at that moment you figure you'll never do anything that stupid again, won't be that person anymore. You'll be somebody who's learned from her mistakes. Sure. Bullshit. Excuse me, but ha.

"Was Sally black?" I asked.

"Yeah. Cal white?"

I nodded, wondering about Leon and Chaney again, wondering how their apparently different circles meshed. I kept recalling Chaney's comment about how difficult it was for him to trust a white person. My Jewish grandmother, my mother's mother, never trusted a non-Jew. Goyim were okay, she would allow when pressed, and she never offered any explanation for her mistrust except that they were goyim, other, separate and apart. I glanced around the crowded, noisy room, at tables filled with flirting couples, rowdy students, multigenerational families, all colors, Korean, Chinese, African-American.

From a small table near the rest room, a woman glared back with hostile eyes. She was middle-aged and pudgy; her husband was husky and had a buzz cut. Both were white. I didn't know them. I wondered if she glared because I was half of a multiracial couple. That way, paranoia, I thought. Maybe she simply despised women with red hair.

My cell phone didn't sound during the meal. I checked it and the batteries were fine, no messages. I didn't want to go to a movie, where I'd need to shut it off. Leon liked the idea of a club, but I didn't want to go anyplace noisy enough that I was likely to miss Chaney's call.

We rented a pile of old movies, enough for a popcorn marathon, and went back to my place, where we couldn't agree on which one to watch first. I suggested we put on some music instead, hoping to listen to a new Chris Smither album. Leon like the idea of music; he wanted to dance. He found an oldies station that specialized in Motown, tried to teach me old Detroit dances I'd forgotten, the Stroll and the Grapevine. One thing led to another, it got late, and we wound up in bed.

I was drifting off, my head on his shoulder, my right arm draped across his chest, which he didn't seem to mind, when the bell rang. Not my cell phone, which I'd thought might ring and which I'd carefully cradled upstairs. The doorbell.

Leon tried to sit up. "Wha— That your sister?"

"She wouldn't ring. She's got a key."

"I might have slipped the chain on by mistake. You want me to—"

"Go back to sleep." The clock said 3:08. If it *was* Paolina, we were going to have words. I slipped on my robe, fastening the sash as I hurried downstairs. My bizarre tenant, Roz, has awakened me late at night, but my thoughts were of Paolina. Paolina hurt, Paolina injured, Paolina in trouble. Even so, I put the chain on the door. I was half-asleep and worried, but habits hold fast.

Chaney tried to push his way past the chain, his bloodshot eyes wide, his hair wild. He brought his face close to the crack in the door and spoke in a voice choked with anger.

"How much do you want?"

My "What?" was simply a reflex, a protest at the fury in his glare and his voice.

"What the hell were you— How could you have—"

"Be quiet. Keep it down!" Pretty soon, porch lamps would flare the length of the block. If he'd been drunk, I'd have smelled it on his breath at such close range. Drugs were harder to rule out. He didn't have a hand in his pocket or a suspicious weapon-shaped bulge in his clothes. He was fully dressed, but he'd done it in a hurry. One of his shirt buttons was undone, his right shoe untied.

I closed the door and removed the chain to the beat of insistent knocking. When I reopened, his charging entry took him clear across the foyer.

"Are you high or what?" I shut the door and turned on him angrily. A bigger man, a less well-educated man, I'd have been more careful.

"*Are you crazy*?" he responded. "Don't think I don't know. The cops—the police. I must have been crazy to—"

"Are you going to calm down, or am I going to kick you out? For a man who doesn't want anybody to know he's seeing a PI, you're pretty damned loud in the middle of the night."

He shot a quick glance at the staircase. "Are you alone here?"

"Chaney, what the hell is going on?"

"I can't believe this. My God, now I am totally fucked."

"I don't know what you're—"

He grabbed me by the shoulders, this intellectual, inoffensive man, grabbed me and tried to shake me like an angry parent might shake a child. "They won't believe me. You'll tell them I hired you. I'll never make them believe me. I could—I ought to kill you for what you've done."

"Let go of me." My voice cut like ice. Before I needed to follow up on it with my fists, he released me and turned away.

I took the single step down to the living room and my desk, lifted the receiver. "Nine one one right now, Chaney, unless you start talking sense. They'll trace the call, even if I hang up."

"Yeah, well, I know you're bluffing."

I made it to the second digit before he yelled at me to stop. For a moment, he looked hesitant, as though his intellect was warring with his fury. I took advantage of the pause.

"Sit down. Tell me what you think I've done before you go off like a bomb." I didn't swear; I didn't shove him into a chair, or whack him with a length of lead pipe. I made my voice deliberately gentle. Meet belligerence with belligerence, you just get more of the same.

To my surprise, he sat, almost toppling into the old butterfly chair that faced my desk. "The police came to my house." He seemed to think that was sufficient explanation but I sure as hell didn't.

"Do they know about the blackmail?"

"They haven't made any connection between me and the dead man, except for the car. But if they do, *when* they do—"

"The dead man." It came out too loud, an explosion of its own.

"Yes," he said, packing venom into the single word.

"Who?"

"Benjamin Dowling."

Benjy Dowling. *Shit.* I tried to pretend I'd heard other syllables, other words, but the name Benjamin Dowling echoed and rechoed till I couldn't stop myself from asking how Dowling had died.

"Like you don't know," Chaney said. "Tell it to the marines."

"And what about you? How do you even know his name?"

"Denali mentioned him. It wasn't important, just conversation, you know. I barely listened. She said something about rowing, a guy she met. But when I heard his name again, a man who *knew Denali,* when the cops told me about the hit-and-run, with *my* car, I thought—and then I knew. When did you take my car?"

"Back up. What exactly do you think—"

He looked around my living room, registering his surroundings for the first time since he'd entered. "This is quite a place. You know, I thought that before. . . . This house in this neighborhood. How does she afford a place like that? You blackmail your other clients to pay for it? You think I'm your meal ticket, but you're wrong. My wife has money; I don't have money. She won't help me. She'll let me sink. I wish I'd told you all this before—before it was too late—but it didn't seem any of your goddamned business. I might have money, money of my own, if I keep my job, if this drug trial goes through. But with the FDA, at this stage, it's hard to say, and Harvard will get the lion's share of the money."

"You think I killed Dowling."

He nodded slowly, as if it were the most logical thing in the world.

"You used my car. *My car.* I didn't even know the damn thing was gone until the cops came. I guess you figured they'd believe me when I said it must have been stolen. As long as there's no connection between me and . . . and the dead man, why shouldn't they believe me? You're the only one who can make the connection, so instead of paying Dowling one thousand or five thousand, now I pay you. God, I ought to call the police and tell them and the the hell with it. I can't believe you'd do this. I can't believe I'd do this. Cover up a murder to shield myself." He planted elbows on knees and lowered his head to his hands. I could hear his shuddering breath. "How much do you want?"

"What did you do today?" I demanded.

"What?"

"I want every minute of your day, Chaney."

"Why?"

"Do it!"

"After I called you, I went to the lab. I was in meetings all day."

"With?"

"Two different sets of drug company representatives. It was exhausting."

"When did you get out?"

"The afternoon session lasted past six. I had dinner at the Faculty Club. I went home."

There must have been gaps. Time when he could have tailed me, realized who the blackmailer was, put his own plan into motion. We eyed each other with growing distrust.

I said, "When did this happen? When did Dowling die?"

He seemed to sink farther into the chair. "The police came after two. Woke me up. They frightened my wife. They asked if I knew where my car was."

"Did they ask where you were at any specific time?"

"Twelve-thirty to one."

"And you were asleep?"

"Yes."

"Your wife will back you up?"

He pulled a face and glanced away. "I'm not sure."

"*Were you asleep?*"

"I didn't kill that man."

"Neither did I."

"If neither of us did it, do you suppose it was an accident? Could it have been an accident? Could—"

"A hit-and-run. With your car? An accident? I hope to hell you don't teach probability in your classes."

He wiped his hands on his knees, then rubbed them together rapidly as though trying to warm them, as though he'd taken a sudden chill. "Dowling was the one then. The blackmailer."

"Yes,"

"What about my letters? Did you find them? Do you have them?"

I must have nodded.

He couldn't keep his hands still. "Thank God. *Thank God.* Imagine what would have happened if the police had found them. Give them to me."

I was motionless. "I don't think so."

"What about the money? Will the police find it? If—"

"I didn't find any money."

He looked at me as if he was sure I was lying.

"Go home," I said.

"But the letters. . . . Are you still working for me?"

"Now you want a murderer on your payroll?"

"I may have spoken too quickly, made assumptions."

"Go home."

"But I need to—I need to order my life. I need to have a plan."

"You want a plan? Hire a lawyer."

"I"—he swallowed—"I have a lawyer."

"A criminal lawyer?"

"Will I need one?" His words were barely audible.

"You might."

"Burn the letters," he said. "Please. If you won't give them back to me, burn them."

"Go home."

"I should never have come." His words were bitter and tinged with regret, for this meeting, for our first meeting, for having sought my help in the first place. He got to his feet like a man who'd aged twenty years in as many minutes and walked slowly to the door.

CHAPTER 14

When a blackmailer dies under mysterious circumstances, you look closely at the person he was blackmailing. That's basic. I reconstructed my earlier phone conversation with Chaney. I hadn't mentioned Benjy Dowling by name; I was certain of that. But Chaney might have known it all along.

I went into the kitchen, yanked the refrigerator door, and inventoried the sparse contents. Three cans of Rolling Rock on the lower shelf were unappealing, cold when I craved warmth. I opened the high cupboard where Roz hides her scotch, found a clean glass, and poured myself a healthy slug.

Shit. Chaney could have followed me after the drop, or this morning in the exterminator's truck. Could have used me to locate his target. Maybe his original approach, that half-assed tail job through Harvard Square, had been a matter of design, a blind to keep me from the thoughts I was currently entertaining. Maybe Chaney had been deliberately awkward and noticeable. Maybe he was actually a skilled stalker.

I know a PI who was hired to find a missing sister, hired by the nicest, most concerned brother, only he wasn't the brother after all.

Turned out to be an abusive ex-lover. When the PI told him where the little sister lived, he beat her so badly, she never regained consciousness before she died. I remembered vowing that that would never happen to me. I'm damn careful when I locate women for men.

I'd been less careful with Benjy Dowling. Because he was a con and a blackmailer. I finished the scotch without tasting it, felt sudden heat in my gut, and poured more.

"Hey, you comin' back to bed tonight?"

Leon stood in the kitchen doorway, eyes narrow in the light, wearing boxers and a frown. I had trouble focusing on his face. He seemed to exist in some other universe, the world of before.

"Wilson having wife trouble again?"

"You listened?" When I set my glass on the table, it made a louder noise than I'd anticipated. "Let me get this straight. You eavesdropped?" My voice was louder, too. Maybe it was the scotch. Maybe it was the memory of my friend's guilty conscience or the churning anger I felt when I considered whether I might have misjudged Chaney, misread him completely.

"Hell no. Calm down. I just saw him out the window. Man, twenty years ago, folks in the neighborhood would've thought you were hosting an NAACP meeting. I don't know what they're thinking now."

"You *saw* him?" It was pitch-black outside.

"Yeah, I love this house. Lookit what I found on the windowsill upstairs. You some kind of pervert?" He brandished my night-vision scope. "Where's a civilian get shit like this?"

"Put it down," I snapped. "Leave it alone."

"Hey, no harm intended."

"Leon, think of this as my office. I'm working."

"This is your kitchen, babe. This is the middle of the fucking night."

"Go back to bed, okay? I need some time to think."

"You let all your clients come busting in anytime? Don't they realize you have a personal life?"

If it had been some other time or place, I might have calmly discussed the nature of emergencies. Now, in the middle of the damn thing, I had no patience. It seemed to me that Leon was turning into all the men I'd ever known who'd chided me for not being at their beck and call, not paying more attention to them, not understanding that their work was more important than mine, starting with my father and moving down a long, long line. Or maybe he just reminded me of Chaney, standing there. I hadn't yelled at my client, but I'd wanted to.

"Leon, I need to think." I rested my head in my hand. For a moment, I thought he'd gone away, but he didn't take the hint.

He said, "If that's how you think, with a glass of scotch, can I join you? Hey, maybe I can even help. Trained and at your service."

When I was a cop, I worked with a cop named Mooney. He was special, unusual; I could have talked this mess over with him. I trusted his instincts, trusted him. Leon was FBI, and until we'd met, I'd never had a good feeling about anybody attached to the feds. I'd worked with him on a single case, a case that had nothing in common with this one. I had knowledge of a crime, two crimes if you counted the blackmail, and I had no intention of speaking my mind to a federal agent, not about Chaney's predicament or my own.

"Please, just go to bed." I tried to keep my voice low, but, like the glass smacking the tabletop, it echoed.

He started to reply, stopped, then muttered something under his breath that I didn't catch. As he turned and stomped upstairs, I considered hurling my empty glass at the wall, then changed my mind and refilled it instead. Maybe I wouldn't drink it, just stare that amber liquid down.

How long before bright-eyed rookie Danny Burkett or desk-bound Kevin Shea made the connection? How long before one or the other decided he ought to question the private eye who'd inquired about a man who turned up dead? How long before Dowling's apartment manager thought she ought to mention the odd salt-and-pepper duo who'd come unexpectedly to exterminate?

Heavy footsteps descended the stairs, hesitated near the bottom, then crossed the foyer. The lock clicked and the door squeaked. I pushed back my chair and walked toward the noise.

"Leon?"

"What?" He turned with the door half-closed behind him. The breeze caught my robe and the sash fluttered.

"Look, you don't have to go. I'm sorry."

"But you don't wanna talk about it?"

"Can't."

"Sorry about that, too." He plucked his jacket off the coat tree in the hall. He was going to leave and I wasn't going to stop him.

"You didn't see Wilson Chaney here," I said.

"I did, but don't worry. I'll keep my mouth shut about it."

I stood on the front porch, watching his retreating form disappear into darkness, ignoring the night chill till it brought prickles to my arms. If the officers who'd gone to Chaney's house had followed him here, if they were out in the dark watching my door, they were getting their money's worth. Maybe they'd figure one lover, Chaney, had found me in the arms of another, Wells. That's the way cops' minds work.

No one seemed to be parked in the tow zones or blocking the fireplugs. The usual cars huddled quietly under the streetlamps. I sucked down a breath of cool night air.

Kevin and the rookie might not make the connection. The building manager, that vague and harried chef, might never mention the exterminator. I went back inside, sat behind my desk, and tugged at my hair, twirling a heavy coil round and round my forefinger.

I'm not a believer in coincidence. I didn't intend to calculate the odds of a blackmailer falling under a hit-and-run driver's wheels the day after hitting up his victim for more money. The cops might not be thinking deliberate homicide, but I was. Would the cops consider Chaney a suspect? Anyone might be upset to learn his car had been stolen and involved in a fatal accident. It would depend on how he'd handled his face when they'd mentioned Dowling's name.

If Chaney had done it, brilliant Chaney, Harvard's own Chaney, wouldn't the man have arranged an airtight alibi? Used someone else's car? Sure, if he'd planned it, but maybe he hadn't. Maybe he'd been following Dowling, waiting to make his rational approach, and then there he was, Dowling, blissfully unaware, crossing the street. In a sudden moment of rage and entitlement, Chaney might have gunned the motor, put an end to his tormentor.

If Chaney hadn't done it, who had? If he had a guardian angel, I figured he or she existed in solidly human form, not nemesis but accomplice. Had the guardian angel followed me? Had Chaney hired not one but two?

If Chaney had done the hiring, why Chaney's car? Rage and entitlement didn't cut it there, not with a proxy. A man smart enough to hire a proxy killer wouldn't let the killer use his car.

I yawned and blinked, sleepy after all. The scotch had done the trick. If Leon had just stayed upstairs, not been so damned nosy . . . Now there was nothing upstairs but tangled sheets on an empty bed, the scent of a man.

I recalled the sour smell of dirty clothes in Dowling's apartment, walked through it room by room in my memory. If I'd entered knowing the tenant would soon be dead, would I have seen it differently? The flat was messy, yes, but was it the mess of a slob, or had someone else searched it before me? Where was Dowling's checkbook, his bank statements? Where were his tax receipts? Why were the blackmail letters so easy to find? Had they been left on the desk deliberately, to give the cops a link to Chaney?

I regretted the unexamined locked garage. I'd decided to go for it another time, to pull a nighttime break-in if necessary. Now time seemed to have run out.

As long as the cops didn't connect the victim with the owner of the car, it would stay a hit-and-run investigation. They'd dust for prints on the recovered car, but they wouldn't be surprised to find Chaney's. Don't kid yourself: a hit-and-run can be treated in different ways. A homeless man goes under the wheels, that's one thing. A politician midcampaign, that's another. The victim always matters. If cops had found the blackmail letters in Dowling's apartment, they'd be on Chaney like ants on sugar.

"Burn them," he'd said.

I didn't burn them. I'm too much a cop at heart to destroy evidence. On the other hand, I didn't want any cop to be able to walk in and take them. I know people who have secret hidey-holes, safes behind switch plates, in baseboards, under the floor. I have a good place, too.

I reread Chaney's love letters. So much trouble for so few words. "Darling Denali, you make me feel like a teenager, like a bridegroom, like a gigolo, evil and pure, darling Denali." Nothing new, no secret code. Simple passion, rising heat. I put each back in its envelope, enclosed them in a plastic bag.

My cat's Kitty Litter tray comes apart. I cleaned and emptied it, stuffed the plastic bag between the two halves, and rejoined them invisibly with duct tape. I don't know a whole lot of people who would search a Kitty Litter tray. And even if someone did search this one, he wouldn't find the love letters in among the litter. Wouldn't even realize the two halves came apart.

Good thing T.C., my cat, can't talk. After the cheap canned-tuna scraps I'd doled out that week, I knew he'd turn me in if he could. Before I closed my eyes, I wondered how Chaney was sleeping, if he was sleeping. And that led me to another thought, just a wisp of memory and query before sleep dragged me down. Why hadn't his wife given him an alibi?

CHAPTER 15

I didn't sleep long and I didn't sleep well. I kept waking abruptly, flipping the pillow, searching for a cool spot against my cheek. It wasn't just the musky smell of the sheets that made me regret Leon's absence; I regretted the reason he'd left. I'd been angry at Chaney, the messenger who'd brought bad news at a bad time. Running straight to me after a visit from the cops was pure stupidity on his part. I'd been furious, and that fury, deprived of its rightful target once Chaney'd made tracks, homed in on Leon like a guided missile.

You learn from your mistakes. Oh yeah, sure you do, and I was getting to be damned good at recognizing them, too, *after* committing them.

Did I dream? I don't remember. I ran over the facts of the case until they became a shopping list, a rote exercise. I couldn't leave Dowling's death alone. It was like a scab I couldn't stop picking at, a sore spot in my mouth that my tongue couldn't leave untouched. I rolled out of bed, knowing that whether the cops treated the hit-and-run as a traffic accident or a homicide made no difference. I couldn't ignore it. I had to know. If I'd fingered a man for a killer, I needed to know. How can you learn from your mistakes if you don't even know which mistakes you've made?

I showered and dressed in khakis and a cotton shirt Paolina had unexpectedly and kindly ironed. Not part of our deal, any more than making her breakfast was for me. Over coffee and toast, I listened to the news but learned nothing. After breakfast, I searched the bushes for the newspaper. The delivery guy must be a hot prospect for the Sox pitching rotation. His velocity is terrific, as demonstrated by the broken branches on the rhododendrons, his location erratic.

Dowling was relegated to a small boxed item inside the "City and Region" section, which used to be called "Metro" before the news execs realized they needed to boost their circulation beyond the city limits. Page two, upper right side, part of a column of disparate items headed "New England in Brief." The subhead read "Police seek witnesses in hit-and-run."

> Boston police requested that witnesses come forward to assist the police in identifying the motorist responsible for the death of a pedestrian. The victim, identified as Benjamin Dowling, 30, of Somerville, was hit while crossing the Birmingham Parkway at approximately 1:00 A.M. The vehicle was traveling west at a high rate of speed. No skid marks were found at the scene, indicating the driver may have been unaware of the pedestrian's presence in the roadway. Anyone with information should call the hit-and-run hot line at 1-800-555-9687.

Three things: First, they'd made the identification quickly. That was understandable. The fingerprint database grows daily, and Dowling was in the system, courtesy of a felony conviction. An easy make. Second, the *Globe* hadn't run with the professor's car. I wondered if the cops were certain his was the hit vehicle. They'd need to do paint comparisons. Still, if he'd worked for a lesser university, his name might have appeared in print. Third, the location was intriguing. The Birmingham Parkway is a short loop of heavily traveled highway between the Mass Turnpike and Soldiers Field Road. Not much pedestrian traffic in the area. I wondered where Dowling had been headed—on foot.

Maybe the *Herald* was more informative. I was getting ready to go out and liberate a copy from a neighbor's shrubbery when the phone rang. I picked it up quickly, thinking it might be Leon.

"Hey, babe." Gloria's rich contralto filled the air. "I just wanna know Leroy's in the clear."

They say that if you go blind, your other senses sharpen, try to compensate for the eyes. That may be an old wives' tale, but Gloria's ears and eyes both seemed to grow more acute when her legs quit on her. She takes in two or three different radio stations while watching TV. She listens to police scanners while dispatching cabs. She makes connections quickly and surely.

I'd eliminated the possibility of Leroy as masked avenger between 4:00 and 4:05 this morning. Leroy would have run down Dowling in a New York minute if I'd asked, no question. Would he take the initiative? Maybe. But for Leroy to somehow grab the car of the man I was working for—no way. I mean, how the hell would he know I was working for Chaney? Leroy's not the most curious of spirits, nor is he exactly unobtrusive. If he'd been spying on me, I'd have seen him, the neighbors would have seen him, and the cops would have seen him. He's huge.

"No problem," I said, "but I'd appreciate it if you and Leroy wouldn't mention yesterday's outing."

"What outing is that?" I could hear the grin in her voice.

"And repaint the van."

"Already done. You follow the guy?" she asked. "You know who did him?"

I liked the way her mind worked, automatically assuming that a smart investigator like me, once interested in Dowling, would have kept him under tight surveillance. I only wished I had. I worked the conversation around to what she'd heard on the police band last night.

"Scanner?" she said. "Whoa, busy, busy night."

"With?"

"Hang on a sec." I listened while she sweet-talked a customer waiting for a belated ride to the airport. She came back to my question without missing a beat. "Night fulla shit, mostly false alarms. I dunno, you'd think kids wouldn't pull that shit anymore, too busy shootin' up the high schools. But last night, they were at it for sure, phonin' in lies."

"The hit-and-run the only fatality?"

"Yeah."

"Anything else in D-Fourteen? B and E's?" D-14 is the police designation for Allston-Brighton. It's a big chunk of town, but most calls run to underage drinking. With parts of BU and all of BC within its boundaries, keg parties take up a lot of response time.

"Liquor store holdup, but that was C-Six." Area C-6 is Southie.

"They call for a tow at the hit-and-run scene?"

"Ambulance, no tow."

You'd think she had it written down, but I knew it was just there in her memory. I'd asked because I was wondering about the location of Dowling's black TransAm.

"Cabbies talking about the hit-and-run?" I inquired, knowing cabbies talk about everything.

"Heard they found the hit car. Owner says it was stolen, but he hadn't gotten around to reporting it yet." I could almost see her shrug her vast shoulders. "Heard he's a big shot."

Talking to Gloria cleared the fog from my brain. After I hung up, I had another cup of coffee and refigured my mission. I wasn't going to investigate just to assure myself I hadn't fucked up and set Chaney on Dowling's trail. Guilt is an overriding theme in my life, but I try not to let it upset my sense of balance.

I'd done my job. I'd succeeded. I'd retrieved Chaney's love letters, Dowling was dead, and the threat of further blackmail was nil. But if the cops found that Chaney had done the deed, I'd be out a substantial fee. Therefore, I needed to prove Chaney hadn't done it.

If I'd had a badge to thrust in her face, I'd have gone to visit Chaney's wife, demanded to know why her husband wasn't sure she'd provide him with an alibi. I couldn't imagine her consenting to speak with me without some form of coercion. I spent some time thinking about what I could use, then decided to go for a source who'd talk to me no matter what.

"Garnowski, J." was how Dowling's parole officer had been listed. I'd worked with Jake Garnowski for only a few months at the end of his cop career, but I'd absorbed his legend. Garnowski wasn't dumb so much as he was lazy. And he wasn't lazy so much as he didn't give a shit. Man hadn't read his morning dispatches in twenty years. I phoned, and, bingo, he was eager to meet for lunch. Chances were that he wouldn't know Dowling was dead. And if he did know, chances were that he wouldn't care.

The tone of his voice on the phone suggested that he remembered me. I decided on a complete change of wardrobe because I remembered him. I chose a low-cut white tank top and formfitting jeans, wore my hair loose and curly.

Jake is old school. He used to be a cop and he used to be a crook. By the time he got booted from the department, he had enough political clout to win a probation officer's slot. After all, he'd never exactly been convicted of a crime. He knew where too many bodies were buried to be threatened with arrest.

Before I left the house, I debated calling Leon and apologizing. I postponed it. I was busy. Besides, I'd already said it once. I hate to apologize.

Garnowski had certain requirements in a lunch place. You had to be able to smoke, which left out a lot of choices. You had to be able to drink hard liquor, which left out a few more. The food had to be American-American. So we were into bars, dark, boozy-smelling places called Whitey's or Smokey's or Joe's, with menus featuring beef stew, hamburgers, and meat loaf. My mouth watered in anticipation; I imagined my arteries hardening into pipelike rods.

I pulled the car into a genuine parking slot, thanked the traffic gods, fed the meter. My quarter didn't register. I carry a slip of paper in my backpack with "Meter Broken" written across the front in large letters. I sighed as I hunted it out and placed it under the windshield wiper once again. Boston meters ought to have a push-button dispenser, OUT OF ORDER signs on demand.

Kelly's Bar and Luncheonette was filled with workmen from the as-yet-and-possibly-forever-unfinished Big Dig. Garnowski was already at the bar, wearing a worn plaid shirt, soiled khakis, and work boots. I always thought that another requirement for a Garnowski place was that it be staffed by some of his former parolees. He always got great service. I'm not sure whether he paid.

He was a big man and getting bigger, growing soft around the middle, with meaty arms. He looked like he used to box, used to throw his weight around, still could if he were motivated. He also looked like drinker, with a shot and a beer already in place in front of him on the bar.

I ordered a beer. I didn't want one this early, but Garnowski was of the old school, like I said, and if you didn't drink with him, you were not one of the guys, and that went double for women in law enforcement.

"Ya look good." There are plenty of men who can say that in greeting and it's okay; not a leer, just a greeting. With Garnowski, the words were accompanied by a searching glance, tip to toe, with a long stop at breast level, then a glance around the room to see if the other members of the herd fully appreciated his drinking companion.

"You, too," I said, staring at his mountainous gut. "Want to move to a table?"

"Sure. Joe, bring us a couple burgers. Cheese?"

"Yeah," I said, surprised he'd offered me the choice.

"Heavy on the fries," he added. "She's paying." That was for the audience, too. Let the guys know that the broad paid to talk to the big man. Garnowski barely made the height requirement as a cop, and some of the shortest ones are the nastiest.

We shot the breeze awhile, parking, traffic, the Dig, the graft, the usual bullshit. Then Jake wanted to know if it was true I was dating some black FBI guy, and what the hell had happened between me and

Gianelli. Was I ratting him out with the Feebs? I wound it around to Benjy about the same time the burgers came.

"The thing about Benjy, he isn't a bad guy."

Garnowski used the present tense when describing Dowling, which was good. His eyes gave nothing away, but I was pretty sure that if he did know Benjy was dead, he wouldn't be able to keep himself from springing it on me.

I nodded. None of the guys in jail are bad guys, you listen to them tell it.

"He's the kind," the parole officer went on, "if he'd lived a nice suburban life, he'd never a seen inside. Typical hard time growing up—no father, no money, kinda bright, but never smart enough."

Benjy was attracted to easy money, he explained. He'd work harder for crooked money than most guys would work for straight pay. Benjy liked the life, the irregular hours, the hanging out, the bragging, the womanizing. He actually used that word, *womanizing*.

"He was like a magnet for trouble. Except not a magnet—what am I trying to say here? He was like one a them metal filings. A crime magnet would come along and yank Benjy clear across the state. That's how he is. Always waiting to feel the tug, always ready to fly across the floor. There's a lot of crooks out there, and I'm pretty sure one a them will get to Benjy again."

Since he was talking about Benjy as if he had a future life in crime, I was careful to do the same. "You'd be surprised if he was heading something, doing something on his own?"

"If Benjy was doing something on his own, it would be ripping off the poor box at a stone-broke parish."

"He get any education in jail?"

"You kidding? Even in this Commie state, we don't coddle 'em anymore. Used to be you could walk outta the can with a fucking college degree. All Benjy coulda learned was how to boost a better car."

"He make friends in jail?"

"Assholes and jerks."

"Ganged up?"

"Not that I heard, but he was buddies with a guy named—lemme see, another one of mine, a Freddie Church, only he never went in one, get it? Never went in a church. Now, I been a good guy. Loose lips and all that. Never can say no to a pretty woman, and you gals all take advantage of me."

He'd raised his voice for the audience, which made me want to slam my boot heel on his instep. He didn't just talk to pretty women; Garnowski talked to everybody. He drank and he talked, and it was a wonder he was still gainfully employed. Somebody must have owed him big time.

"Why ya wanna know about Benjy? What's he done?"

"Boring old due-diligence shit."

"As in a job?" He gave me the eye. He didn't like it when women swore. Drinking was fine, because then they might let him score, but swearing—well, that wasn't ladylike.

I said, "What kind of jobs would he be likely to take? Restaurant work?"

"Nah, he hated that shit, said they were all grab-ass places. Worked cleaning buildings, mostly. Janitorial, but had trouble getting jobs, keeping them, too."

"You know where he's working now?"

"Nope. He's offa my list. Did his time, paid his price."

"How'd he get caught?"

"Couldn't leave well enough alone. Ya know, that's another one of Dowling's sins. He's always—whatchacallit?—gilding the fuckin' lily, ya know. Has to do you one better. He and a buddy rob a place, he's got to take it on himself to beat the shit outta the manager. Makes the manager remember the robbery a whole lot better, that much pain. Then when the cops question him, he's gotta give 'em all these details that they can check, tell he's lying like a rug. Can't shut up. Gotta go you one better. Ambitious, but can't leave well enough alone."

"I heard he was a rower. You know anything about that?"

"Like rowin' boats? Nah. He's in good shape, though. Weight lifter. Prison athlete. Gotta be strong, protect yourself from the ass-grabbers."

I was waiting for him to make a move. If he tried to pat my ass, I was going to plant my knee in his jewels.

"Known associates besides Church?"

"Really, Carlotta, what's it matter?"

"Hey, I'm buying you lunch, aren't I, Jake?"

"He did something, right?"

"That would be telling."

"You don't have to. People don't change. Trust me on that. When I started out, I was like idealistic. Really, I fuckin' was. But people don't change. Same old, same old. They come around in a big revolving door, and Benjy'll waltz right through my door again. You'll see."

Benjy wouldn't, but I didn't want to disturb the man's worldview. We finished our cheeseburgers. I got him to promise he'd leave Freddie Church's last known address on my answering machine. He urged me to have another beer or two, on him, really. He hadn't spent time with a woman as good-looking as me in a long, long time.

I wanted to tell him that with breath like his, it was no fucking wonder, but a source is a source, so I smiled and told him I had to run. I fed the coins I hadn't fed the meter into a vending machine and grabbed a *Herald*.

A meter maid was fast approaching my car when I retrieved it. You're not supposed to park at a broken meter. It's a ticketing offense, one of the many *gotchas* of Boston driving. I mean, where's the logic? There aren't enough meters, and most existing meters are broken; therefore, let's make it illegal to park at broken meters. I pulled into a loading zone to escape the rampant meter maid, spread the newspaper across the steering wheel.

The *Herald* had dug up some stuff on Dowling, unearthing both the mother in South Easton and his criminal record. The mother said, "He was a good boy," with predictable lack of originality. What are you supposed to say when some cop comes to the door in the middle of the night and tells you your kid's dead? The words the reporter chose to paint Dowling made him a working-class hero, a man who'd paid his debt to society and was well on the road to rehabilitation when tragedy, in the form of a dark blue van, struck him down. The article made much of the grieving mom, but it didn't name the van's owner.

A van seemed an odd choice of vehicle for Chaney. I was banking on his innocence, and I didn't know him well enough to predict what kind of car he'd drive. I didn't want to go home because I didn't want to be there if Officer Burkett stopped by. Instead, I parked four streets away from Dowling's apartment and figured out how to approach the garage from the street behind Chestnut. I wasn't planning to do anything in daylight, but a full-light reconnaissance seemed advisable. I reconfirmed that the garage had no windows.

Leon didn't call and I didn't call him. I phoned Gloria and gave her the plate on the black TransAm. She'd hear if it had been towed or reported stolen. Probably it was parked in the damned locked garage, with the kayak still perched on top. But if it was, how had Benjy Dowling gotten from his place to Birmingham Parkway?

All day, I felt like the shoe was poised to drop. When it finally fell, it didn't land with a thud, but with a shrill ring. It wasn't Chaney's voice on the line this time. This time, the call came from a lawyer. Todd Geary, Wilson Chaney's attorney, would appreciate it if I would be at his office on Monday morning at nine o'clock. It sounded more like a summons than a request.

CHAPTER 16

I knew Todd Geary by reputation. He used to work for one of the hot-shot firms in the financial district, until he made the fateful decision to divorce his wife, aka the boss's daughter. Now he toiled at a smaller firm, of which he was sole proprietor, located in Kendall Square. He wasn't a criminal lawyer, never had been, more of a financial wheeler-dealer.

At nine o'clock, I found a parking place on Binney Street and hiked toward the river, pushing against a chilly wind. Geary's Cambridge Parkway building seemed to have no security, just a board in the dismal lobby, giving the names of tenants and their office numbers. The elevator was empty and slow, a private cubicle, so I took advantage and tugged my panty hose higher at the waist. I was wearing my best Filene's Basement black meet-a-lawyer suit, sleek light-weight wool. The suit was comfortable enough, but the damned panty hose were coming off the minute the meeting ended.

Geary's furniture outclassed his surroundings, which made me wonder whether he'd lifted the rosewood desk and credenza from his previous office. There was no receptionist, although there was a reception desk, so it was possible he'd timed our get-together for a moment when his receptionist was taking a break. Also possible that he had no receptionist. He rose to greet me, a man in his thirties with the spare look of a long-distance runner. He wore a crisp blue shirt with a sharp white collar, Turnbull & Asser quality. His slacks were charcoal and matched the jacket neatly arranged on a wooden hanger behind the door. When he resumed his seat, I noticed that his expensive shoes were worn at the heel.

"I hear you do good work," he said with forced cheerfulness.

There are people in town who say nice things about me, but I'm not sure they outnumber those who voice complaints. He didn't volunteer his source, so I waited.

"I suppose you know Dr. Chaney from Harvard?" He smiled engagingly. He had very even white teeth, a longish nose, opaque gray eyes.

"No." I displayed some teeth, as well.

"Wilson hasn't told me a great deal."

I stayed silent. I like to stand mute around lawyers, and most of the time they enjoy the sound of their own voices so much, they hardly notice. So far, the meeting appeared to be a fishing expedition with Geary trying to find out exactly why I was sitting in his office chair.

"Does he know you from Harvard?" I asked when the conversation showed signs of grinding to a complete stop.

"No."

An impasse. I was debating whether to ask if we might send out for coffee when he decided to continue.

"I represent Dr. Chaney vis-à-vis his interests in Improvisational Technologies. The commercialization of academic research in 1999 alone resulted in more than forty billion dollars in economic activity, supporting more than two hundred and seventy thousand jobs. That's from the AUTM, just out."

"AUTM?"

"Association of University Technology Managers."

"Are you a member?"

"No." Geary looked as if he was enjoying our conversation about as much as he'd enjoy sitting on shards of glass. His restless fingers tapped the desktop. "Um, there are potential areas of conflict whenever a university and a private enterprise are involved in a joint venture. I represent Dr. Chaney's interests, both with Harvard's Office of Technology and Trademark Licensing and with outside firms, venture capital, so forth. Ah, good, here he is. I was getting a little worried; it's not like Wilson to be late."

Chaney wore a lightweight navy suit over a sky blue T-shirt. He'd pushed his sunglasses onto the top of his head and carried a slim black attaché case.

"Everything okay?" Geary asked intently as he shook hands and waved him into the chair next to mine.

"If you mean, have I been arrested yet, the answer is no, I haven't. Fording told me to take a few days off, but don't worry, I'll still be at the lab."

"But not teaching?"

"No." Chaney turned to me, nodded, then focused on the attorney. "Have you given her the money?"

"I was waiting for—"

"Do it."

Geary's lips tightened. "Ms. Carlyle, I have been instructed to hire you, and to pay you a retainer of one thousand dollars. Unfortunately, I cannot tell you what services you are expected to perform for that fee, or for any other monies you may receive."

Using a tiny gold key, he unlocked the top drawer of the rosewood desk, then removed a thick envelope and passed it to me. It wasn't sealed. The ten one-hundred-dollar bills were crisp.

Chaney said, "Now go for a walk, Todd."

The attorney bristled. "That's not necessary. If she's working for me, and I'm working for you, I ought to know what this is about."

"What you ought to do is keep my name out of the papers, Todd. And keep your ears open."

"Well, I have. Kept them open, I mean. Is she allowed to know what I've heard?"

"Yes."

The attorney lowered his voice. "The police haven't found who-ever stole your car. But they have found a witness to the accident." He shuffled through a pile of papers on his desk until he located a folded yellow square. "Here it is. An elderly woman pulled into a parking lot along Soldiers Field Road to change from her reading glasses to her regular lenses. Woman named Myra Crump. Looked up when she heard a loud noise. Says the victim was carried on the front of the van for almost two hundred yards. According to her, the driver must have known he hit someone."

"Unless he was drunk out of his mind," I offered.

"She felt certain he hit the man on purpose."

"Why?"

"Something about the movement and speed of the van."

"That's no good," I said, "not if she says she looked up when she heard the thump."

"I agree."

"Plus, it doesn't speak to Dr. Chaney's involvement. His car was stolen."

The lawyer said, "But he hadn't reported it."

I said, "Look, I live in Cambridge, too. My car's been stolen twice and I do everything but chain the damn thing to a tree. Professor Chaney didn't realize it had been stolen yet. Thieves don't ring your bell and tell you it's gone."

"Exactly," the lawyer said. "I agree. I think the police are overstep-ping themselves on this."

"So they don't have anything else?"

He pressed his lips together and rechecked the small slip of paper. "Well, they may. The Brighton station got a phone call early this morning. The caller described the driver as a black man in his forties, well dressed."

"Shit," Chaney muttered under his breath.

"Have they asked you to participate in a lineup?" I asked Chaney. "Did they take your photo?"

128

"Not yet."

"Wilson," Geary said, "I'd seriously advise you to hire a criminal attorney. I can recommend some very good people."

"No, Todd."

"In fact, at this point, I'd advise you to hire a lawyer you trust."

"I do trust you, Todd. You know that; you're the best."

"But—"

"Why don't you take that walk?"

"Wilson, if I didn't consider you a friend, I'd—"

"I know. I appreciate it. Someday I'll tell you all about it, but right now—"

"Fifteen minutes." The lawyer clipped off the phrase, shrugged into his suit coat, and abandoned his office.

"Have the police come to see you?" Chaney asked as soon as the door closed.

"Think he's running a tape?"

"No."

"I haven't heard from them."

"Good."

"I expect to," I said.

"My letters?"

"They're safe."

"You won't destroy them? Or return them?"

"Not yet."

"You don't trust me," he said reproachfully.

"I haven't given them to the police," I said.

"Yes, well, listen, we don't have much time. Friday, when I came to see you—was it Friday?"

"Yes. The middle of the night."

"I haven't slept for so—"

"What?" I tried to keep my impatience in check.

"I told you I'd been at home, asleep, when the accident occurred."

"And then you said your wife wouldn't confirm your alibi."

"Couldn't. Because I wasn't there."

I settled back into my chair and crossed my legs, taking care not to display my new underwear.

"I got a phone call," he went on. "On my cell. Very few people know my private line."

"Who was it?"

"I thought it was, um, a student of mine, Sarah Bigelow. She said she needed help. She asked me to meet her on the Weeks Bridge. You know where that is?"

The Midnight Tango Bridge.

"She sounded confused and worried. Desperate. If someone you knew had killed herself recently, and then you got a call from a woman rambling almost incoherently, well, you'd have gone, too. But now, I think I—"

"What?"

"I don't know. It got me out of the house."

"You're telling me you think you were set up for the hit-and-run."

"I'm telling you she didn't show up."

"Did anyone? Is there anyone who can alibi you?"

"I didn't see anyone I know. And now I'm not even sure there is a Sarah Bigelow in my class. I know there's a Sarah, but the intro classes are so big and I've taught for so many years."

"Why didn't you tell the police about the call?"

"Well, first of all, I hadn't told Margo I was going. I knew it would upset her. She's a—she's been ill."

"Okay."

"And I thought she'd back me up. I didn't realize she'd heard me leave. And frankly, does it sound likely to you?"

I could see his point.

"Do you think I should tell them now?" he asked.

It's not like I've never lied to a cop.

I said, "I'd leave it. There will be plenty of time to spring it on them, and in the meantime, they might find something to exonerate you."

Chaney expelled a breath. "I don't think they're looking to exonerate me. I think they're looking to prove I did it. And if I'm not mistaken, the evidence will turn up."

"You mean someone will provide it?"

"Yes. The same way they got me out of my house. I want you to find out who is doing this to me. I mean, isn't it reasonable that Dowling was blackmailing more than one person? Don't blackmailers tend to do that?"

"You're saying somebody else Dowling was blackmailing decided to kill him—and that person knew Dowling was blackmailing you as well."

"So he used my car. Yes. Exactly."

I hadn't found anything in Dowling's apartment that indicated he was blackmailing anyone else. On the other hand, it had been too easy altogether to find Chaney's love letters. After my meeting with Garnowski, I was wondering whether Dowling might have had a partner in the blackmail, a partner who'd tired of him.

I said, "They won't arrest you unless they have more than an old woman and a phone call saying the driver was black."

"Something will be provided," he said. "Some type of trumped-up evidence."

"You need to hire a criminal attorney."

"Geary's qualified to arrange bail if it comes to that. And he's good. He can keep my name out of the papers."

"And that's more important than hiring somebody who knows the game?"

"Right now, yes."

"Todd Geary used to specialize in companies going public. This is the same man, right?"

"Yes."

"What's he doing for you? Is Improvisational Technologies going public?"

"This is a bad time for public offerings."

"Is that a no?"

"Improvisational Technologies has been looking for an outside partner, someone with considerable funds to invest. Several meetings have been set up, and my presence at those meetings is imperative. I need to be totally focused on presenting our findings to potential investors."

"I thought Improvisational Technologies was partnered with Harvard."

"We are."

"Harvard has more money than God."

"But the more money Harvard puts in, the more money Harvard expects to take out."

"What does Improvisational Technologies do?"

"The major thrust is research." He stared at his wristwatch. "I have one of those meetings in fifteen minutes."

"Research in what area?"

"In alternative therapies to methylphenidate."

"You're developing something new for ADHD?" Methylphenidate is the generic name for Ritalin. If he thought he could shut me down by using the chemical name, he was wrong.

His mouth twitched. "You must know someone with ADHD."

"Yes. Or I should say possibly. One psychologist thought my little sister might have it."

"Not surprising. There's a huge potential market, particularly for a substance with fewer side effects than CNS stimulants, like Ritalin, Concerta, and Adderall. How old is your sister?"

"Fifteen."

"Was she younger when it was diagnosed?"

"It was five years ago."

"CNS stimulants can have a very different effect, depending on the age when the drug is first given. Is she medicated?"

"No."

"At fifteen, I would probably advise against it. There are so many variables when dealing with the brain. We're only now seeing lasting neurological changes, elevated levels of certain proteins like CREB.

That's why a new approach, a unique approach to the disease—or rather, to the symptoms—would be invaluable."

"Unique meaning patentable?"

"Yes."

When Chaney'd walked into the lawyer's office, he'd looked exhausted and worn-out, but as he spoke about his research, his eyes brightened and his back straightened. I remembered Denali's roommate, Jeannie, describing Chaney as a vital, exciting lecturer. In the lecture she'd recalled, he'd issued a warning against educational medicalization. Now it sounded as though the man who'd preached against the overuse of drugs was developing his own.

Todd Geary didn't knock, maybe hoping he'd overhear something to his advantage. Or maybe he didn't want to get in the habit of knocking on his own door. Chaney practically leaped from his seat as soon as the door opened.

"I have to be going," he said. "I'll be at the lab the rest of the day. Leave me a message on my cell and I'll get back to you, either one of you."

Geary had his mouth open to ask a question, but Chaney was already gone, his footsteps retreating down the hall. The lawyer shook his head and seated himself behind his big rosewood desk. He seemed surprised to find me still seated in the chair when he glanced up.

"Possibly," I said, "you can help me."

"Possibly." He was tight-lipped, still angry at being dismissed from his own office.

I smiled. "You seem to know Dr. Chaney well. Would you be able to tell me whether he has any enemies?"

The lawyer steepled his hands, brought his fingertips to his mouth, then rested his hands on the desk. "I'd advise you to talk to his wife."

Fine with me. I wanted to meet Chaney's wife. If she was sharp enough to realize he'd left the house, maybe she was sharp enough to verify the oddball phone call. Maybe she'd listened in.

"You think she would know?" I asked.

He displayed those even teeth in another smile, not a pleasant one. "That's not what I meant. Have you met Margo Chaney?"

"No."

"Well, what a treat you have in store."

I waited for him to smile, to share the joke, but his face stayed deadpan.

"Would you be willing to call her and arrange an appointment?"

He picked up the phone and dialed.

CHAPTER 17

The house, which adorned one of those tree-lined streets northwest of
Harvard Square, was secluded and private, with a high wall and a
large yard. A Colonial among Colonials, vintage 1700s, or a good imitation, with plenty of elegant houses to copy on nearby Brattle Street,
once called Tory Row, due to the sympathies of those living in the
fancy mansions during Revolutionary times. I eyeballed the address
the lawyer had given me, wondering whether he'd made a mistake,
transposed a number. Don't get me wrong; Harvard professors earn
good money, but this was a massive house in an expensive area.

I rang the bell and waited. The professor had told me his wife was
ill. Todd Geary's arched eyebrows and odd manner when discussing
Mrs. Chaney made me think I might be facing something more exotic
than physical infirmity.

The garden fence was seven feet high, designed to stop peeping
neighbors cold. Even in heels, I couldn't peer over the top. Footsteps
proceeded down a flagged path, and then a cool male voice inquired
whether I had an appointment. When I said yes, a slot opened and the
same voice asked me to please place my card on the tray. I scribbled
my name on the back of one of the lawyer's cards and handed it

through, wondering if the Chaneys had recently been burgled. Seemed like a lot of security—a big ADT sign on the lawn, this elaborate ritual by the fence.

"Just a moment, please." The footsteps receded, leaving me stranded on the wrong side of the gate. I measured the height of the multichimneyed roof. Three floors at least, maybe twenty rooms. I counted mullioned windows, gave it up at thirty-seven, wondered whether Chaney would be proved right and some physical evidence would magically turn up linking him to the hit-and-run on Birmingham Parkway. It's tough to manufacture evidence. Police procedure has gotten pretty damned sophisticated when it comes to physical evidence.

The gate opened soundlessly. The man attached to the voice was young and wary, filled with undergraduate earnestness. He had blond hair that fell in waves over his ears, a round face, wire-rimmed glasses, and an Adam's apple that lurched up and down as he spoke.

"Mrs. Chaney will see you in the withdrawing room." He blushed when I raised an eyebrow at the quaint term. "She is returning the house to its pre-Revolutionary condition, so she prefers to use that word. A previous owner had actually removed walls, but she was fortunate to find the original architect's drawings. It's one of her hobbies."

I followed him onto a wide enclosed porch and then into a fan-shaped foyer—gray, with white trim. The place smelled like rose blossoms. I wondered whether Mrs. Chaney would wear a hoop skirt.

I was disappointed, but not by much. She wore what might be described as "invalid's garb," a long off-white nightgown, almost entirely covered by a woolen robe. Her dark hair was caught and elaborately looped at the back of her neck. She was pale, formidably thin, and perfectly groomed, in spite of her boudoir getup. She was either much younger than her husband or remarkably well preserved—hard to say which. Her glance was positively terrifying. I had the feeling that she'd priced every garment I wore within thirty seconds, right down to my underwear.

At first sight, she didn't seem to be black. Her dark hair was smooth but braided, and her features—well, again, hard to say. After what Chaney had told me about not trusting white people, I decided his wife was most likely a woman of color.

"I hope you've come to explain," she said irritably. "I've tried speaking to that worthless twig of an attorney. I have no intention of paying him extra to handle this. And now he tells me he may have to hire another attorney, and you as well, just because Wilson has gotten himself into this ridiculous trouble."

Once she'd finished evaluating my attire, she picked up where she'd stopped in her knitting. A ball of pale blue yarn rested on her lap and steel needles flashed.

"Perhaps I could sit," I said.

She was posed in a semireclining position, her back elevated by pillows, her slippered feet propped on a sort of a chaise longue. From some distant history lesson or long-forgotten book came the term *fainting couch*. That's what the piece of period furniture must be; I hesitated to ask.

"Yes, sit, if you must. I hope this won't take long. Mark? Mark dear, could you bring coffee for Miss—"

"Carlyle."

"And some cocoa for me."

He didn't click his heels before leaving the room, but he came damned close. I waited for Margo Chaney to say something, but she merely stared at me as if I were some interesting form of insect life until I spoke.

"Mr. Geary thought you might be able to help me."

"I'm sure I don't know how." *Click* went the needles.

"You said your husband had gotten himself into trouble."

"Yes, well, we are all sinners, every one." *Clack*.

I didn't know how to respond. Coffee and cocoa might arrive at any moment, so I thought I'd try small talk. "You have a lovely home."

It wasn't anyplace I'd want to live. More like a museum than a place to eat and sleep, with glossy paint, ornate molding, and gleaming chandeliers.

"Yes, well, you may tell Mr. Geary that this home will go unmortgaged to my children, along with my home in Oak Bluff. Both have been in my family for generations, and they will remain so, unencumbered. There is no use pretending that Wilson is made of money at the present time. What money there is is my money, and I will not squander it on a man who has behaved foolishly."

Vehicular homicide may be careless or brutal, but I'd rarely heard it described as foolish. If she had a family home in Oak Bluff on Martha's Vineyard, she was not only a woman of color; she was a woman of money, too. The so-called talented tenth vacationed on the Vineyard.

"Miss Carlyle," she said, "what is your work?"

"I'm an investigator."

"A policewoman?"

"I was a policewoman."

"But you're no longer one. Perhaps you're not entirely corrupt."

"Let's hope not. I'm working for your husband."

Her needles were small, the yarn thin. She worked quickly, but I couldn't tell what she was making. "Running down some hooligan with his car. Imagine—" She stopped abruptly, and I realized she'd caught Mark's faint footsteps. He carried a silver tray laden with floral china. He stooped and placed it on a mahogany table with practiced ease.

"Cream?" asked my hostess without rising from her chaise.

"Yes, thank you."

"Sugar?"

"Please."

She dismissed Mark with a frown as soon as he'd doctored my coffee. A plate of what seemed to be pound cake made me realize I was starving. The cocoa smelled wonderful and I wished I'd requested it as well. On the other hand, the room was warm and stuffy. If I'd ordered cocoa, I'd probably have fallen asleep.

"Please, help yourself," said Mrs. Chaney.

"May I cut you a slice of cake?"

"No, I couldn't possibly eat, but do have some."

I did.

"It's a Colonial recipe, with cranberries and currants."

It was dry as dust. If I hadn't chugged coffee to moisten it, it wouldn't have gone down. She watched me like a hawk while I ate, as though she were going to do her dissertation on my table manners, or lack thereof. That and the dry cake killed my appetite.

"Miss Carlyle." She paused, as though she'd forgotten what she was going to say. Or maybe because she felt too weak to continue.

"Carlotta," I said helpfully.

Most people would have responded with their own first name. Hers, I knew from the lawyer, was Margo, but she couldn't bring herself to divulge it, or to use my given name. "What I wish to— I do not wish this matter to appear in the newspapers."

"I don't plan to speak to any reporters."

"Don't be rude. Are you having an affair with my husband?"

"No." How many affairs did she imagine Chaney was capable of carrying on simultaneously?

"I like to get things straight from the beginning."

"I see." And that wouldn't be rude, I thought. "Let's talk about Friday night, if you don't mind."

"Yes, what about it?"

"Your husband says he was here with you Friday night when he received a phone call."

"I don't recall hearing the phone." She made a noise that in anyone less delicate would have been a snort. *Click, clack* went the needles.

"But you heard him when he went out that night?"

"The side door is underneath my bedroom. I would hear it. I *often* do."

My bedroom, not our bedroom. And not a slip of the tongue, either.

"Is there a phone in your bedroom?"

"I generally turn off the ringer at night."

"What time was it when you heard your husband leave the house?"

"I didn't look at the clock."

I thought she was lying. I let her words settle into the cool silence of the room, hoping she'd amend them, but when she spoke again, it was to ask, "Are you the sort of person one hires if one suspects one's husband is unfaithful? A hypothetical question, you understand."

"Let's give it a hypothetical no."

"I—if I'd realized at the time why the police were interested, I might have lied and said Wilson was home. It was unwise of me not to say he was home; I don't know what came over me."

A sudden desire for revenge, I thought.

"Perhaps if I told the police I'd been mistaken, that Wilson actually *was* here—"

"Reverse yourself now that you know what it's about?" Oh, the cops would enjoy this, I thought, both halves of the couple revising their tales.

"You don't think that would be a good idea?"

"The police might not believe you."

She smiled. "I'm a very convincing liar."

I smiled to let her know that was not news to me.

She said, "Perhaps Wilson might tell you with whom he actually was at the time. And then she could discreetly go to the police with her information."

"But you have no idea where he might have been?"

"No. Tell me, Ms. Carlyle, do you have children?"

I didn't see what that had to do with anything. "No, but I have an almost-adopted sister."

"What does that mean?"

"I was paired up with a little girl through the Big Sisters Association a long time ago. We're still together, but it's more a mother-daughter relationship than a sister thing."

"Are you married?"

"No."

"You should be, for that girl's sake. I have a son. He's fifteen now, away at school."

For the first time, she set down her needles and made eye contact. Hers were deep-set and coal black.

I said, "You must have had him when you were very young."

"Thank you. I did. And then I divorced his father. I thought I was in love with Wilson, that he was the great love of my life. I thought it was the right thing to do, that my happiness and my son's happiness depended on it."

Sometimes when reluctant witnesses open up, it's like a dam breaking. They begin with monosyllabic grunts, progress to sentences, and then, bang, you're going to hear the story of their lives. I stayed motionless, my coffee cup raised to my lips. I didn't intend to do anything to stop the impending flood.

She said, "I have had six miscarriages since I married Wilson. A single child—my father used to say that no one should have an only child. It's too risky for your genealogical line, and for your child, as well. You invest too much in him. I know I do. That's one of the reasons Byron's away at Groton. I can't keep my hands off him, my attention off him, when he's here. I used to be an active person, and now, when I'm not going to one doctor or another, I lie here recovering from one pregnancy, hoping another will take. I feel terrible all the time, bloated and ill."

"I'm sorry." She was using baby blue yarn and small-gauge needles. Hoping another would take.

"If I knew for certain that Wilson were having an affair, I don't know what I'd do. How I'd feel. Jealous, yes. Angry, yes. But I can't say I'd blame him. I'm not the woman he married. I take my basal temperature twelve times a day. I call him to come home and do his duty, and that's what it's become, a duty. I keep imagining that he's going to leave me and have children with another woman, and then sometimes I *want* him to leave. *I* want to leave and have babies with another man. They can't find anything wrong with either of us, but I had a healthy child with my first husband. I know I could have more babies. I know I could."

A fifteen-year-old son. Not legally old enough to drive, but fifteen-year-olds do drive. There would be an ex-husband, as well, although it seemed to me that any man would be grateful to Wilson Chaney for taking this peculiar woman off his hands. I'd known other women obsessed with making babies, having babies. I was seeing signs of it in my own baby, Paolina, and it scared me to death.

She said, "I would divorce him today if—"

"If?"

"I'm sorry. I didn't mean that. Of course I couldn't leave him at a time like this, with people accusing him of something so vile. I wouldn't desert him now." She pulled a lace handkerchief off a small table and dried her eyes. "I'm sorry," she said, "I don't usually— You're a good listener." She made the compliment sound like an accusation. "Tell Wilson I'll tell the police whatever he wants me to say." She picked up her knitting and the needles slowly clicked to life.

"Mrs. Chaney, does your husband have any enemies? Anyone who might wish him harm?" Chaney's lawyer, Todd Geary, considered Margo to be Chaney's enemy; that suddenly seemed clear to me.

She pressed her lips together in a frozen smile. "Well of course he has enemies, dear. He's a full professor at Harvard. Do you have any idea how many people envy that, how many want his job? Everything Wilson does is measured and tested and ranked. Is he smart enough? Is he published in the right journals? And then there's extra pressure because he's black. I'm tested and ranked, too; don't think I don't know it. I used to entertain the right people, try to make things easier for him, but now— I don't even know the younger people in his department. If you want to know who's sharpening their knives for Wilson, you'd have to ask Fording or someone else on the spot."

"Who?"

"George Fording, Wilson's department head. He would do anything to help Wilson. I'm sure he would."

Was this the same department head Chaney'd described, the one who'd cheerfully toss him to the wolves?

"Do you think he'd see me?"

"Certainly. George would do anything for me. Would you like me to call and pave the way?"

When I nodded, she summoned Mark and asked him to fetch a telephone. I wondered whether she ever moved, whether prolonged lounging was in some way connected to increased fertility, what she did with all her baby knitting. No matter how hard I tried, I couldn't see her following her husband, stalking him, running anyone down with the van. Too much energy required.

She barely seemed to notice when I left. Mark ushered me to the gate.

"I assume you're not related to the Chaneys," I said.

That drew another flush. "I'm her secretary."

"How long have you worked for her?"

"Long enough to know she wouldn't want me answering questions."

"Do you like your job?"

"It's better than washing up after the chosen ones in the dining halls, thanks."

He shut the gate behind me, and I walked in the shade of the elm trees, heading toward my car. If Chaney was right, if he *was* being set up, I didn't have much time. If someone wanted Chaney to take the blame, the telephone witness would show up with a dead-on description of Chaney. Or an anonymous note would tell the cops some tasty morsel Chaney had neglected to tell me. I wondered if all of Chaney's love letters to Denali Brinkman were safe and accounted for in the plastic bag stashed under my cat's business.

I used my cell phone to call my message machine. Garnowski sounded drunk, but he'd come through with an address for Freddie Church. If Church was home, I could fit him in before my appointment with George Fording.

CHAPTER 18

If this had been the movies, Freddie Church would have lived in Allston, within walking distance of the Birmingham Parkway. He didn't; he lived in an apartment complex off LaGrange Street in West Roxbury.

It was maybe a half hour's drive, but I didn't bother with a phone call. If he wasn't home, I'd visit his neighbors, inquire about his recent visitors. I stopped by the house and grabbed a photo of Benjy Dowling to flash. It wasn't a great one. Roz had done her best in the basement darkroom, but the rain had been heavy the night of the payoff. Still, the features were recognizable. Dowling had thick eyebrows and deep-set eyes over a well-shaped nose. A good-looking man. I stuck the photo in my backpack and drove, wishing I'd asked Garnowski more about this Freddie Church. Was he the kind of guy, unlike Benjy, who'd head up a criminal enterprise, an idea man, a leader?

There's no quick route from Cambridge to West Roxbury. I took cabbie shortcuts, turning every few blocks, twisting my way through the back streets of Allston-Brighton and Brookline in sporadic traffic, sitting almost two minutes behind some driver too chicken to enter a busy Brookline rotary.

I crossed the VFW Parkway, turned right off LaGrange, then right again into a rutted alley. I didn't see any visitor parking, so I took a numbered resident-only slot. There must have been a hundred apartments in the complex, but no visible inhabitants. It looked like the sort of place where you didn't want to hang around outside, an isolated clutch of yellow brick buildings, half still under construction and half already falling apart. On my left was a sorry playground, a barred basketball court with steel nets, another dusty gravel parking lot. It wasn't exactly a project, but it had the air of a place with plenty of subidized Section 8 housing. Kids in school, Mom drunk or sleeping it off, Dad bagging groceries or living elsewhere. It looked a lot like a prison, so Church probably felt right at home.

I removed my suit jacket and folded it neatly on the passenger seat. Visiting a place like this, I would have been better off in jeans or sweats, maybe a splatter suit.

Church's apartment, 5G, was a "garden" flat, meaning it was almost entirely underground, a habitable basement. I eyed the narrow windows. Barely visible behind straggly shrubs, they'd provide all the natural light he got.

Jail security had it all over Church's apartment complex's security. His vestibule door was heavy, steel-reinforced, and had a good lock to boot, but, like most of the other doors, it was propped open with a wooden board. Easier for construction crews to gain access; easier for thieves, too. It enabled me to walk right up to Church's apartment without sounding a warning bell. I could hear the TV blasting, a good sign somebody was home. I knocked, waited, then knocked again loudly.

"Yeah? Yeah? Hang on, for Chrissake."

I knocked again.

The man who answered the door didn't look like a crime titan, but who knows? He was in his thirties, skinny, bare-chested, and wore his wrinkled khakis low on his hips. His narrow face was covered with stubble and he smelled of booze and sweat. His eyes were pale gray, the whites veiny.

"Whatcha want? Quit yer banging. I gotta helluva headache. Bad enough the crews start work crack a fuckin' dawn, ya gotta—" He stopped yapping and gave me a long look, registering my presence in much the same way parole officer Garnowski had. "Hey, lookit you, now. Ain't you a big girl!"

Big is a comparative term. I'm tall for a woman, yes. I'm not a heavyweight, but I'm not scrawny, either; no fashion-model famine victim, thank you. But if I'd been six inches shorter, I'd still have been big compared to Freddie Church. He was no more than five two, but he stood erect, a little rooster of a guy, with a hint of a Tennessee accent and bad teeth.

"Jake Garnowski sent me." As I spoke, I stepped into his apartment and the smell hit me, a pungent mix of unwashed clothes, unwashed dishes, rancid food, spilled beer, and overflowing ashtrays. He could have used about a bushel of Margo Chaney's rose-petal potpourri. Sometimes I think I quit being a cop because I couldn't stand the stink.

"Hey, how 'bout a drink?" said the little man, a blast of liquor on his breath.

"Bet you started without me."

"Yeah, yeah," he said. "Well, I know it's early, but I'm havin' myself a li'l wake here. Friend a mine died. Hit by a fuckin' car."

"Benjy."

He brightened. "You know Benjy? My man Benjy? Hey, you and me'll have a drink to him, then."

"No, thanks. I just want to ask a few questions."

"Don't tell me you're a cop. That would be too damned depressing."

"I'm not a cop."

He smiled like he'd put one over on me. "Hah, if you ain't no cop, I don't have to answer shit." He waved a finger at my nose.

"Up to you," I said. "Depends how much you want to go back to the can. Way I understand it, you're on parole, Freddie, and unless my eyes are bad, you've got some serious weed sitting on your sofa. Probably your own personal stash, but your record, any prosecutor would go for distribution."

He stared at the sofa, saw the Baggie plain as day. He tucked it under a cushion, marched back to the door, and made as if to hold it open. He was pretty well looped and having trouble walking. "Whyn't you just leave? You're pretty, but you gotta bad attitude."

I smiled. "Hey, Freddie, you got a beer?"

"That's better. That's sociable." He closed the door and staggered off into an alcove that passed for a kitchen because it had a hot plate and a refrigerator. Meanwhile, I investigated the Baggie under the sofa cushion. Damned if I could tell whether it came from the same mother lode as Dowling's stash. Leroy probably could have.

Church came back with an open bottle of Michelob and a smudgy jelly glass. I wiped the lip of the bottle with my sleeve and drank from that. Seemed safer.

Church said, "You're kiddin' about the weed, right? I could just flush it, and how'd you prove it? You ain't no cop."

"So when was the last time you saw Benjy?"

He took awhile, trying to decide whether I was bluffing. The pint of store-brand whiskey on the battered coffee table was freshly opened and a third gone. Two roaches sat in an ashtray otherwise filled with cigarette butts. He took a seat on the sprung gray sofa and slugged from the bottle. "Hell, the man's dead, right?"

"Yeah." His brain was operating and he was asking himself why he should risk jail to protect a dead man.

"I used to see Benjy at meetings, AA and that shit, but we both quit going. I ain't seen him more than three times this past year, and, man, we used to be tight."

"You argue over anything?"

"Nah. It's women. Women is what does it, gets in the way of men staying friends."

"Your woman or his woman?"

"Does it look like I got a woman hid in here?"

He made an expansive gesture that took in the filthy room. If he had a woman, the gesture said, by God, he wouldn't be living in a sty.

Guys like that never seem to understand why women aren't lining up to do their cleaning.

"I don't know," I said. "Do you?"

"Hah. Wished I did, hon. I'm talking 'bout Benjy's babe. He never said nothing, but that's what I figure. Babe like that, what's she wanna hang out with me, classy little babe like that? Don't want him hanging with lowlifes like me, either. Man, Benjy was always a lucky one with the broads, I tell you. You know what he had?"

"Nope."

"You never met him?"

"Never had the pleasure." I'd searched his apartment, but it wasn't the same as a personal introduction.

"Confidence. Course he had a dong long's a horse, too. That's what gave him confidence. He wasn't a big man, you know. Just hung, the way some of us small guys are."

He gave me a look to make sure I knew what he was telling me. Two in as many days, Garnowski and now this runt. My cup runneth over.

"Jake a buddy a yours?" he asked. Do you sleep with Jake? was what he meant.

I said, "Probably you've got more than an ounce of dope in this dump, right?"

"Hey, hey, let's keep it civil."

"Let's keep it professional, too, Freddie. I want to know what you had going with Benjy."

"And I'm telling you. I ain't even seen him lately."

"I heard you were storing stuff for him."

"Yeah, well that's horse shit. Who tole you that?"

"Your pal had a lot of cash when he died."

"Good for him."

"How do you think he came by it?"

"Was he working something?"

"You tell me."

"Well, if he was he was working it without me. I told him come to me he finds something, but once that girl got with him, he didn't hang with me no more. You know her? You talk to her? She was a looker. Blond hair, looked real and all."

"Where did you meet her?"

"Some bar, one of them places over on Harvard Street. Wished I could remember her name. Probably see her at Benjy's funeral, you wanna talk to her."

"About five two, little oval face, good body?"

"That's the one."

"She won't be there. She died."

He gave a soft grunt and placed the bottle carefully back on the coffee table, moving with the caution of a man who knows his sense of balance can't be trusted. "Her and Benjy both? Jesus. When did she go?"

"In April."

"Christ on a crutch, I didn't know. Man, Benjy didn't even call me or nuthin'. Girl had a funny name, like a hill."

"Denali."

"Yeah, yeah. You tellin' me that pretty girl's dead and gone?"

"Killed herself."

"Whoa." He grabbed for the bottle and took a long drink. "Go figure. You think that's why Benjy was playing in traffic? Shit, I never thought a that. I mean, maybe he didn't want to go on without her, you know?"

"I think Benjy was into something that got him killed."

"You think he was offed?"

"Hit-and-run. I do."

"Damn."

"Who else did he hang with, Freddie?"

"Shit, lady, I dunno. I tole you I—"

"When you last saw him, what was he doing?"

"Lookin' for work, like always."

"What kind of work?"

"What kind— Hell, maybe he figured he'd try brain surgery, lady. You got a record, you take what you get. Benjy used to clean places. Me, I paint houses. Fuck, what time is it, anyway? What day?"

"Benjy ever take you out on the river?"

"Huh?"

"He was a rower, right?"

"Oh, yeah, he used to stay in shape on one of them machines up at Concord. Machine, boat, same shit, he says. But he liked it on the river. I got no use for it. I go to the gym, but the river, man, it stinks. You fall in, they gotta give you a shot."

"He store his kayak here?"

"I didn't even know he had a boat. Look, maybe he was into loan sharks. That's all I can figure."

"I told you. He had money."

"Well, shit, maybe that's where he got it from. Jesus, he finally gets some money and now he's dead. You know, I ain't gonna go to work today after all. What the fuck good is money anyway? Get some, you die. Your buddy's dead, you should get to take the fuckin' day off, right?" He lifted the bottle and took another swig.

I tried to get him back on the track, but the liquor glazed his eyes and made him repeat my questions instead of answering them. He grew increasingly maudlin and increasingly incoherent, and I didn't learn much beyond the fact that he wasn't Benjy's partner in blackmail. I figured I ought to cut my losses and get out before somebody stole my car. Church told me to be sure and drop by again. I think he'd forgotten who I was and why I'd come.

I kicked the board out of the way so the vestibule door would shut. Let the construction workers press the buzzers and wake the tenants. Two Latino boys had materialized on the basketball court. They looked at me with dead eyes. I walked down the narrow path to the parking lot, then stopped and turned suddenly. The boys were shooting hoops, feinting and dribbling, trash-talking in Spanish. No one else was there, but I had the same feeling I'd had when Leon walked away from my house in the darkness—that someone was watching. I walked some more, listening for footsteps behind me. Nothing. Probably someone looking down from one of the apartment windows.

My car was there, unharmed. I checked the time on the dashboard clock and decided I could afford a brief detour. I took Market Street through Allston-Brighton, sneaked onto Parsons behind St. Columbkille's Church, then drove the loop of the Birmingham Parkway, looking for the place where Benjy Dowling's life had come to an abrupt end. No broken glass on the pavement. No brownish stains. A Buick honked as I slowed to check for yellow crime-scene tape. I didn't see any. Nor did I see any pedestrians, not even in the middle of the day. A couple of bicyclists, yes, but no walkers.

Damn it, I wanted the accident report. I wanted details. I phoned Todd Geary and left a message on his line, telling him to get in touch with the officer in charge, have the police report Xeroxed and sent to my house.

CHAPTER 19

From Greenough Street on the Cambridge side of the river, the Charles looked gray and sullen. I scanned the riverbank as I drove, looking for boathouses, wondering whether Dowling, who'd used the river as a road the night of the money drop, might have traveled it again the night he died. Stands of high cattails blocked my view.

By the time I found a parking place in the Square, I was eight minutes late for my appointment with Chaney's enemy and department chair, George Fording. I donned my jacket, smoothed my hair, and then dodged Rollerblading students over the cobblestone paths, wishing I'd worn sneakers and a fuller skirt. I had no trouble entering the building or making my way unchallenged to the third floor. The olive-skinned young man behind the desk in Fording's outer office gravely informed me that Fording was also running behind schedule. It would be another five minutes, possibly more.

I told the young man I'd be back, then retreated down a flight of stairs. I sat on a bench underneath a poster advertising an upcoming lecture in Askwith Hall. The subject: "Theory vs. Research in Education." It was subtitled "Intended and Unintended Consequences."

I grabbed my cell phone, dialed information, and got the number for Groton Academy before I realized I didn't know Mrs. Chaney's son's last name. Damn. It wouldn't be Chaney. It would be her first husband's surname. I asked for the headmaster's office, identified myself as Mrs. Chaney's personal assistant, and asked whether Byron had safely returned from his weekend.

There was a pause. "Let me check," quavered a middle-aged alto.

I was zapped on hold and treated to symphonic dreck, the sort of middle-of-the-road slop no one would listen to outside a dentist's office or an elevator. Two chattering students passed, hunched under heavy backpacks. I checked my watch again. I'd stay on hold three minutes, no more.

The shaky alto interrupted. "Excuse me, but Byron has no scheduled overnights until the end of term. Byron Chase?"

"Right."

"He hasn't been off campus in weeks."

"I must have misunderstood." I apologized for taking up her time and crossed Byron off my list of suspects. Good. I didn't have to worry about some stepfather-stepson intrigue.

I glanced at my watch again and considered calling Leon. Later, I told myself. Not enough time now. I went back upstairs, and as I approached Fording's office, the olive-skinned man stuck his head out the door and waved me onward. He rapidly ushered me to an inner office door, rapped three times, and shoved the door ajar.

Dr. Fording sprang out of his chair, a small man in a three-piece suit. He stood by his desk, bobbing his head, and declaring himself delighted to meet me. His assistant's eyes took in his smile and raised me from the level of peon to prospective lecturer at the ed school. I attributed Fording's courtly greeting to Mrs. Chaney's self-trumpeted influence.

He was narrow across the shoulders, long-waisted, and short-legged. His gold-rimmed spectacles shortened the bridge of a snub nose. He had smooth pink skin, silvery hair, the genial features of an aging elf. He wore pinstriped navy wool and invited me to sit with a smooth and practiced gesture. When he sat, he looked taller than he was.

The olive-skinned man closed the door with a discreet click.

The carpet was a vintage Oriental, the desk antique cherry. The chair into which I lowered my rear end was covered in a rich tapestry-like fabric. I wondered if Fording had another office somewhere where he worked. This one looked like a stage set. It was so perfect and the little man fitted into it so perfectly that it made me suspect him of something: impersonating a Harvard professor, if not actively pursuing a career as a blackmailer on the side. I inhaled the aroma of apple-scented wood from the picture-perfect logs on the fireplace and automatically scanned the mantelpiece for a pipe rack. Surely such a carefully cultivated image required a pipe. Bet he used to smoke one before the threat of mouth cancer made him give up the show.

"Bad business, this," he said.

Out of sheer perversity, I said nothing. I like silence myself. Doesn't bother me at all, and I find it revealing to watch others squirm their way through it. The two windows were draped in heavy velvet, the lighting indirect.

"I understand you work for Wilson's attorney?" Fording said.

I nodded.

"May I see some identification?"

It amazes me how often otherwise-responsible people accept strangers for who they say they are. My respect for the man shot up. Of course, if I'd wanted to fool him, I'd have taken pains to provide myself with exactly the sort of laminated photo ID I now passed politely over the desktop.

He scanned it briefly. "Well, anything I can do to hurry Wilson's return, I'm more than happy to do. I just don't understand what that can be."

"Why did you feel it necessary to restrict Dr. Chaney's teaching? He hasn't been charged with any crime."

"Nor do I believe he will be. The idea that anyone could imagine

Wilson Chaney running down a stranger in cold blood! I work closely with the man. His judgment is not impaired. He is not an alcoholic or a drug abuser."

"I don't think anyone claimed he was."

"Then what? Do the police believe he did this as a deliberate act? What reason have they given? Are they implying he did it to test some psychological theory? Some Raskolnikov crime and punishment thesis gone mad? Guilt and its repercussions are not Wilson's areas of study."

Fording used his hands when he spoke, waving them in the air. I bet he missed the comforting business of his pipe.

"Then why isn't he teaching?" I asked. "If you believe so strongly in his innocence?"

"Dr. Chaney is simply taking some personal time off, by mutual agreement. He is not forbidden to teach his classes. Far from it, in fact. He's working very hard under considerable pressure, and we agreed that, with this added complication, perhaps it would be best for all concerned if he were to concentrate on his Medical School responsibilities and his very substantial research."

He gave the impression of absolute sincerity, but Chaney had reported the event differently—as a suspension. I wasn't sure which one to believe. After all, Chaney had lied about being home with his wife, thought it better not to mention that Denali had died by her own hand.

One corner of Fording's elegant desk held a glass bowl filled with smooth dark pebbles. He seized one and placed it in his palm. It weighted his hand, restricted his gestures, and seemed to calm him. "What is it you want?" he asked. "How can I help?"

"Dr. Chaney maintains that his van was stolen."

"If he says, so, I believe him. Absolutely."

"If he was not driving his van, someone went to considerable trouble to make the police believe that he was."

He smiled. His top teeth were white and gleaming, but no one had taken the same care with his unevenly spaced lowers. "Surely it's more likely that the police are mistaken, or actively malevolent. He is a black man. Possibly they act out of prejudice. You know what they are."

"I used to be one," I said.

He shrugged, as if to say he meant no offense. "There is also an ancient prejudice at work here, town versus gown. I understand the man who was run over was an ordinary working-class type?"

"An ex-convict."

"Ah. The new working-class hero. Now, it's my belief that a man like Wilson Chaney ought to be the working-class hero, a man of no particular background, who by the sweat of his brow has made himself into someone who can and should be held up as an example to others of his race."

I hadn't been in his office five minutes and Fording had mentioned Chaney's race twice.

"Chaney lied to the police," I said. "They don't like that."

"Wilson must have had a reason."

"He said he was at home; his wife says he wasn't."

He shook his head with a rueful grin. "You have met Margo?"

I nodded.

He passed the smooth pebble from palm to palm. "Well, frankly, I adore her—not for who she is right now, but for the memories I have of her. I always try to humor her when I can." He stopped, and it became clear that he was not about to proceed without prompting.

"She rarely leaves home, I understand."

"Well, believe me, it wasn't always like that. She is a very unusual woman. You know she divorced her first husband to marry Wilson? Margo is a—she was a magnet, a glorious presence, ten, fifteen years ago, a dynamo, a force of nature. If she wanted Wilson, and she did, no one would wager against her."

"Why him?"

He smiled and clasped the pebble in his right hand. "I'm an educational pychologist, not a psychiatrist. It's easy to sit on the outside and speculate, isn't it? Tempting, too. I'm not saying it was a question of race, but Margo's first husband was Caucasian, and her family disapproved strongly. Wilson was Harvard, plus he was black, and that must have seemed a potent combination."

Three times. Oh, he was good. He was "not saying," but he *was* saying in terms so twisty, I wondered if he could keep track of his implications and inferences. Race kept coming up in responses that required no reference to race.

"As for the conflict in what the police no doubt call Wilson's 'alibi,' I will say that lately poor Margo has not been as much of a companion as she might have been in previous years. You might wish to discreetly ask Dr. Chaney whether he's having some kind of an affair. I know that would be the old-fashioned, honorable type of thing he'd be likely to do. If he was with someone other than his wife, in that way, well, he wouldn't want to harm the other party's reputation or hurt his wife's feelings. Margo is quite a wealthy woman, with a battery of lawyers, and they say that once a woman has weathered that first divorce, well, some do get the hang of it."

"Are you married, Dr. Fording?"

"No." He was too surprised at the question to refuse to answer.

"Do you know for a fact that Dr. Chaney's having an affair?"

He hesitated, fiddled with the pebble, and popped it back in the bowl. He smiled slowly, then shook his head to indicate that he didn't. I was sure he had more than an inkling that Chaney had strayed.

"When I spoke to Mrs. Chaney earlier, I asked her whether her husband had any enemies," I said. "She sent me here." I left it deliberately ambiguous to see how he'd handle it.

That smile again as he carefully rephrased my statement. "To inquire whether Dr. Chaney had enemies? Enemies." He tasted the word. "So melodramatic. Has Margo filled your ears with tales of academic back stabbing? I assure you we have no junior faculty members stealing cars and running down strangers in an attempt to move into positions of seniority. We tend to confine our battles to committee assignments and class schedules. Don't get me wrong: It's not peace and bliss at all times. We disagree on methods of defining learning disorders, the effectiveness of biofeedback techniques, and behavior-modification strategies. We are becoming more aware of the biochemistry required for proper learning. Our Mind, Brain, and Behavior Program, with its cross-disciplinary thrust, is a model for other universities. Many of our educators are close to becoming psychopharmacologists. It's a vast new field, and an exciting one."

He came up for air and quickly interpreted my glance. "Ah, a scary one, you think? *Brave New World* and all that."

"It crossed my mind."

"And yet you wouldn't raise an objection if I said every child ought to have a nutritionally sound breakfast before beginning the school day. Education on an empty stomach is wasted education. The school breakfast program is valid; it's a great success. But children are regularly sent to school who can't organize, who can't process information, who can't differentiate between important and unimportant data."

"Maybe I'll take a class some other time," I said, "but right now, I want to know about Dr. Chaney's enemies."

"Yes. Excuse me, I got quite carried away. I don't get into the classroom as much as I used to. Perhaps I should."

"Chaney's enemies?"

He held a finger momentarily to his lips. "Helene Etheridge, who used to be his secretary, has absolutely no use for him. He saw that she got transferred to another department, but I believe that now she actually likes it over there. In the past eight years, he has refused three doctoral theses. Normally, your doctoral candidate in education is not prone to hit-and-run revenge, but I can give you their names if you wish to waste time. Dr. Chaney is a very successful member of the faculty. He is on the cutting edge of what we do here, and perhaps some faculty who hold with more traditional approaches to educational theory and practice are resentful of his ascension. A medical credential is a very attractive one."

"Do you know any of his colleagues at the Medical School?"

"Any who wish him harm? Certainly not."

"And at the lab, the research facility?"

"Dr. Chaney is a prominent researcher. Other faculty members might envy the sort of financial rewards that can bring. He has a drug in clinical trials, human trials."

"And those are progressing smoothly?"

"No clinical subject under the influence of Dr. Chaney's therapeutic ministrations has yet taken up an AK-forty-seven and positioned himself on a rooftop. There has been no adversity in the clinical trials. Far from it."

"Would you say that his research—I understand he's developing some form of Ritalin substitute—would make him a lot of money?"

"Well, that depends, of course, on interpretation. What is a lot of money these days?"

"Millions."

"I wouldn't think so. There are a great many drugs similar to Ritalin, mixed salts of single-entity amphetamine products, Adderall and the like, and lately there are nonstimulants as well, like Strattera, which I believe is atomoxetine. I wouldn't think so, because frankly, Chaney's is not a revolutionary change. He is using a stimulant approach, but he hopes to develop a drug with far fewer side effects. All I can say is that I imagine there are those who are jealous of his success. There are even those who would tell you that I am Dr. Chaney's enemy."

"Really. Are you?"

"We have had our differences. He is more concerned perhaps with his individual reputation, while I am concerned for the reputation of this department and the ed school and the university. We are not temperamentally alike. I wish he would publish more scholarly articles, spend less time on his research."

He grasped another pebble and clutched it tightly in his hand. "But make no mistake about it, young lady, his success reflects well upon me. I believe Wilson and I understand each other. As long as his work enhances this institution, I will protect him and intrigue for him, and make sure that he sits on the right committees. Loyalty for loyalty. Is that all?"

"Is there any particular reason you believe Dr. Chaney is having an affair?"

"Will you be speaking to Wilson today?"

"Probably."

"Perhaps you could give him a message?"

"Certainly."

"Give him my regards, first of all. Tell him I assume his innocence and am certain he will be back with us shortly. And you might tell him that I received a phone call from a friend of mine in Legal Services. Tell him Ms. Brinkman's name has been dropped from the lawsuit."

"Ms. Brinkman?" I kept my voice flat, pretended I'd never heard the name.

"A student, a former student. Her people were misguidedly suing this institution, but they've evidently seen the light."

"How does that concern Dr. Chaney?"

"If he wishes to tell you, that's his business entirely. Good day."

He knew. He knew Chaney'd been sleeping with Denali Brinkman, and he wanted Chaney to know he knew it. He rose and I followed suit. I shook hands with him at the door. His skin was as cool as one of the pebbles in his glass bowl.

Did he also know about the blackmail? Damn, no matter how I tried, I couldn't see him as Dowling's accomplice. Working with Dowling, a commoner, a townie, an ex-con, would be impossible for such a flagrant elitist. Oh, he was a blackmailer all right, but not for cash, not for a piddling five thousand bucks. For power, for prestige. I bet he had the secrets of all his faculty indexed, filed, and memorized, ready to trot out when he needed them.

No wonder Chaney had described the little man as his enemy. No wonder Mrs. Chaney felt he'd do anything for her. The little man was as slippery as silk, as changeable as New England weather, as treacherous as a rocky cliff. Whether he supported Chaney or not would have little to do with Chaney and everything to do with what Fording perceived as being to his own advantage.

I wondered about his personal life, or lack thereof. Maybe he had no personal ties, no life outside the office. Like a puppet master, he seemed to enjoy being above it all.

CHAPTER 20

So absorbed was I in my admiration of Fording's deviousness, I almost tripped over a man fixing the electrical socket on the ground floor of Thompson Hall. I mumbled an apology and was halfway down the corridor before I suddenly halted, turned, and stared back at him—an ordinary Joe wearing ordinary coveralls similar to the ones Leroy and I had worn to impersonate exterminators. The man didn't react to my glare. He probably was exactly who he seemed to be, but how could I tell? I took a few more steps, recalled the coveralls hanging from the hook on the back of Dowling's closet door.

The blackmailer didn't need an accomplice within the ed school, be it department chair, student, professor, or secretary. Dowling could have gained entry to the ed school the same way Leroy and I had gained entry to his flat. Who'd think twice about a man in coveralls kneeling by Chaney's office door?

Harvard has its own janitorial services, but what if one of the cleaners called in sick? Would they use a temp service for replacement help? Hadn't Freddie Church said that his buddy Dowling was looking for cleaning work?

A huge SUV had parked nose to my bumper, so it took me longer to extricate my car from its slot than it would have taken me to walk home. Once I'd regained the street, home I went, eager to peel out of my suit and plan my next move. I'd have gotten out of the suit a lot sooner if I hadn't been confronted with a visitor, Cambridge rookie cop Danny Burkett, smack on my living room sofa.

A cop on the doorstep is one thing, a cop in the living room another. You're not required to open your door to a cop. You can pretend you're not home, or openly refuse entry. Your house is your castle.

My house, alas, is also Roz's castle. Did I mention that Danny Burkett was a very handsome and well-built man? Roz doesn't care so much about the handsome. She doesn't go by faces, and she certainly doesn't care about such niceties as intellect or personality. A well-muscled body is all it takes. Music spilled out of the speakers, the same damn oldies radio station Leon had tuned to, the same Motown soul. The lights were dim. Should I mention that there was heavy breathing involved and that both sofa gropers quickly reacted to my presence and got vertical once I shut off the radio?

I didn't make any hasty remarks like "I see you two know each other," because with Roz, that's not a given. She sees a dude she fancies on the street, she goes up to him and makes arrangements. Lucky her. I had a pretty good idea this one had walked right up to the door and rung the bell.

You ring my bell three times, you get Roz. From the dazed look on Burkett's face, she was his vision of paradise. Me, I flat out don't know how she manages it, juggling all those guys, not getting involved, not getting diseases. One way she manages, she neglects the goddamn housework.

"Uh," Burkett began eloquently, patting his uniform into place, his face aflame.

"Glad you're home," Roz said cheerfully, although I knew she was anything but. "I let him in to wait. A cop, I figured, how much could he steal?"

"You came to see me?" I asked Burkett.

"Uh, yeah. I had a couple questions."

"Did you happen to have a warrant?"

"Huh?"

"Just kidding. Roz?"

"Yeah?"

"Got anything to do? The dishes, maybe?"

"Very funny." She was wearing—well, how shall I describe the look? Cheap and ready? It's not the clothes, though, not the skimpy Day-Glo green tank or the black microskirt. It's the body. I've tried to explain it to Paolina. There are clothes that some girls wear and they look fine, and then a Roz, with boobs, tattoos, and attitude, dons the same outfit and it's the wrong side of porno. She made tracks for the stairs.

Burkett called after her, "Uh, can I call you?"

"Sure."

I said, "I'll give you her number. Scram, Roz."

She gave me a look, but she stomped off.

"Wanna lie back down?" I asked the rookie. "Sorry. Hey, don't worry, I won't mention this to Kevin." No way would I mention it, but I wanted to keep Burkett rattled.

"What do you mean?"

I raised an eyebrow. "Just that it's a novel way of questioning a witness. What was it you think she saw?"

"Hey, come on. I—"

"I know. But it's been a long day and I think of this as my office." To emphasize the point, I sat at my desk and did my impression of Paolina's high school principal. "What can I do for you? You need a PI?"

"No. It's just I'm working a little thing for myself. I noticed an odd thing."

Damn. "What's that?"

"You came asking about that guy, Benjy Dowling, right before he got killed."

"No," I said. "Wrong. I came asking about the fire on Memorial Drive. You told me about Dowling. File it under coincidence."

"Sure. But then I thought, What if it doesn't belong there? What if the lady followed up on it?"

"Didn't get around to it."

"Why did you say you were checking on that fire?"

"I didn't."

From the look on his face, he'd run out of things to say, so I took a turn. "It would have been nice to know he was a con right off."

"So you did follow up." He looked like he thought he'd scored a point.

"Didn't take much to find that out. You could have given it to me, but you didn't."

"Hey, why should I?"

"'Cause that's how it works. You give; I give."

"Hey, I gave you a lot, the whole load—the scene at the fire, the delay with all the fucking false alarms, the smell, the names of the witnesses."

"You didn't say anything about false alarms."

"Sue me. I thought I mentioned it. We were late—I told you that—'cause my fat partner hates to hustle. Well, the fire guys were late, too, 'cause they were all to hell and gone chasing their tails out to Somerville."

He planted his feet and leaned back on my sofa, grinning, and I didn't think he'd go away unless I tossed him some kind of bone. "Look, you were doing Kevin O'Shea a favor."

"Yeah. And a lot it got me."

"You could do yourself one."

"Yeah?"

"You could find out about Dowling's car. Black TransAm. Mass plates. I can give you the plate number."

"I can find it."

"I'm sure you can. If it turns up in a tow lot, I'd appreciate a call."

"And then?" He licked his lips. He was trying to be serious, but he looked like a puppy who wanted to play.

"And then I might be able to give you another lead."

"Is there anything else you can tell me *now*?"

"Yeah," I said. "Watch out for Roz. She'll break your heart."

166

"It's okay." He gave me a wider grin. "I'm a cop. I don't have one."

"Call me if you find the car."

"Call me if you want to have a little chat."

I ushered him out the door, then kicked off my heels and peeled down my panty hose while still standing in the foyer.

"I'm a cop," he'd said. "I don't have one." The words seemed to echo and reverberate in the small space. Did I still have a heart? I hadn't called Leon, and I wondered if it was over already, over before it had really begun. I wondered what Sam Gianelli would be doing this evening while I changed into something more comfortable. More comfortable—unless I heard from the rookie cop that the TransAm had been found—for breaking into Dowling's garage.

CHAPTER 21

I considered wearing all black, top to toe, face mask, the whole deal. I really did. Maybe if it had been winter, maybe if it had been New York. But for Somerville, I figured my best disguise was looking like a totally ordinary person on the street. I didn't have to debate long. Jeans, sneakers, navy hoodie over navy T. My height's not a problem; I don't stick out on the street unless I want to. My hair can be a problem, so I brushed it straight, restrained it with a scrunchy, and plunked a Red Sox hat over it. The ultimate disguise. *Officer, stop that thief! What thief? The one in the Sox cap.* In Times Square, at La Guardia, a Sox cap might stand out. Near Davis Square, it's camouflage.

It would have been better if I'd had a buddy to stroll with, a guy to walk with hand in hand. Who looks twice at strolling lovers? Well, I wasn't going to invite an FBI agent to accompany me on the night's prowl, so I shoved that regret to the back of the deck.

I parked my car about eight blocks from my destination, and lucky I was to find a legal slot so close. It was past midnight, but porch lights were still on to discourage burglars, occasional cars circled to find spaces, and the never-sleeping students passed in tight knots, bound for the Davis Square subway or one of the bars. I navigated my way toward the house where Benjy Dowling had lived, not too fast, not too slow. Walk too slow, you're a potential victim; too fast, you draw the eye, as well. Walking too fast at night makes you look nervous, like you're scared of the shadows, maybe like you're carrying too much cash.

My chief worry was passing patrol cars. Drivers at night look straight ahead; it's only cops who give the street the real once-over, who regularly swivel their eyes side to side to take in all the action. If Roz hadn't pissed me off by trifling with the cop in my living room, I might have asked her to come along and watch my back. Too late now. What the hell, the street was lightly traveled; I'd treat all vehicles as though they might be cop cars. Better that way. Even Somerville has a few unmarked units.

I abandoned the sidewalk when I came to the house directly behind Dowling's, took to the driveway I'd explored earlier, and vaulted the fence that separated the two yards. Easy and uneventful. No dogs. I reached into my backpack and made sure my cell phone was off. I didn't want it playing a C scale at an indelicate moment.

The garage lock was not a problem. I'd checked it previously; I'm good with locks. I was worried about the door, about the possible— no, the likely—squeak. I hadn't heard it raise a ruckus the night I'd watched Dowling open it in the pouring rain, but that night the rain had been bucketing down, obscuring noises. I'd brought a spray can of WD-40, but that wouldn't ease the initial groan. The way the garage was built, I'd have to lift the door high, then roll under it in order to gain access to the creaky springs.

I studied the back of Dowling's building, imagining Mr. and Mrs. Hooper safely in bed after a yummy dinner of barley soup. Mrs. Maguire, on the second floor was the one so concerned about the cockroaches. Her lights were out and I pictured the little critters scurrying around her kitchen, partying with her condiments.

As I began easing down the driveway toward the front of the garage, a Somerville cop car cruised slowly by. I pressed myself into a niche behind the chimney of 157 Claremont. Oh bliss. The chances of another cruiser coming down this narrow street in the next half hour? Slim to none. I counted slowly to ten.

One of the things some thieves don't think about is light. I'd already scoped the neighborhood and knew the location of the closest streetlamp. It was two and a half houses down, distant enough that the garage door area stayed dark, which was good for all purposes except cracking the lock. To that end, I carried a pencil flash cleverly adapted to clip onto a belt buckle. A thief showed me the technique. Most door locks are just about waist level. You pop the flash into position and stand on your toes or bend your knees to aim the thin beam.

I did. Dowling hadn't shown area burglars much respect with his choice of locks. Really, my high school locker's combination lock had been about as good as the thing on the garage door. It took me under two minutes, and that's not bragging, because a real thief would have been home in under a minute.

There was a good chance that even if Mr. or Mrs. Hooper heard the garage open, they'd simply roll over and go back to sleep. After all, Dowling had opened it in the middle of the night, with no reaction from the first-floor tenants. It wasn't an inherently alarming sound, unless one of them recalled that their tenant was dead and wouldn't be opening any more garage doors, middle of the night or high noon.

I took a deep breath and shoved upward. *Crack. Creak. Groan.* It was bad, and I stopped with the edge no more than ten inches off the ground and kicked my waiting backpack into the gap to hold the weight of the door. I'd loaded it with heavy books as well as burglar's tools for the purpose. I lay flat and inched under the door. Once inside the garage, I used my flash to locate the working parts, sprayed them with faithful WD-40, removed the backpack, and lowered the door.

Easier said than done. The sudden flurry of tasks left me breathing hard. I listened for approaching footsteps, any alarm on the street. Hearing nothing, I released a breath I hadn't realized I'd been holding. City people haul up the window and yell, "What the hell ya think yer doin' out there?" before taking drastic steps like calling the cops. Ya call a cop, the night's sleep is ruined. It could take 'em forever just to show up, and besides, it's only kids out for a lark, they think, did the same when they were young.

The dark was oppressive, the air utterly still. I was inside a closed black box, crouched, waiting, listening, my leg muscles tensed. If I heard footsteps, if someone opened the door, I'd be down the street as fast as my legs could move. This wasn't a situation I wanted to try to explain.

No one came and my legs slowly relaxed. I swallowed and tried to moisten my lips with a dry tongue. After three more counted minutes, I opened my backpack and removed a larger flashlight.

I already knew the car wasn't there. I'd stuck out my foot in the darkness, waved a fully extended arm, felt nothing. The kayak was also a no-show. There were boxes, cardboard cartons, a small workbench, a Peg-Board hung with hand tools. A rusty kid's bike, a battered red wagon, a pogo stick. Two cans of old paint, one unused. A semiflat soccer ball, a vintage badminton set, a dead mouse, dirt, leaves, and cobwebs.

I opened every box. Most were cartons for stereo components and contained the foam imprint of whatever gizmo they'd once contained. I untaped the cardboard cartons and sorted through old clothes and clutter. I found a carton filled with papers and my heart took a leap, but on closer examination they turned out to be nothing but the Hoopers' ancient tax returns. I didn't find anything a person might have been blackmailed over, or any blackmail notes. I didn't find any money. I didn't find anything that looked like it might have belonged to Benjy Dowling.

I stood and played the flashlight beam over the floor. I couldn't read footprints, but there was a pattern of sorts. Oil stains where the car had once stood, leaves and dirt surrounding the outline of the car, surrounding the boxes. On the left side of the garage, a spot maybe two feet by two feet looked like it had been swept with a broom. Maybe that was where Dowling had stored his things. Gone now, swept away.

I had nothing to show for my night's labor aside from filthy clothes and cobwebby hair. I returned the large flashlight to my back-pack, set the pack in position for a replay of the garage opening and closing trick. The WD-40 made my exit less noisy than my entrance. No car lights caught my less than graceful retreat. The Hoopers lights stayed off.

During the walk back to the car, the backback felt like it was loaded with bricks, not books, and it was hard not to hurry. I passed two men going in the opposite direction. They smelled of beer and cigarette smoke, and one ventured a smile. I didn't return it.

I drove conservatively, parked deep in my driveway, and went in the back door. The dishes had disappeared from the kitchen sink. Roz must be trying to get back in my good graces, I thought. I opened the fridge, thinking I'd have some milk, or maybe orange juice. I smelled Leon's aftershave just as he came up behind me. He placed a hand on my shoulder.

"Roz let me in."

"I hope she didn't take advantage of you," I said dryly.

"I'm saving myself for you. Assuming we're still speaking."

"If that's the price, we are. But you might want to back off till I shower."

He massaged my shoulders, then ran his right hand the length of my spine. Cool air spilled out of the refrigerator, but I realized I wasn't thirsty after all.

"Room for two in the tub," I said, grateful it wasn't one of Paolina's nights.

He didn't remind me of my father or my ex. He didn't ask where I'd been, didn't ask how I'd smudged dirt over the back of my sweat-shirt and jeans, simply helped me shed them quickly and get under the warm spray. One thing I've got in my aged house is a modern showerhead, a handheld gizmo that doubles as a sex toy when you're not washing alone. I love fooling around in the tub. Water is my com-fort zone, my element. Broke as I may be, there's always bubble bath tubside. Bath brushes and fancy sponges, too.

I washed Leon's hair and he washed mine, carefully loosening the tangles. We compared battle scars: His, on his abdomen, was from appendix surgery; mine, on my left thigh, was from line of duty. He had bite marks on his left arm from line of duty, and he told me the story, making it a lot funnier than it must have been at the time. We laughed and took our time with each other, didn't rush. It was good and slow and easy, and I never thought about Sam. Well, maybe once, later, in bed, when he spooned in close and kissed the nape of my neck.

I thought I'd sleep like a stone, but I was restless, reviewing the day, wondering whether I should have called Chaney, warned him that Fording knew or suspected. Tomorrow morning, I'd call Geary, find out if he'd gotten the police report on Dowling's accident, get the lawyer to find out what he could about the lawsuit Fording had mentioned and why Denali's family had bowed out of it. I was disappointed that I'd found nothing in Dowling's garage; I'd need to go through what I'd taken from his apartment again. Maybe Leroy had noticed something I hadn't. And there was something else, something hovering at the fringe of my memory, tantalizingly close but elusive, taking shape one second, infuriatingly shapeless the next.

"Relax," Leon murmured.

"Have you ever had a case where the facts keep whirling around and around and you can't—"

"I try not to bring my work to bed." He rolled slowly onto his side, hoisted himself on one elbow, and said, "Yeah, I know what you mean."

"So what do you do?"

"I sleep with a good-looking woman. Helps me relax."

I smiled. "Maybe women are more relaxing than men. Ever think of that?"

"No." He leaned over me, his teeth white against the darkness of his skin. "Hey, babe, what I do, I get my mind off it, go at it sideways, like a crab. Let your mind wander; go to sleep." He put his lips on mine to end the conversation.

Still, I couldn't sleep. I let my mind wander, tried to think of something other than Dowling's death, Chaney's peril, and wound up thinking about men, thinking about sex, thinking about techniques and differences and similarities. Same basic equipment, same basic urges; the same parts go the same places, and yet . . . There are times when you go through the paces, hoping the fire will spark, and then there are the breathless moments when both of you are on the same page, playing the same note. Leon and I were good together. But Sam, sometimes with Sam, it wasn't simply playing the same note; it was harmony. Close and intricate harmony.

I was thinking about him when it came to me, sideways, like a crab: false alarms.

CHAPTER 22

I came awake with the same glimmer at the back of my mind, *false alarms,* and rolled over with a strange sense of urgency, prompted not by an event but a memory. The night the Cambridge Fire Department recovered Denali Brinkman's burned corpse from the partially finished boathouse addition, aid was delayed because equipment was tied up responding to false alarms. Danny Burkett had said so; I was sure of it. And when I'd asked Gloria about police-band activity the night Benjy Dowling died, she'd remarked on the unusual number of false alarms, all the damned false alarms. . . .

I was alone in bed. The pillow next to mine was dented, the sheet thrown back. Leon's clothes were gone, no longer piled on the chair, pant legs dragging on the floor. I sighed, showered, and dressed, reacting against yesterday's meet-the-lawyer suit with jeans and a white scoop-neck T. Instead of panty hose, I chose sandals. I keep a good black suit jacket and black low-heeled pumps in the car. Add the jacket, substitute the heels, and there aren't many places I can't go.

I caught the scent of coffee, faint and tantalizing, and let my nose lead me downstairs. False alarms . . . I didn't know how frequent they were, or whether the Boston area was currently experiencing a false-alarm epidemic, but the coincidence ate at me.

Leon, dressed in neat khakis and subdued plaid shirt, was in the kitchen, peering into the refrigerator. His jacket was slung over the back of a chair. The coffee—takeout in white Styrofoam—smelled wonderful.

"Bless you, thank you." I removed the top from a container with difficulty. He'd brought four huge cups, but as far as I knew, we weren't expecting company. Logy from the night's half sleep, I thought I could probably down three on my own.

"Damn," he murmured, head still in the fridge. "I was going to make you my world-famous scrambled eggs. I put chives in 'em, cream cheese, too."

"No eggs?" The chance of chive or cream cheese, I knew, was remote.

"Two cartons. That's what fooled me. One's dead empty and the other's got one measly egg sitting in the corner. Cracked, too. Your milk's sour, and the butter—well, I wouldn't use it to grease a cookie sheet."

I mumbled something about the case keeping me busy.

"I can understand running out of coffee, but how can you—"

"Leon, hey, I appreciate the thought, but if you're planning to make scrambled eggs here, you have to shop first. That's the way it plays."

"Do you even know what you've got in the kitchen?"

Yes, I know what I've got in my kitchen. I have whatever the hell Roz buys. She's erratic, I'll be the first to admit, but I'm not fussy. There are basics, like cinnamon-raisin bread, Paolina's favorite, and slices of Swiss cheese, which she nibbles carefully around each hole, preserving a latticework until the slice collapses. If there's no orange juice, I'm grumpy; no peanut butter, Roz can't survive. As for the rest, it's catch-as-catch-can, and I do a lot of takeout. Usually, there are eggs. Leon was looking at me like I'd flunked seventh-grade home ec. Truth is, I opted for wood shop instead.

"There's probably some cold cereal—shredded wheat or some- thing."

"With no milk? There's stuff in there with sell-by dates older than you are."

"Leon, why are you going through my refrigerator?"

He glared at me. "I wanted to make you breakfast."

The false-alarm business was pounding in my brain. "I've got stuff to do this morning. I'm not interested in—"

The phone shrilled, interrupting words I'd have regretted later. I grabbed the receiver off the wall and marched it into my office.

"Chaney's been taken into custody." Todd Geary sounded flus- tered, a quality I'm never prepared for in a lawyer.

"When? What happened?" I sank into my desk chair.

"Margo just called. Two plainclothes officers were at their door a little after eight. They asked questions. She doesn't know what; Wilson wouldn't let her stay in the room, said it might upset her. She tried to listen in, but she didn't hear much. They took him to headquarters."

"Cambridge police? Boston police?" I picked up a pencil.

"Boston."

"Has he phoned you?" There was no notepad. Where the hell had I put it?

"No."

"You figure they're just harassing him?" Maybe the telephone caller had come in and given them a stronger ID, yanked Chaney's photo from a six-pack.

"I have a source at the station," Geary said.

"Excellent. What does he say?"

"The cops got something in the mail, an anonymous communica- tion."

The other shoe, I thought. "What?"

"I'm not sure I have it exact, but it was something like 'Find out why Chaney paid Dowling five thousand dollars to keep quiet about their relationship.' Does that mean anything to you?"

"Shit." I scrawled the words on the back of an envelope.

"Well, it's nonsense, of course," Geary blustered. "I can't—"

"It means the cops will go to his bank," I said. "They've probably already been there." The point of the damn pencil broke with an audible snap.

"But—it is nonsense, isn't it?"

"Look, Chaney said you could get him out on bail."

"Yes."

"Do it. Get over to the Brighton station and make a stink. If he's charged, get him out of there. Did you get me the accident report?"

"What?"

"The accident report on Dowling. I left a message."

"Yeah, yeah. I have it here. If you come and—"

"Messenger it over."

"All right."

"And then get over to Brighton."

"But I have an eleven o'clock meeting with—"

"Cancel it. Wilson needs you. Hey, wait! Are you still there? Good. I need something else. Details about a lawsuit. The defendant is Harvard. Yeah, that Harvard. Brinkman was one of the plaintiffs until yesterday."

"Who's Brinkman? What does this have to do with springing Chaney?"

"You're supposed to cooperate with me, remember? I can call Harvard's Legal Services and ask who the plaintiff's attorneys are and get the runaround all day. You can use whatever pull you've got, professional courtesy, whatever, and find out in ten minutes."

"Possibly."

"I'm sure you can. Then get me in to see whoever's representing Brinkman and the others against Harvard."

He gave a long-suffering sigh. "When?"

"As soon as you can. Call me on my cell."

"Okay."

"And send the messenger, and get Chaney out."

"Yeah, sure." The line went dead.

I pressed the button, bit my lip, and stared at the silent phone. I wasn't surprised by Geary's call. If Chaney was being set up, the initial frame hadn't taken. I'd removed the blackmail notes from Dowling's apartment before the cops arrived. Now another incriminating tidbit had been dangled in front of their noses.

Leon made a noise. He stood in the doorway. I had no idea how long he'd been there, how long he'd been listening.

"Wilson," he said. "That was about Wilson Chaney, right? Come on, don't tell me it's none of my business. He's a friend."

I placed the pointless pencil carefully on the desk. "Leon, what can I say? He may be your friend, but he didn't ask for your help. He came to me. Not as a friend. How am I supposed to help him by blabbing, when he came to me for confidentiality?"

"He's in trouble."

"Go see his wife, ask her how he is."

"Margo doesn't like me."

Score one for you, I thought. "How long have you been Wilson's friend?"

He pressed his lips together. "Notice I'm not asking why it's any of your business."

"If you don't want to say, fine with me." The tension was back, thick as the night we'd argued. I felt like I had as a child when my dad would force too much air into party balloons. "Stop," my mom and I would beg, hands over ears, waiting for disaster, for the balloon to burst and my father to curse the cheap balloons, the shoddy goods. Why the hell didn't he blow them up to the proper size, quit before they burst? Last night's gentle caresses seemed like they'd happened weeks ago, months ago, with a different man.

Abruptly, Leon relaxed. He took four steps into the room, sank into the canvas butterfly chair across from my desk. "We're old neighborhood, me and Wilson, back in Philly. We're Oxford Circle boys, and old OC is not a nice place. Amazing the two of us are where we are, since most of the guys we palled around with are probably doin' ten to twelve."

"Chaney's smart," I said. "So are you."

"Takes more than smart. Takes lucky, too. And Wilson—I don't know—he's smart, but he's dumb."

"How so?"

"Smart in school, you know? Couldn't touch him in school. But dumb with people sometimes, dumb with women, for sure."

I'd met my client's wife. "The two of you stayed in touch?"

"Nah, but I looked him up when I got transferred here. My old aunty Beth, she keeps tabs on Chaney, always holding him up to me like some kind of god. 'Chaney's at Harvard and you're a flatfoot; too bad you didn't make good like your friend Wilson.' That's why I don't call Aunty Beth more often. But it's not Wilson's fault. He doesn't behave like that. He knows I remember him when. He likes to get together, talk about old times. His family, once they stayed with us four, five months. We shared a room like real brothers when their place burned down."

I didn't show my interest on my face or in my voice. "How did that happen?"

"I don't remember. I'm not even sure I ever knew. Electrical fire, I think. Space heater or something. We all used space heaters back then, landlords turned the heat off so early. Why?"

"Doesn't matter."

"Carlotta, let's go out for breakfast. Charlie's Kitchen's good."

"I don't have time, Leon."

"Aren't you going to eat?"

"When I'm hungry, I'll find something."

He glanced in the direction of the kitchen. "I wouldn't guarantee that."

"If I don't find anything, I'll skip it. Nobody starves to death missing one crummy meal." God, I sounded like Paolina. "I know I'm not the perfect housewife; it's not my goal in life."

"What is, babe?"

"What do you mean?"

"Where's this thing of ours going? Where you wanna be ten years from now? Do you wanna wake up in the morning with one cracked egg in the fridge?"

"I'm sorry, Leon, but this conversation's going to have to wait."

"That's what I keep hearing. It'll have to wait. I'll have to wait. I'll have to bide my time till you're ready. You call the shots."

"Leon, I've got a client in trouble. I have to make calls."

"Yeah, well, I can play that, too. I have to go to work, and it's always something important. It's the goddamn FBI!"

He turned on his heel and I heard the front door slam. Christ, we might as well be married, I thought. Damn. You need time for a relationship, time to build it, time to nurture it, and nurturing has never been my strong suit.

Fuck that, I thought, and I don't use those words often, even in my head. It's a guy's curse, equating lovemaking with violence and anger and all the things I don't normally choose to bill it with. Fuck that. I do fine nurturing Paolina. Maybe it's pretense that has never been my strong suit. I took a sip of coffee that was too damned hot. Oh, pretense was my strong suit when I married. I played sweet and patient and understanding when Cal didn't come home till four in the morning. I played grateful when he'd spend the night at home. I was all the things I thought he'd want a wife to be, and none of it was enough. Now, jaded veteran that I am, I want someone who wants me for who I am, and damned if I'm going to pretend to be interested in eating scrambled eggs when I've got a client heading for a cell.

I sipped the coffee more cautiously. Leon had abandoned the other three cups on the counter, hadn't even taken his own. I called the fire department's dispatch center in Boston and, passing as a journalist, one of my favorite ruses, found that there was no general rash of fire alarms, although there had indeed been false alarms the two nights in question. I never asked about those two nights directly, just keyed my questions to other events, school vacations and the like, until I got the information I needed.

"You use the same instant ID the police department uses, right?"

"Yes, the number comes up on our screen when you make the call."

"But that hasn't cut the number of false alarms?"

"It cuts the number that kids make from mama's phone. But people still yank the call boxes. And we can't get a trace on cells and mobiles."

"Thanks."

Two sets of false alarms . . . I admit it: I was starting to wonder not where my investigation would lead but where it should have begun. I'd been hired to stop the blackmail, but was the blackmail the first crime in the series? I'd had trouble imagining Denali's suicide from the get-go, and now it seemed like part of a pattern. Two deaths—and I knew Benjy Dowling's death was no accident. So what did that make Denali Brinkman's? Arson? Murder? Dowling, the man whose emotional testimony had helped the cops settle on suicide, was dead. Yes, the medical examiner had agreed, but Boston's MEs have a spotty reputation. It was years ago, yeah, and times have supposedly changed, but one once wrote "natural causes" on a mobster with a garrote still embedded in his neck. The ME might have seen what he thought he was supposed to see, primed by the police report and the recent MIT suicide by fire.

I phoned a source in the ME's office and arranged to buy some information. I thought about the gas station on Mount Auburn Street, about the pump jockey identifying Denali as the woman who'd requested gas for her stalled car. Eyewitness testimony is notoriously unreliable. Could it have been another woman? Could Denali have been tricked into playing the scene? Maybe it was the black TransAm that had run out of gas. Maybe Dowling had arranged it so that he'd stay with the vehicle, waiting for help, and she'd go for the gas. If Dowling had killed his girlfriend, had someone killed him, seeking revenge?

I considered the matter as I scrounged for food. Who cared about Denali Brinkman? Chaney came to mind. Great. Suspect number one: my client. I was hungry, damn it, and there was nothing to eat in the house. I hated it that Leon was right about the way I lived, but what the hell gave him the right to criticize? Another phone call or two and I'd hit the Central Square Dunkin' Donuts, play volleyball, smash hell out of a round, unfeeling ball till my anger died.

I yanked open my desk drawer, pulled out the receipt I'd found crumpled in Dowling's filing cabinet. Graylie Janitorial Services. I recalled the unmarked coveralls on the back of his door. A phone number was printed neatly at the top of the small yellow sheet, along with a Medford address. I dialed.

It rang and rang, six times, eight times. I thought every modern business had an answering machine, but I guess not. I was about to hang up, when a voice came on the line, a semihysterical woman's voice, heavily accented. I gave my name, but she didn't let me go on.

"Please, you call back later, no? I leave this line open, no? For *la policía*. Oh, *madre mia,* they say they call right back. You call later, *sí*?" Click. A dull, empty hum echoed in my ear.

I checked the address again. Medford's not far, and I decided I wasn't hungry after all.

CHAPTER 23

With caffeine pulsing in my veins, I wanted to move, to drive, to get to Graylie Janitorial Services as quickly as possible. I didn't want to wait for a messenger to make it from Geary's Kendall Square office to my North Cambridge home. It's no more than a ten-, eleven-minute drive, given good traffic, but that's a thing Bostonians are seldom granted; plus, Geary might have consigned the envelope to a cabbie. The cabbie—if I knew cabbies, which I did—would pick up a passenger along the way. They're not supposed to, but they do.

I yelled upstairs, and, hallelujah, Roz was home and awake enough to promise she'd listen for the bell and sign for the police report.

I considered the hour and the traffic, decided on the Alewife Brook Parkway, winding through East Arlington to the Mystic Valley Parkway and into the working-class city of Medford. I turned right on Forest Street, crossed the Mystic River into Medford Square, better known to townies as "Medfid Squayah." The address put Graylie Janitorial Services on a mixed block, half residential apartments, half small businesses. It was a squat square building with fresh blue paint and a discreet sign on a tiny patch of lawn. There weren't any police cars parked in front, and I took that as a good omen. I grabbed my jacket, slipped it on, skipped the pumps. The semihysterical woman hadn't sounded in any condition to criticize my choice of footwear.

I rang the bell, and there she was, a tiny woman with a round face and long dark hair caught in a single braid. She looked like a china figurine, a statue of the suffering Madonna.

"I called earlier," I said. "I'm a detective." Two truths; both statements honest. *I am a detective. I had called earlier.* Two truths can constitute a lie, but I didn't feel obliged to explain that to the woman as she muttered welcoming words in Spanish.

"Oh *sí*, you come at last, you look. I don't know yet what is missing, what is gone, but I call."

She was thirty, I figured, maybe less, her skin impeccable porcelain. Not a wrinkle, but that may have been because she was plump. Honduran or Guatemalan, probably, with black eyes round as stones. She didn't ask for ID, and I found myself nodding, encouraging her misapprehension without coming right out and impersonating an officer.

"I go in already," she said, waving her hands. "*Ai*, I know I shouldn't, but I do. When I see the lock broken, I must go like a strong wind blows me there."

"*Comprendo, señorita.*"

The simple Spanish called forth a rush of speech so rapid, I had to use both hands and voice to stop the flood. "*Mas despacio, por favor.*"

She slowed down. "I am so stunned, I don't even think, but maybe there's someone still inside."

"Do you want me to check?" I asked in Spanish.

She shook her head. "*No es necessario.*"

She'd gone inside; she couldn't help herself. She hoped she hadn't done the wrong thing, going in, even starting to straighten up, but·it was as if she were on automatic pilot. That was the work she did: You saw a mess, you cleaned it up. And she hadn't thought to put on rubber gloves, although she understood all the *ladrones* did now; all the thieves wore gloves.

While she was speaking, she opened the door wide and stepped into a ten-by-twelve-foot office that had been turned upside down. The two desks were toppled, the drawers extracted and shaken until empty. Posters that had been on the walls were on the floor. Potted plants displayed their roots and the potting soil had been dumped on top of file folders. The shaken woman hadn't gotten far with her cleaning.

"Look," she said. "*Madre de Dios*. Who does such a thing? *Ai*, beasts, not humans. Pigs. It makes me sick."

"What's your name?" My Spanish runs to things like that, basics.

"*Pardon*. I should tell you, no? I am Fidelia Moros Santos."

"And you work for Graylie?" I didn't give my name, but she didn't seem to notice.

"Is no Graylie. Is my business, no? I don't have the English so good, but I am here many years. A citizen, no? I am owner, but I am clever, no? I think, who comes to a business with a name like Moros Santos? Only maybe the women who want a clean house cheap, but I do more. I clean for the big companies. They like more English, no?" She folded her arms under heavy breasts and awaited my approval.

I smiled. "You made up the name?"

"*Sí*. I have a man here speaks good English, works for me. I have him for answer the phone. When Anglos know there is an Anglo in the office, they are more happy. They don't care who owns, just they need to know someone understands good English. I understand good, but I sound not so good."

"You sound fine," I said.

"Look. Look what they do. Animals." She held up a mound of disordered receipts much like the one I'd salvaged from Dowling's drawer. I should have identified myself, asked her whether she remembered the client who'd paid her for services on at least two occasions, shown her his photo, but she was eagerly leading me around the room, pointing out the outrages visited on her office. In addition to the two dismembered desks, pillows had been tossed off a saggy couch. Magazines and papers were strewn across the floor. A file cabinet was upended, one corner dented.

"Did you keep money here?" Something seemed wrong, but I couldn't yet pin it down. If you break into a business, you go for cash; you go for a safe. Maybe kids had broken in, but there was no gang insignia, no graffiti, no shit smeared on the walls.

"Not so much, no. A little only for when one of the crews goes for coffee, maybe. In a gray metal lockbox."

"I don't see it," I said.

"Is gone," she agreed.

All the time we were talking, I kept one eye on the window, an ear open for the sound of an approaching patrol car. The Medford cops wouldn't come racing down the street, sirens screaming and lights flashing. An over-and-done-with B and E at a small business is not a bank robbery in progress. Before they came, I needed to work the conversation around to the receipt and what Benjy Dowling had purchased from a cleaning company.

"We ought to wait for a crime-scene team," I told the woman gently. "I saw a doughnut shop across the street. We could wait there and talk. You look like you could use some coffee. And I could use a doughnut." I doubted the Medford cops would call out a crime-scene team for such a small-potatoes crime. I just wanted out of there before the cops came.

"That's so sweet," she said. "You're no like a cop at all."

Inwardly, I cringed.

"I no can lock the door," she protested.

"It's okay," I said. "Just close it. We can see it from the window."

She needed to find her bag, which she'd put down somewhere in her panic, and now she couldn't remember even which bag she'd brought to work that morning. *Ai*, she moaned over and over. What would she do about the crews that were to work the next shift? She'd come in early because she had to do all the office work this week, what a mess, how hard it was to be alone in a crisis. She went on and on, until I found her bag and led her across the street to a coffee shop that must have been spanking new in the fifties and hadn't changed since. Round vinyl stools poked up from the warped linoleum flooring. The counter faced cases of doughnuts that hadn't been made within the past four hours. I hoped they'd been made sometime that week.

I glanced around cautiously, knowing that cops and doughnut shops go hand in hand, but the place was deserted. Didn't bode well for the coffee. No sirens, no prowl cars. No activity across the street. I ordered two glazed doughnuts and coffee for myself, the same for Señorita Moros Santos. The middle-aged waitress had dull eyes.

At first, Señorita Moros Santos seemed too nervous to eat, but once she took her first bite, the doughnut disappeared in a few ravenous swallows. Then she started to talk again, and it seemed as though she'd keep going forever. Most of it was in Spanish, but the occasional phrase came out in English. I didn't have trouble following her.

She loved her business and she loved Medford, which was also where she lived, and nothing like this had ever happened to her before, and it was terrible, *terrible*, that it had happened now, when she was so busy and understaffed. She wasn't a grand cleaning business like the ones that did the big skyscrapers in Boston, but she didn't have the union problems they did, either. She had lots of family members on her crews and she'd brought over friends and family from Guatemala, sponsored them now she was a citizen, and everyone was willing to work long hours because they were used to it and they wanted to stay in this country, and the money she made was very good, very good. Even her lone American was happy to work for low wages because, well, he was so very interested in the future of her firm.

An employee willing to work for low wages always catches my attention. The way she spoke about his interest in her future made me check her hands again, looking for an engagement ring. She blushed and paused, and I got a chance to insert a couple of questions.

"Do you sell uniforms? Coveralls for cleaning?"

"No."

Dowling hadn't bought the coveralls from Graylie; so much for that theory.

"Do you work for any of the universities in the area. Tufts? Harvard?"

"No, no."

She was off again, and I learned she had an indirect connection to Harvard, cleaning many of its research labs. She was very proud that she was a licensed and bonded agency. No one ever complained about her work. Prompt, her people were, and they cleaned very well.

"Do you want another doughnut?"

She looked at the case longingly, then patted her round stomach and declined.

I said, "The American man who works with you, he has the other desk in your office?"

"*Sí*. We work together most days."

"He only answers the phone?"

"*Ai*, no, he is so good with customers. He does everything. Even he heads one of the cleaning crews. He doesn't want to be the favorite, the owner's pet boy, my Ben."

I was glad I hadn't been drinking coffee when she gave his name; I'd have choked while trying to swallow. "Excuse me, but what's Ben's full name?"

"Benjamin Dennison." She smiled as if it were the most beautiful name she'd ever heard, said it like the syllables were musical notes. The way her tongue caressed it, I wondered if she sat and practiced writing it over and over like some high school girl: Señora Dennison, Señora Dennison.

"And how long has he worked with you?"

The blush reasserted itself. "Almost a year now. We are such very good friends."

"And so you've told him about the break-in?"

"*Ai*, no. I cannot. He is gone away. Very sudden, he goes. I don't even know he is planning to go, but maybe it is his family. You know, sometimes things happen, and there's nothing you can do but go yourself."

"Where is his family?"

"I think maybe New York. I don't really know. We have not yet been acquainted, but soon we will all meet. Maybe he goes to tell them about me."

"When will he be back?"

"He didn't say. The note he left is so very short. He say not to worry. He knows me—always I worry. And now look, see what has happened, and he is gone." She gave me a wry smile, but the worry predominated, shadowing her black stone eyes. I thought she had more reason to worry than she knew.

"So you're engaged?"

"*Sí.*"

"A handsome man?"

"*Sí.* Very."

"You have a photo?"

"No. Ben hates it to have his picture taken. He hates it."

"He is tall?"

"No, not so tall as you, señorita. You are tall as a man."

"He has dark hair?"

"*Sí.* Dark hair, dark eyes. *Muy guapo.*"

She'd grown to rely on Ben because his English was so very good. She absolutely depended on him. He was such a devoted employee. She trusted him so much. Really, she hadn't realized how much she'd placed on his plate. She didn't actually do the cleaning much anymore, not that any of them were above pitching in. She kept coveralls at the office in case she had to fill in for a sick worker. The big firms expected things to get done. They didn't want their efficiency hurt by a slow cleaning crew.

Shit. If her Ben was my Benjy, I bet she didn't know about the ex-con stuff any more than she knew his real name. Maybe he'd told her he had trouble with the IRS so that she'd pay him in cash. Maybe she paid all her employees in cash.

I said, "Tell me, do you work for a company called Improvisational Technologies?"

"*Sí,* that's one of Ben's places. Always he goes with the team to Impro."

Impro. That word was emblazoned on a mug on Benjy's windowsill, next to an unwatered plant.

"Excuse me," I said softly. "Did you drop this?" I had placed the photo of Benjy in my jacket pocket, just in case. Now I mimed plucking it off the floor under her seat.

"Oh," she said. "No, but look, that is Ben, yes. Maybe he put it in my bag for a surprise. It's not so good a likeness, too dark, but you see how he is handsome? *Muy guapo.*"

I agreed with her, then deliberately glanced at my watch and looked out the window. "Where can they be? Really, a team should have come by now. I'd better see what's holding them up."

"Shall I go back to the office? Leave things alone? Fix things?"

"No, no, you finish your coffee, Señorita Moros Santos. If I'm told to report to another crime scene, you remember to tell the new people everything you told me." I patted her on the shoulder, but I couldn't offer any more reassurance, couldn't make myself say that everything would be all right. Because it wouldn't.

I called the Medford cops from a pay phone, reported the crime again, but this time I added an untruth, saying the thief might still be on the premises, possibly armed and dangerous. I thought that might speed them along sooner. I wondered if the señorita would ask them about me, about what had become of the tall Anglo woman cop with the so very red hair.

If my deception came home to roost, so be it. I couldn't worry about it now. I had other fish to fry, plenty of them. For instance, I wanted to see exactly what Benjy Dowling had cleaned at Improvisational Technologies.

CHAPTER 24

I drove the twisting parkways on autopilot, considering the break-in at Dennison/Dowling's workplace, dismissing the possibility that some clueless thief would choose *that* office to rifle and rob, not the shop next door or the liquor store down the block, but the office in which Dowling had a desk. Did Dowling's killer imagine he kept blackmail materials at the office rather than at home? Would I need to visit his house again? If I did, would the woman cooking barley soup downstairs make me for the exterminator?

I recalled the photo of Dowling I'd left with the señorita, the hooded dark eyes, straight nose, and heavy brow. What in that face had made Denali Brinkman, small, blond, delicate but strong Denali, take notice? Question: How does a Harvard girl meet an ex-con? Answer: She spots him shoving a mop across the floor of her lover's research facility and, boom, it's love at first sight. Something wrong there.

But, of course, Denali and Benjy had rowing in common. Maybe she'd met him on the river, never known his interest in her lover's business. I tried to make the couple work. I thought about the men I've dated, the men I've seriously dated, not the one-night stands or the blind dates recommended by friends you realize you don't really know. The men I've dated have stuff in common. They're tall, for one thing. I've wondered about it, about whether I harbor some secret desire to be dominated, but I think it's just the culture; I'm not immune to it. I've never really dated anyone much shorter than my own six one. It limits the field.

Beyond the physical, there are other similarities in my men: humor, sensuality, intensity. Plus, like a lot of women, I tend not to date down, not to date guys less educated than I am. That doesn't mean I need to see a prospective date's college diploma—or proof of professional employment. It just means I look for a guy who's quick on the uptake, a guy with something on the ball. No one I'd spoken to had stressed Dowling's brilliance. Everyone I'd spoken to had stressed Denali's.

Had Dowling been a break in her pattern? Or had Chaney? What was there about both men that had drawn Denali Brinkman? Had the choice of Dowling been a reaction against the overly intellectual Chaney? Had the girl felt so outranked, so outmatched by her Harvard peers that she'd rebelled and chosen a townie like Dowling? Had she been on some precipitous mental decline? Had Dowling been part of the disease that led to her decision to die?

Always supposing she'd made that decision herself . . . I kept coming back to that: Had Denali chosen to die? I sighed, punched on the WUMB-tuned radio, lucked into Chris Smither singing "Drive You Home Again," and let his intricate guitar work overwhelm the throb of unanswered questions in my head. Times like this, you follow the leads, do the work, take it doggedly step by step, and hope something makes sense. Usually, I excel at theorizing, at speculation, if you will. Mooney used to tease me about my vaunted "intuition." I wondered what he'd make of this mess, wondered if the Cambridge cops and the Brighton cops and the Medford cops would ever realize they each held a piece of the same puzzle.

I knew it. Did it do me any good?

I decided on a quick stop at the house to grab the police report on

Dowling's accident. Roz heard my key in the door and wanted my opinion on a prospective tattoo, an abstract bow and arrow design of indelible weirdness that she was planning for her left breast.

"You need money?" I asked, only partially to change the subject.

"Why?" She was wearing what looked like a slip, black and shocking pink, barely covering her butt. Her legs were bare until you got to the big furry puppy slippers. If she'd opened the door to the messenger wearing that outfit—well, I was surprised he wasn't still panting on the doorstep.

"Impro," I said. "Improvisational Technologies, a research lab affiliated with Harvard." I told her I wanted every scrap, who stood to make money, who stood to lose it. Anything and everything she could find, as quickly as possible.

"Oh," she said. "You got a message. Woman. Jeannie St. something."

"Cyr."

"Yeah. She says you should come by and grab a trophy. Does that make sense?"

"Did she leave her number?"

"Yeah."

"Call her back, tell her you're my—" What? I thought. Not assistant, not associate. Friend would have to do it. "Say you're my friend and that I asked you to pick it up for me. Okay? Then do it. Be really nice to her, okay?"

"What? You think I'm not nice?"

"Just be yourself. And take along one of those photos from Magazine Street Beach. Ask Jeannie if she knows the man in the picture."

"Just knows him?"

"Yeah. And if she ever saw him with Denali."

"Denali. Like the mountain? Am I supposed to know Denali?"

"Don't complicate it."

"Way cool name, Denali."

She saluted and I took charge of the police report. Before I left, I picked up another photo of Benjy Dowling as well, and a Pepsi from the fridge.

Improvisational Technologies was in north Brighton, the scene of the hit-and-run an easy detour. I headed west on Memorial Drive, took Greenough to Arsenal, crossing over Soldiers Field Road, then turning left to join it. Traffic was light on the Birmingham Parkway, no pedestrians, not even a cyclist. I drove the complete loop of roadway, retraced my route, and pulled into the narrow access road near the Day's Inn. In the small, deserted parking lot, I came to a halt between yellow lines.

The Birmingham Parkway runs almost parallel to Soldiers Field Road. There's not much ground between the two big streets, a football field's worth, maybe. The businesses, a McDonald's, a Staples, a party store, front on Soldiers Field and turn their backs on Birmingham. Only an oldies radio station and the motel face the parkway. Traffic is heavier on Soldiers Field, cars heading downtown. Trucks take the Birmingham Parkway, the quickest path to North Beacon Street. Across the parkway, a rusty six-foot fence barred pedestrians from the slightly elevated Mass Pike. Farther on the left lay a construction site littered with massive lengths of pipe, wide-diameter pipe big enough to sleep in if you were homeless. But Dowling wasn't homeless.

I couldn't imagine what had brought Dowling on foot to this ugly urban stretch of roadway, any more than I could conjure what Denali had seen in him. Maybe he'd hitched a ride as far as Mickey D's. I wondered if the cops had questioned the burger-flippers and fry cooks. I opened the envelope, read the typed double-spaced report, then exited the car.

Nearly lunchtime. A stream of cars was starting to pull into the McDonald's drive-through lane, but I could have stood in the middle of the road for five minutes without a car passing the spot where the van had smashed into Dowling. I traced hypothetical footsteps. If he was coming from the river, he'd have had to cross Soldiers Field, scoot through the McDonald's lot, walk in near darkness down an unpaved path almost as far as the construction site, then cross four more lanes toward the inaccessible turnpike. I considered the path in reverse; no illuminating insights.

According to the police report, all area businesses had been canvassed, all workers, customers, even motel guests questioned, with no results. I walked to the the site the diagram specified as the place the body had been found, an upgrade near the Mass Pike fence. The grass was brown and matted by heavy feet. I yanked out the scene-of-crime photographs.

Dowling looked more like a bloody rag doll than a human, his neck bent at an impossible angle, his legs crushed, his body torn, and yet it was hard for me, even with the awful photos in my face, to regard him in a sympathetic light. Ex-con, blackmailer, deceiver—he might be all of those, I reminded myself, but he was still a victim, dead before his time. For a moment, a thought flickered like a dying bulb and I saw a possible link between Chaney and Dowling. Both victims.

I crossed the road and stared at the construction site. It looked abandoned. I kept walking, found Market Street closer than I expected, over a shallow rise.

The Birmingham Parkway came to a dead end at Market. Faces stared at me speculatively from behind the wheels of Hondas and pickup trucks, and the prickly feeling at the back of my neck made me glance around sharply, searching for—I don't know—maybe a black TransAm. Everything seemed normal. I was simply the lone pedestrian as far as the eye could see, a curiosity.

I took note of the buildings, the number of FOR SALE signs, the new construction. Harvard had bought up a lot of the land here. There was speculation in the newspapers as to which of the Cambridge colleges might be asked to move to this less-desirable location, on the same side of the river as the Business School but without the ivied redbrick splendor of the Cambridge campus, without the storied history.

I walked back to the car, got the address for Improvisational Technologies. Life Street. Off Guest Street. And Guest Street was off Market Street, close, very close. Dowling could have been heading toward Impro when he died.

Chaney's baby, Improvisational. An attempt to improve the lives of those with AHDH through a new drug, an alternative to Ritalin and Adderall, a better, safer, stronger drug. Fording had pooh-poohed it as a moneymaker, but what had Chaney's wife said? Her husband wasn't a wealthy man *yet*. She wouldn't divorce him *now*. I wondered whether she was waiting for a big score, whether Impro figured into her plans.

I placed the police report on the passenger seat, keyed the ignition. I'd go there, trust to the moment, see what I could learn.

My cell rang. I glared at it, considered ignoring it, then answered. It was Geary, the lawyer, feeling pretty full of himself. He hadn't had to arrange bail for Chaney after all. The cops didn't have a leg to stand on. Not only had he fearlessly wrested his client from their clutches but shark-to-shark courtesy had prevailed, and if I could be at 500 Federal Street in fifteen minutes, Mr. Fitch, attorney for the plaintiffs suing Harvard, would grant me an audience.

"Can he see me later today?" I asked. "After lunch?"

"He can see you for five minutes in fifteen minutes, period. Then he's going to New York and then to Washington, and you'll be lucky if I can get you in to see him in six weeks."

There are times I miss being a cop. Not many, granted, but this was one. A cop doesn't work alone. A cop is part of a team, and right now I wanted to send a member of my team to cover the lawyer while I continued on to Impro. But there was only me.

Fifteen minutes was cutting it close, but I'd absorbed enough caffeine to know I could make it. Hell, I could probably make it if I had to abandon the car and run.

CHAPTER 25

The rowers on the river glided along like exotic waterfowl, lifting their oars in unison and flowing gracefully under the bridges. The traffic on Storrow Drive, tracing the curve of the Charles, was stop-and-go. Drivers, penned in their stuffy cars, honked and gave one another the finger. The Leverett Circle jam stretched back toward Charles Street, so I took the exit, edging through narrow Beacon Hill streets, using my cabbie know-how to avoid main drags and stoplights. The parking gods smiled, and I hastily pulled into a just-vacated slot. I stuck bare feet into pumps, fed the meter, and rushed down the street, only three minutes behind schedule.

The lobby was marble-tiled, the sign-in desk mahogany, the offices of Hawthorne and Fitch a giant step up from Geary's Kendall Square den. I admired the Oriental rug in the twelfth-floor waiting room and imagined that Harvard's lawyers commanded even plusher digs in a more luxuriously appointed building.

A receptionist kept me waiting in a blue velvet armchair for eight minutes before ushering me into a corner office and abandoning me to another blue velvet chair. Had she known me better, she'd have kept me in the outer office. The assumption that clients—and how was she to know I wasn't one?—don't snoop is not a good one for a young receptionist to make.

Alas, Mr. T. J. Fitch, Esquire, kept no incriminating papers on his desk. Matter of fact, he kept nothing on his desk. Its shining empty surface, broken only by a vase of tulips and daffodils, made me flat-out suspicious.

In spite of the disappointing desk, I had plenty to admire. The view from the window was superb—blue sky, jagged rooftops, the cranes and shovels of the Dig, the aqua ocean. There must have been fifty pictures on the far wall, not counting certificates. Every honor Theodore Jackson Fitch had garnered in his life, he'd framed, including his high school diploma, which was from Boston College High. The Boston College diploma was there as well, which made him a double eagle in local lingo. I looked for his law school diploma. If he'd gone to BC Law, he'd be a triple. Nope. He'd gone to Yale.

I recognized several faces in the photos and started to make the connections you make in a small city like Boston. I recognized a group of lawyers known around town as "the Big Tobacco boys," guys who'd made the industry cry uncle and pay up. Many had pocketed million-dollar fees. I identified Fitch from his presence in so many shots. He had a nice even smile, which he bestowed on many politicos, Republicans and Democrats alike.

"Sorry to keep you waiting," he said pointedly, apparently unhappy to find me standing behind his desk instead of sitting in the supplicant's chair. "I haven't got a lot of time, but Todd Geary was extremely insistent."

Good for Geary, I thought.

He wore a suit that must have set him back a thousand bucks, Canali or Zegna, one of those Italian labels they carry at Neiman Marcus or Bloomingdale's. His shirt was snowy white, his tie hand-painted silk. Maybe he was expecting to have his photo taken again. I regretted not wearing my suit. I was definitely outclassed, but what can you do?

"So what is it you want?" He settled behind his massive desk, nodded me back into the blue velvet chair.

"Did Mr. Geary tell you I was in his employ?"

"He did." The lawyer kicked back in his chair, placed one leg on the corner of his desk, displaying a Bally loafer. I wondered if he'd worn such nice footwear before the tobacco firms settled.

"The name Denali Brinkman has come up in an investigation relating to one of Mr. Geary's clients."

"Brinkman."

I thought it odd that he chose to repeat the last name. Denali's the odd name, the one anyone hearing it for the first time would be likely to echo. The vague politeness of his voice told me he had no recollection of the name, but the brief flash of interest in his eye said something entirely different.

I said, "I'd like you to tell me what you can about her connection with the suit you've filed against Harvard."

"Because you ask."

"Because Todd Geary asks."

I watched him sum me up, trying to decide how little he could get away with revealing. He assumed a bland and pleasant demeanor.

"We live in a age of corporate responsibility," he began. "Corporations used to feel they could boss everyone around. 'What's good for General Motors,' you know?"

" 'Is good for the country,' " I responded.

"Right. And what's good for the chemical companies and what's good for the tobacco industry, and then people realized what they've always known: Might doesn't make right. And look at things now. Big Tobacco took a huge hit. The Roman Catholic Church is going to have to sell major property to settle its sex-abuse cases. McDonald's is going to have to face the fact that it's poisoning its consumers every bit as much as Big Tobacco ever did. These giants do not police themselves."

I nodded because he seemed to expect a reaction.

"Here's a corollary: If we hold corporations responsible for their actions, shouldn't we hold colleges responsible for theirs? We give them not simply our dollars but our most precious thing, our children."

He stopped, as though waiting for applause from a crowded courtroom. I was obviously there to warm him up for a courtroom appearance.

"Brinkman's name," he went on, "was part of a class-action suit brought against Harvard University."

"And the class?"

"Parents who've lost their children."

"It can't be a very large class," I said. A very sympathetic class, though, I thought. If I were bringing the suit, I'd go for a jury trial.

"Larger than you might think," he said. "And there are other suits, against other prestigious universities."

He didn't finish the thought, but he didn't have to; it was there on his walls, in the photographs. He was thinking of bringing all the suits together. One big class, like the tobacco suit, but more exclusive.

"Excuse me," I said, "but are you talking about an extension of Tarasoff?"

"Very good," he said. "You've come across it?"

I nodded. It was an old decision, 1976 or thereabouts, that talked of a "duty to warn." Psychiatrists, in particular, had been held liable for not warning the parents of suicidal minors, or the potential victims of homicidal patients.

"It's my understanding that Miss Brinkman is no longer involved in the lawsuit," I said.

He smiled. "If she was, I wouldn't be talking to you, in spite of any favors I might owe Todd Geary."

"Can you give me a time line? Was Brinkman one of your first clients?"

"My last. This suit has been building for a long time. My initial clients lost their child eight years ago."

Eight years is a long time. I wondered if the lawsuit were a way of holding on to the lost child, a way of refusing to accept the death.

Since college students are no longer considered minor children, I wondered if the parents had a legal leg to stand on.

"So Brinkman joined when?"

"Barely a month ago."

"Can you give me the exact date?"

He thought about refusing for the hell of it, because he was a lawyer. He must have owed Todd Geary a big one, because he reconsidered, opened one of his desk drawers, and rooted in a file.

"I'd also like to know who contacted you on behalf of Brinkman's family, an attorney, a—"

"It was the girl's fiancé. He intimated that he had the support of a great-uncle, the next of kin, who resides in Switzerland."

"The fiancé would be Mr. Dowling, correct?"

"Yes."

"And the uncle?"

"Albert Brinkman of Lausannne."

"I would appreciate both of their addresses. Todd Geary would."

"Ask my secretary on your way out." He was hoping I'd take the hint, but I stayed seated as he consulted a sheet of paper. "They joined the suit April fifteenth."

"You met Mr. Dowling?"

"Yes."

"Did he impress you favorably?"

Fitch was very good at controlling his face, but his lips pursed slightly. "Reasonably so."

"You accepted him as Denali's fiancé?"

"He had letters from the woman, a photo of her. He was upset—justifiably, considering what had occured."

"Did you happen to copy the photo, keep it?"

"I request photos of all the victims. These are young people, bright, energetic, with all their lives ahead of them."

He was going for a jury trial all right. "May I see it?"

"You can have it. Tell Todd I'll put it on his bill."

If the *Globe* had run this one instead of their grainy rowing shot, they'd have had people leaving flowers at the boathouse, turning it into a shrine, à la Buckingham Palace the day after Princess Diana died. Denali Brinkman was sitting on a bed, or maybe a couch, looking away from the camera. I wondered if she knew the picture had been taken, if she'd glanced up a moment later and protested. One hand was behind her, splayed on a coverlet or a throw; the other was at her temple, smoothing back her hair. She had a small, secret smile on her face. High cheekbones, long lashes, a thin, elegant nose. I wondered if she'd ever modeled, then thought, No, her face is too individualistic.

"And when did Mr. Dowling and Mr. Brinkman change their mind about the lawsuit?" I asked.

He pressed his lips together, deciding whether to keep talking, weighing the pros and cons. "This week."

"And which one changed his mind, or was it both of them?"

"Mr. Brinkman said he wanted no part of any action against Harvard."

"Do you know why he changed his mind?"

"No."

"But you have a suspicion."

"Not really."

"A speculation."

"I need to wind this up, but I'll say this: I was relieved when Brinkman bowed out. I felt he would weaken my case. I might have asked him to withdraw if he hadn't taken that choice away from me."

"Why?"

"Whom do you represent?"

"Geary."

"Whom does he represent?"

"I can't say."

"Then I can't say, either."

"Mr. Geary will be disappointed."

We sat on opposite sides of the sleek desk, each waiting for the other to speak. The silence grew. I wanted Fitch to take his time, review whatever it was he owed Todd Geary, decide how much getting me peacefully out of his office was worth. The view from the window was fine, and I had a lot to think about.

In my experience, cases have patterns. There was a pattern to the blackmail and a pattern to the lawsuit. Each had a purpose: to make money off Denali Brinkman's death.

But there was another pattern as well, one that didn't fit, one I didn't understand. I considered the events. The blackmail had drawn me into the case. The lawsuit served the same purpose as the blackmail. But what about Dowling's death? What about the withdrawal from the lawsuit? I couldn't see the purpose, so I couldn't find the pattern.

Fitch spoke. "Tell Mr. Geary he might try the other side."

"The other side," I repeated.

He smiled. "I don't mean the dark side here, although maybe I do. I'm a Yalie, you know. We often call Harvard 'the dark side.'"

"You're suggesting that Geary try Harvard's attorneys?"

"Well, yes, although Harvard's lawyers, like most, tend to err on the side of discretion. It was good to meet you." He stood, impatient to end the interview.

"Mr. Geary's in a hurry on this. He needs to know."

"Then you might try someone less discreet."

I waited. There was no point pleading. If he wanted me to know, he'd mention a name, a place.

"If I were you," he said, crossing the room and opening the door to the hallway, "I'd try Harvard Admissions."

I decided to press. "Anyone in particular?"

"That's it," he said. "That's enough. Tell Todd when I say five minutes, I mean five minutes, not fifteen. Good-bye."

After thirty long seconds, I gave up and walked through the doorway. The door closed softly behind me. You can't slam doors in places like that. The carpet's too thick to allow it.

CHAPTER 26

What was the name of that mythological beast, the nine-headed serpent killed by Hercules? I bet a smart student like Denali Brinkman could have dredged Hydra from her memory in a flash. If I recalled correctly the least attractive thing about the Hydra was the fact that when you cut off one head, two more popped forth to take its place. Same thing with this case. Instead of finding answers to my questions, I was finding more damned questions.

I wanted to get back to Improvisational Technologies, I needed to visit the Harvard Admissions office, but the medical examiner's office was closer than either, which put it next on my list. I used my cell, got my pal Beaubien on the first ring.

Jackson Beaubien, my prime source at the ME's office, is about forty years old, small, white, and stooped. He has a slight southern drawl and gives me the creeps, not the least because he always wears a shower cap and is eager to discuss corpses. We first got to know each other when I was a cop, and he's one of the contacts I maintain with strategic Christmas bottles of scotch. He's an orderly, a gofer, a nobody at work. He makes not standing out an art form.

"You get it?" I asked him.

"Easy as pie, but Xeroxing's gettin' expensive," he told me.

"You have it in your hand?"

"Ready to go."

"Where can we meet?"

"I'ma goin' for lunch in Chinatown. Ya wanna eat?"

"No time." It was the truth, but I'd have made any excuse rather than have lunch with Beaubien. Like I said, he loves to talk about what he sees at work. The last time I ate with him, the people at the next table moved to a corner booth.

"I'll start walking," he said.

"Corner of Kneeland and Albany?"

"Fifty bucks."

I fished two twenties and a ten from my backpack, wondered if the autopsy report on Brinkman would be worth its freight. Earlier, when I'd phoned Beaubien, I'd been full of the coincidence of the two sets of false alarms, eager to know whether Denali Brinkman's suicide might have been murder in disguise. The discovery that Dowling worked at Impro had distracted me, but I still found the possibility fascinating. I gunned the ignition. Chaney would pay the fifty, and inquiring minds want to know.

He was waiting on the corner, looking furtive, as always, wearing the shower cap, as always. I gave Beaubien the bills and he handed me an envelope. It could have passed for a drug deal.

I used my cell to locate Chaney while I plotted a course toward Brighton and Improvisational Technologies—no mean feat, considering the ravages of the Big Dig project on city roads. He wasn't at Harvard; Fording hadn't reconsidered. I made it onto the Mass Pike, tried the Cambridge house, and got the sweet voice of Mark, Mrs. Chaney's secretary. I identified myself and asked to speak to Chaney.

I could hear Mrs. Chaney's voice in the background. "Is that the Realtor?"

"Hang on, please. I'll see whether he's able to take your call." Mark was nothing if not polite. I thanked him.

More female vocals, but I couldn't understand the words.

Mark again: "I'll transfer you. Hang on."

Music, then another ring.

"Have you got him?" Chaney's tone was intense and demanding.

"Who?"

"The bastard who set me up. You have no idea what I've been through. The police—I came very close to getting arrested." He lowered his volume abruptly, as though he'd suddenly realized he could be overheard. "They'd been to my bank. They knew I'd taken out money in cash. They had some idea that it involved Dowling, that I was paying him off for something, but I guess they had no proof he'd received the money. They kept asking me what I did with the cash."

"What did you tell them?"

"I told them it was a personal matter. I refused to elaborate."

"And what did they say?"

"Don't leave town."

I wondered how long it would take before another scrap of evidence arrived at the cop house, telling them where to find Dowling's stash.

I said, "You're not thinking of moving, are you?"

"Moving?"

"Your wife thought I might be the Realtor."

He made a noise somewhere between a snort and a laugh. "No, no. It's nothing. Just something she does, looking at real estate on the Vineyard, a fantasy thing. Are you making progress?"

I dodged a massive pothole on the Pike. "Did you know Dowling worked with a cleaning service?"

"I didn't know Dowling at all."

"Would it surprise you to know he was part of the cleaning crew at your lab?"

"At Impro? That *is* odd." He sounded genuinely puzzled.

"I'm heading over there now."

"Now?"

"Yes."

"That's not a good idea."

211

A GTO passed me on the right and honked; I was only going ten miles over the speed limit, not fast enough for him.

I said, "The man who was blackmailing you has a connection to your place of business, and you don't think I should find out how long he's worked there, or whose offices he cleaned?"

"Look, there's sensitive work going on and I don't want the staff upset. How's this? I'll be there later this afternoon. Come at four, and I'll be happy to show you around."

"Sure," I said. "No problem. See you then."

What the hell is he hiding? I thought.

The Impro parking lot was small, and in order to maximixe the number of cars, someone had simply drawn the lines so tightly that the SUVs and vans barely fit. It probably didn't make the drivers park any worse than usual, but it sure didn't seem to help, so I wound up parking in a larger lot at a nearby steak house, ignoring the threatening notices that said parking was strictly for patrons and all others would be towed at their own expense.

The steak house smelled wonderful. I could have a drink and eat a leisurely lunch while I waited for Chaney to arrive. Maybe go for a stroll afterward. Bird-watch. Do some goddamn macramé.

Not likely. I checked my cell battery, called Roz.

"Yo."

"You probably meant to say 'Carlyle Investigations,' right?"

"Hey," she said cheerfully.

I gave up. "What can you tell me about Improvisational Technologies?"

"First off, Paolina called to remind you she's going to Adele Guzman's *quinciana* tonight. Is that right, *quinciana*?"

"Yeah, Sweet Fifteen. Listen, when we finish, call Fannie Guzman and check it out. She's in my Rolodex."

"Check it out?"

"Make sure it's a legit party. Make sure it's girls only for the sleepover part, or else make sure they've got a wall between the guys and the girls. Chaperones, shotguns, whatever."

"You don't trust your little girl?"

"I was fifteen once, Roz. Were you?" By the time I was fifteen, I'd given birth to a child and given her/him up for adoption without ever knowing the gender of my child. It was an experience I never mentioned, and I sure as hell didn't want Paolina to repeat it, didn't want her ever to have to make such a devastatingly irrevocable choice.

"Improvisational Technologies," I said.

"Okay, well, up till 1980, you worked for a university, you invented something, the university owned it. So the universities were having a brain drain. Professors would invent things, yeah, but they'd keep them a secret, take a leave of absence or quit entirely, and then they'd have a product and the university could whistle for its share of the profits."

"What's this got to do with—"

"I'm giving you background. In 1980, we got the Bayh-Dole Act specifically to encourage the translation of university research into useful products and services and shit. So now every university has got an Office of Technology Transfer or an Office of Technological Advancement, or something like that."

"What's it do?"

"Helps professors set up ways to market the stuff they invent on company time. The university gets its share, but the professors make enough moola that they're not tempted to split for the private sector. The universities play it like, Why should you have to learn to market your product? Stay in the ivory tower. We'll handle all the nasty details for you. They take a fat cut, but their point of view is that the guy invented it on company time, right?"

"Okay, so what did Chaney invent?"

"He's a hotshot in brain chemistry, but with the educational psych background, too, and he's looking for chemicals, drugs, that ease psychological conditions. ADHD is one biggie, but they're so many fucking brain disorders, you know? Autism and depression and anxiety, bipolar syndrome, all that shit. Improvisational Tech is Chaney's baby, with Harvard's support. Oh, and I didn't mention that Harvard will also put you together with venture-capital firms because they don't want to bear the whole cost. I mean, this stuff is freaking expensive."

"On what order of magnitude?"

"First of all, time. We're talking ten years, and then there's money, two hundred and fifty million to get one drug from start to finish. Even after you file with the FDA, it can take another ten years for them to approve the drug."

"Ten years?"

"It's more like thirty months, average. And it's not like there's only one guy working in a little office, either. It's the biotech boom. There're more than three thousand clinical trials taking place right now in Boston-area hospitals and clinics."

"And one of them belongs to Chaney?"

"Yeah, he's finishing up phase two, which is very cool."

"What's phase two?"

"Okay, you start with chemical and animal tests, then you go to phase one, where you try out your drug on a heathy population, like twenty to a hundred healthy people. You gotta pay them. I'm thinking maybe I'll volunteer someplace."

I held my tongue. They'd probably ask what drugs she did regularly and toss her out. Hell, they'd take one look at the hair and the tattoos and toss her out.

She went on. "Phase two. Now it's safe, you gotta show it's effective, right? Most of these are randomized trials, where one group gets the experimental drug and another gets a placebo or a standard treatment. These are usually blinded or double-blinded trials."

"Nobody knows who gets what."

"That's double-blinded. They used to just do it blinded, where the patients wouldn't know if they got the new stuff or the placebo, but then some shrinks figured that the docs treated the patients differently, talked to them differently, that kind of shit, if they knew who was getting what. So they double-blinded the studies."

"Right."

She went on. "And this is a biggie—only about a third of all drugs successfully complete phase one and phase two. Phase three is killer expensive. You gotta run the tests with anywhere from several hundred to several thousand patients. Phase three lasts several years."

"Blinded?"

"Yeah, doubled and randomized. They're so many of these damn studies, they have trouble enrolling enough patients, but seventy to ninety percent of drugs that enter phase three successfully complete testing, and after you pass your phase three, then you can go for FDA approval to market."

"Chaney's phase two is looking good?"

"Very good, that's the word on the street. So if this was ten years ago, Harvard would take the company public, but the market sucks for IPOs right now."

"Chaney's been meeting with people."

"Well, I imagine the name Harvard in his résumé doesn't drive the moneymen away, but the hot thing now is takeovers. Selling out to a big pharma for big bucks. Novartis, the Swiss pharmaceutical firm, is moving into Cambridge soon, and everybody's hoping they'll buy up some of the smaller fish, and probably so is Novartis."

"Why?"

"They need new drugs. Most of the big pharmas, GlaxoSmith-Kline, Merck, Novartis, Roche, they don't have enough late-stage drugs in the pipeline to make up for the money they're gonna lose when the patents expire on their older drugs, their major moneymakers. They need blockbuster drugs or they can't keep generating the big profits and their investors will bail. So they're buying little firms like crazy. Novartis just bought Idenix, and the deal could be worth eight hundred and sixty-two million."

"Is anybody courting Impro?"

"That's what I'm checking now. I've got calls into people at Pioneer Investment and I've got a pal at Nutter, McPherson."

"Good. How many people does Impro employ?"

"Thirty-eight."

"And Chaney's the CEO?"

"No. Can't be. Harvard has rules and regs to avoid conflict of inter-est. He's on the board of directors; plus, he's listed as a consultant."

"Who's the CEO?"

"Dr. Nigel Helving."

"Check him out. Is there a George Fording anywhere?"

"Doctor?"

"Of course."

"Yeah, here he is. Member of the Scientific Advisory Group. There are a ton of other names, plenty of initials and degrees after all of 'em."

"Print out a list so I can look them over. One more thing. Are they hiring?"

"Let me go to their Web site. . . . Okay. Hiring. . . . Yeah. Techni-cal. Hey, here's one for a receptionist. You want me to go for it?"

"Tell me more about the technicals."

"Okay, they've got an opening for a high-throughput medicinal chemist. You need your B.S. or your M.S. in chemistry, along with practical experience in conducting multistep organic synthesis, isola-tion, purification, and characterization of novel compounds. You want more?"

"That should do it," I told her. "Thanks. Remember to call Mrs. Guzman."

I locked the car and walked across the street.

Improvisational Technologies was a low-slung two-story yellow brick square, with one side broken so you could pass between thick brick walls to an inner courtyard. The exterior walls looked fortresslike, but the walls of the inner courtyard were patterned with picture windows, more like a hotel than a prison. I wondered how much of the building Harvard had funded, how much of it Harvard owned. Surely this was their land.

Chaney worked here and Dowling had cleaned here. Dowling had been blackmailing Chaney when he died. If Chaney was right and Dowling had been blackmailing others as well, it was possible he'd learned enough during his work hours at Impro to fuel his illegal

216

activities. Yet Chaney didn't want me interrupting his staff to question them about the possibility.

As I opened the heavy door to the foyer, I noted the camera installation in the upper right-hand corner. It was meant to be noticed, boasted a small red light that indicated it was active. Peering through glass double doors, I could see a tiled lobby with a reception desk to one side, a woman typing diligently at a keyboard. I pressed a bell. The receptionist didn't look up, but after a time, the door buzzed and I opened it.

I figured the bell must ring in some security office linked to the door by the camera. If you didn't pass muster in the foyer, you didn't gain entry.

The receptionist looked up when the door opened. I fastened a smile on my face.

"May I help you?"

"Yes. Who would be the best person in Human Resources to see about a job?"

It was a calculated request. Not "May I see someone in Human Resources?" Not "Are you hiring?" I needed an opener that would make her think about the suitability of the people in Human Resources, not about my suitability.

She was no dummy. Her smile glazed from welcoming to rueful.

"I'm afraid we do no on-the-spot hiring. You'd need to call ahead for an interview, or submit your CV on-line. If you tell me what sort of position you think you'd be qualified for, I can give you a name, so you can send your résumé to the proper person."

"And then it'll get stuck in a pile of other résumés, and I'll get a call in two months, when I'm no longer out of work."

"I'm sorry."

"Look, I was talking to Wilson Chaney at a party last Saturday and he suggested I drop by."

She licked her lips. "Did he, by any chance, leave a message with anyone at HR? If someone were expecting you . . ."

Chaney's name had power, but not enough.

I said, "I don't think anyone's got my name on an appointment list, but what would be the harm in letting me—"

"I'm sorry, but that's not the way we do things here."

I had no intention of leaving without gaining an inner sanctum. I'm stubborn, but she was no pushover. The look in her eyes made me think of a bulldog.

After a few more minutes of an argument that was getting us nowhere, her voice turned steely. "I'm sorry, but if you don't leave now, I'll have to call Security."

"Why don't you do that," I replied.

And that's when I lucked out. The man who responded wore a Foundation Security uniform.

CHAPTER 27

The head of Impro's security force sat across from me at a dark wooden table, his mouth a thin line in an inexpressive face. He was a tall, loose-limbed man in his mid-thirties, wearing the Foundation uniform, light blue shirt with a patch on the left arm, dark blue pants with a light blue stripe up the side. The TV in the bar area of the steak house was tuned to Red Sox baseball, a day game, and he was conscious of it, looked like he wanted to turn and face the set, ignore me completely. He'd just refused my offer of a drink but had sullenly accepted a cup of coffee. I was starving and more than willing to buy the man lunch, but he didn't seem happy at the prospect.

"Eddie said you had some questions." He bit off the words, staring at his watch.

I used to work with Eddie Conklin, the big man at Foundation Security, back when I was a cop. I'd done some recent work for Foundation, and Happy Eddie and I had emerged from the ordeal as friends. A quick call once I'd been bounced from Impro had resulted in Joe Spengler turning up quickly at my table. What Eddie had said to get Spengler there so fast, I didn't know.

Possibly, Spengler thought I was checking up on him for Eddie.

Before we started, I had to get a few things straight or the man would never open up. I slipped a card from my wallet and passed it across the wooden expanse.

He studied it. "Carlyle Agency, huh?"

"Just me. I used to work with Eddie."

"You went out on your own. You like being your own boss?"

"Money's not great, but the hours are terrible," I said.

He almost smiled.

"You're working something that ties in with Impro?"

"Yeah."

"Well, I wanna know what you got."

"That's what I figured," I said. "You'd want to know what's going on. And in exchange, Eddie thought you'd give me some answers."

He weighed it as if it were a trap that might spring shut. "Sounds okay."

The waitress brought watery coffee in heavy dark mugs. The lighting was bad, the way it is in steak joints when they don't want the customers to be able to tell the difference between medium-rare and well-done meat. I ordered a quarter-pound burger, and Spengler decided to go along. He even agreed to split an order of onion rings. Progress.

"So who goes first?" he asked when the waitress disappeared. "How about ladies?"

I ignored his baiting smile. "First, I want you to tell me about the job. What does Foundation do for Impro? Are you decorative, or serious security?"

"Hey, it's a real gig."

I waited, hoping he'd continue. It would have made me feel better if he'd accepted a beer; he probably still considered me a possible spy.

He said, "Company's been around—I don't know—more than five years, but we only took over like five months ago, kind of sudden. They wanted us fast, to beef things up."

"What kind of things? Due diligence? Computer security?"

"Due diligence, yeah, we do that."

"How? Through Foundation's central office?"

Eddie's smart, but he tends to hire more muscle than brain. Plus, he keeps things too centralized for my taste.

"Look," Spengler said, "a lot of these guys have already been run through the Harvard mill, and that's one mill grinds pretty fine, you know, so if it's a Harvard postdoc, I gotta admit, probably guys down at Eddie's don't do that much digging."

"Thirty-eight people, I hear."

"Yeah. Small but growing. They get more financing, they bring in more people. Started out like, you know, a garage band—two, then four, then eight. A core group, then the group expands. They got some grad students, man, I don't know if they ever go to class, 'cause they're here all the time. Postdocs are worse, practically sleep here. Most days, it's quiet, but sometimes they have these big meetings. Then, if it's gonna include outsiders, we check ID at the door. Photo ID."

The waitress brought our burgers on dark red plates. Dark plates, dark wood, dark lighting—I decided I'd give the joint a miss at night. I opened the pale bun and removed the wilted lettuce and limp tomato slice.

"Can I have those?" Spengler asked.

"Sure."

"My girlfriend asks if I ate vegetables for lunch, this way I can say yes. She's vegan and I'm a meat guy. I don't think it's gonna work." He gave me a regretful smile.

"Far as vegetables go, I like artichokes," I said.

"Me, too. On pizza. The only place I like vegetables, on pizza. They blend in."

I nodded, my mouth full. I have nothing against veggies, carrots, brussels sprouts, broccoli, but I wanted to be on his team. He ate meat; I ate meat.

"This tastes great," he said, chewing the burger. "Man, I've been eating a lot of pizza lately."

We talked odds and ends for a while—how I'd met Eddie, where he grew up—but he kept coming back to food and how much he wished he could convince his girlfriend to eat meat.

"It's not natural," he said. "I mean, look at me, look at my teeth. Why would I have teeth like these, God didn't want me to chew meat?"

He was really trying to cut down, but the less meat he ate, the more he craved it. I was starting to like the guy. He was trying to work it out with his girlfriend, trying to figure a compromise. It made me sad, made me wonder why I couldn't work it out with Leon, considering all we had in common, both of us carnivores. By the time I aimed the conversation back to business, the atmosphere was easier, more relaxed.

"So let me see if I've got this straight," I said. "Harvard vets your people, Foundation's home office verifies, and you check IDs. Okay. I got that. What's the policy on incidentals?"

In security work, incidentals are the wives and kids who come to visit, the mailman, the gardener, the electrician.

"We don't run a check on every Federal Express guy. FedEx doesn't get past reception, ya know?"

"The way I didn't."

"Yeah, that lady on the desk, man, she scares me."

We shared a smile.

"Cleaning crew?" I asked.

"Bonded," he said firmly.

Sounded to me like Foundation was going on people's reputations, not doing the groundwork. Spengler had finished his burger. Now he concentrated on the onion rings. I was wondering whether I'd be lucky enough to grab a couple, when he stopped eating abruptly, and wiped his hands on his napkin.

"Your turn," he said. "What's this about?"

I wasn't planning to discuss Chaney's troubles with anybody associated with Happy Eddie. Eddie knows too many cops and owes too many favors. The police might be trying to make a financial link between Chaney and Dowling, but as far as I knew, they didn't know about the blackmail, and I wasn't going to be the one who spilled those beans.

"Cleaning service," I said. "One of their people wasn't who he seemed to be. An ex-con, and I'm checking up on whether he stole from the places he cleaned. Has anyone missed anything at Impro?"

He shook his head slowly. "Money?"

"Money, jewelry, information. How do you make sure people don't take stuff out of the building?"

"Shit. The cleaning crew?"

"Not the whole crew, just one bad apple. What could he do?"

"Let me see." He leaned back, seemed to be running a floor plan through his head.

I said, "Maybe you could let *me* see."

"What do you mean?"

"I'd like to look around the place, if that's okay with you. It would help if I could see the setup."

I watched him decide. Eddie had told him to cooperate. He'd enjoyed his lunch.

"Sure," he said. "Why not?"

I paid the bill and we walked back, right past the startled receptionist and down the hall. Once through another set of doors, I could see that a designer had made an attempt to counter the sterility of the reception area. The walls were pale gray, the carpet an agreeable blue. Tall floor plants and an occasional ficus tree added green to the color scheme. It could have been a stockbroker's office or a suite of medical offices. I inhaled. The air was chilly and I couldn't identify the faint underlying odor.

"Foundation bring in the camera unit in the foyer?" I asked.

"Yeah," he said. "Before, they didn't have shit. We got cameras at all the exits."

"They lose anything before you got brought in?"

"Not that I know of."

"I was just wondering why they decided to beef up security."

He shrugged.

We passed several doors with see-through glass panels.

"Main lab," Spengler said.

"Is that on-camera?"

"No, just the exits."

Dowling, once inside the place, would have had free reign. A low hum came from the general direction of the lab. I peered inside, saw long flat tables, racks of tubes and flasks, microscopes hooked up to computer screens. Some of the machines looked similar to those in the forensic-technology lab at Schroeder Plaza, the new police headquarters building. Two walls were covered with whiteboard, and a complicated series of letters, numbers, arrows, and tree formations was scrawled on them in vivid primary colors. Two figures in lab coats, one of them Asian, stood in front of an equation, pointing and gesturing. I couldn't hear what they were saying.

"Are there limits to what employees can bring in and out?" I asked.

"You bet. No discs in, no discs out. Guys gotta open their briefcases or backpacks if we ask, but, tell the truth, once we know the guy's a legit hire and he's been around for a while, we don't ask, because if these guys want to get stuff out, they're gonna get stuff out. They sign agreements when they sign on to work here, nondisclosure and shit, so the best defense is the legal department. A lot of this stuff, it's not patented yet, just ideas. So you gotta trust the people you hire."

"I see," I said, trying to keep him juiced, keep him talking.

"That's one of the reasons I'm not killing myself over the cleaning crew. You know, maybe they'll take a few bucks somebody leaves in a drawer, but what else are they gonna take? They wouldn't recognize what's worth stealing."

I smiled. "What is worth stealing?"

"You kidding? Read the newspapers. Most of these little biotech shops, they're hoping Johnson & Johnson or some other big pharma's gonna come in here and buy them, take 'em over. Only suppose Johnson & Johnson doesn't need to buy what they got, suppose they can just steal it?"

"Drug formulas."

"Yeah, and processes. How you put it together. Till the patent's fixed, till it's all registered in Washington, D.C., everything's up for grabs. Shit like that happens. It's like there's stuff in the air, ideas. One scientist reads the same article as another, and, wham, the lightbulb goes off at the same time."

As we walked, the architecture of the place became obvious. The big lab was the central block, with windows onto the courtyard and several doors onto different corridors. The individual offices were in the outer square, windowless cubicles. We passed a corner office with Helving's name on the door. Spengler kept walking toward another door, one without a nameplate.

"This is where the security people hang out. I thought we'd check and see if there are any theft reports I'm not aware of."

He spoke as if this would be a remote possibility. I was wondered why Fording held a position on the Scientific Advisory Group's board, and what that position meant in terms of his relationship with Chaney, his subordinate at the ed school. Chaney had assured me Fording would toss him to the wolves if he were accused of sexual misconduct. Fording had maintained his support for his colleague. Which one was telling the truth?

In a small room, a scrawny man in Foundation garb stared at a bank of security cameras. As soon as he heard Spengler open the door, he slipped headphones off his ears, tried to stuff them into a drawer, forgetting in his haste to turn the power off. The sound was cranked up so loud, I could hear it, and I could tell by the look on Spengler's face that he could hear it, too.

"Hey, Joe," the scrawny guy said, fastening a phony smile across a round face. "How ya doin'? Introduce me to your lady."

"She's a PI, jackass, and I told you not to listen to that heavy-metal shit while you're watching the screens. Fire alarm goes off, you won't even hear it. Miss Carlyle, meet Gordo."

"She's a PI?" He sounded like he didn't believe it.

"Look, we had any trouble with theft lately?"

"Nah."

"Any other kind of trouble?" I asked.

"Such as?"

Spengler jumped in before I could reply. "Looks like we got a con working a cleaning crew."

"No shit. That place is fucking bonded. We should get their ass."

"There haven't been any complaints?"

Gordo bit his lip and furrowed his brow. "Nah. Hey, the con, she a woman?"

Spengler shrugged, glanced at me.

I said, "No, a man."

"Oh," the moon-faced Gordo said, "okay, then it's not what I thought."

"What are you talking about, jackass?" Spengler asked.

"Remember?" he said. "I'm sure I told you. You know, about that other PI—can you believe it, a broad, too—excuse me, a lady, a woman, the one who wanted to take a look at everybody on the cleaning crew, everybody came in for the clinical meetings, everybody in the whole damn place. Smoked like a chimney, and when I ask her to put it out, she launches into this whole shit storm about fucking Massachusetts, how we don't leave anybody alone, no smoking, no drinking, no—"

"I don't remember you saying anything." Spengler's tone was ominous.

"She find what she wanted?" I asked.

The guy shrugged, sorry he'd mentioned it, but I didn't intend to abandon the subject. Two PIs nosing around one business was out of the ordinary. It gave credence to Chaney's theory: Dowling might have been blackmailing another employee.

"You said the PI was looking for a woman?"

"Nah, it was just . . . well, *she's* a woman, and she didn't seem right somehow. But if you know the con's on the cleaning crew, well, then it isn't her, is it? Plus, she said she'd be back, but she didn't come."

"Then maybe she did find what she was after," I said. "You showed her the surveillance tapes?"

"Yeah. Nothing wrong in that, is there, Joe?"

"How many did she look at? She have a specific time period in mind?"

"February, March, but like I told her, we only keep tape for two weeks. It's not like we got tons of room to store old tapes. We reuse 'em."

"But she still wanted to look."

"Right. While she smoked and swore at me. She was pretty gung ho, pretty damn eager, like it was gonna mean a fat promotion for her or something. Said she'd be back, seemed pretty damn sure about it, too, but then she never shows up. Can you believe that?" He sounded angry, as though she'd promised him cash and never delivered.

"Can you show me the tapes?" I asked.

"Which ones?"

"The ones she watched."

"Nah. Ones I showed her, they been taped over already."

"Did she say why she was going to come back?"

He shrugged. He knew all right, but he was lying. He wasn't skilled at it.

"What did the person look like, the one she was watching for on the tapes?"

"She didn't say."

"Yeah, but you're not dumb. She'd stop the tape, freeze the frame when a certain type came on-screen. A certain person. You must have noticed." I was shamelessly flattering the man. Often, that works.

He made a face. "I dunno. I wasn't payin' all that much attention, tell the truth."

"You remember her name?"

"Nah."

"She *tell* you her name?"

"I think so, but I can't remember it."

"She give you a card?"

"Hey, jackass," Spengler said. "How about some cooperation?"

"Hey, yeah, I believe she did."

The business card wasn't in the top drawer of the desk, the place Gordo seemed to think he'd find it. Wasn't in a file marked "miscellaneous," which is where Spengler expected it to be. Once he saw that the search was going to be a protracted one, Gordo reluctantly realized he must have stuck the lady's card in his wallet by mistake.

Spengler said, "You dupe a tape for her? What did she pay you?"

"Shit," Gordo said. "Just one. Hey, for a hundred bucks, you'da done it."

"I'd have told my boss about it," Spengler said.

"Hey, I figured it didn't have anything to do with this place. You know what those PIs do. It's some guy cheating on his wife is all. None of Foundation's business."

Spengler blew out a breath and looked at me. I shrugged.

"I want that tape," Spengler said.

Gordo said, "Well, I ain't got it no more. She didn't show, so I tossed it."

"Which one was it?"

"We ain't got it no more. Some February, March shit. Nothing special. It's been taped over five times by now. Hey, sorry. Sorry I brought it up."

Spengler asked him a couple of other sharp questions—about the female PI, about missing packages, mail gone astray, everything down to lost umbrellas, but to no avail. Gordo had decided to clam. I didn't think he was holding back. Spengler offered me the other PI's business card and I gave it a quick glance before tucking it in a pocket. No one I knew.

"I'll be sure to let Eddie know how much I appreciate your help." I shook Spengler's hand.

"Thanks," he said. "You give PIs a good name."

"Not like that other bitch," Gordo muttered.

Spengler gave him a look that said his days with Foundation were numbered.

CHAPTER 28

My cell shrilled as I walked back to the car. It was Chaney. He said he couldn't meet me at Improvisational Technologies after all. His teaching assistant desperately needed to go over tomorrow's class work; a review was essential.

I accepted the weak excuse without protest. "Not a problem. Tell me, did Denali Brinkman ever work at Impro?"

"No. She was an undergrad."

"Did she ever visit?"

"I think so." He sounded hesitant. "Occasionally. We went in late at night. None of my colleagues would have seen her with me."

The lovers would have appeared together on the surveillance tapes. I pictured the unknown PI in the small room I'd just vacated, viewing the flickering screen, watching. Watching for what? For whom? If I hadn't already known the identity of Chaney's blackmailer, I might have imagined that the other PI, someone less than honest, worked for him, scouting possible victims.

I'd seen Dowling pick up the money with my own eyes, but maybe I'd jumped to the wrong conclusion. Maybe Benjy was the one working for someone else, someone who'd tired of him, killed him, and now wanted Chaney to pay for the crime.

My client murmured another apology and hung up.

Who else would have hired an investigator? A competing drug-development company wouldn't be interested in exits and entrances. Margo Chaney's aristocratic face flashed through my mind, Mrs. Chaney, practically bedridden. She'd asked whether I was the kind of investigator you hired if you suspected your husband was unfaithful.

I glanced at my watch: 3:30. The business card I removed from my pocket was battered, as though Gordo, the guard, had crumpled it before smoothing it into his wallet, but it was legible, black print on cream-colored stock. Helen Orza, Investigations. No address, but a phone number with a 603 area code. New Hampshire, the Live Free or Die state. I settled into my car, which had been neither towed nor ticketed, despite the steak house's dire warning, and reached for my cell.

I got a recorded message. "Hey, it's Helen. Leave your number, hon, and I'll get back to you." Very professional, I thought sourly. I left a message, emphasizing that it was urgent. The lack of address was frustrating, but I didn't think it odd, not for a woman in this business. I wondered fleetingly if the phone was a cell, if the woman worked out of her local Starbucks. I could find her in a cross-referenced directory if I had to, provided the number wasn't for a cell.

All I needed was for this damned hydra case to sprout a head from New Hampshire. Not that New Hampshire's far away, but why couldn't Helen Orza have lived on Memorial Drive, along my pathway home? On the way to Harvard's Admissions office?

I checked my battery, then used the phone again, this time to call Fitch's office. Yes, the receptionist recalled my visit. I told her how extremely grateful I was for her help, explained that while she'd given me Albert Brinkman's address and Brian Dowling's address earlier in the day—she did remember that, didn't she?—I'd forgotten to get the name of the gentleman at Harvard's Admissions office who'd been so helpful to Mr. Fitch in the Brinkman matter.

She informed me that Mr. Fitch was unavailable. News flash. I feigned dismay, intimated that I'd probably lose my job because of my dumb, dumb mistake. My boss *really* needed that name.

She was young, new to the job. She wanted everyone to like her and she didn't want me to get in trouble. She zapped me on hold, then came back a few seconds later to eagerly reveal that Horace Matheson was the name I wanted. I thanked her gravely. She wasn't going to last long in the legal business.

I hung a quick left out of the steak house's lot. Fitch, the lawyer, had given me the gift of advice: Don't discuss Brinkman's sudden withdrawal from the case with Harvard's legal representative; talk to someone in Admissions instead. Was it genuine advice, or a stall? You don't get to work in Admissions unless you have some discretion, and I wondered what tool I could use to pry information out of Matheson. Brinkman was dead; there was no compelling reason for her file to remain confidential, but there was no compelling reason to release information, either.

The office for undergrad admissions is housed in Byerly Hall, one of three main buildings linked by colonnades in dignified Radcliffe Yard, between Brattle and Garden streets. The building's known less for its architecture than for the multiple chimneys that vent the laboratories inside. They worked well; instead of stinking of chemicals, the entryway smelled of old books and fresh coffee, and I wondered if Harvard had found a way to bottle the scent, like new-car spray.

I followed discreet signs to the Admissions office. It was high-ceilinged and spacious, with a reception desk set far enough from the door to allow easy entry. When I asked to see Mr. Matheson, the receptionist gave me raised eyebrows and a quick once-over.

"You have an appointment?"

I handed over a card. "I can wait."

I can wait—the most fearsome words a receptionist hears. The dark-haired woman eyed my card, caught private investigator, and hesitated, one hand on the telephone, considering, perhaps, the effect the announcement that a private investigator wished to see Mr. Matheson might have on the assembled doting parents and potential students.

"I'll be right back," she said firmly as she disappeared down the hall.

The waiting area had twin sofas, four upholstered chairs, two reading lamps, and a coffee table stacked with copies of *Harvard Magazine* and the *Harvard Crimson,* the undergraduate newspaper. A young man with a stalk for a neck and wire-rimmed glasses sat next to his similarly long-necked mother on one of the sofas. They clutched various maps of the area. A teenage girl, wearing a black suit, occupied one of the armchairs. Her attire was designed to make her look more sophisticated, but it wasn't working. She kept staring around the office and grinning widely. Every time someone entered, she glanced up eagerly, as though expecting Tommy Lee Jones to stroll through the room. No, not Tommy Lee. Her age, she'd be happier with Matt Damon or Ben Affleck. Natalie Portman. I wondered whether Harvard would live up to her expectations. A youngster who looked barely sixteen had another chair. He read the *Wall Street Journal* with devoted intensity.

One reason I was so willing to wait was that I'd brought my reading material with me. I sat as far as I could from the door, the desk, other people. I didn't want anyone peering at Denali Brinkman's autopsy report over my shoulder.

Here's the deal: When I was a cop, the guys made a big production out of trying to gross out the rookie broad. They made book on how long I'd be able to stand waiting in a stifling bedroom with a bloated corpse for the ME's crew to show up and haul the body away, on whether I'd puke during autopsies. I'd steeled myself, and little by little, by not passing out, not crying off, refusing to react, I passed the stupid hazing ritual.

The yellow envelope measured ten by fourteen. I opened the string closure and slid out seven typed pages.

The name on the initial sheet was Jane Doe, but someone had crossed it out with typed *X*'s and written in "Denali Brinkman." "Approximate Age" came next: "20–30 years." "Sex: female. Height: 60" (residual). Weight: not applicable."

Residual height meant the body had been so badly charred that portions of it were missing. I skipped to the findings section, read that the cause of death was asphyxiation due to the inhalation of smoke, with carbon deposits in the tracheobronchial tree. The inhalation of carbon monoxide was also listed, with carboxyhemoglobin saturation at 15 percent. Global charring with some body mutilation. Inhalation of smoke meant that Denali had been alive when the fire was set. She hadn't been murdered first. The arson wasn't a blind. So much for that theory. I flipped the pages, looking for the tox-screen results.

Ethanol: negative in the blood, positive in the urine. I wasn't sure what that meant. Positive for carbon monoxide. I scanned the list. Amphetamines, barbituates, benzodiazepines. A positive hit on the benzos, but what did that signify? Anyone planning to kill herself, certainly anyone planning to kill herself in such a terrible way, might have taken whatever drugs she had on hand. Why save them?

The receptionist's voice startled me. "Miss Carlyle?"

I shielded the pages. "Yes."

"Mr. Matheson will be tied up for some time. Perhaps you'd care to make an appointment for another day."

"No," I said. "I'm fine."

"Perhaps you'd care to mention what this concerns?"

"I've just spoken with Ted Fitch, and I have some questions concerning Denali Brinkman."

She nodded crisply, turned, and made tracks down the hall again. I went back to the beginning of the autopsy report, learned that the body had been presented to the ME in a blue body bag, that it was wrapped in a tannish white sheet, that the remains were mixed with a quantity of collapsed and burned construction debris, including drywall and fragmented glass. The body had been basically intact, but the distal phalanges of the right foot were broken away. Soft tissue was extensively charred and macerated, and had a moist, pasty texture. I turned the page to the internal examination, read about Brinkman's cardiovascular, pulmonary, and gastrointestinal systems. A life weighed in grams. The last line on page seven read "Identification made from dentals records."

Beaubien had included a glassine envelope of autopsy photos. I hoped he'd copied them, not stolen them. I'd known he'd get them somehow, wouldn't want me to miss the gore.

The room smelled faintly of lilac. There were soothing paintings on the walls, one of them a view of the old Yard, dominated by Massachusetts Hall. A stern-faced portrait hung over the fireplace, probably one of the early presidents of the university. There was a framed photo of a young John F. Kennedy in graduation robes and mortarboard, one of seven U.S. presidents who had attended Harvard. Every so often, the young man with the newspaper cast a reverent eye at the picture.

Where had they come from, these young people? Harvard admits from every state in the union, as well as from overseas, and takes pride in the diversity of its freshman class. These kids all looked the same, polished and well dressed, bright and white.

I was avoiding the autopsy photos. Another young woman entered the room, glancing around with apparent delight, her face dimpling as she gave her name to the receptionist. Had Denali Brinkman come here to take her freshman tour? Had she sat on the edge of her seat, wondering whether JFK had sat there before her?

Photos are photos—no more, no less. They don't include the smell of charred flesh. Still, I'd never seen a body so badly burned, so blistered and charred. It was a human figure, no doubt about that, but— I inadvertently raised my hand to my mouth, but I don't think I made a noise.

The photos were safely back in their envelope, so I must have put them there. I could understand why the ID had been made through the teeth. I couldn't see anyone—father, mother, lover—recognizing that ghastly, blackened, skeletal face. I paged through, found the dental chart. All thirty-two teeth, three cavities.

The cheerful young woman in the black suit was ushered to an inner office. The stalk-necked boy and his mother followed. I felt inside my backpack, found a banana with intact skin, fairly well browned, but edible. I wasn't hungry after what I'd been viewing, but it was nice to know I'd have something to fall back on when it got late.

The receptionist called my name. I stood, anticipating success, and approached her desk.

"Mr. Matheson said to tell you he's referring all queries concerning Ms. Brinkman to Legal Services. He suggests you make an appointment."

"He won't see me."

"Correct."

I considered my options. I could lurk by the back door of Byerly. Fine, except I didn't know what Matheson looked like. I could stake out the parking area, but I didn't know what kind of car he drove, if any. If I worked smack in Harvard Square, I sure wouldn't bother with a car. I'd take the T.

Frustration ate at me, but I had no string to pull. I didn't know why Albert Brinkman had changed his mind about suing Harvard, and I didn't know what it had to do with the office of undergrad admissions. Possibly, Theodore Fitch had pulled a fast one; maybe there was nothing to know.

I'd go home, call Geary. Call Beaubien, thank him for the report. I swallowed a bitter taste and took a final look around the elegant room, trying not to think about what fire had done to perfect Denali Brinkman, rowing champion, petite, blond, brilliant Denali. At perfect Harvard.

I glanced at the young man with the *Wall Street Journal*, who was still waiting, still hoping for the big yes, the dream future. I felt sad, and it wasn't just from staring at the photos of Denali's body. I felt sad for the teens who sat in the perfect armchairs, and for the teens who'd never sit there, for the hopeful and the hopeless. I considered the earnest young man. What did he expect? That this storied place would somehow change him, mold him, make him into someone special and different and unique? I pondered the new crop of Harvard freshmen, culled from the best and the brightest, the small fish about to take a dive into the big pool.

Would they find success here, or failure? Would they find despair? Like Denali Brinkman.

CHAPTER 29

My cell had been getting a workout. I decided to make a few calls from home, use the bathroom, grab a Pepsi without paying two bucks for the privilege. I'm glad to report I'd already visited the facilities when all hell broke loose.

"All hell" may seem extreme when used to describe two teenage girls, but believe me, it's not. When I encountered them as I stepped out of the bathroom into the hall, I didn't recognize the first one, period. What the hell is she— I stopped even as my mouth opened to ask her the question. The second one was Paolina, but not Paolina as I'd seen her before.

My little sister, five three, barely fifteen years old, has got the all-American ideal figure, the heavy breasts and boyish hips, and the whole package was practically on full display. She wore shorts that started low on her hips and ended high on her thighs, with a waistline drawstring begging to be tugged. Her shirt was—well, it was transparent, and she wasn't wearing a bra. She was perched on heels I wouldn't wear to impersonate a hooker, a thankless task I used to perform for the police department.

"That's not what you're wearing to the party." The words were out of my mouth before I could stop them.

She and her friend goggled at me. The friend—I recognized her now—Aurelia—my God, she'd grown—wore a skirt the size of a Band-Aid, paired with a low-cut tank top. Both girls wore makeup, their lips glossily painted, their lashes caked with mascara.

"You gotta problem?" Aurelia asked.

I considered possible retorts, knew enough to watch my mouth. "Halloween, right?" wouldn't go over big, and they wouldn't know what I meant if I asked whether I should drop them off at the Greyhound bus station, where the professionals congregate.

I sucked in a deep breath. One of the things about kids, one of the saving graces, is that when you look at them, you see more than a simple imprint; you see layers. When I look at Paolina, I see her at fifteen, yes, but underneath I see the faint outline of the twelve-year-old, the ten-year-old, the little girl. When she was small, Paolina dressed up as a policeman, as a fireman, trying on life. She was trying on femininity now, and I knew I had to be careful.

"Paolina," I said. "Look at me."

She clenched her jaw.

"Aurelia, you're not my responsibility. You can wear whatever you like. You can leave or you can stay, but if you stay, you'll be quiet."

She pulled a face but kept her mouth shut.

"Come into my room. There's a better mirror, better light."

I led them in, watched as they pranced in front of the full-length glass. To my eyes, they were just this side of ridiculous, just this side of pathetic. They looked like plastic dolls, like wanna-be Barbies. But that was through my eyes. Through theirs, they were glamorous, sexy women. Hot.

"Do the shoes hurt, Paolina?" I sat on the unmade bed, feeling creaky and ancient, at least ninety-five.

"No. Not really."

"They *will* hurt," I said. "You could sprain an ankle. No more volleyball."

"So?"

"I think we need to compromise here."

"I'm not gonna wear the same thing I wear to school," she said. "It's a party. And I was gonna wear a bra. I just couldn't decide what color."

What color would be moot with a different shirt. It's so damn unfair, I thought, how quickly kids grow up, how fast their bodies mature, how slowly caution catches up.

"Do you remember the perfume?" I asked Paolina. "My very best perfume."

"That Sam gave you." She sat on the floor, cross-legged, a child and a woman, and Aurelia joined her, a tumble of color on the rug. I should have known that's what Paolina would remember about the perfume, that a man gave it to me. She'd always adored Sam.

"What about perfume?" asked Aurelia. "Oops, sorry. I'm like not supposed to talk."

Paolina said, "When I was like a baby—"

"You were nine."

"I poured it all over me. I must have used a tablespoon."

"A shovel," I said. "She had to take two baths," I told Aurelia. "We could have bottled the bathwater and sold it as eau de cologne."

"It wasn't that bad," my sister said, but she was smiling. It's one of her favorite tales. She's always loved retelling the stories of her childhood with me, the time she almost got lost at Fenway Park, the day she crashed her bike into a rosebush. Once, she told me she didn't think her mother remembered any stories about her, just stories about her brothers.

"You remember what I said?" I asked.

"I'm not sure." She knew; she was teasing.

"Come on," I said.

" 'A little bit goes a long way.' " We spoke it together, singsong. She said it in Spanish and I stuck to English.

"I think we've hit another one of those moments, honey. You are beautiful. You are both so beautiful." Girls, especially girls who grow up without fathers, need to hear those words often, I think. I tell Paolina how beautiful she is at every opportunity, but I'm afraid she'll never believe it until she hears it from a man old enough to be her father. "But right now, the way you're dressed is like way too much perfume."

"The boys like it."

"You like a guy wears his shirt open to his belly button, his pants so tight that you can see everything he's got?"

Aurelia giggled.

"It's better to be cool," I said. "Understated. Sophisticated. Give them a hint, a little taste." I wanted to wrap them both in heavy over-coats, but I knew it wouldn't fly. "Paolina, if you wash your face and start over, pick some clothes that whisper instead of shout, you can wear my perfume tonight. Just a touch."

God knows it wasn't what I wanted to say. I wanted to lock her in her room and forbid her to ever wear anything half that revealing. I wanted to preach at her, warn her to be careful what she pretended to be, because when you dress up for a role and play it in the real world, it's a role you can get stuck with forever. I remembered my father's angry red face as he yelled similar phrases. I remembered how little they'd meant to me then, and I held my tongue.

"Could I still wear this blouse? With a black bra?"

"A white one would look better. But different pants, maybe those pale blue ones. And sandals? You've got such pretty feet."

Aurelia asked my opinion on her outfit then, and the conversation loosened up. They scrubbed off the mascara and started over. I let them use some glittery powder I'd gotten as a free sample, and they took turns sniffing my special-occasion perfume. Finally I took charge of the flask and told them that if they passed muster when they came down to my office, I'd instruct them in the art of perfume application.

I paused in the hallway and inhaled deeply, aware that I'd escaped a potential disaster, escaped to fight another day. Why, I wondered as I made my way downstairs, do I keep my temper in check when I deal with Paolina, let it rip when I'm with Leon? I care about my little sister. We've been together a long time. I love her and I need our relationship to last. I guess I didn't feel that way about Leon, not yet. Maybe I was testing him in some way, trying to see what he'd put up with. Maybe I was good with kids, lousy with men.

I didn't fight with Sam Gianelli. That's not how I lost him. I could go back to him tomorrow; he'd be there. I almost laughed, almost. There I was, a grown woman, telling myself a fairy tale as "happily ever after" childish as any the girls in my bedroom could have invented. If I went back to Sam, he'd still be who he was and I'd still be who I am. He'd still be mob and I'd still be a cop.

Downstairs, I phoned Geary, but he wasn't in. I didn't leave a message, decided to bypass the lawyer completely, place a call to Albert Brinkman in Lausanne, Switzerland, instead. Hear it from the horse's mouth.

It was six hours later in Switzerland, night. I might haul old Monsieur Brinkman out of a soft bed. I had a picture of him in my head, white-haired and frail, too ill to attend his niece's funeral. I didn't want to alarm the man. I twisted a strand of hair around my index finger, yanked, decided to risk it. I punched fifteen digits, the phone rang five times, and then the answering machine addressed me in rapid-fire French. I left a message in English, kicked back in my chair, crossed my legs on my desk, and closed my eyes.

I imagined Paolina showing up at the Harvard Admissions office in her ill-chosen party clothes, the glances she'd attract. How did kids learn to present themselves when they came from backgrounds like Paolina's? What chance did they have? And yet, should everyone have to march to the same drummer, pass through the same cookie cutter, buy the same black suit in order to enter the hallowed portals?

How Denali Brinkman's application must have delighted Harvard's Admissions officers. Here was no cookie-cutter kid. What could be better, a smart athlete, a student from a nontraditional background who could be counted as a minority to boot, part American Indian? Harvard keeps track of all sorts of statistics on the makeup of its freshman class, from racial background to the state from which they hail. Where was Denali from? The rower at the Weld had mentioned a western state, Idaho or Wyoming. Not many applied to Harvard from those big open-air states, nothing like the stacks of applications from New York and Massachusetts. Harvard tried for balance in its freshman class, and with so many applicants, it could pick and choose. Denali was tailor-made, a perfect fit, I thought, and the phrase was still in my head when I opened my eyes and noticed the new and unusual paperweight on my desk.

The statuette was small, no more than six or seven inches high. It had a base of silver, topped by crossed oars in gold. It was battered, the rightmost oar bent. I touched it hesitantly, thinking that Denali Brinkman, the beautiful woman in the photo, the terrible corpse in the morgue shots, had touched it as well. Her fingerprints were on the statuette, but what did that matter now? I picked it up.

The note underneath was in Roz's eccentric hand. "Got this from Jeannie St. Cyr at Phillips House. She says thanks. Likes her doctor. Hopes this will help you remember your friend Denali."

I turned it in my hand. It didn't look like a reward for winning a major race, an Olympic qualifier, more like a high school or camp trophy. Maybe it had been a big race, but a third-place finish, an honorable mention. I checked the silver base for printing, had to pick up a magnifying glass to make it out.

Harsha Lake. Junior Women's IX. 1987.

I read it a second time, fingering the engraved letters. In 1987, Denali Brinkman would have been five years old. Someone else's trophy? Who keeps other people's trophies? You might keep your mother's cherished awards or your sister's. If Denali's mother had been old enough to bear a child in '82, she would hardly have been a junior rower in '87. Denali had no sister.

I considered Denali Brinkman, the Admissions officers' dream come true, recalled the fairy-tale quality of Chaney's reveries. So sophisticated, so mature. Not like the others. Amazing for a girl her age.

What if Denali wasn't a girl her age?

I stared at the silent phone. The entire house, seemed eerily quiet and I wondered what Paolina and her friend were up to now. Why had Albert Brinkman dropped the lawsuit? Because the people at the Admissions office had finally done some belated research, knew that Denali had falsified her application, threatened a countersuit for theft of services? It was certainly possible that Denali Brinkman had falsified her application, that she was older than she claimed to be. I reopened the autopsy file, shuffled through the pages. Yes. "Approximate Age," it said, "20–30 years." No one had made a note of the discrepancy because they saw what they were meant to see: Denali Brinkman, Harvard freshman. And what was a year or two in the scheme of things?

I thought of the girls upstairs, striving to look older, more sophisticated, then considered the opposite: a woman dressed as a girl. It would be easy, especially for a woman as slight as Denali Brinkman.

"Roz," I yelled. No answer.

I grabbed the statuette, holding it tightly, as though it were the only solid thing in this whole damn case, and maybe it was. What else did I have? A fistful of blackmail notes hidden between the layers of T.C.'s litter box. What was the term Roz had used to describe Chaney's clinical trials? *Double-blind,* that was it. I felt like I was groping in the dark. If Denali hadn't been the person she claimed to be, was my client off the hook? I didn't think so. No. He might be off the hook for screwing a student under twenty, but that was the least of his problems now. He was in danger of getting caught on a sharper hook—for running down Benjy Dowling.

Footsteps. I glanced up as Roz came pounding down the stairs, her hair dyed a brassy gold, which looked almost normal till she turned around and displayed the blue stripes in back. She started talking as soon as she entered the living room: "Mrs. Guzman knew all about the *quinciana.* Leon called and wanted to know whether you could—"

"Where is Harsha Lake?" My inquiry stopped her.

"Is there a prize?"

"Find an atlas," I said. "My aunt had one. It's in the guest room, I think, or—"

"Find it faster on-line," she said.

"I don't care how you do it. Just find out where it is, what race was held there in 1987, and who won this trophy."

"Right now?" she asked. "But I was going to—"

"I'll try the atlas; you go on-line."

My great-aunt's old *National Geographic Atlas*, which I found after a lengthy search under a clump of laundry in Paolina's room, went straight from Harsewinkel, Germany, to Harskamp, Netherlands. When I hurried back to the living room, Roz was still hunched over the screen and the girls hadn't appeared to claim their perfume. I tried the New Hampshire number again, left another message for Helen Orza, used the word *urgent* again. I considered calling Leon, leaving him a message, too, saying I was thinking of him but was too busy to talk, too busy to meet. I knew what he'd think of that. I wished we'd known each other years ago, maybe when I was in school, when life wasn't so hectic.

I didn't know how to tell him that finding out who'd won a race in 1987 on a lake I'd never heard of took precedence over spending time with him. I only knew it was true. I could pretend it was otherwise, but who the hell would I be pretending for? I ate leftover Chinese food, drank a Rolling Rock. The phone rang just as the two girls came parading down the stairs. I waved them off, holding up my index finger to indicate I'd only be a minute, and answered.

A man. I'd been hoping so hard for the female PI, I'd convinced myself it would be her. If this guy was selling aluminum siding, he was going to get an earful.

"Hey, Miss Carlyle, right? You called to speak to Helen Orza?" If I'd had to pick one word to describe his voice, it would have been *gravelly*. If I'd gotten a second choice, I'd have gone for *annoyed*.

"Yes."

"From Massachusetts, right? Six one seven?"

"Yes."

"You seen her?"

"I want to speak to her. I'm a private investigator, and I'm wondering if we might be tugging on ends of the same case."

"Oh. She come to see you when she was there?" He also sounded like he'd had more than one beer.

"No."

"Well, thanks for calling."

"Wait a minute. Who are you? When can I speak to Ms. Orza?"

"Hell if I know. Sorry, sorry. It's been a long day and I thought maybe—" His voice drifted off.

"When do you expect Helen in?"

"I dunno. Long time since she's gotten a call."

"Who are you? Do you work with Helen?"

"Not all the time, but sometimes. I'm freelance, pretty much."

"Would you know if Helen was working for a woman named Chaney? Margo Chaney?"

"Name's not familiar. Don't ring a bell, ya know? If you've got something you want Helen to work on, maybe I could help you out. Anything Helen could do for you, I could do. Pretty much. I'm not licensed like her, but I'm good. I'm Phil. Phil's my name."

"Phil what?"

"Gagnon."

I wrote it down. "Phil, you have a number for Helen down here?"

"Ah, no."

"You have access to her files?"

"Well, yeah, but I—I don't know if I should—"

Shit. He sounded dumb as a brick, and slow to boot. "Phil, what's your address? What city are you in?"

He rattled numbers and streets. Epping, New Hampshire.

"Listen, Phil. I'm going to be in your office in an hour, maybe less."

"What?"

"You or Helen should be there to meet me. I'll make it worth your while."

"What's that mean, worth my while? I'm not sitting on my fanny no hour."

"Solid money," I said, "for solid information. I need to know who Helen's working for in Boston. You'd be able to tell me that, wouldn't you?"

"Well, yeah," Phil Gagnon allowed.

"An hour." I drive fast, and New Hampshire's not far. I wasn't sure, but I thought Epping was near Exeter. Had a speedway. Near Rockingham Park, too.

"It's gonna cost you at least a C," he said.

"Fine." I hung up before he changed his mind. If he were smart, he'd have waited and let me make the first offer.

Paolina still looked old enough, sexy enough to bring a lump to my throat, but she'd toned the tramp factor way down. I convinced her that she'd look better with her hair styled differently, then finished her off with a light touch of perfume. I gave Aurelia only a cursory glance before anointing her as well. I didn't want Gagnon to get tired of waiting and leave.

CHAPTER 30

I could have dialed Leon, arranged to eat dinner at Centro, quiet, with a candlelit table, savory soup, flavorful pasta. We could have hashed out our troubles over martinis or a bottle of Italian red, come back to my place, spent a very agreeable night. I could have driven to New Hampshire in the morning.

Instead I took Cambridge Street to the Monsignor O'Brien Highway and the O'Brien to the Gilmore Bridge, all the while trying to isolate the concrete facts, the line-by-line justification for jumping behind the wheel now, at the tail end of rush hour, but all I could locate was a deep and undefined sense of urgency, a cloud of menace, a visceral tug.

I'm not given to premonitions. I disregard shooting stars, looming ladders, and black cats that stray across my path. Shit like that annoys me, if it has any effect at all, but I couldn't help myself. I needed to follow up on the Orza business *immediately*. I felt uneasy, for Chaney and for myself. The prickles down my spine I'd experienced on and off since visiting Dowling's buddy Church were strong, an undercurrent I couldn't ignore.

I cast a glance at the rearview mirror. It was twilight and growing darker by the minute. Only a few drivers had flicked on their headlights. Cars seemed gray and shadowy in the fading light. I reached into the compartment under the center armrest, grabbed a tape at random, got Rory Block's *I'm Every Woman,* and stuck it in the deck.

Whenever I head north from Boston, I try to take the coast road, old route 1A, so I can hug the coastline, watch the small fishing boats dart out to sea and back to port. I admire the grace of the sailboats, but the small fishing boats are my favorites, the working boats. Today, opting for speed over beauty, I took Route 1 to Interstate 95, the impersonal eight-lane monster roadway. I felt the lure of the coast towns as I passed the tempting signs, pictured the rocky Gloucester coast, the long, low dunes of Crane's Beach in Ipswich. The speed limit was sixty, the traffic doing seventy. The drivers in the left lane were doing eighty and so was I. I watched for state troopers, slowed whenever passing southbound drivers flashed their lights in the universal warning, and made it as far as Portsmouth, New Hampshire, in good time.

The sun sank slowly, the clouds growing suddenly pink before giving up their color as the sky turned gray. Headlights bloomed and I added mine to the glow, stretching my spine and yawning from the sheer repetitiveness of the broken white lines and speeding cars. I love to drive, but highway driving's not my thing, no challenge to it, just join the herd and press the pedal. I consider city driving a competitive sport. I relish narrow, curvy coast roads. I took the Route 101 exit toward Exeter and the Hamptons, put my car on autopilot and my mind on the Chaney case.

Five months ago, in January, something must have happened, something must have changed at Improvisational Technologies. Their long-term security service had been suddenly deemed inadequate and Foundation had been hired instead. Foundation wasn't a small-time outfit, nor was it cheap. Spengler had insisted it was a real gig, not window dressing. Possibly Chaney's affair with Denali Brinkman had been cooling down at about the same time. The lovers had supposedly split a month before she died in the April blaze. The fire department's response time had been compromised by a spate of false alarms.

Chaney got the first blackmail note, then the second, then hired me to stop the blackmailer.

There were false alarms the night Benjy Dowling died, as well. Dowling had cleaned offices at Impro under an assumed name. Denali Brinkman had been close to Chaney, but then she got close to Dowling. Dowling was an ex-con, who always got caught because he gilded the lily. According to his parole officer, the man couldn't leave well enough alone.

I took the Route 125 exit, fewer cars on the road now, three ahead of me, a couple in the rearview mirror. I hoped Helen Orza would be waiting at her office when I got there, but if not, I'd deal with Phil Gagnon. On the tape, Rory Block sang an a cappella spiritual called "Ain't No Grave Can Hold My Body Down," and it seemed as if I could almost see Denali Brinkman's face superimposed over my faint reflection in the windshield, the grainy face in the news photo, the beautiful face in the shot I'd gotten from Theodore Fitch, the lawyer.

"Who are you?" I thought, and was surprised to find I'd spoken out loud. Too much solitude. Too many miles over too much road. Where did you come from, girl, and why did you lie about your age? Was Denali your given name? When and why did you decide to become Denali? How did you make the cut at Harvard? How did you die? What did you mean in that last cryptic note—"Time to delve for deeper shades of meaning"?

I made a right onto a narrow road more to my liking, killed the music, picked up my cell phone, and punched in Danny Burkett's number. He was off duty, so I tried his home number, which I'd gotten courtesy of Roz.

He didn't sound pleased to hear from me. Quite possibly, he'd have preferred a call from my tenant.

"You find Dowling's TransAm?" I asked.

"Not a trace. Coulda been stolen. It'll turn up. They always do."

"You read the autopsy report on Denali Brinkman?" I asked.

Silence. "Yeah. Why?"

"You wonder why she was so badly burned?" A car passed on my left and I quickly checked my speedometer. I hate it when cell-chatting drivers slow way down. I was doing better than the limit. Guy probably knew the road better than I did.

Burkett said, "It doesn't keep me up nights. One of the fire guys, he said maybe she soaked a sheet in gasoline, spread it over herself from top to toe. That was one woman who wanted to die."

"What if she didn't?" I said.

Silence. "You there?" I didn't think I'd fallen into a cell-reception black hole, but his lack of response made me wary.

"Yeah."

"Come on, let's take it without our buddy Benjy Dowling, without the boyfriend who turns up and tells the sad story. I looked at the tox screen, and she was positive for benzos. Could have been Rohypnol, you know, 'roofies,' that date-rape shit."

"This wasn't rape, Carlyle. It was *suicide*."

"It looked like suicide. But think about it. How do you get somebody to lie down quietly and not make a fuss no matter what the hell you do to her? You give her that roofie shit, she's out of it in maybe twenty, thirty minutes. You cover her with a sheet soaked in gasoline."

"Gasoline she bought herself at the station on Mount Auburn Street, telling that whole tale about running out of gas when she had no fucking car."

"Benjy Dowling's TransAm could have run out of gas. Benjy could have sent her to the station, told her the guys would raz him but that a girl would get sympathy."

"That's weak."

"But possible. Don't you think Dowling was a little too helpful?"

"You think he killed her?"

I'd been conscious of lights in my rear window for some time, slowly gaining on me. I hadn't sped up; I was going fast enough for this road. There were plenty of places where the yellow line gave way to a broken line and passing was possible.

"I think he was involved," I said.

"And she wrote herself a snuff note because he asked her to? What is this shit? Who are you working for?"

This time when I glanced in my rearview mirror, the headlights were almost on top of me. They changed to brights, dazzling my eyes. The bastard wasn't slowing down, either, wasn't pulling out to pass. I floored it and swore.

"What's the hell's that?" Burkett said. "Where are you?"

"Burkett, listen, I'm on the road. I've got a drunk or some lunatic on my tail."

"You on the Artery?"

Damn it. I let go of the phone, grabbed the steering wheel with both hands, and wrenched it to the right. The road here was tight, suddenly hilly and narrow. Dark, fewer streetlamps, fewer cars. The vehicle behind me was bigger than my Toyota, some kind of small truck, or maybe an SUV. It smacked against my rear bumper and for a moment I was almost lifted off the road. Then the car came down with a thud and a sag of the rear axle.

I had to wrestle the wheel just to keep the car on the road at this speed. If I accelerated, I didn't think the tires would hold the tight turns. On the other hand, if I didn't speed, I'd get rammed.

I steadied the wheel, pressed the accelerator, consciously relaxed my shoulders, and ordered myself, Breathe, damn it, breathe. Telephone poles zipped by the windows, trees, fields bordered by stone fences. By the time I spotted turnoffs, it was too damn late to take them, and even if I could have taken them, where the hell would I have been headed? Signs passed in unreadable blurs. I honked at a Honda, pulled out, and passed him at a lunatic speed, the SUV on my tail. Use your cell, I silently told the Honda's driver. Call the cops. Turn me in. I could hear Burkett squawking from the phone somewhere on the seat, but I couldn't lift a hand off the wheel.

"New Hampshire," I yelled. "I'm in New Hampshire. Epping, I think. No, I'm not on the main drag; I took a left and then a right fork. I don't know what the hell the name of the road is!" I kept up a crazed monologue, describing the surroundings. No urban landmarks, no

251

Store 24, no Citgo sign, just stands of dark oak and maple, aspen and birch, mile markers that flashed by too quickly to read. Where were the gas stations, the other cars, the hunky truck drivers with CB radios? This was southern New Hamspshire, not the Great Sandy Desert. This stretch of road was probably well travelled six nights a week, and I'd picked lucky seven.

I crested a hill, saw the diamond yellow sign too late, then the sharply curving arrow to the left. Still, I might have made the adjustment if the SUV hadn't bounced off my rear fender, shoving, pushing, grinding me into the guardrail with a metallic shriek. The guardrail ended too soon, abruptly, and then my car left the road and I was braking and steering through trees, careening downhill. There were saplings at first; small, they broke like matchsticks, making sharp cracking sounds. The car bucked and leaped. My head smacked the padded ceiling, then something harder. I strained to keep my hands on the wheel. Larger trees loomed. *Turn off the ignition!* I had to turn off the damned ignition, but how the hell could I with my hands tight on the wheel, clamped to it like a bolt? How could I let go? I rode the brake, tried to guide the car down a treeless path on a wooded slope at night, bring it safely to a halt.

Impossible.

CHAPTER 31

I may have been conscious when the ambulance came. I have a bumpy memory of people and noise and searing pain, of figures in jumpsuits and hands probing and testing, of getting strapped onto a gurney, but the images faded in and out, clear, then fuzzy, and then something was over my face. I struggled against the mask and the restraints, fought against going down, down.

I knew he was in the room when I woke the second time. Before I opened my eyes, I knew by the scent, by the hand on my wrist, by the gold band of a pinkie ring that Sam Gianelli was present, so I kept my eyes closed for one delicious second longer, unwilling to let go of the fantasy.

He was there when I opened my eyes, seated in a metal chair at the side of my narrow bed. I blinked, shut both eyes quickly, reopened them to narrow slits. Without turning my head, I could see the sharp creases in his gray pants, the pearl buttons on the deep blue shirt. Gold cuff links. A lock of hair at his left temple had lightened almost to silver. The sight of it made my throat contract, my eyes blur.

The room was small and the smell, aside from the faint odor of bay rum, said hospital. White walls. No windows. Machinery crowded the space to my left, but I wasn't hooked up to any monitors. No tubes.

"What are you doing here?" I spoke softly because I didn't want the illusion to shatter, turn into some intern or resident who looked like Sam.

No response. I moved my right arm, then my left. My left shoulder felt odd, not so much painful as stretched. It was difficult to swallow. I wanted to ask whether I was going to die. Was that why he'd come? To watch me die? I felt logy and awful and my mouth tasted like the inside of a copper pipe.

"What the hell did they give me?" I spoke louder this time, resigned to the unreality of the image. If he were real, why hadn't he answered?

" 'Where am I?' " he said gravely. "That's what you're supposed to say."

It was Sam's voice, gravelly and deep. I turned my head. He looked rock-solid and steady, unfazed, but relieved, too. Familiar, but different. A little older. The tentative crease in his forehead was now a definite one. Uptilted wrinkles faded in and out at the corners of chocolate-colored eyes. A faint gray tint shaded the flesh beneath them. His chin was just as stubborn, his mouth soft and full-lipped. His suit jacket hung on the back of the wooden door.

A round clock over the door, a schoolroom clock, read 10:35. Night or morning?

"How— What—" I'm not sure what I started to ask. Sam put his right hand over my left, squeezed.

"It's okay," he said. "You dislocated your left shoulder, but it's back in the socket now. I understand putting it back hurts like hell. The medics admire your vocabulary. You also have what they're calling a mild concussion. They put a number on it, but I can't remember."

"But why—"

"Why me? You were talking to a cop when you went off the road. Remember?"

254

Danny Burkett. I tried a nod. Not a great idea. The room floated for a moment, then resettled with a lurch I felt deep in my gut.

"He did his best to give the local cops an estimate of where you were. Did a decent job. Then he rang Roz let her know what was going on. He got Paolina."

"She was at a party."

"She had a fight with somebody and went back to your place to cool off. Roz wasn't home. She didn't know what else to do, so she called me."

Paolina could have called Roz. Roz has a cell, and even if she forgets to turn it on, she can almost always be found through her boyfriend, Lemon. Paolina could have called Leon. She knows Leon's last name, and my Rolodex is centered on my desk. She could have called Gloria. But she'd called Sam.

"Sorry," I said.

"I'm not."

"No?"

"No."

"You didn't have to—"

"I know. Paolina was pretty worried. I've been calling her."

"Thanks."

"No. I mean I've kept in touch with her. I don't know whether she told you or not."

"Not."

"It wasn't a secret. She could have told you."

"She didn't." I tried to sit, then, remembering the ways of hospital beds, pressed a button on a controller that hung from the side panel of the mechanical bed. It was shaped like the remote control on a TV. "Is there any water around?"

"Hang on." There was a metal pitcher, a plastic glass. "Do you need a straw?"

"I can manage." The water was warm, but it took the copper taste away, made swallowing easier. The silence in the room grew. If the

255

schoolroom clock had made an audible tick, I'd have heard it. "Sam, that's nice of you—to call her, I mean. She's fond of you. And coming here—I don't know what to say."

He smiled. "Hey, took me an hour to knock the dents out of the armor."

"Still fits, though. On you, it looks good."

"You, I've seen look a helluva lot better."

"No fair."

"It's mainly the shiner."

I winced.

"Color's not so bad yet," he went on, "but you know how those things get."

"You're enjoying this." I'd spent time at his hospital bedside after he'd been blown up by a bomb at Gloria's cab company. I'd always thought his injury spelled the beginning of the end for us. I'd felt guilty for not preventing the bombing, not realizing the danger, and guilt eats at you. He'd almost lost the use of a leg. He still limped, but you had to study his gait to notice.

"At least you didn't break your nose," he said.

I've broken it three times, what with police work, cab driving, and volleyball.

"And your hair's back to red. I missed that the last time we—last time I saw you. I'm supposed to holler when you wake up." He made no move to press the button attached to the low railing of the bed. Instead, he edged over, sat next to me, lifted his hand to my face, and gently touched the area under my right eye. "How's that feel?"

"Okay."

He lowered his face and kissed me gently. "I've been wanting to do that for hours. I think it's some sort of Sleeping Beauty compulsion. I kept sitting there thinking that if I kissed you, you'd wake up."

"You shoulda tried it."

"I wasn't sure you'd want me to."

"Now you are?"

"The Gianelli men have healthy egos."

I didn't need any reminder that he was his father's son. What had driven us apart was his allegiance, not just to the old man but to his father's way of life. Gianelli means mob in the North End. Other Catholic kids grow up, become doctors, lawyers, priests. Gianellis go into the family business. For a while, both Sam and I thought he'd be different, but when his brother died and his dad needed help, Sam answered the call, and we said good-bye.

Now we indulged in some fairly passionate kisses, considering my condition and the restrictions of the unromantic bed, and I thought maybe it would be okay if the nurses and doctors didn't look in on us too soon.

"You're not married?" I asked him when we parted for air.

"Nah. You?"

More kisses stifled my reply. The more urgently his lips brushed mine, the more awake I felt, the more aware I became that there was some compelling reason I needed to get out of this hospital bed.

"Where am I, Sam?"

"Aha," he said. "I knew you'd get around to it. Exeter Hospital, Exeter, New Hampshire. What happened? You're too good a driver to miss a turn and fly off the road, even if you were speeding. The cop told Paolina—"

"I was shoved off the road." The anger came back, so hot that I could feel it, and with it the helplessness and rising panic: riding the brakes to the bottom of the hill, almost the bottom, certainly the bottom. The jarring, creaking stop, the echoing silence, the hiss of the engine. Fire. I'd been so afraid of fire after seeing what it had done to Denali Brinkman's body, after those terrible photos.

"Road rage?"

I swallowed. "I don't think so, Sam."

"You should file a police report."

Sure, I thought. "I've got nothing. I couldn't get the plate. I can't even give the cops a make or a model. It was dark."

"It's okay," he said.

"No," I said. "It's not."

"Why not road rage?"

Because it's too damn convenient, I thought. "Because I'm working a case. Because I came up with a lead."

"You think somebody didn't want you to follow it up?"

"Yes." I bit my lip. "So I need to find out why."

Once, he would have tried to talk me out of it, to humor me, tell me it was the concussion talking, that I needed to sleep.

"Who's Phil?" he asked.

"Phil?"

"You were talking about Phil when they brought you in. The medics wrote it down, and I wondered—"

Phil Gagnon. "Not a boyfriend, Sam. The lead."

"Not that it's any of my business," he said.

We shared a glance.

"Not that I wouldn't want it to be my business. More water?" he asked.

"Please. I ought to ring for a doctor."

"Feeling bad?"

"No." I closed my eyes. "I'm lying. Yes, I feel bad, but I've felt worse. I've got to get out of here, get discharged. I need to leave. As soon as possible. Now. I have to— Sam, what about my car? Where's my car?"

"Towed. It's not repairable."

"Shit." I stared down at my blue cotton hospital johnny. "I'll need a loaner. Did my backpack make it out of the car? I have my insurance company's number in my wallet. Damn, I'll probably need a copy of the police report."

"Everything's here, but I'm willing to provide chauffeur service."

"I can't go home yet, Sam. I appreciate it. You're wonderful. But I need to find this man."

"Hey," he said, "isn't that always how it goes?"

"Sam, he's a witness, a source—I don't know what he is. It could be a woman. I was going to talk to whichever one showed up. Or both."

"Do they live near here?"

"Pretty close. I was on my way to an address in Epping."

"If the docs will let you go, I'll drive you. Don't look a gift Porsche in the mouth."

"Sam, I can't tell how long it might take. If these people aren't in their office, I'll have to wait for them. I might have to follow this lead somewhere else."

"If it's too much, I'll drop you at a rental-car company. You'll call your insurance office, get a car. I'm not signing on for a month here, Carlotta. Just a day."

"It's morning?"

He nodded. "I tried to make them move you to a room with a window, but they were booked."

I was in a spacious single, and now I knew why. I was surprised they hadn't bowed to Sam's wishes, commandeered a room with a view. Maybe in New Hampshire, the Gianelli name didn't inspire the same kind of fear it did in Boston.

"Sam, is there a closet in here? Clothes?"

He gave me the eye.

"Sam."

"Okay, okay. There's one of these ominous hospital bags. You want me to look?"

"Hand it over."

My jeans were intact. Ditto my black jacket, which I'd placed on the seat beside me while I drove. My cell phone was there. Underwear. My white shirt was blood-spattered and ripped, sliced completely through sleeves and sides, as though they'd had to cut it off.

"Need help?"

"They probably sell some kind of T-shirt in the gift shop. A tank top, anything that'll go under the jacket. Nothing cute. If everything in the gift shop makes you shudder, don't bother. I'll keep the jacket buttoned."

"You want me to go now?"

"Yeah, but—"

"But?"

"Be sure you come back."

"Fifteen minutes. I'll send in a doc if I find one."

"I'll start doing the release routine. Sam—"

"What?"

"I don't know. I—" I wanted to say how touched I was that he'd come, how cared for he made me feel just by his presence, but I was afraid I'd start crying. I smoothed the beige wool blanket, fingered a flaw in the weave. Whatever painkiller they'd given me when they fixed my shoulder—or maybe it was the concussion—my emotions felt uncomfortably close to the surface.

"It's good to see you," he said.

"Yeah, that's what I wanted to say. It's good to see you."

As soon as the door closed, I dragged myself to a sitting position. My stomach rolled, but nothing came up, and I thought I might simply be hungry. I started to press the button on the bed rail, but my bladder advised me to delay till I'd visited the bathroom. Once there, I discovered a shower stall as well as a toilet and a sink. The lure of the shower proved stronger than my desire for immediate escape. I managed to untie the johnny, with my right hand doing most of the behind-the-back work.

I examined myself as best I could in the small square of mirror over the low sink. Sam was right: I'd looked better. The area under my eye was starting to turn purple. My shoulder didn't look half as bad as it felt. I'm a quick healer, always have been. There were welts along my right leg, the familiar scar on the other. My left side under my arm and farther down my hip had a couple of abrasions.

A well-constructed car, that Toyota. I felt a stab of keen regret, as if I'd survived a fall from a favorite horse, only to be told that the now-lame animal had to be put down. I stood under the stinging shower and let the water restore me.

Underwear, jeans. I couldn't bring myself to refasten the johnny. I slid my bra and jacket on, favoring my left shoulder, fastened the buttons. The neckline was too low for business attire, no doubt about that. I hoped Sam could find me something to fit underneath. I touched the swelling under my eye, traced the pattern of Sam's fingertips, wondered for a moment if I'd imagined his bedside presence, conjured him from dreams.

I made my way back into the small room, found my muddy shoes. I must have managed to get out of the car under my own steam. Yes, I remembered the struggle to find the keys, turn off the ignition, the terror of fire. I sank onto the bed, my legs suddenly weak.

If Paolina had called Leon instead of Sam, would Leon have forgotten our disagreements and come to fetch me? I thought so, but I wasn't sure. I felt guilty about Leon, guilty about leading him on, shutting him down. I felt as though I'd never given him a chance. Maybe we'd never had a chance, pretending from the moment we met, both working undercover, each deceiving the other. I'd been a pseudosecretary; he'd been a pseudocarpenter, each of us supposedly working a construction site. Maybe I'd always wondered why he'd fallen for that mousy-haired secretary. Maybe he'd always wondered why I'd been attracted to the carpentry foreman.

Had I known who Sam was when I'd fallen for him? He'd been my boss at Green and White Cab, Gloria's unlikely pal, co-owner of the firm. I'd been young enough to think that sleeping with the boss had nothing to do with power or politics. Just chemistry, I thought. Just the way we feel together between the sheets. I didn't ask what Sam's prospects were; he didn't say. He didn't ask whether I'd make a good Italian Catholic wife and mother. I was a future cop and a cop's daughter, and he was a born mobster, and I didn't know it. Where's the honesty in that? The lack of pretense? And what did it matter? Which was better, pretense, or the bitter knowledge, the certainty, that the person you want is a person you can't have?

The door swung open and a stern-featured woman with a stethoscope hanging around her neck like a dogtag asked me to remove my jacket so she could check my vital signs previous to discharge. I took it that Sam had muttered a few magic words in passing.

We were out in less than half an hour, me wearing a man's white ribbed undershirt, which Sam rightly thought I'd prefer to a pink T-shirt embellished with flowers and the hospital's logo.

"You're sure you're up to this?" he asked as he closed the car door.

I adjusted the leather seat via push button till it conformed to my body. The Porsche smelled like he'd just whisked it out of the showroom. Leather and wood, deep pile carpet. Sam had always had fancy cars, even when I first knew him. How had I imagined he afforded them, the co-owner of a small-time cab company?

"We'll need a New Hampshire map," I said.

"Bought one in the gift shop. Plus some chocolate bars."

"I love you, Sam."

He was who he was and I was who I was, but what was the use pretending I didn't love him? It didn't mean we were going to spend the rest of our lives together, playing Cinderella and the Prince, but what was the point in denying it?

I was surprised our combined breath didn't smoke the windshield. I know I'd have liked to find the way to the nearest hotel. Instead, I opened the map on my lap and plotted the quickest route to Epping.

CHAPTER 32

Sam drove, big hands easy on the wheel, and I found myself telling him about Chaney, the blackmail, Benjy Dowling and his hit-and-run death, grateful to be able to talk to someone who wasn't FBI or a friend of Chaney's, someone who didn't have advice to offer or an ax to grind. When I got to Denali's suicide and my reasons for believing I might be investigating two murders, rather than a murder and a suicide, his lips tightened.

"I trust you're carrying some self-defense in your backpack?" When I didn't reply, his eyes narrowed. "You were run off the road."

I hadn't been able to use my hands to grab a cell phone, much less aim a pistol. It wouldn't have helped one damn bit if I'd been carrying a rocket launcher. I was about to expound on this, when Sam mentioned that the car was equipped. It took me a minute.

Guns.

"Just thought you should know." He glanced at the rearview mirror.

I could probably be arrested for sitting in the passenger seat of Gianelli's Porsche. I sighed and told myself no, whatever weapons he had, they'd be legal and registered. Or illegal and untraceable. I didn't want to ask. Sam and I used to disagree about the usefulness of firearms. I used to be more opposed to carrying firearms than I am now. I should have been carrying, a case like this, I admit it. What good was my S&W .40 doing locked in my desk? When a case comes down to murder, a professional ought to carry.

We drove through one of those perfect New Hampshire towns, with Victorian houses and a white-steepled church, a velvety town green. We must have looked like wealthy tourists passing through in our shiny car, but there was a Beretta in the dash compartment, something with more heft in the trunk. Made me wonder what lurked behind the proper Victorian facades. I felt disoriented by the sun-dappled lanes, the luxurious car, the familiar yet unfamiliar man, as though I'd jumped backward or forward in time. I squeezed my eyes shut, hoped the queasiness was simply another aftereffect of whatever medication they'd used when they'd shoved my shoulder back into the socket.

I asked myself why whoever'd rammed me off the road hadn't come back with a gun of his own and finished the job. I'd been help-less, barely conscious down in the ravine, a sitting duck till the ambulance arrived. Had the driver figured he'd done enough? Had he thought I'd die in the crash, be seriously injured, forget about my job? Was the whole run-'em-off-the-road business unrelated to the case? Was I a raving paranoid?

Roz has a T-shirt with a tongue-in-cheek warning: JUST 'CAUSE YOU'RE PARANOID DOESN'T MEAN THEY'RE NOT AFTER YOU.

Sam's voice slipped in and interrupted my thoughts. "This guy you're supposed to meet in Epping, could he be the one who ran you off the road? I mean, who else knew you were coming?"

"I think I was tailed." I hadn't noticed the truck, but would I have noticed, with the traffic, in the twilight, in the dark?

"You want to stop for real food, or just make do with the chocolate?"

The sense of urgency was with me again, the dread, the uneasiness. "If we pass a coffee shop, I could do with about a gallon of takeout."

Belatedly, I checked my cell for messages, found that Geary had called twice, Chaney once. Face it, Sam's unexpected appearance had knocked my professionalism for a loop. I wanted to call Paolina, scold her, praise her, reassure her, but knew I wouldn't get through. She has a cell, but they make her turn it off in school.

Geary was in and had news, but first he needed to express his annoyance that I hadn't gotten back to him immediately. Just who did I think was paying my fee?

I cut him off. "I'll explain later. What's the deal?"

"Chaney was picked up. They actually arrested him. Finger-printed him, took a mug shot. He's out on bail now. I had it set to go the last time. This time, they surprised me. Picked him up last night. Margo called me every five minutes; I'm not kidding. At first, I didn't think they were going to charge him. I thought it was gonna blow over. I thought he'd have some sort of explanation."

"For what? What happened?"

"They linked that guy Dowling to the money Wilson took out of the bank. Evidently he had an alias, a second identity, as Ben Denni-son. This Dennison deposited the exact amount of cash that Chaney withdrew, the day after Chaney withdrew it. So now it looks like some kind of payoff. You know anything about it?"

I ignored his question. "How did the cops make it?"

I could almost hear him shrug. "They're cops. They investigate."

The woman who ran the cleaning service, what was her name? Fidelia Moros Santos. She could have gotten in touch. Or the anony-mous tipster could have been at it again.

"Find out," I said. "And tell me what happened at Improvisational Technologies five, six months ago. Why did they hire new security? Was there a break-in?"

"I don't think so."

"A breakthough? A new discovery?"

He took his time, then said, "No."

"Think back. We're talking December, January."

"Is it important?"

"It could be."

"Let me check my calendar." He put me on hold. I watched Sam's profile, studied his hands on the wheel. "Yes. Well, near the end of January, that's when the Swiss came over. A medium-sized Swiss firm, not one of the giants. They were interested in buying Improvisational, but it didn't work out."

"Why?"

"These deals are immensely complicated. It usually doesn't come down to one single make-or-break item. I know Chaney was opposed to it."

"Do you know why?"

"Sorry. Can't say."

But do you know? My fingers tightened on the phone. I felt like forcing the issue, knew it would be a waste of time.

The lawyer's voice turned demanding. "Look, Chaney wants to see you, wants to know what you've got. When can you make it over here?"

"I don't know."

"You don't know?" He sounded incredulous.

"I'll be in touch." I hung up.

We stopped for coffee at a convenience store. Sam went in; I stayed in the parking lot to make more calls. The sun was high overhead, but I felt like it ought to be midnight. I decided to try Helen Orza, make sure she or Gagnon would be there, before going any farther. Maybe I ought to give it up, go back to Cambridge, deal with the lawyer, deal with Chaney, I thought. I wasn't feeling all that great, that was for sure.

"Hello." A woman picked up after four rings.

"Helen?"

"No, you've got the—"

"I'm looking for Phil Gagnon," I said.

"Oh."

"Is he there?"

"No."

"I was supposed to—"

"Are you the lady who called from Massachusetts, the one—"

"Yeah."

"He said if you called again, and if you had the money—"

"I do."

"Then try him in Brentwood."

"Brentwood?"

"Not like L.A., not like whatchamacallit, the wife-killer, not O.J.'s Brentwood. Brentwood, New Hampshire. South of Epping. He'll be at Wiseman's, across from the county courthouse."

"Change of plans," I told Sam when he came out carrying two enormous Styrofoam mugs. He handed me one, our fingers touched, and the electricity sparked.

"I know what you mean," he said.

I leaned in and kissed him, thinking, God, if Paolina could see me now. I climbed back into the car, again wanting nothing more than to travel the quickest route to the nearest Victorian inn with flowered sheets and scented candles. A canopied bed, a rug in front of a fireplace. Hell, I'd settle for a secluded lover's lane, a quick encounter in a cramped car. I wondered if Sam felt the same way.

He went back into the convenience store, got directions to Brentwood's county courthouse from the clerk.

"I don't know. Maybe I should just go home." We hadn't gone more than half a mile. I was chugging aspirins with my coffee.

"Maybe," he said noncommittally.

But what if I'd been run off the road just so I wouldn't connect with Phil Gagnon? What if that was the reason for the attack?

We kept driving. Picture-postcard New Hampshire gave way to poverty New Hampshire. Smaller houses on narrower streets. The infrequent larger homes had battered signs in front of them, posted on unruly lawns, advertising inns and rooming houses, antiques, and legal services. Low flat buildings that might have once been warehouses or factories looked abandoned, with broken or boarded windows, brick walls covered by grafitti. Then we'd take a turn, and another town center with perfect grass and white clapboard houses would appear. The towns were small, the changes sudden—built-up, run-down, rural, city, someplace in between. We got lost twice, in spite of the map and the directions, and twice yellow detour signs made me grind my teeth.

The county courthouse was a big square building, granite and brick, with an ornate dome. The county jail was almost next door, on the next block, an imposing edifice that looked more like a high school than a jail. Wiseman's had to be Wiseman's Bail Bonds, located in a row of similar shops across the street from the courthouse, as the woman had said.

Sam pulled up across the street.

"Bail bonds?" he said.

"I guess that's where Gagnon works."

The place looked like a pawnshop, or, if you took in the whole row of shops, a cheap motel. Each featured a storefront window, some barred, some with pull-down metal awnings. One had a hand-lettered sign over a boldface phone number: YOU RING, WE SPRING. Wiseman's slogan seemed inevitable: A WISEMAN STAYS OUT OF JAIL.

"You going in?"

"Well," I said, "that was the point."

"Want company?"

This chauffeur role did not come easy. It cost Sam even to ask permission. Gianelli men don't just have healthy egos; they tend to have women who stay home, don't ask questions about work, have lots of kids, do what they're told.

"Why not?"

"Good. You gonna be who you are?" He knows I don't always tell the whole truth and nothing but when I'm on the job.

I nodded.

"Okay."

I put a hand on his arm, thought better of it, and let go. I wanted to tell him I'd prefer it if he didn't go in strapped for bear. I was sure he had a carry license, but if he didn't—well, none of my business.

To my relief, he made a discreet stop at the trunk of the car. You sometimes find a cop or two in a bondsman's shop. A night in the hospital's bad enough. I didn't relish the prospect of a night in jail for a chaser.

CHAPTER 33

A tinny radio blasted seventies rock and roll in the entryway, but the din receded as I crossed the linoleum floor to the counter. Behind the counter, an old man, late sixties, early seventies, ran his palm over his grizzled chin. He wore a plaid shirt, a skinny tie, a knitted vest, and suspenders, and his hair stood out in a puffy gray cloud over a broad forehead. He made a tsk-tsk sound with his tongue, started talking before I had the chance.

"Hello, cookie," he said, talking fast, like a transplanted New Yorker. "Is that a shiner I'm seeing or what? This a domestic, right? You gonna go his bail and it ain't even turned color yet?"

Sam started to protest and I bit my cheek to keep from laughing. "How'd you figure that?"

"Lookit youse. I don't gotta be no Einstein. What? You're a drug dealer, a gang banger? Unless you're trying to sell me something I don't need, you're a domestic. What I advise is you let him sit in the tank and think it over, young lady. You don't gotta bail out no guy does that to ya."

"If he did it, trust me, I'd let him rot." I handed the chatty gent my card. "Guy smacks me around, I'm not going his bail. You Mr. Wiseman?"

"Howdja guess?"

"I'm looking for Helen Orza."

He spread his arms wide, glanced around the perimeter of the shop as if he were seeing it for the first time. "Search me. Ain't got her."

"Phil Gagnon, then."

"Hey, you're the one with the money for Phil? He told me you promised him a C to sit tight last night, but then ya didn't show."

"I was detained."

"Well, Phil says you can give me the money. You trust me, don'tcha? A guy old as me, where can he run?"

"Where's Phil?"

"I sent him on a job."

Shit. I didn't want to sit around all day waiting for Phil Gagnon.

"Maybe I can help yas," Wiseman said. "Gagnon doesn't know much. What he knows, probably I know. Probably I know twice what Gagnon knows. Four times."

"Do you know where I can reach Helen Orza?"

"Hang on," he said. "Gotta take a call."

The phone was ringing so loudly, it felt like a drill working its way through my forehead. I was grateful when he plucked the receiver off the hook. Everything about the place was loud—the music in the foyer, Wiseman's voice, Wiseman's shirt, the general decor, which continued the cheap motel motif. There was a square of bright green carpet in front of the counter, like a putting green, clashing with the bright blue paint on the walls. I wondered if Wiseman was color-blind as well as slightly deaf. He hollered into the phone, yelling numbers: "That's a buck and a quarter; that's nineteen ninety-eight." I didn't think he was talking single bills. A buck and a quarter bail would be a little over a thousand, very cheap.

Sam summoned me with a nod so small it almost didn't count, more a movement of his eyes than his head. On one end of the counter stood about a hundred windup toys, small sets of teeth, beer kegs, tiny animals made of bright-colored plastic. Sam wound up a giraffe and set it moving in a jerky splay-legged rhythm. I frowned at him.

"Go 'head and play," Wiseman called from ten feet away. "Calm your nerves. Let the lady talk to me some more."

I walked back while Sam wound up a boxing kangaroo. "So can you help me?"

Wiseman nodded his shaggy head. "You wanna know about Helen?" He rubbed his chin again. He'd done a bad job shaving. "Man, Helen's giving me trouble. I can maybe give you a number for her, but she's never there when I call."

"A Boston number?"

"Six one seven anyway. That's eastern Massachusetts."

"Does Helen work for you?

"Yeah. Her and Phil, the both of 'em. I'm an equal-opportunity employer."

"She's a bail agent?'

"Yeah."

"She do other stuff on the side? Regular investigative work?"

"Far as I know, she just does bail."

So much for her working for Mrs. Chaney trying to document Professor Chaney's extracurricular activities.

I said, "So who's Helen looking for? In Boston."

"Well, that would be telling." Wiseman offered me a crooked grin.

"Look, I drove up here because Phil Gagnon said he'd be able to give me some info."

"*Sell* you some info."

"Yes."

"Phil's an ass."

"I kinda suspected that." We shared a smile.

"You like my windup toys?" he asked, nodding at the far end of the counter, where Sam had about a half dozen of them in motion now, making herky-jerky movements, a clatter of small noises.

"They're extremely cool," I said.

"You *did* say you'd pay him?"

"I did. I intend to, if I get something of value."

"Whicha the toys is your favorite?"

"I'll tell you later."

"Okay, I gotta ask. You a retriever, too?"

Retriever. Skip tracer. Bounty hunter. "No."

"'Cause your card says PI, so you could be, and if I got a skip out there who's into two bondsmen, I'd like to hear about it. Guy over there, playing with the toys, he could be your muscle. He's kinda overdressed for it, but who knows with guys?"

"He's not my muscle. He's my driver."

"Okay, see what I mean? Now little Helen, she's been working for me—what?—six, seven months is all. Nice young kid; I know her brother. He's in the can. Family's got a bail history, you know what I mean, so she needs dough. I figure she's got a lot of the wrong kind of connections. You know what I mean?"

"I know." I couldn't help liking the old coot. He was wizened and crabby, but he had laugh lines all over his face.

"Used to be, I didn't use no women in retrieval work. Used to never see many women here, period, except cryin' mamas pledging their jewelry and stuff. Women in the can, you know, they get picked up, their pimps bail 'em. Cost of doing business. But now they're bringing in girls for all kinds a shit. Domestic disturbance, gang fights. I'm not complaining. It's good for business. But you know, as a father of daughters, a grandfather of granddaughters, it stinks."

"I couldn't agree more. Who was Helen looking for?" I was starting to feel a little woozy, but I didn't want to sit. If I sat on the wooden bench to the side of the counter, I'd feel like a felon, first off, and second, Wiseman would talk my ear off.

"You got Phil's money?" he asked.

I handed him two fifties.

"She had three, maybe four files out. Which one you want?"

"I don't know."

He made a sound in his throat. "Then I figure you're not a jump specialist. Least we know who we're after. We just don't know where to find 'em."

272

"Does it matter, me not knowing?"

"Well, four files. I don't know."

"How's this? If I locate any of your skips, I'll let you know."

"On the house?"

"On the house."

He still looked undecided. I counted out another twenty, another fifty, another hundred.

"Now you're broadcastin' on my wavelength," he said.

We made a deal—for copies of the files, plus Helen Orza's number. He threw in the windup giraffe when I declared it my favorite, and he warned Sam that if he ever hit me again, he'd go looking for him personally. We were both giggling by the time we got back in the car.

"You've got an admirer," Sam said.

I settled myself into the leather seat, pressed my hands over my eyes. "Whoa. That was some vicious old-guy breath back there. I thought I might faint for a minute."

"Seriously, you look like you're going to faint. How about some food?"

The block had pawnshops, bail bondsmen, beer cans in the gutter, the bleak air of failure. "Not around here."

"We passed a diner a mile back."

"Fine."

I leaned back and closed my eyes. I'd thought I'd crack the files the minute I was out of Wiseman's door. Instead, I clutched them against my chest and concentrated on breathing in and out, told myself I'd look them over in the diner.

There were only two other people in the place, singles at the counter. Sam commandeered a booth and a bowl of whatever soup was on tap, as fast as the lone waitress could bring it. I think a bill changed hands. The next thing I knew, I was spooning minestrone soup greedily into my mouth while Sam consulted a plastic menu and ordered.

My cell rang and one of the two men on the counter stools glared at me like I'd just interrupted his elegant meal in the whispery softness of the Ritz dining room. I thought about letting the damn thing ring, but then I grabbed it out of my backpack.

Leon. I told him I was okay, couldn't talk, that I'd be in touch. Sam was watching with a carefully neutral expression on his face.

"A guy I'm seeing," I said when I hung up. Then I thought, damn it, I didn't have to say anything. It's not like I owe him an explanation of my life.

"FBI?"

I raised an eyebrow, spooned more soup. My stomach was starting to settle, my headache diminish. The red counter stools looked less abnormally bright.

"Couple guys thought they ought to warn me. You like him?"

"I like him. Let's not talk about this now, okay?"

"Okay."

The waitress slammed plates in front of us. The grilled cheese sandwich came with a bag of potato chips. There was another bowl of soup, and I chose that, along with a packet of saltines and a Pepsi.

Sam said, "So who do you figure is in Wiseman's files? Your dead con, Ben Dowling?"

I swallowed, took a breather. The soup still felt good going down, but I was getting full. "No. I'm figuring the con's partner, the blackmailer, also possibly the murderer. Somebody Dowling was working with."

"How will you recognize him?"

"Probably I won't. I'll go back to the head of security at Improvisational Technologies and convince him to let me run through their tapes." I tapped Wiseman's files with my index finger. "I'll spot one of these bail jumpers going in or out of Impro. Then I'll find out why the guy has it in for Chaney, the whole deal, give it to the cops."

"Sounds good," Sam said between bites of his sandwich. "Maybe we could have dinner tonight?"

"Sam, you know I'd love to, but let me see how I feel later. I may need a nap."

"That would be good, too." He gave me a long, meaningful glance from under hooded eyelids. "You going to finish that soup?"

"It's yours."

I opened the first slim folder. It contained two sheets of paper concerning a fellow named Domingo Gaston, arrested for felonious assault, with a side of drunk and disorderly on October 18 of the previous year. Juan Marie Franciosa, Gaston's brother-in-law, was listed as his indemnitor, the man who'd come up with the $3,200 bail. There were addresses and phone numbers for both men, scribbled notes saying that Gaston had missed an appearance in court on January 3, and that Juan Marie had disavowed any knowledge of his whereabouts.

Wiseman had posed Domingo Gaston in front of the counter, taken a Polaroid shot for future identification purposes. My copy of the snapshot was paper-clipped to a sheet of lined paper that said "Height: five eight, weight: 145; brown, brown." I took the last two to mean hair and eyes.

The waitress brought me another Pepsi. It was in a tall glass full of ice cubes and flat as pond water. I stuck Gaston's file at the bottom of the pile, opened number two, studied a photo of Markham Rodney Yarrow, and read about his arrest for breaking into a 1999 Mercury Sable while toting a master key and a pry bar. His cousin, Marilyn Sue Yarrow, had cosigned for him, and he'd repaid her $2,900 worth of faith by skipping town. I was surprised at the minimal amount of information Wiseman collected. He didn't list Social Security numbers, evidently didn't ask for dates of birth, almost like he was daring his clients to run.

I opened file number three.

"Sam," I said. "We have to go."

"Let me get the check."

He took one look at my face and slapped a twenty on the counter. I was already halfway to the door.

In Polaroid number three, Donna Barnette stood in front of Wiseman's counter, eyes staring straight at the camera, expression defiant, her whole body sullen and resentful. She had ruffled short hair, wore jeans and a tank top. The notation on the attached sheet of paper said "Height: five two; weight: ninety-five; blond, blue."

She was Denali Brinkman.

CHAPTER 34

No wonder the Harvard Admissions office didn't want to talk about Denali Brinkman. I sat at my desk and shielded my eyes from the lamp. They felt bruised by the light, and I wondered if the curious overbrightness was due to the mild concussion. I wondered how much my insurance company would pay toward a new car, and what I'd buy. I wondered where I'd hidden the aspirin.

Sam was gone, as abruptly and completely as if he'd disappeared in a puff of smoke. The whole New Hampshire interlude was taking on the shape of a dreamlike fairy tale, "Sleeping Beauty" morphing into an offbeat version of "The Frog Prince," in which the enchanted frog remained amphibious, but the beautiful princess turned into a beast.

Denali Brinkman was Donna Barnette, who'd been charged with forging driver's licenses and running a confidence game in Epping, New Hampshire, a little over a year ago. Who'd posted $3,800 bail, indemnified by a nonexistent cousin, and evaporated, only to reappear as a Harvard student.

I flipped off the lamp and sat in the shadows. I wondered whether she'd taken the SATs and ACTs herself or found a way to borrow someone else's scores, how she'd managed transcripts and essays. Had she stolen her essays off the Internet, or composed them herself? She'd have needed a confederate, someone to mail her application and respond to her acceptance, preferably from far away. Maybe from Switzerland. I wondered who old Albert Brinkman really was, a fellow con artist, a stooge?

I felt a grudging tug of admiration. What impressed me most was the planning, the long-term thinking. Most cons have a hard time planning from Monday night till Tuesday morning. Donna Barnette had to have been uncannily bright, driven, Harvard material in an unusual guise.

I leaned forward, head in hands, the heels of my palms massaging my temples. I admit it, I felt wretched. My head ached like hell. The small abrasions along my right side itched underneath the bandages and my shoulder throbbed. Sam Gianelli had dropped me at my doorstep and left.

True, he'd kissed me thoroughly. True, he'd promised to call. True, I'd chased him away, insisting I had work to do that couldn't wait. There was an added strangeness to the interlude that I was only now starting to appreciate. What had Sam been doing in New Hampshire, alone, with no bodyguards, driving his own car? Not once had he been interrupted by the shrill ring of a cell phone. Since he'd taken over his terminally ill father's mob job, Sam's movements had been circumscribed, his time not his own. And yet, he'd been there.

I forced my mind away from Sam and back to the case. How did the knowledge that Denali Brinkman was not who she seemed to be help or hurt Wilson Chaney? I recalled his early raptures, how different she was from the ordinary student, how much more mature than the other girls, what a different life she'd led. The truth about Brinkman made Chaney seem more truthful, and one item he'd emphasized was that Denali had made a play for him, not the other way around. I'd discounted his claim at the time, but now I accepted it as fact: *Denali had made a play for him.* So what had she hoped to gain by seducing her teacher?

My head was pounding like a snare drum. The area under my eye felt tender and my shoulder was on fire. I swallowed aspirin dry from a bottle I finally located in my desk drawer.

Denali Brinkman had entered Harvard under false pretenses. She had seduced her professor, a man currently developing a new ADHD drug. A medium-sized Swiss pharmaceutical firm had wanted the company and presumably the drug, but Chaney had refused to sell. Denali Brinkman had a Swiss connection, possibly the same Uncle Albert who'd neglected to call me back. Denali Brinkman had partnered up with another ex-con, Benjy Dowling, who'd worked at Chaney's lab. Why?

I slammed the flat of my hand on my desk in frustration, recoiled from the sharp smack. Denali Brinkman was dead. Possibly Benjy Dowling had tried to carry on with her plan, whatever it was. Now Dowling was dead, too. Had Denali/Donna been killed by someone from her former life, or had she been killed by Dowling? Had she killed herself after all, knowing that Helen Orza, New Hampshire bounty hunter, was on her trail, that Harvard would find out who she was, that she'd be kicked out and publicly disgraced?

I chewed another aspirin, shuddering at the grainy bitterness on my tongue. What the hell was public disgrace anymore? Chaney might be a target for blackmail, but he was a university professor. Wasn't it more likely that Denali/Donna, con artist, once identified as a fraud, would have beaten the New Hampshire charges and gone on the *Jerry Springer Show* to tell the world how she'd made a fool of Harvard? Wind up an instant celebrity, the subject of some made-for-TV movie? Not kill herself.

I still thought she'd been murdered, but did it matter? I didn't know. I just knew I had to keep moving. The more time passes, the less chance there is of solving any crime, especially murder. Like a shark, an investigation has to move or it dies. I couldn't stop it, couldn't slow it down, couldn't take time to consider what it meant to have Sam come back into my life, Sam, sitting patiently at my bedside till I woke. Damn. This investigation felt more like a runaway train than a shark.

I tried Chaney's lawyer, Todd Geary, got a recording, listened to tape spooling in my ear until it stopped and began to hum. I clicked the receiver down, closed my eyes, tried to catch the train of the investigation, to remember where I'd been headed before the damned truck rammed my car and temporarily derailed me. I'd been talking to Officer Burkett. I'd asked him about the missing TransAm, speculated about the benzos listed on the autopsy report.

I phoned Burkett at his home, his office. Nothing. I left messages, thanking him for his rescue efforts, asking him to call. I tugged my hair and bit the rough edge off a fingernail. Why didn't he have a cell? Why didn't Geary have a cell? I bet both of them did, but neither had given me the damned number. I drummed my fingers on my desk in time with the throb in my shoulder.

I needed to know who'd turned Chaney in this time, who'd told the cops that Dennison and Dowling were one and the same. Who could I call at the Brighton station? Who would talk to me? Who owed me? I recalled and discarded several names. Damn it, wasn't there anyone? I remembered the Hispanic woman who ran the cleaning service. If the cops hadn't received another anonymous tip, they'd most likely learned about Dowling's dual identity from Fidelia Moros Santos. If she'd seen Dowling's photo in the news, linked it with her Ben, she'd have run to the cops in full cry.

She answered the phone with a dispirited droop in her voice, but her tone changed as soon as I identified myself as the redheaded woman who'd visited after the break-in.

"*Ai*, it is finally you," she said eagerly. "Who are you, really? What is your name, *por favor*? The *policía* say they don't know you. Please, you will come again? I must see you." She spoke so quickly, I could barely understand.

"What is it?"

"I must see you now. Today. I must ask you— I have decided you are someone I can trust."

I took the aspirin bottle out of the drawer again, tried to read the tiny print on the label. How many were too many? While I screwed up my eyes, I explained to Señorita Moros Santos that I had no transportation. She was adamant: I must come. I tried to ask her whether she'd spoken to the cops about Dennison/Dowling, but she shut me down cold. She would say nothing on the telephone. She knew about those things—bugs. She knew the telephone was not safe. I shrugged, blew out a deep breath, told her I'd be there, then called Gloria, who agreed to send Leroy with a cab.

"I thought I saw you pull up in a Porsche?" Roz came clattering downstairs, perched on platform shoes. "Whoa, what the hell happened?"

"A crazed New Hampshire motorist."

" 'Live Free or Die,' " she said matter-of-factly. "Was that Gianelli's car?"

"It was, and I don't want to talk about it. I want you to get all the insurance crap together on my car. You'll need a copy of the police report—Epping, New Hampshire—but first I need everything you can get on this woman." I handed her Wiseman's slim report on Donna Barnette, my copy of his Polaroid.

"But what about Dorothy Boyd?" she asked plaintively.

I rested my head in my hands. "I give up. Who the hell is Dorothy Boyd?" I was thinking I'd need to find sunglasses before venturing outdoors.

"Just a girl who won a trophy on Harsha Lake."

The battered silver and gold cross-oared trophy. The first hint that Denali was not who she seemed to be.

"Tell me," I said.

"Well, I started with FISA.com, which is the world rowing Web site, but I shoulda gone right to USRowing.com, because *lake* is, like, an American word, and sure enough, Harsha Lake is near Cincinnati, Ohio. The Cincinnati Junior Rowing Club is there, and they've been hosting the Junior Invitationals forever. They attract rowers from everywhere, nationally and internationally. They do eights, lightweight eights, fours with coxswain, coxless quads, singles, doubles—"

"Roz."

"Yeah, well, I had to go through a lot to find this out. I want you to appreciate my research."

"I appreciate it."

"I had to go from person to person to get to somebody who remembered back to the 1987 race. Mrs. Belden sent me to a Mr. Harris, who sent me to—"

"Roz."

"Finally, I got to this Felicia Giddings woman, who could talk the ear off an elephant. She thought I was doing a magazine article on the competitors in that race, what happened to them later on in life, that kinda shit. Isn't it great what people believe? Like who'd care about some old race? And did she remember the singles, because her daughter was supposed to win."

"But Dorothy Boyd won."

"Yeah, and old Mrs. Giddings holds a grudge. The girl shouldn't have been allowed to enter." Roz stood tall, stuck her nose in the air, and imitated Mrs. Giddings's snottily languid tone. "Really, she didn't belong. She'd just turned up at the high school a few weeks earlier, registering at nearly the end of the year. A transfer student, but really, Mrs. G. didn't know where she'd come from. She was with her father, and old Mrs. G. left no doubt that she didn't think the man was Dorothy's father at all, more like a funny uncle. She wouldn't come right out and say it, but she thought the man was sleeping with the girl, no doubt about that."

"And?"

"Girl won the race going away. She was a fabulous rower. Even Giddings wouldn't take that away from her. Left town right afterward, and little Heather—that's Giddings's girl—came in second, totally upset about losing. Didn't enter another race for like a year. I had to listen to it about ten times."

"Did Mrs. Giddings remember the man's name?"

"Mr. Boyd."

"Great."

"Hey, that's all she could remember."

"Sorry. Nice work. Now you need to do both of them, Donna Barnette and Dorothy Boyd. Same person. Run them through Merlindata.com and SearchAmerica.com, all those places, then get onto someone in the police department, like your pal Burkett, and sweet-talk him into running the names through NCIC. I have a hunch there's a criminal record." As I finished speaking, a horn started beeping outside.

"Okay," Roz said.

"And tell Leroy to cool it. I'll be there as soon as I can."

First, I found my sunglasses. Then I looked up Helen Orza's phone number, the one Wiseman had given me, in the cross-referenced directory. A Somerville address, not much of a detour as the crow flies. We could hit it on the way back from Medford. Last, I unlocked the bottom drawer of the file cabinet that supports the left side of my desk and inhaled the sharp scent of oil. The black case that contained my S&W .40 still looked new. I opened it, swallowing a bitterness beyond aspirin residue. I remembered going shooting at the police range with my dad; cherished the memory of his pride at my skill. I recalled the man I killed when I was a cop, a bad day in a lousy part of town. I remembered being on the wrong end of a bullet, lying helplessly prone, the sound, the flash, the pain and shock, the welling blood. I ran my finger over the raised scar on my thigh and fitted the weapon carefully into the waistband of my jeans.

CHAPTER 35

Boston cabbies are required by law to wear shirts with collars. Leroy wore a Hawaiian number, open like a jacket, over a vivid gold basketball jersey. Heavy silver chains circled his massive neck. He wore sunglasses, too, huge wraparounds you'd have to call shades. I wondered what Gloria had told him about my New Hampshire off-road driving adventure. I wouldn't have put it past her to know every juicy detail of Gianelli's rescue mission.

We made good time into Medford. I couldn't imagine Señorita Moros Santos choosing to unburden herself in front of Leroy, so when we turned onto her street, I asked him to stay in the car. He grunted and I considered how many of Graylie Janitorial's crime-conscious neighbors might spot him idling in the cab and instinctively call the cops. I advised him to visit the nearby doughnut shop and keep a low profile.

Fidelia Moros Santos opened her front door before I had a chance to knock, her porcelain complexion blotchy, her single long braid twisted into a lumpy knot on top of her head. She'd aged since the last time I'd seen her. She wasn't wearing mourning black, but her gray suit was shapeless and wrinkled, as though she'd put it on without glancing in a mirror, as though she no longer cared how she looked.

"So," she said, taking my hand and clasping it briefly, "you are no cop."

"I am a cop, a private cop." *Investigadora privada.*

"*Madre de Dios,* but you are hurt."

I'd shoved my sunglasses up over my forehead, forgetting the shiner. Well, what else could I do? I couldn't wear sunglasses indoors without blundering into chairs, not to mention looking like an addict. "I'm okay," I told her. "It's nothing. What's so urgent?"

"If you are like you say, *privada*, why you come here before?"

"The English-speaking man who worked here, your boyfriend, was involved in something I was working on."

"*Ai,* my Ben." She sank into the chair behind her desk with a heavy sigh, nodded me into a guest chair. The office had been cleaned since the break-in. The plants were back in the pots, but no new posters hung on the wall. She hadn't bothered to open the blinds. The photo of Benjy Dowling, the one I'd snapped near the old powder magazine, was taped to the side of her computer screen. Stacks of paper and file folders piled near the monitor made it look as though she'd fallen behind in data entry. "He is dead, no?"

"You told the police that he's dead?"

"*Ai,* no, I don't say that. I tell them nothing about Ben." She looked so astonished by my assumption that I decided she was telling the truth. Someone else had told the police that Dowling and Denni-son were one and the same. Who? An anonymous adviser?

"I do not know what to do," she said. "Almost, it is funny. In my family, I am the clever one, you see? The one who knows. Also the old maid, no? The one who will never marry but who will take care of everything, of the old people, of the money worries. I think it will always be like that, getting dressed up for my sisters' and my cousins' weddings, and then I meet a man and I give my heart. He is not one of ours, and I should know better, but what can you do?"

I said nothing, but I thought about Sam. *He is not one of ours.*

"Now I think he must be dead." She shrugged and tried to force her lips into a smile. "He does not come back, and I have not heard from him. My family has not heard. Maybe he is just gone away, I think first, but I know in my heart he is dead. I found something at my apartment that makes me even more sure he is gone, but I don't know what to do with it. I—I don't know, *la policía*, they have been good to me, but I worry that if I give them this thing—"

"What worries you?"

"*Ai*, maybe there is something inside that will ruin my business. Before this terrible week, I have two things—I have my business; I have my Ben. I am a happy woman. If I no longer have Ben, I must have something. To lose both, it would be too much. I don't know, but I am uneasy. I cannot sleep, and I go to church, and I decide I will do what you say."

I hoped her priest hadn't advised her to put her trust in a stranger who'd bought her a doughnut when she was distraught.

"What is it?" I asked. "What did you find?"

She groped in a huge satchel, beige cloth covered in embroidery, and withdrew a thick envelope. She stared at it for the count of five, then passed it solemnly across the desk. It was sealed, but it wasn't stamped. It hadn't traveled through the mail. Across the front in a bold scrawl, it said "Open in case of my death."

"Do you know when he left this?"

"*Ai*, no. I know nothing. I understand nothing, except that he is gone away. He did not come back here for work. No one knows where he has gone. My younger sister, she says he made a fool of me, but I know he would be here unless something terrible happened."

"You didn't open this? Read it?"

"*Ai*, no. How can I read it? When I don't truly *know* that he is dead, not really, not for sure."

Okay, Carlotta, I thought, this is where you leave. This is where you take the envelope and lie to the poor woman. Say you'll give it back to her if it turns out her fears are overblown. I found myself fumbling for the Spanish, my mouth shaping different words.

"*Señorita*, you are right in your heart. He is dead. I am sorry to tell you like this, suddenly, but your feelings are true. The man in that picture is dead."

"Thank you," she said with enormous dignity. "It is important that I know."

I reached across the desk and touched her icy hand.

"Now you read," she said.

I considered taking it to the cops unread, considered it for maybe ten seconds. Then I took a letter opener from a mug, slit the top of the envelope, and spread the pages on the desk.

Handwritten. Five pages long. Three feet away, Fidelia Moros Santos sat as though she were carved out of stone, except for the tears that ran slowly down her round cheeks.

> *To whom it may concern:*
>
> *I'm starting like that because I don't know who'll be reading this first, but I hope sooner or later it gets to the cops. She thinks she's so smart. I told her I was going to do this, write it all down so she'll have to leave me alone, but she thinks she's so damned smart, she probably thought she could find it at my place, or at work, but she didn't know jack about Fidelia and me. Thinks she's so smart. Ha.*
>
> *Well, if you're reading this, I guess she was smart enough. I saw it coming but not till it was too damn late, and then this was the only thing I could think to do, so I'll have my revenge, but I sure wish I'd got away and managed to grab a big chunk of the money. I don't think she was playing square with me from the start.*
>
> *She is Denali Brinkman, and don't believe for a second that she is dead, because she isn't.*

I read the last line twice.

"I have to go, *Señorita*," I said, standing, holding out my hand to shake hers. "Thanks you for trusting me with this. You were right to do it. If there is anything in here that compromises your business, I'll try my best to keep it out of the hands of the police."

She stood as well, took my hand. "He is dead?"

"Yes. You did the right thing. The absolutely right thing."

I half-ran, half-walked to the doughnut shop, rousted Leroy from a table, where he sat with half a dozen doughnuts on a platter. The waitress bagged them while I waited impatiently. I gave Leroy Helen Orza's Somerville address, read the rest of Dowling's letter in the car, speeding toward what I knew would be an empty house.

> It went great, at first. She had that fool Chaney eating out of her hand while we waited for him to finish off his patent stuff. We're almost ready to grab it, when the shit starts falling. See, first, Denali gets hurt, so she can't row. I mean, she'd been having trouble with a few classes before, not turning shit in and stuff, but who cared, with her being such a great rower and all? But that stupid Chaney keeps delaying, and now she's worried about people nosing around, asking questions, kicking her out because she can't row. So she comes up with this idea about how it would be better if she were dead. I kinda laugh it off at first, but I think she'd been thinking about it for a long time, starting over clean, ever since she got arrested in NH.
>
> She asks me to drive her to some shit town up there. I'm suppose to wait in the car while she hangs around the jail, but not looking like her, in a black wig and fat-girl clothes, and then later she changes to her cleaning overalls and I do, too, and we go to this dentist office place, wait till dark. I never busted a dentist office before. Easy. A favor for Denali is all, and she came out smiling like a cat.

A dentist's office. Someone else had mentioned a dentist's office. Yes, the only time Denali had ever started a conversation with her roommate, Jeannie St. Cyr, she'd inquired about a local dentist.

Then later, she asks me to call this number in NH and tell this girl Helen that she can find "Donna" easy in Boston, give her a hint or two where. This Helen, she even stayed at my place for a while. I bet sweet little Denali, "Donna," whatever, saw her when she was posting bond, not the same looks, not drop-dead pretty like her, but same height, same shape, kinda gave her the idea.

Helen Orza, Wiseman's unlucky employee, must have been working at the bondsman's office that day. Maybe she was the one who'd snapped the Polaroid of Donna Barnette, posing against the grid that showed her height. Wiseman himself might have commented on the similar size of the two women. Possibly Donna/Denali alone had noticed, filed it away for future use.

Orza's address in Somerville was a corner convenience store with a phone, nothing more, nothing less. Denali would have paid some clerk to say that Helen was out whenever Wiseman phoned. She'd have left a few letters for the clerk to post at certain intervals. What had Donna Barnette been charged with in New Hampshire, after all? Forgery. I didn't bother to go into the store, confront the clerk, listen to his outraged denials.

Well, the place Denali went wrong was, she didn't reckon with me. Thinks she's the only one with half a brain. This patent shit's taking too damn long. I don't see why Chaney shouldn't pay my expenses while I wait, and I don't see why I shouldn't make a chunk of change off Harvard while I'm at it. I mean, think of it, deep pockets, right? She says no, wait for the big score, forget about it, but she's wrong. Chaney paid up like a baby, and Harvard will, too.

Wrong, I thought. You paid, Benjy. Hell, that's why I'd sensed two patterns in the case, because there were two crooks, each trying to outsmart the other. Two patterns, one slow and crafty, the other hasty, eager to get rich quick. Two crooks, two plans. Denali wanted something big from Chaney. She was willing to wait. Dowling, the con who always went too far, who gilded the lily, was the blackmailer. He was the one behind the lawsuit. I wondered whether Denali would have killed him if he hadn't branched off on his own, if that had always been her plan.

"Carlotta? You okay just sitting here?"

"Hang on a minute, Leroy."

> *Anyway, I'm sorry it went down the way it did. I had nothing against that Helen, seemed like an okay kid. I'm not saying I didn't know Denali would kill her—I mean, she stole her dental chart, right?—but I wasn't really in on it, more what you call an accessory. I was real good. I shoulda been an actor, probably won an Academy Award. The cops took Helen's hairbrush from my place when I told them I had it, case they decided to do that new DNA thing. Well, I'm smarter than Denali thinks I am. There's hairs here in this envelope. Don't throw them away. They're Helen Orza's hairs, from her hairbrush, I swear to God, and they're just like the ones I told the cops were Denali's. This is the truth, so help me God.*

"Start heading to Cambridge, Leroy."

I phoned Burkett, left a message telling him I'd messenger Dowling's confession. I called Geary, Chaney's lawyer. Still the recorded message. I called Spengler, head of security at Improvisational. He put me on hold while he checked, then told me Chaney wasn't in the lab, that he'd been there but had left. "Alone?" I asked. "Did he leave alone?" Did I want him to pull up the video? Spengler asked. I did. We were still tracing the curving path of Alewife Brook when he reported that Chaney had left with a small blond woman, a real looker.

I called Chaney's house, got Mark, the secretary, then Margo, the wife. The connection was bad. My cell battery was running down.

"What?" I said. "What did you say?"

Her voice sounded muffled. "Can you come over right away?" she asked. "Now?"

"Is your husband there?"

Static almost muffled her reply. "No."

I told Leroy to drop me at the Chaneys', then take the envelope to Burkett at the Cambridge Police Department, give it into his hands and his hands only. I tried for a dial tone on my cell, got nothing, picked up the cab's two-way and got Gloria.

"Urgent," I told her. "Call Leon at the JFK Building." I didn't have to give her a number; Gloria knows numbers. "Tell him his buddy Wilson Chaney is probably on the way to Logan Airport with a killer. Tell him I'll be heading there in a few minutes, the international terminal, with a gun. Tell him if he can clear the path for me with the staties, I'd be obliged. If he can meet me, so much the better. Tell him the BPD will have paper. Chaney's not supposed to leave the state, much less the country."

"Got it."

Leroy said, "Maybe I better stick with you."

I said, "Come back here as soon as you've given the envelope to Burkett. If I'm already gone, meet up with me at Terminal E, Logan. Gloria, you still there?"

"Here."

"Make the call. And send me another cab." I gave her the Chaneys' address.

CHAPTER 36

The high gate was open, not hanging ajar, but unfastened. That should have rung a bell, but the warning was muted because my mind was focused on the fact that Denali was Donna was Dorothy. That the golden girl was alive, not dead, a killer, not a victim. I pushed past the gate and took the flagstone path to the front door.

When no one answered my knock, I turned the knob. The door swung in, stopped abruptly, stuck. I put my shoulder to the wood and shoved until I could slide sideways through the narrow gap.

Mark, Mrs. Chaney's secretary, was dumped on the foyer floor like a sack of trash, the cause of the blocked door, the object I'd moved. I put a quick hand to his throat. His carotid artery pulsed weakly. He gave a faint snorting sound when I touched him. I slid out of my shoes, found my gun in my hand, eased down the hall toward the withdrawing room.

Silence hung over the house like a coiled and waiting snake. I kept my gun in both hands, used it to point around corners and into empty doorways. I found Margo in the withdrawing room, stretched on the chaise. She seemed to be asleep, but she was bound with the cord from the fancy telephone, the white lines almost invisible against her pale frilled nightgown. The instrument dangled near the floor, dead and useless, but Margo was alive, breathing, gagged with a scarf. Her eyes fluttered and she struggled weakly against her bonds.

I grabbed my cell, punched 911, got nothing, not the feeblest dial tone. The red light gleamed. RECHARGE BATTERY appeared in the small window. I was debating my next move, whether or not to untie Margo, whether she'd prove an asset or a helpless disaster, screaming in terror, when her imagined scream seem to materialize, echoing through the house, a wail of anger and rage, followed by a sharp report, the unmistakable sound of a gun. Not a backfire, gunfire.

I left Margo and raced back to the front door. Mark hadn't moved, but I could hear groans and low murmurs, coming from the right of the foyer, down another hall. I pressed my body against the wall, making myself a smaller target, and inched forward. My thigh started to ache; the old gunshot wound seemed to tingle at the harsh smell of cordite.

Freeze frame: An office, small, disordered, lined with bookshelves. A desk, a sprawled chair. A painting leaning against a wall, a flash of color. A wall safe, door yawning. Wilson Chaney prone, a trickle of blood seeping from his temple; wearing a white shirt at first glance, a lab coat at second; his face twisted in pain, his eyelids flickering. A leather briefcase, open, papers scattered across a wooden floor. A woman bent over Chaney, kneeling near his waist, a spill of blond hair.

"It was his fault." She seemed to know someone was in the doorway, but she didn't look up. "Tried to trick me—bastard had a gun in the safe. Would you believe it, Wilson, with a gun?" She lifted her head and the silky hair framed her face like folded wings.

What had I expected? A devil in a dress? A femme fatale, cheap, gaudy, and obvious? She was beautiful the way angels in church are beautiful. Her chin was pointed, her cheek smudged. The left knee of her jeans was torn, and her breasts were bare under a tank top. Her nose was smaller than a true classic, but she was a stunner all the same, her lower lip full, her wide eyes cornflower blue. Calm, but with depth. They said, How could a girl like me do anything wrong? They said, I didn't mean it. They said, Please take care of me.

"Back away from him," I said. "Let me see your hands."

She didn't move anything but her sullen lips. "It's his fault. He pulled a fucking gun. He—I don't know—you can never tell with men, can you? So happy to see me, that's what he said. He used to be happy to see me."

"Get your hands in the air." There was a gun in the room, but I couldn't see it. Her hands were spread, one on each side of Chaney's motionless body—one near his shoulder, one disappearing under his waist.

She smiled at me, showing small white teeth, staring unflinchingly into the gun barrel. "I thought you were still in the hospital."

"I thought you were dead, Denali."

"Your mistake."

Wilson had yanked a gun from the safe, whirled, shot? No. He'd pulled the gun, aimed it at beautiful, beautiful Denali, stopped and spoken, tried to reason with her. She'd dazzled him, grabbed the weapon, fought him, shot him. He'd fallen.

Where was the gun?

"Move away from him," I said.

She kept her hands where they were, her knees on the ground. I watched her feet. Beige sandals. Scarlet toes like drops of blood. If she was going to charge me, she'd need to shift her feet, get some leverage.

She smiled. "You work for him, don't you?"

"Yes." Was the gun under Chaney? Was she scrabbling for it? Had she reached it?

"You work for him. Right. So now I'm going to tell you why you're going to back off and let me walk out of here. Listen, or you'll regret it. He'll regret it, and so will you."

She had a low voice, gruff and throaty, almost like a teenage boy's when it starts to change. I kept the pistol pointed at her chest.

"You give me to the cops, I'll nail your boss for rape, first off. You know, we had a thing going, but I'll say it was rape, and who's to say it wasn't? That'll fix the bastard. He'll never get another job like the one he'll lose."

"Maybe. Maybe not." Once the cops pull her record, no one will believe a thing she says, I thought.

"He wouldn't want you to keep me here. The shooting was a mistake. Just let me go and you can rush him to a hospital. He's still bleeding, see? He'll be okay."

I didn't move. Neither did she.

"Hey, he's no saint, believe me. None of this would have happened if he hadn't been trying to cheat Harvard in the first place. Oh, I'll talk about that, don't think I won't. He's no angel in this. Does that surprise you? It does, doesn't it? You fell for him, didn't you? Such an important man, such a brilliant man."

My eyes flicked over the floorboards, the rug, her splayed hands. Had her right hand, the hand near Chaney's waist, disappeared farther under his body? His lab coat blocked my view.

"You know what an unintended consequence is?" she asked.

Oh yes, I thought. "Yes," I said aloud.

"There's more going on here than you could possibly know. And it's worth millions, hundreds of millions."

I watched her watch me, looking for the gleam of interest when she mentioned money. I tried my best to supply it.

"Sure he's been talking about an ADHD drug, help all the poor kids. Sure that's where he started. But when you mess with the brain, you don't really know what's gonna happen. These guys, they think they're so damn smart, but they don't know."

"What do you think he found?" I asked.

"What *did* he find." she said, correcting me. "I'm no fool."

I've seen politicians claim they were bankrupt and mobsters swear their innocence on their mothers' graves, but I have never seen a more calculating face. I watched her clear blue eyes decide what to tell me, and I knew that whatever it was, it wouldn't be the truth, the whole truth, and nothing but.

"He's in late stage clinicals now. You know what those are, right? You're not dumb, either; you read the papers. A woman in your business, you must be sharp."

She was working me, trying to get me on her side, flattering me. I watched her bait her hook. It was like taking a master class in con artistry.

"One of Impro's clinical trial groups, at a certain dosage, had an unexpected outcome. Totally unexpected. Chaney couldn't have been more surprised if they'd sprouted wings and flown away. They all, every single man, woman, and child, lost weight. Brilliant Chaney didn't expect that. That hadn't happened before, not in the animal control groups, not ever. He was so excited, he had to tell someone."

Poor Chaney, blabbing to his sweet little lover.

"And nothing else bad happened to those people," she went on. "No adverse effects. They all lost pounds and kept on losing. He had to stop the trial. Imagine. You know how many fat people there are in this world? How many who aren't fat but think they're fat?" Her right hand moved just a little. She licked her lips and tossed her hair to cover the movement. If I'd been male, the tricks might have kept me looking at the wrong things.

I pretended I hadn't seen her move. I could see the ease flow into her eyes then, the idea that she was going to walk away, that she'd found herself another sucker.

"Fifteen percent of kids in this country are fat, for Chrissakes, and that's just kids. You know what people will pay to look good? You know what women pay for Botox shots, poison shots? In this country, weight loss is a fifty-billion-dollar-a-year thing. Imagine what they'll pay for this. Imagine. Chaney did. Chaney said, Why should Harvard get all that money when I did all the work? Why shouldn't I walk away with the giant's share? Why shouldn't I be able to leave my bitch wife, go off with my girlfriend? Have all the money in the world?"

"There's a problem, Denali. If Chaney were gone, if he'd disappeared with his drug formula, well, then people might believe it, but here he is, and you shot him."

Her eyes blazed. "It was a fucking accident. It should have happened like I said."

"'Should have' isn't going to cut it."

"If he hadn't been so fucking slow, everything would have been fine. He kept saying it would only be a little longer, a little longer. He had to be able to replicate his results, make sure he could duplicate every little thing. I needed him to fill out the damned patent application." She waved at the papers scattered on the floor. "It's all done now. We could walk away with it, you and me. There's plenty for two, plenty for three. You can have Wilson's share, for doing nothing, for walking away. I know a man in Switzerland who knows people at drug companies. I could really use some help. I hurt my shoulder and—"

Yes. Which shoulder? How much would it slow her down?

"If I hadn't hurt my damn shoulder, Harvard wouldn't have given a damn about my grades. They would have had their fucking rower. They wouldn't have asked questions, wouldn't have—"

The situation was finally getting to her, the gun pointed at her heart, the man bleeding beneath her, her whole easy-money paradise going up in smoke. She heard the desperation in her own voice, paused, and tried a smile.

"But that's water under the bridge," she said. "The question is, What could you do with a cool million?"

"You shot Chaney. The cops are going to want somebody for that."

"We can fix it. There's nothing we can't fix. There's a can of gas in the trunk of my car. I can write a note, forge his signature. From Wilson, saying his wife was driving him batty, saying he killed her first, then decided he couldn't live with it."

"Shot himself and *then* burned the house down?"

"Started the fire *before* he killed himself. Who's to say he didn't? The house burns, nobody will be looking for any patent applications, that's for sure. They went up in smoke. And when some firm in Europe comes up with the same drug, well, things like that happen all the time." Her voice was soothing and persuasive.

I let myself look interested. "You shoot the wife, somebody might hear."

Her laugh was easy, like she didn't have a care in the world, much less a gun pointed at her heart. "You hear any sirens? Nobody called the cops on the first shot. People like this, people who live in houses like this, they don't hear anything. And if they do, they don't do anything. They don't want to get involved." Her hand slipped half an inch farther under Chaney's waist. "If you're worried, we can forget about using a gun. I've got some pills I can give the wife."

"The same pills you gave Helen Orza?"

Her hand came out from under Chaney's lab coat so fast, I only registered metal, not a weapon, just metal, a dull metallic gleam. I shot her, low on the right shoulder, stepped close, and clubbed her with my gun to bring her down. She was unconscious when I wrestled Chaney's .22 out of her hand.

CHAPTER 37

Mount Auburn Hospital: ivory walls, machine-chilled air, antiseptic smell. I sat at Wilson Chaney's bedside and wondered whether Dorothy Boyd/Donna Barnette/Denali Brinkman would make it through surgery. A clock ticked, a round schoolroom clock with a sweep second hand. Chaney's small room looked so much like the New Hampshire hospital room in which I'd awakened this very morning, I felt as though time had slipped a gear, as though I ought to be lying in the narrow bed instead of my client. I couldn't get Denali Brinkman out of my head, couldn't stop seeing those cornflower-colored eyes. I wasn't glad I'd shot her. I wasn't sorry I'd shot her. I was glad she hadn't shot me.

Chaney slept, a drug-induced slumber, his temple heavily bandaged. Tubes ran from his arm to an IV-drip stand that held two plastic bags of colorless fluid aloft.

How much of Denali's tale was true? Had Chaney found some wonder drug, tried to cheat Harvard out of it? I eyed the clock and wished someone would relieve me. Margo Chaney was being treated on another floor, for bruising, superficial cuts, and a panic attack. She'd begged me: "Could you please, please stay with Wilson?" She didn't want him to be left alone. She would send someone soon, she'd said.

Footsteps hammered down the hall, sharp steps, not the rubber-soled swish of the medical staff. Please, I thought, not another cop. There'd been too many of them, demanding, accusing, taking notes for my statement, revising my statement. All in all, not so bad. They seemed to believe my account of the events leading up to the shooting. Just like they'd believed Benjy Dowling about the fire.

Then there'd been Leon, to whom I'd passed on the harried doctor's words: Wilson would recover. He'd been lucky. Fired at an angle, the small .22-caliber bullet had glanced off his skull. No brain damage. Leon had been anxious, relieved, angry. We'd started another quarrel, stopped only because I couldn't sustain it. He'd told me next time to back out the door and yell for help.

"Sure," I'd said sarcastically. That's my style; that's my nature.

We'd agreed to call it quits, stay friends, whatever the hell that means. He'd asked whether it had anything to do with him being black. I'd told him no, maybe it had to do with him being in law enforcement. I hadn't mentioned Sam, but I knew it wouldn't be long before he heard, long before he knew.

Knew what? What did I know? A brief moment, a few caresses, and what?

The footsteps tapped past my door, down another corridor, and I thought again about Denali Brinkman, Dorothy Boyd, somewhere in the same hospital, beautiful body under harsh white lights, behind metal doors.

Dorothy Boyd, Dorothy Louise Boyd, a dull, stolid name for someone who'd christened herself for a soaring Alaskan peak. Brinkman . . . Why Brinkman? Living on the brink? I put aside speculation and read facts, as delivered by Roz, along with a merciful sandwich, an hour earlier. The pages were photocopies of faxes, blurry, or maybe there was something wrong with my eyes. I stared at the wavery print.

Dorothy Louise Boyd, born December 12, 1972. Twenty-seven

years old, not nineteen. What an advantage that must have given her, competing against kids eight years her junior. She'd made it into the criminal justice system as a juvenile, but that record was sealed, and the earliest offense Roz, working with Danny Burkett at the Cambridge cop house, had been able to find was August 1988, for soliciting an undercover officer in Cleveland. Sixteen years old. I wondered why she hadn't been treated as a juvie. Maybe she'd pretended to be older, or had so many offenses on her sheet by then that they'd bumped this one up. Sentenced to juvenile detention, so the judge hadn't gone for her as an adult. Probably an older man, I thought. Next stop, Denver, Colorado, selling drug-related paraphernalia. She'd given her place of birth as Alaska, and been sent to a girl's rehabilitation school.

The machine at the side of Chaney's bed traced his heartbeat. It was mesmerizing, hypnotic. My shoulder throbbed and my head hurt. The colored line on the chart blurred and I thought about pressing the buzzer on Chaney's bed, calling the nurse, requesting a couple of aspirin. I went back to the file instead.

The rehab school hadn't changed Dorothy's ways. By 1990, she'd worked her way back into the system, this time for writing checks on the account of a gentleman in Provo, Utah, where she'd been sporadically attending high school. There was a change in the quality of the paper, a few sheets of lined loose-leaf stuff tossed in with the faxes, handwritten notes from Roz, who'd tracked down and spoken to an old high school teacher, a Harvard alum, no less. Had he filled Denali's head with college memories? I struggled to read Roz's scrawl. Good grades. Captain of the rowing squad. Living on her own. Only after she'd left school had the teacher discovered that lovely Dorothy had been supporting herself via prostitution.

She'd landed a less sympathetic judge, spent three months in the county lockup. She'd been taken in by a deputy sheriff and his wife after completing her sentence, repaid them by leaving town in the middle of the night with $780 and the wife's gold jewelry.

That warrant was still outstanding when Desiree Brent was picked up in October '92 in Des Moines, Iowa, arrested for grand theft auto.

Working with a man. He got the big years; she pleaded down. Spent eighteen months at the state pen in Fort Madison. I tried to square the black-and-white words with the images of Denali Brinkman offered by her roommate, her resident adviser, her lover, with the fallen angel bent over Chaney's prone body.

She was smart, knew how to row, but she couldn't stay out of trouble. She'd started out working alone, but later in her criminal career, she'd worked with a partner. Or a stooge. There were gaps in her history. I wondered if she'd filled them in with honest jobs, rowing, traveling to Europe, Switzerland, any of the fantastic places she'd rhapsodized about to Chaney.

If she'd done her crimes in California, she'd have been a lifer, a three-times-and-out loser. But she'd moved around, committed her offenses in different jurisdictions. She'd been nailed six times; I wondered how many other crimes she'd walked away from clean.

Roz had also spoken to the Iowa prison psychologist. Good for her. I squinted my eyes, pored over her notes. Bits and pieces of the story Denali had told Harvard and Chaney were part of the tale she'd told the shrink, but she aimed to please—she'd altered the facts to suit the occasion. She was an orphan with Chaney, the abandoned daughter of alcoholics for the shrink. Her American Indian heritage showed up in both tales. The shrink had termed Dorothy an exceptionally gifted manipulator. She'd also used the term *narcisisstic personality disorder*. Roz had underlined the words *borderline personality* and placed a string of question marks after them.

She'd labored in the prison infirmary as an orderly, in the library as a trustee. A perfect prisoner inside, but outside, she couldn't keep away from the Benjy Dowlings, the get-rich-quick schemes. Her last prison release was in '98. Royal Oak, Michigan. She'd been involved in a bar fight. Hit a man with a broken bottle. Aggravated assault. And now, if she came out alive from the room with metal doors, she'd go back to prison. A waste of beauty, a waste of intelligence, a necessary jailing. I recalled those icy, calculating eyes.

"Time to delve for deeper shades of meaning," she'd written in her supposed suicide note. Time to delve for deeper pockets than Harvard's, that's what she should have written. What was a hundred-thousand-dollar education, what were any damages she could win by claiming she'd been raped by a professor, compared to the millions the pharmaceutical industry might pay for a quick and easy weight-loss drug with no side effects?

I didn't hear George Fording's footsteps, just the rasp of his subtle cough as he stood in the doorway. He wore a dark blue suit, a maroon tie, a shirt so relentlessly white, I blinked. He wasn't alone. The man beside him was a stranger, wearing an elegant suit as well, carrying a briefcase.

"Is he—" Fording whispered the words, as though afraid to wake Chaney.

"He'll be fine."

"Good of you to stay. Margo is frantic, but I'll take over now."

The second man stared at his watch pointedly. His small slit of a mouth curled, as though he'd just tasted something unpleasant. Fording introduced him as Mr. Hitchens, from Legal Services.

"With a writ?" My tone was sharp. I felt seriously underdressed in dirty jeans and a men's T-shirt purchased that morning at a hospital shop. Underdressing makes me defensive.

"A friendly visit," Hitchens assured me, his voice like butter. "Just to stress that we would appreciate it if all statements to the press concerning this unfortunate matter were to come from one source, so as not to confuse the issues. And as these matters are likely to become the focus of legal proceedings, it would be best if nothing appeared in the press that might prejudice a jury at some point down the road."

"In other words, you don't want anybody to know Harvard admitted an ex-con. Well, I can understand that. What I'd like to know is how long you've known about it."

He moistened his thin lips but didn't respond.

"I mean, did you know before she supposedly killed herself, or did you just suspect? Were you actively pursuing her? Did you let her know you were on her trail, hoping she'd do something, like leave of her own accord?"

"None of these questions is likely to lead to a productive line of inquiry, Ms. Carlyle," he said smoothly. "If I have to get a writ to keep you from asking them in the press, I can have one in ten minutes."

"Yeah? Well, I can talk to a reporter in five."

Fording said, "Mr. Hitchens, perhaps you'd let me speak to her."

"Be my guest," snapped the attorney.

"Alone, please."

Hitchens pursed his small mouth, then turned and left.

"He's too late," I told Fording. "I already talked to the cops."

Fording's mouth twitched in what might have been a smile. "I shouldn't imagine Mr. Hitchens is terribly concerned about the police."

"Yeah," I said. "Sure. Loose lips sink endowments. The fix is in. Why am I not surprised?"

"You look tired."

"I am tired. I wonder if Chaney can hear all this, if he's tracking it on some subconscious level."

Fording eyed the sleeping Chaney as though considering the possibility. "What are you reading?"

"Criminal record. Denali Brinkman's."

"Poor girl."

"Save it. You want to talk about a poor girl, talk about Helen Orza."

His brow furrowed. "I don't believe I know the name."

"She's the one who fried in the boathouse fire. Guilty of looking like Denali Brinkman, guilty of having a crummy job. And you can feel sorry for Benjy Dowling, an ex-con she ran down like a dog in the street, because he got too ambitious, got in her way. Feel sorry for them."

He glanced around the room. There was no other chair and I wasn't about to relinquish mine.

He said, "I feel sorry for Wilson Chaney, as well. Wilson's a decent man and a fine scientist, a civilized human being. Possibly a weakness in times like these."

I raised an eyebrow. "He thinks you despise him."

"That's a strong word, *despise*."

"He told me that if you had any evidence he'd slept with a student, you'd toss him to the wolves."

There was no change in the little man's demeanor, no alteration in his dry tone. "Intriguing. Of course, it's in my interest to keep my department members on their toes. I try not to show favoritism, like a father with his children."

"Would you have fired him if you'd known?"

"You think I didn't know?" He gave a tiny half smile, a tilt of the corners of his mouth. "People in my department belch during class in the morning, I know it by noon."

"How about this? Did you know he was trying to cheat your precious department? Cheat the university?"

"Ah," he said softly.

"I suppose you know all about the magic weight-loss drug? The unintended consequence?"

"Ah," he repeated. "That."

"Yes, that."

"It's an interesting development certainly, really quite a promising possible therapy. Why do you inquire? What does—"

"Then why not file for a patent immediately? Why wait?"

He glanced around again, but no chair had materialized. "What did Wilson tell you?"

"Not Wilson. The girl." I told him what she'd said, just what she'd said, but all the while I was remembering the feel of the pistol in my hands, the cool blue eyes assessing me, evaluating me, trying to read my mind.

"A fantasy," Fording said in his dry academic tone. "An utter fantasy."

"You're saying there is no drug?"

"Not at all. There is—there may be a drug."

"You're saying it wouldn't be valuable?"

"Oh, it would be. It might very well be. Wilson and I discussed it. We discussed filing sooner rather than later. We agreed to delay."

I raised an eyebrow. My head was starting to ache again. Maybe I should call down the hallway, forget about the aspirin, inquire about the availability of a bed.

"Why?" I asked. "Why delay?"

"For a number of reasons. Wilson is a scientist, and he knows the value of being first. But he also wanted to be completely confident of replicable results. He needed to make sure it wasn't some sort of fluke. Often, when results can't be duplicated, reputations are jeopardized. And he wished, as any scientist would, to comprehend the phenomenon, not simply report it. That's understandable, surely."

"Yeah," I said. "Not to mention the money. You're a member of the the Scientific Advisory Group at Improvisational Technologies, right?"

The little man took a step toward me. "Ms. Carlyle, don't jeopardize Wilson's reputation or mine. Don't do it. Not on the word of a girl like that."

"She was good enough for Harvard," I said.

"Please." He lowered his voice and his eyes darted around the small room as though checking under the bed for spies. "Wilson has no desire to cheat Harvard or to leave Harvard. He isn't planning to defraud the university or anyone else, with the possible exception of his wife and her lawyers." He dropped his voice on the last phrase, as though he didn't want anyone, not even the unconscious Wilson Chaney, to hear.

"I don't understand."

"Wilson may have delayed. He did delay. I tell you this in confidence and I hope that confidence will be respected. He intends to file the patent application. Yes, he certainly does. But only *after* he divorces his wife. You've seen what she's like. You can understand that, can't you?"

Wilson Chaney slept, a tan blanket stretched taut across his chest, an IV line trickling liquid into his veins. He looked younger asleep, his forehead unwrinkled, his expression placid. If he were awake, how would I frame the question? Why keep the discovery secret, Wilson? Fording had his view: Wilson had never intended to run off with his dream girl. He'd delayed, but only until he could see his way clear to make a break from his wife. I could understand that, the man-woman tension, the man-woman problem. Of course I could understand that.

Could I believe it?

The machines tracked Chaney's vital signs, but no collection of silicon chips and circuitry could track his thoughts. Fording believed he was planning to leave his wife. Denali/Dorothy may have thought so, too, might have assumed he'd cooperate eagerly, blinded by lust, help her steal the drug from Improvisational. He might have gone along. Or he might never have known her plans. As long as he stayed unconscious, his heartbeat skittering across the screen, a pulsing blue line, it was anyone's guess. Asleep, Chaney was a blank canvas. Fording painted him in noble colors, believed him innocent, and I suppose I did, too, both of us shading him with our own beliefs about his character, just as he'd embellished his own picture of beautiful Denali Brinkman, just as we all see people through the lens of our own vision, through a dirty window or a shiny pane of glass.

I didn't shake Fording's hand when I left. I told him to keep his lawyers away from me and I'd keep quiet. Slap me with a restraining order and I'd find a way to break it.

My shoes made their own *tap-tap* down the tiled corridor. I felt light-headed and sleepy and unable to walk a straight line, but I made it to the front door. It was dusk. Trees shaded Mount Auburn Street, and I thought it wasn't more than a mile home, too short a distance for a cab.

The Porsche drove up beside me, silver paint glinting. The tinted window gave an electric whine and descended. Paolina, crammed sideways into the tiny backseat, stuck her head out of the gap.

"North End," she said eagerly. "Spaghetti with clam sauce."

Her hair was back to normal, dark and glossy, hanging loose. I couldn't see what she was wearing, but she had a grin on her face. I swallowed a sudden thickness in my throat and thought, Sure, "happily ever after" land, here we come. Not my daughter in the backseat, not my husband behind the steering wheel. No future in that, no long-term plan for this relationship. Hell, it wasn't even my car. I didn't have a car.

I said, "I owe you some perfume, sweetie. Who'd you fight with at the party?"

Sam said, "Are you going to get in?"

In the distance, a dog barked. A trio of pigeons darted suddenly across the dusty street.

I got in.

I damn well did. I sank into the leather seat and kicked off my shoes. I'll take my happily ever after in small doses, thank you. I'll take it when I can get it. No guarantees, no promises, day to day.

Denali Brinkman died in surgery.

I think she did.